I0584103

Second Edition September 2021
by Indies United Publishing House, LLC

Cover design by Damonza

ISBN 978-1-64456-362-5 [paperback]
ISBN 978-1-64456-363-2 [Mobi]
ISBN 978-1-64456-364-9 [ePub]

Library of Congress Control Number: 2021943135

INDIES UNITED PUBLISHING HOUSE, LLC
P.O. BOX 3071
QUINCY, IL 62305-3071
www.indiesunited.net

Dedication

To the HHC, 3-16th, 29th Infantry Division.
Keeping the Valley safe.

COL'M

BOOK THREE

D. KRAUSS

INDIES UNITED PUBLISHING HOUSE, LLC

Col'm: Saint Columba, a warrior monk from Ireland who killed 5,000 men in a battle over a stolen Psalter. Banished to Scotland, Columba wrestled with the Loch Ness monster, fought the druids, opened locked gates by invoking the sign of the Cross, established monasteries, and converted the Picts to Christianity, often at the point of a sword.

Part I: Trampling Out the Vintage

1.1

Middle of October
This evening

A car was coming up the mountain.

Collier leaned on the rake and watched it, tracing its labored progress by the degree of black smoke belching from the jury-rigged chimney sticking out the back. Coal-powered, quite inefficient, especially for this steep ascent. Horses had a bad enough time with it, let alone a POS steam car. But, obviously, someone wanted to impress him.

Gee, I wonder who?

Collier looked across the valley at the opposite peaks, the setting sun turning them into black spearheads framed by fire. Dazzling, to the point he could no longer make out the glorious reds and yellows of the maples and oaks and sycamores putting on their autumn best. He could, though, see pinpoint lights bobbing about, marking the torches and the rare oil lamp of other 'posters still working their piles of leaves. One advantage of being on the east side of the valley: he got more daylight. 'Course, it also meant a later start in the morning, but he showed up pre-dawn anyway because he had other things to do, like measure the pits, arrange for deliveries, send the crews off and do his rounds before ending up here alone to tidy up the leaf lines and calculate loads and volume for tomorrow. At least, that's what he told the brigadistas, who might consider such individual effort a sign of counter-revolutionary impulse. If he ever told the truth, that he took on these late tasks simply to enjoy a moment of solitude, well, to the camps with him.

Which may be why the POS was struggling up the valley. To the camps with him.

Again.

He grinned. Wasting your time, fellas. Got the routine down pat. Endure a couple weeks of torture and sleep deprivation and then break down and cry and confess to error and I'm glad to be back in the embrace of the State and I will never, ever do that again … and then he would go back and do it again. As they well knew. Their best bet was to simply shoot him.

Which may be why the POS was struggling up the valley.

He sighed and turned away and eye-measured the lines of leaves he'd sculpted. About two more weeks on this site, then spend the remainder of the season back in the valley. By the end of November, he'd have his last batches of compost delivered, freeing up the pits for the new crop. Based on the quantity so far, he'd need to dig another set of pits before the snows arrived. Hopefully, his sons had picked up the last loads of manure and positioned them for mixing. He chuckled and whispered, "Pay your dues," in anticipation of his eldest's on-going complaint about doing the literal shit work.

Pay your dues.

The car had reached the flat right below this rise and it shuddered and coughed and belched an incredible cloud of black smoke before the fireman in the open back, sweating in this cold, threw dampers and cut off the steam. It looked like an old Buick, a car even Collier's dad would have found ancient. They'd probably found it stored in some old codger's garage, rust free and pristine and big and decadent and perfect for the cadre. Cut it apart to add boiler and pipes and there, a working car, so to speak. Best they could do after twenty years of enlightened rule.

The driver was bent over the wheel, probably throwing other switches and valves, and more intent on that duty (because one wrong move and the car blows up) than on Collier. The passenger, though, was not making that mistake.

He stared at Collier through the windshield. The sunset glow obscured him somewhat, but Collier saw and felt his scrutiny. He also saw the Party uniform, crisp and ironed and no worse for the cloud of cinders and soot it must have endured, major's gold leaves on the shoulders winking at him. The guy was not wearing his cap; black-and-gray curls swept back from his forehead and fell past his ears, definitely not within party regulations. So, this guy was a maverick. Or a favorite. Collier examined the apparatchik's pointed face, cheeks volcanoing to a prominent nose, and, after a moment, knew who he was.

"Hello, Deavers," Collier greeted the former Ghost, former soldier, and current traitor, as he slid out of the car, stood and brushed at the uniform. "How'd you survive Pemberton?"

Deavers smiled. "Hello, Rashkil. Same way you did." He paused. "I ran."

"Before the battle, if I recall correctly," Collier said and cast casual glances around for the best escape routes.

Deavers waggled a hand. "Before, after, point is, I made it. As did you."

Collier could belabor the point that running away from a battle was of a different character than surviving the onslaught, but decided it was a bad course. The Blues had lost that battle, lost the war, and anyone who'd been a Blue – much less a Ghost – was still, technically, the enemy. Unless you threw in with the winners, like Deavers had. Like Collier hadn't, so why compound his obvious troubles? Because Deavers, of all people, showing up here was trouble enough.

"So this is like the Mafia, right?" Collier observed, "Send someone I know to whack me?" Collier casually leaned on the rake and figured he could throw it at Deavers the moment the craphead reached for a weapon then off the cliff side – the one with all the boulders – and hope the darkness and steepness would cover him enough to prevent a bullet in the back. And hope he was still agile enough to avoid smashing his head into the rocks.

But, apparently, no need because Deavers laughed and shook his head and held up placating – and empty – hands. "I'm not here to whack you. I'm here to say hello."

Uh huh. "A postcard would have been easier," Collier said and gazed significantly at the still-smoking car.

"Mail isn't reliable."

Collier raised hands in mock horror. "After twenty years of the Five-Year Plan? How can that be?"

Deavers wagged a semi-serious finger. "Careful. Someone might consider that negativism. Which is an offense against the State."

"Yes, I know," Collier said, dryly, "Some of your best torturers have explained that to me."

"Three times, I think." Deavers fished around in his tunic – Mao-like, of course. Despots loved that look – and pulled out a pack of cigarettes. He tapped out a couple and offered. Collier shook his head and Deavers lit one, puffing luxuriously and releasing a cloud of smoke and wondrous perfume into the air. Ah. Good stuff, that. Real tobacco, not that corn silk garbage the masses got. Man, what Collier would do for a pre-Event cigar …

Collier savored the memory for a half second and then returned to reality. "What do you want, Deavers?"

Deavers feigned injury. "No small talk? No asking how I've been, where I've been, for the last twenty years?"

Collier brushed a hand at Deavers's uniform. "You seem to have done all right."

"And you." Deavers brushed his own hand at the leaf lines. "Haven't."

The retort rising to Collier's lips summarizing how sellouts like Deavers usually did better than the loyal almost broke out, but he suppressed it. Why compound your obvious troubles? "It's a living," he said.

Deavers shook his head mockingly. "Now, see right there? The language you use. 'A living.' How bourgeois. How … counter-revolutionary." And he gave Collier a hard stare.

Collier almost burst out laughing. Almost. A hard stare from Deavers was a gnat challenging an elephant, but why compound your troubles? "I see you've got the lingo down," he said, coolly, "You always had a finger to the wind, didn't you? Even before Pemberton."

Deavers frowned. "I had the good sense to see how things were going."

"And the better sense to run away before you had to fight."

Compounding my problems now, Collier thought as Deavers reddened and his eyes narrowed. Never could keep my big mouth shut. Dad had repeatedly warned him about that, so did Mom, so did Rosa …

Rosa.

In the woods between the creeks. Her desperate, clawing kiss, and a last glimpse of her as she led the remnants of the Ghosts away. Away.

Deavers's anger visibly turned into weariness. Looked like a genuine weariness, too. "I didn't come up here to fight old battles. What's done is done."

"Why did you come up here, then?"

"Like I said." Deavers drew another puff. "To say hello. See, I've been assigned here."

"Really." Suspicion clouded Collier's face. "Lose a bet?"

Deavers chuckled. "No, nothing like that. It's a promotion, actually."

"To …"

Deavers was neutral. "Case officer."

Collier stilled. Case officer. Which meant … "You're Directorate," Collier said quietly

Deavers said nothing, merely looked at him. Collier furiously went through the implications: a new Directorate case officer, someone Collier knows, a traitor, a sellout, who conspired with Colonel Caldwell (may he burn in hell) to destroy the Ghosts and the Blues and what was left of the United States, facilitating the rise of this godawful, murderous, quasi-Marxist regime; a case officer not from this area (New England somewhere, if Collier remembered correctly), who'd presumably spent the last twenty years climbing the ranks of the Directorate while torturing and murdering in the name of the People's Republic, obtaining the powerful rank of major on a bloody stack of bodies, a rank far above what this pissant little backward District needed, just showed up.

Why?

"Why?" Collier asked.

Deavers looked puzzled. "Why am I Directorate?"

"Well, that is one question, but you can tackle it after you answer the question I meant. Why you, and why here?"

Deavers smirked. "You, former Sergeant Rashkil, wonder why orders make no sense?"

Good point. If there was one thing Collier had learned in his five or six years as an upstanding member of the late, lamented Blues, nothing ever made sense, especially orders issued by the jumble of idiots constituting the Blue command structure. It was endemic to the beast; Dad, who had served in the real US military – the one that had existed before the Event – had regaled Collier with similar tales of idiocy. How much improvement would a scurvy bunch of neo-Marxists bring?

"There is no such thing as a coincidence," Dad whispered in his ears.

"Why are you really here?" Collier's tone let Deavers know he wasn't buying it.

Deavers sighed and shook his head sadly. "Wow. So much suspicion. Has anyone told you that you're paranoid?"

"With good reason," Collier intoned.

"Yes." Deavers's look darkened. "You do have good reason, don't you?"

A slow pulse beat in Collier's temple. "I would say so. I would say anyone with half a brain, even a smidgen of common sense, is paranoid these days. Because having half a brain, even a smidgen of common sense, earns you Directorate attention."

Deavers examined his fingernails coolly. "Other things do, too."

Collier's shields went up. "Whatever could you mean, Deavers?" he asked, maintaining the facade. "I'm just a poor, humble composter trying to improve crop yields for the State. Since we no longer have fertilizer. Or tractors. Or enough food to feed everyone." Collier blinked slowly. "By the way, how ARE things in the Midwest? Heard there was some mass starvation."

Deavers frowned. "Who told you that?"

"A little birdie. We get lots of them out here in the woods."

Deavers was quiet for a bit. "Still on the wrong side,"

he spoke low, dangerous, "Still getting people killed."

Still?

Shields went to full power. "What do you want, Deavers?"

"I want us to be friends."

Collier said nothing.

"Oh, no." Deavers waved a hand. "Not in the old bourgeois sense, you know, hoisting a few beers together, playing poker on Wednesday nights, all that rot." Said with genuine scorn. "No, I mean a friend in today's sense. Someone harmless. Someone I can talk to from time to time, get a ... feel, for what's happening. Someone who will then remain ... unbothered." And he gave Collier another hard look. Another gnat.

"You know," Collier said, softly, "that could be construed as a threat."

Deavers shrugged. "Call it what you want. But consider the offer."

Collier made an exaggerated show of considering the offer. And then rejecting it. "Be your ... friend." He gave that last word its proper emphasis. "As you've defined it. Problem with that ..." Collier stretched luxuriously and gripped the rake for possible combat "... when I look at you, I see too many bodies. I see Swift getting blown to atoms by an exploding tank. I see the Wilson brothers getting plastered by an F-16. I see..."

Rosa. Jonesy. So many. Too many.

"... and I don't see you by their side. I don't see you at all." And he prepared to hurl the rake.

Deavers said nothing, simply stood there with eyes half closed and arms crossed. After a moment, he said, "The war is over, Collier, has been for years. You lost. We won. You should accept that. You should help us rebuild."

Collier made an exaggerated turn toward his leaf lines. "I think I am."

"You know what I mean."

Yes, Collier did. "The best I can do for you is just stay up here. I'm not bothering anybody up here. No one."

Deavers quietly puffed the cigarette down.

Collier sighed and turned to the dying light, the mountains now stark and black against the blood red sky, the fireflies over there winking out as sane men went home. "You should probably head back now, Deavers. I don't know how familiar you are with these roads, but your little Tinkertoy," Collier made a contemptuous gesture at the car, "might have trouble with them. Could be an accident." And he gave Deavers a significant look.

Deavers's crew standing near the car exchanged glances, their hands drifting toward their belts. Collier got ready to throw the rake.

"Perhaps we should," Deavers said, raising a quelling hand to his crew, who froze. "After all, it is getting late." He took a lazy glance at the deepening sky. "And I think we've said all we can say." A pause. "For now." A glance at Collier, a tossing of the cigarette butt into the dirt, and the three of them got back in the car.

"Be a stranger," Collier called, and watched with some amusement as the firemen worked frantically to get the boiler back up to pressure, taking at least five minutes before there was enough steam for the driver to gingerly back up, obviously conscious of the drop-off, and drive the vehicle back down the slope. The days of fast getaways were long gone.

Deavers stayed on him as the car jinked and jerked, Collier still feeling his regard even as darkness and distance obscured the windshield. He followed the slow progress of the vehicle down the trail, the fire from the boiler marking its position. The light had fallen fast, the only illumination now the backscatter of sunset bouncing off a few clouds dotting the October sky. He took in a deep breath, the smell of leaf mold and turned earth and the coming winter flooding his lungs. He then walked over and picked up the cigarette butt, inhaling it deeply. Ah!

Collier melted into the dark, his feet finding a familiar trail on the edge of the leaf lines. He skirted one of the ridges and stopped about halfway up, probing a stone outcropping until he grasped a canvas bag. He pulled it to himself and felt his way back along the trail.

An hour or so later, there was a low whistle off to his front. Collier whistled back and nodded at the two shadows-against-shadows in the larch stand, and then slipped through the hedges and brake. A low rough building, barely discernible at the bottom of the hollow, had a single candle in a window giving it form.

Collier walked in and strode down the pews as the congregation silently rose, the candles giving enough dim light for him to see his way. He stepped behind the podium, reached into his bag and pulled out the book, adjusted the candle next to him to give more light, then, without looking up, intoned, "Open your Bibles to 1st Timothy."

1.2

Yesterday

"EEEEEEEHAAAAA!"

Price almost burst into laughter as the call came up the hill. What city boys considered a holler was downright a joke, something they'd no doubt heard from some other city boy. Or TV. Price had a vague memory of some show … Duke of Earl or something like that … with actors pretending to be good ole boys and doing exactly the same holler the yutz down the hill had just done. Pap had taught him the real calls, offspring of the terrible Rebel Yell that Early and Ewell's troops screeched as they thundered down on the Yankees, those calls, themselves, offspring of the ones used by Comanches and Celts and whoever else in misty times got their blood up that way. "EEEEEE OOOOOO, WOOOO EEEEOOOO!" Price screamed back. That's how you do it, city boy.

Cass and Slickie, sitting beside him in the grass, guffawed their appreciation, whether of Price's authenticity or the city boy's silliness, didn't matter. More that Price could still do the call after all these years, and that he'd actually gotten off his lazy ass and came out here with them to do the drop. Little things mean a lot, Pap had told him. You wanna keep your men's respect, show 'em you can still do the job. And Price could still do the job. If he had his way, it's the only thing he'd do.

"Want me to go get it?" Cass asked

"Nah," Price said, "I'm gonna run this whole shebang. You two watch my back."

With a petulant toss of her head, Cass nodded. Price grinned. Cass was a tough little thing. Nothing she loved more than a good fight, something you'd never know looking at her because she was slight and thin, a dove-like blue-eyed wispy blonde, closer to a porcelain princess than anything. But she was all cord and tendon and stronger than a lot of men, almost as strong as Slickie next to her, who was also nothing but ligament and muscle and so thin he could step sideways behind a tree and disappear, and so silent he'd swipe a wallet before the victim heard the first swish of jacket sleeve. He looked a lot like his sister, the same blondness and ivory skin, and some people thought him albino, but the resemblance stopped at his eyes, which were dark and fathomless. While Cass would fight for the sheer joy of it, her brother did so only when necessary, but with efficience.

Just the kind of people you wanted at your back.

After the requisite five minutes, Price looked at them and said, "All right," then slid noiselessly around the stump, pulling the canvas bag with him. "Shouldn't be long."

"You sure you don't want me to …" Cass bubbled up. Man, she was a bug!

"No, young'un, I can do this. I ain't that creaky." He paused. "Yet."

"But …

"Just stay here unless it sounds like I need you."

Cass began another protest but Price shushed her. "And don't get any ideas about messing with those boys down there," he warned. "They're scared enough of us."

"Taking all the fun out of it, Uncle P," she groused and glanced at her brother but he nodded acquiescence. Boy was all business, something Price appreciated. His sister could learn a bit of that. He gave her a warning look. "Make sure you do what I say. Don't want to tell your Daddy about it."

She paled a little at that and Price inwardly grinned and then crouched below the ivy and underbrush that sheltered the stump. He wasn't really her uncle because her daddy wasn't really Price's brother, but Price had forged ties so close with his gang that they all called each other by family titles. And while Brother Dinwiddie let his only daughter get away with everything up to and including murder, he would tolerate no disrespect of Price.

No one disrespected Price. No one.

Price sat for a minute longer and studied the terrain. Still pretty thick, even this late in October, with lots of reds and browns in the tangle as various leaves changed color. There was a lip on the slope that blocked his view of the hill base, but there was so much undergrowth between here and there that if anyone was doing anything untoward, the racket would alert him. City boys couldn't move through the woods quietly. Price could. He moved.

The bag was a bit of a weight, the three quarts of 'shine in there sloshing around but not enough to give him away. No clinking because he'd silenced them with some old newspapers he kept for that purpose. Silly things, all pre-Event with stories about wars in scumbag Middle Eastern countries that didn't exist anymore (or no one cared about enough to go see if they did), and some politician on one side complaining about some politician on the other. Every once in a while, Price showed the papers to the few people who could still read, especially the young'uns like Cass, and say, "You see how things used to be?" And she would look at him like he was from another planet and go, "Uh huh," and sidle off.

Damn kids.

He couldn't blame them. How many times had he rolled his eyes when Pap had regaled him with tales of an America made of bone and muscle where men were men and women were frightened? Price's America had been a marshmallow where MTV and video games defined your worth; that is, until the Event had turned it back into a place of bone and muscle. And Byzantine and murderous, and Corporal Price smuggled stolen goods for Colonels, who thought his talents were best used enriching themselves instead of fighting Reds, a decision Price heartily seconded, until a Colonel stabbed him in the back and Price, in turn, stabbed him and got the gold …

… the gold. Still safely hidden, still a legend and a rumor among his men and the target of other gangs (which ended up buried in dark woods in dark vales); a piece of it here and a piece of it there to buy checkpoint guards who overlooked what was on the back of pack mules or in the back of wagons, buying cadres and commissars who lost incriminating pieces of paper or who reassigned overzealous Directorate officers and tipped him about pending raids so the converging brigidistas found an empty barn or a clear spot in the woods instead of the expected loot. The world ran on gold, not slogans or philosophies. Price had built his country on it.

Price Land.

He chuckled. Sounded like one of those old pre-Event big box stores. And maybe it was. Price Land offered food to the starving, clothing for the naked, currency exchange for the speculator and precious jewels and art for the discriminating. In its back rooms and storage facilities and safes, Price Land piled up more coin and barter goods and promises and alliances and was profitable and a law unto itself.

So screw you, Reds.

Okay. Let's get this show on the road.

Price dropped to all fours and, carefully picking his way along the slope, low-crawled to the lip. He pulled up a bit of bluegrass and raised it above the edge, making little movements. If anyone had set up, an arrow should fly through the air about now. Or, a gunshot, if anyone were stupid enough or extravagant enough to use a rifle. No one had guns anymore except Directorate troops. At least, that anyone admitted. Hee hee.

No arrow, no slingshot, no spear, so Price rolled to his right and into a small tunnel cut under the blackberry stand and wiggled through, catching his back on the thorns from time to time and cursing them as appropriate. The things we do for safety. About ten minutes later, Price piled up at the end of the tunnel, winded. Man, he was getting old. What *was* he now, forty-three, forty-four? Something like that. No one knew the real dates anymore since the Directorate had abolished the bourgeois calendar and imposed some silly thing that marked the fall of the Blues as the First Year of the People. What nonsense. Some people did a thriving business producing illegal old style calendars, the more daring of them still listing holidays like Easter and Halloween, but business required knowing the People's dates, so Price had lost track. But he was definitely somewhere north of forty, which was a problem. These days, most people didn't live much past fifty. Thank you, People's Republic, and your systematic destruction of bourgeois concepts like health care and medicine in favor of your "People's" Clinics, waggishly nicknamed Roach Hotels because you don't check out. Fortunately, there were a couple of pre-Event doctors – well, an RN and a PA – living in Price Land with access to a well-stocked pharmacy that Price's boys kept up. But, they were getting old, too, as were the medications, and their apprentices could only learn so much. Before too long, they'd be back to using wise women and voodoo for health care.

Progress, comrade.

Price peered through a surreptitious break in the brake and scrutinized the Drop Off Stump. There it was at the bottom of the slope, suspiciously clear of undergrowth; that is, if you were a country boy. The city boys that made up most of the local cadre wouldn't give a cleared area surrounding a stump in the middle of the woods a second glance. Price gave it third and fourth glances, looking for something wrong: a shape where there shouldn't be one, a gleam of metal off an arrowhead, dark where there should be light. Not that he expected an ambush, but circumspection was his middle name and you never knew when some idiots would get it into their heads to not only keep the product but keep their payment also. An old story, going back to the days of drug deals. Even Pap, who did not like to handle the drug side of the business, only the popskull (little pat on the canvas bag at this point), had to deal with the occasional idiot who got it in his head that he was smarter than he. Even Price, who *did* handle the drug side of the business because Pap considered it a young man's game (but still kept an eagle eye on it), had to, deal with an idiot or two himself.

Because people were, overall, idiots.

The proof was overwhelming. Pre-Event, the arrogant self-regard that made an entire country believe it was invulnerable, that it was smarter and better and oh so much more sophisticated than those backward narrow-minded generations that pre-existed it … and what happened? Devastation on a global scale. Post-Event, the survivors believed they were so much more sophisticated and brighter than the dead around them … and what happened? Breakout and civil war and more death and areas of the country still quarantined after all this time (like DC, which was a death trap: if the Flu didn't get you, the cannibals would). And the people today, putting their faith in a bankrupt system like gol'damned Commynism, as Pap called it, which left them starving and impoverished and enslaved.

So the chances of an idiot waiting for him down there by the stump were purty good.

The chances of idiocy popping up right smack in the middle of any given situation were so good that Price had made it an operating principle …well, Pap had, and had beaten it into Price's brick-hard brain. He, in turn, had beaten it into his gang's brains. At least, he had tried. Some of them – I'm looking at you, Cass – suffered from an overabundance of confidence that made them dismiss idiocy as a motivating factor. That, in itself, was idiocy, and Price had imposed ironclad SOPs for every transaction, like always bring backup, keep your backup hidden, approach with great caution, and be ready to abort should anything even whiff of wrongness.

Price spent a good hard five minutes in scrutiny. Nothing whiffed. Okay.

Carefully extricating himself from the brake, Price slowly rose to his knees and waited for his movement to elicit a reaction. Nothing. Pulling the bag to himself, he slipped its handle on a shoulder and boldly marched to the Stump. At this point, it was better to trigger the attack then go pussyfooting around, which would force the idiots to move before they were ready, and idiots, being idiots, were never ready. Price was. One hand on his throwing knife, he stepped up and pulled back the sheepskin cover. There was a canvas bag fit snug in the middle of the stump. He looked around one more time and then pulled it out and and looked inside.

Scrip. Sonofabitch.

Price almost threw the bag down in disgust, ready to stomp off because, goddamn, how many times did he have to tell people, we do not want any of that effin' People's Republic funny money? Price could print up as much of that crap as he wanted and in better quality, at that. His engraver was a true craftsman, had actually worked at the Mint and knew how to run a manual press to boot. Even the guy's apprentice could do a half-assed enough job to pass muster. So who did this city boy asshole think he was, trying to pay in it? Price was going to have words with whoever had found this customer ... wait. There's something else inside.

Price fluttered the scrip aside and smiled. Ah now, that's better. Reaching in, he pulled out a necklace. A sapphire one. Nice ...

Nice? It was freakin' awesome!

Price, who prided himself on never being impressed, gasped, because he was freakin' impressed. The stone was huge – had to be at least seventy karats – and cobalt blue, set in ... platinum? Wow. And not plain platinum, either, but dressed with an array of diamonds and smaller sapphires and ...

What. The. Fuck?

Price stared at the necklace, glittering and strobing in the sunlight. What the fuck? Even the dullest of the dull had to know this thing was priceless; even if it was fake, the craftsmanship alone marked it as pre-Event and, ergo, worth a whole helluva lot more than a measly three Mason jars of popskull. Heck, with this, coulda bought fifty cases, even your own still, bucko. So why in the blue blazing hell of Loch Lomond (thanks for that one, Pap) would you pay with something this exquisite?

Set up.

Price dropped the necklace and bag and flipped his own bag off the shoulder simultaneously, the shattering of glass followed immediately by the reek of almost pure grain alcohol gassing the area as he whipped around to flee, but he was too late.

"Halt!"

Followed by a sound that Price had not heard in decades:

Bolts on rifles being released.

Fuck.

He froze.

"In the name of the People's Republic of America," shouted the same voice, "you are under arrest!"

Directorate.

Double fuck.

"Okay, okay!" Price yelled. "I surrender! Don't shoot!"

"Put your hands on top of your head!" Halt Voice shouted and Price was happy to comply. He was happier to comply with the next order to drop to his knees because that gave him an opportunity to sneak a look around.

Five of 'em rose from deeply concealed strategic points so well done around the stump that Price hadn't made 'em, all pointing black rifles that looked a lot like M-16s at him, all dressed in Directorate black, all wearing balaclavas ...

The Faceless.

Triple fuck.

A lot of things ran through Price's mind as the perimeter closed on him, like how in the blue blazing Loch Lomond had this ambush even got planned without him getting word of it? What was he paying those guys in the commissar's office for, huh? And how is it this ambush gets sprung on one of those rare occasions when Price hisself showed a little bit of leadership by personally running the drop? That seemed to indicate Price had a leak somewhere, a conclusion shocking enough to make him almost forget the most important thought swirling around his brain:

What the eff was the Faceless doing here?

One of them – probably Halt Voice – stepped around to Price's front and placed the barrel of the rifle against his forehead, giving Price an exquisite view of it. Yep, an M-16, and an old school one, at that, Vietnam era, if he was not mistaken. Talk about retro. Price was pretty sure his own M-16s, buried here and there in various safe stashes, were later variants, including numerous M4s, but this one ... duckbill flash suppressor and chrome carrier ... was an antique. And there was only one person among the Faceless who was a true aficionado of antique M-16s, the rumor being he would pay top scrip to anyone bringing him an AR-10, and that person was its commander, Maj Rickard Lawless.

Fuck beyond fuck.

"You blink," Lawless said, "and I ventilate your skull."

"But the sun's in my eyes," Price responded, because it was in his nature to be a smart ass.

In response, Lawless pressed the duckbill against Price's forehead, no doubt leaving a mark. Price kept his eyes wide open past the point of comfort and endured the tears and the stinging because that was infinitely better than a ventilated skull. Infinitely.

But eyeballs demand blinking and, right at the point Price decided he'd opt for ventilation, Lawless stepped back as another barrel pressed against the back of Price's neck and still another into his ribcage. Squeezing his eyes shut, he made a show of extreme discomfort as he took stock of the situation.

It wasn't good.

Two of the Faceless were at his back, pretty much covering him except for his right side, which could have been an opportunity except another Faceless stood there about three yards away, watching him, while the fifth one was doing perimeter security. Maybe, if Price was lucky, he could swipe the guy immediately behind him with the blade and then twist it into the leg of the guy on his ribs, but he'd never get past the guy watching and the guy on perimeter. Much less Lawless. Best to stall for time until Cass and Slickie came to his rescue – a dim prospect given that this was the Faceless – or something else occurred to him. Like something else would.

Okay, time to punt.

"Bit out of your jurisdiction, aren't you, Rickard?" Price said.

Yep, good, the surprise he was hoping for on Lawless's face, caused by the fact that Price knew his first name, much less who he was. Had to be a bit disconcerting to hear some pissant gangster out in the boondocks greet you thusly. Maybe it would disconcert him enough for Price to try the blade swipe.

Good luck with that.

Because surprise almost immediately gave way to coolness in Lawless's intense, neon green eyes, made all the more terrible by his almost invisible eyebrows. He silently studied Price for a moment before reaching down and grabbing the necklace, the barrel of his lovely old M-16 not wavering a smidgen as he did so. Guy was under control, that's for sure.

"Henry Price," Lawless said.

Now, whose turn was it to be surprised? Outside of the gang, nobody knew his name. Further proof he had a rat somewhere in the basement.

"For violation of the People's Antiquities Act," Lawless flourished the necklace, "you are hereby arrested and immediately forfeit all rights and privileges of review within the beneficial courts of the People's Republic."

Well, that certainly came out of left field. "Um, wha'?"

Lawless held the necklace up in the air, a look of admiration crossing his face. Couldn't blame him. Even the most ascetic of murdering, cold-blooded Faceless assassins would be dazzled by it. "This is the Bismarck Sapphire."

Price's blank look told Lawless all he needed and the guy actually smiled; at least, Price thought he did because the corners of his mask turned up. "It is a property of the State, stolen from the Smithsonian and therefore, outlawed in anyone's hands other than the Secretary's."

Hmm. Price wasn't sure what Bismarck, North Dakota had to do with something like this, but out of the Smithsonian ... let's see, if Price was accurately recalling the murky events immediately post-Event, that meant one of the quarantined groups systematically looting DC had grabbed it and probably sold it to a collector like Colonel Leideig (may his soul burn in hell) and, from there, who knows? Point being, it was a rather valuable piece of jewelry that the Secretary Himself, Lord and Master of Us All General Frederick Santos Kant, would want to keep in the hands of "the People." Which was him. Hence, the effrontery of a pissant like Price gaining possession was enough to get him shipped *toute suite* to the coal mines farther south. Do Not Pass Go. Do Not Get the Benefit of a Bribable Jury. Go Directly to Hard Labor for Life.

"I must point out," Price said, mildly, "that you're the one who gave it to me."

"So!" There was a note of triumph in Lawless's response. "You admit, in front of witnesses, that you possessed it."

"Well." Price remained mild. "Hard for me to deny that when you, yourself, were the one who gave it to me to possess. Which, of course, begs the question of where you got it from?" Price raised mild eyebrows.

Lawless waved that away. "Immaterial. The State may

use its resources to prove the guilt of a social criminal."

"The word you're searching for here is entrapment."

Lawless cocked his head, clearly amused. "They said you were a cool one. And you're obviously stalling for time but you shouldn't waste any more of your breath because no help is coming. And won't be any trial, so your entrapment defense won't get the time of day." He let that sink in. "Let's go. I'm very eager to have a conversation with you before the mines claim you. I'd really like to know how you know who I am." He nodded at the Faceless behind Price.

Crap, Price thought, as the two rifle barrels jammed viciously into his ribs. That's a discussion I don't want to have. That's a job I don't want to have, coal mining, that is, although it's supposed to be honorable work. If you live through it. And Lawless is right, there is no help coming so let's go down fighting, shall we? Price made an exaggerated lurch forward off the gun barrels, like he'd been pushed too hard, his hands slapping the ground in front of him and ready to pull the first of the throwing knives.

Thwap! *Thwap*!

Followed by, "*Erf*! *Oogh*!" The sounds usually made by targets of Slickie's two crossbows, in this case, the two Faceless behind Price.

As Price threw himself flat, he saw Lawless whirl and drop his barrel on the blackberry brake and cut loose on full auto, the roar of .223 rounds not heard in this Valley since the War, startling, loud, and deadly as Lawless systematically mowed through the underbrush. Two more full autos joined him as the two other Faceless added their firepower, more intent on the hidden threat in the bushes than on Price.

Move.

Spinning to his knees, Price side handed the first

throwing knife at the closest Faceless, catching him neatly in the upper right chest. Without stopping to examine his handiwork, he flipped the second knife underhanded at the farther Faceless. Not as good a throw, but it caught the rifle and threw the Faceless off balance enough to send his bullets wild. A second later, another crossbow bolt blossomed in the middle of that one's chest.

Four down, one to go.

Continuing his spin, Price had the third knife up and behind his ear and ready to split Lawless's back with it when he saw that he wasn't facing the assassin's back. No, he was facing the barrel of Lawless's lovely antique-but-definitely-in-working-order rifle, pointed directly at Price's lovely head. One skull ventilation, coming up.

Wham!

Cass had burst out of the brake and, with the jodo stick in her right hand, slammed the barrel of Lawless's rifle down to the ground, where it ventilated a lot of ants. She then slapped him across the forehead with the jodo stick in her left hand, the two moves so simultaneous and fast that Lawless was on his back, stunned, as Price sat there, equally stunned.

"Come ON!" Cass shrieked at him as she continued her momentum around and headed pell-mell for the brake.

Price was about to raise an objection, that, instead of running away, they should take advantage of this situation to finish off one of the most notorious assassins of this regime, one who had, somehow, managed to penetrate Price's once-thought-impenetrable organization and gained a lot of information on him, but there was a lot of shouting and crashing coming from down the hill. Of course. Reinforcements. And not Price's.

Leaping to his feet, Price hit full stride in one run, slipping another knife in his hand as he came alongside Lawless. Hate to cut and run, but ... Lawless, though, rolled away and all Price managed to do was catch him deep in the shoulder. Lawless's grunt of pain would have to satisfy and Price hit the edge of the brake at full speed, diving through to avoid the majority of the tangle and gain the tunnel. Low crawling at the speed of light, he emerged below the lip. A big push and he was standing on the other side where Cass crouched, panting.

"What the hell—" began the impromptu chewing out that would emphasize the foolhardiness of taking on a superior fighting unit like the Faceless but, then, thank you, when she fell flat on her face. "Get down!" she yelled. You didn't have to tell Price twice; he hit the dirt.

Dien Bien Phu.

The entire lip and the brush behind it exploded as about ten thousand various rounds from various automatic weapons shredded the area into hay. Price swore he heard the deeper sound of something bigger, 7.56 or even .50, helping shred the area into hay.

All for me?

As Price puzzled over this extraordinary display of very rare firepower dedicated to a little pissant like himself, Cass crawled up the protected side of the slope, as protected as a little bit of rock and overhang could be under such an onslaught, and Price followed. After what felt like a year, and under the serenade of what sounded like every last round in the People's Republic inventory, they crawled around the stump and fell, gasping, into the little depression behind it.

Better protected here, because even the lip of the slope couldn't keep all the rounds out, especially the big ones but Price was disturbed to see some of the trees on either side of the stump splintering under the assault. "We need to get the hell out of here," Price said.

"Way ahead of you," said Slickie as he appeared on the back of the dip, crossbow strapped to his back, four jars of popskull in his hands.

"Go now," Price urged, "Drink later." And he gathered his knees to flee.

Slickie set the four jars down, grabbed one, and hurled it against the trees on the right, shattering it. He did the same to the trees on the left, and then the front of the stump leading to the lip. He then knelt, pulled out a striker, and threw sparks into his tinderbox.

"What the hell are you doing?" Price said.

The tinder caught and Slickie blew it into full flame and lit some sticks he was carrying and tossed them into the underbrush.

Whoosh! The popskull, splashed across the terrain, caught immediately. Good batch, that.

"What the hell are you doing?" Price repeated.

"They can't follow us," Slickie explained as the flames caught at the dry, thick underbrush, suddenly roaring all along the slope, making for the lip. And for them, if they didn't get their butts in gear.

Didn't have to tell Cass twice; she was already beating feet up the opposite slope. Slickie squatted there, waiting for Price's old man's brain to catch up and spur him into action. "Sure wish I'd grabbed that necklace," he groused and ran for his life.

1.3

Late Evening

"So tell me," Collier said to the gloom around the table, "how it is that we get a new Directorate chief, a major, no less, and no one hears about it? And," he added, with emphasis, "a chief that I know." He paused to let that sink in.

There was an uncomfortable shuffling in the gloom and the sounds of chairs shifting, a reflection of that discomfort. Collier watched shadows against shadows bob about each other in an attempt to get someone, anyone (other than themselves), to speak up.

A tinder flared at the end of the table, lighting Washburn's heavily bearded face. "We don't know," he answered as he dropped the tinder into his pipe, getting the tobacco he cultivated in a surreptitious plot in the back of his house to light.

Any other member of this group giving Collier such an answer would earn themselves a vicious rebuke and a dressing down, much the way Collier used to brace privates who didn't know why their rifles were so effin' dirty, but this was Washburn, and the guy was a straight shooter. "So tell me why we don't know," was all Collier asked.

"Because." Washburn twisted the pipe around the tinder, getting better purchase on the tobacco. "He just showed up."

"No one expected him?" Collier asked.

"No one." Ben Whittaker, sitting opposite Washburn, confirmed.

The room was quiet for a moment. "Well, that's a bit disturbing." Collier turned to Whittaker. "Perhaps, Ben, you can tell me how that happened."

Ben blinked somewhat in surprise, glancing nervously at Washburn, who glowered at him. No love lost between those two, Collier not sure if it was Washburn's hillbilly attitude toward black people or Ben's cosmopolitan one toward hill folk. But they did respect each other's abilities, which was the main reason they hadn't knifed each other. Yet. That Ben had, apparently, screwed the pooch on this one lessened Washburn's restraint.

"Uh, well," Ben dithered, "one day things are normal, then one day he's here. Unannounced."

"None of your sources gave you a heads-up?"

"None of them knew he was coming."

"When was this?"

"Last week."

Last week. And Deavers's first order of business was popping by for a chat. Disturbing. That Deavers knew exactly where to find him, even more so.

Collier sat back, letting the gloom cloak him. "You didn't think it important enough to let me know last week that some Directorate major, replete with a staff and a car, shows up out of the blue?"

The dim light hid it, but Collier could imagine the contortions of incredulity crossing Ben's face about now. Calling him out like that, right in front of everybody … pretty rude, especially because Ben had shown great loyalty and effectiveness these last ten years, bringing Collier every jot and tittle of info he'd gleaned from all the contacts he had in all the little Byzantine offices and bureaux and departments covering a three-District range.

But, Ben, if you had served in the military, either Red or Blue, instead of hiding out in the hills (not a criticism, man. Given everything, I wish I had done the same thing), you would know that it takes just one intelligence failure to kill us all.

Like it killed us all back then.

"Puh!" You could hear the protest in Ben's splutter of indignation. "Because he didn't come *in* like a Directorate major! He was quiet, showed up at the Strasburg Ministry of Agriculture by himself in a private's uniform, like an overage, and was put to work on the Cattle desk. The cadre was annoyed but you expect personnel screw-ups. He didn't reveal himself at all. First I heard about his true nature was from you." The protest had turned into hurt.

Collier pressed his lips. "Quiet, hmm?" Collier considered the implications of that and then said, "All right," the forgiveness implicit in his voice and he could picture Ben's face now collapsing into relief. He could actually see Washburn's face in the pipe light retain its glower. Gonna have to address that.

"Uhm hmm," a throat cleared, interrupting Collier's intent to voice the implications of a Directorate major sneaking in like that and his focus shifted to the end of the table where another tinder flared and another pipe blazed, raising the ambient light enough to reveal the gray-haired old man sitting there.

"Mr. Cody," Collier acknowledged, and waited. Of all his section chiefs, Eulen Cody was the only one Collier addressed so. Too much respect to call him by his first name.

Eulen dipped his pipe in salute to Washburn, an appreciation of the tobacco they exchanged, and then said, in his gravelly, time-ravaged voice, "Think we might be up against something we ain't been up against in a long time."

"What's that?" Felicia piped up from the dark, saving Collier from having to ask. Eulen liked his drama, and Collier usually waited for someone else to feed it.

Eulen savored his moment. "Professionals," he said, finally.

Collier let the others absorb that. "Mr. Cody, do you mean pre-Event?" When everything was better. Even the intelligence agencies.

There was enough light now for everyone to see Eulen shrug his shoulders. "At least trained by someone with pre-Event experience." Like I was, he left unsaid. A former Marine of Dad's generation who became a CIA Special Ops guy then an analyst, which was impressive enough. That he was still alive, given the events of the last thirty years, was even more impressive. Hence Collier's respect.

"It may be natural talent, too," Collier said. "Deavers was a smooth operator when we served in the Ghosts."

"He was a Ghost?" Felicia exclaimed with the proper amount of awe in her voice. Ghosts were legends.

"Yes," Collier responded, grimly. "But he was part of Caldwell's circle. Almost got me killed." He didn't need to elaborate. Everyone knew how Colonel Caldwell had sold the Ghosts out, a plot foiled by Collier's willingness to distract the Red forces as Rosa ...

... Rosa ...

led the surviving Ghosts to safety.

Rosa.

"... snake in the grass," Felicia huffed and Collier came back to reality.

"Indeed," Collier said, raising a hand to interrupt further commentary, "That he is. But snakes are dangerous. This guy is dangerous. He's more capable than most."

They chewed on that. "So why's he here?" Darra

quietly asked.

No one spoke. Then Eulen did: "To crush you, Collier."

And there it was.

No other reason made sense. The Directorate sneaks in someone who has a history with Collier, knows his MO and capabilities, and was sufficiently ranked to command resources, such as steam cars.

"So why announce himself?" Felicia asked. "Why not mosey up here with a squad of Ds, or even some Faceless, and wipe us out while we're sitting around the table?" And she slapped it with some irritation.

"Because he doesn't know everything yet," Washburn said, poking the pipe at Felicia in emphasis.

She snorted. "Knows enough to let Collier know who he is."

"True," Collier interrupted, "but that might be designed to rattle us, cause us to make a mistake, and use that to fill his info gaps." He drummed the table thoughtfully. "All right," he said, after a moment, "Let me throw this out. Deavers is a bad guy, but a finger-in-the-wind kind of guy. I always got a sense he was following self-interest, not a creed. So, yeah, he's let me know he's here and he's Directorate and they have their own agenda, so rattling us may be part of some longer action and he wants to look good."

"Soooo …" Eulen drew a slow hand across his chest.

Collier followed. "He needs to break this," a gesture around the table, "up but with minimum fuss—"

"And he's hoping you'll take the warning and fade away," Washburn finished for him as he refueled the pipe.

Collier smiled in the dark. Count on Washburn to grasp the implications.

Quietly, Darra asked, "Will you?"

Collier let that sit for a moment before saying, "No."

A pause. "Here's what we're going to do," and he made assignments. Simple ones: Alert the troops. Move supplies. Increase readiness. "Got it?" he said and the others acknowledged and got up because there was nothing further to discuss and shuffled toward the door.

"Ben. Washburn," Collier said softly and those two paused and returned to the table as the others continued on.

The door closed, Collier looked at the two of them, Washburn's pipe-glow providing enough light for him to make them out. "I need to know," Collier whispered low enough the two had to lean forward to catch it, "who's with Deavers. What he's got, where's he got it, and what he intends."

They stared at him a moment, then at each other, nodded, and slipped out. Collier smiled slightly. The two may not like each other, but they worked together well. Very well.

Collier waited a decent interval then stood and carefully made his way to the door, more by memory than sight. He opened it and peered around the sanctuary, the two candles at either end almost like strobes in comparison to the pitch blackness of the meeting room.

"Ready, Mr. Rashkil?" a soft voice carried to him from a back pew.

He grinned. "I am, Mrs. Rashkil," and he strolled over to the nave, snuffing the candle on the table there, and then down the middle until he stood opposite the last pew, locating the shadow in the farthest seat. The shadow rose and moved into the golden glow of the last candle. It was like the sun illuminating an angel, the light finding beauty and throwing it out for all the world to enjoy.

She *was* an angel, otherworldly, elfin, with a bronze cast to her skin and hair that spoke of fairy and Tu'ath and ancestors from other universes. Her eyes saw other planets and had witchery in them. Collier still remembered the first time he saw her. It was a couple of months after he had given up the search for Rosa in the hills of central Pennsylvania, her trail going cold somewhere near Harrisonburg. He'd drifted down the Valley Pike to Waynesboro and had been exiting the wreckage of what used to be Fishburne Military Academy, grieving over the damage done and resolving to dig the weapons storage locker out of the rubble and seize the old WW2 M1s (war tested, mother approved) for his own use and he looked up and saw a fairy queen standing quietly near a crushed porch column. Her eyes contained everything of the last thirty years. Everything.

"Hello," she'd said, voice of wind chimes.

"I'm lost," he'd replied, and he did not mean his location.

Standing there in the rubble of Collier's adolescence, she said her name was Evelyn and she was born in Waynesboro and her parents had worked as teachers at Waynesboro High School and it was astonishing for Collier to realize he may have actually known her father because he'd been an assistant football coach and Collier had played against them. But it was a lost memory. And he had never seen her anywhere around the town before, and after, the Event, because that would have been a memory he'd never lose.

But she had seen him.

During the Draft Gang attacks, townsfolk often teamed up with Fishburne cadets to beat them back. She was part of that. Her dad had taught her to shoot right after the Event because he wasn't going to have his daughter dragged off to serve whatever government or President was in charge of the country this week and, on at least five occasions, she had helped man the Fishburne ramparts.

"I never saw you," Collier insisted.

"I know," she'd said.

Her family had remained in Waynesboro after the war started, and that's where Breakout caught them. Fleeing the monsters, they had, unfortunately, run smack into a bunch of them at Swift Run Gap. Evelyn had watched from some hillside rocks as her family was raped and dismembered, the monsters throwing body parts at her but unwilling to climb up to get her. They finally left, jeering and laughing and wearing parts of her sister and her mother around their shoulders, and she began coughing, the first signs of Phase 2. She wandered delirious through the mountains and ended up at the ghost town of Elkton, strewn with the bodies of other Phase 2 victims, and lay down in the middle of the street to die alongside them, but she didn't. She recovered, she stayed there, a ghost among ghosts, hunting deer and bear in the surrounding mountains and trading with passing Blues and sniping passing Reds. As the Blues disappeared and the Reds multiplied, she drifted back to Waynesboro and her wrecked house and found Collier in his wrecked school.

"I was a Ghost," was all Collier said to explain his own travels. And that was all that was necessary.

She came with him as he wandered down the Valley (which is northwards in the odd geography of the place) and he took out his (Dad's) Bible in places where there seemed an interest and preached what he felt. In the unknown ways that things occur, they ended up in the mountains somewhere near Bluemont and Collier became a composter in service to the Brave New State and a secret pastor in service to God and they married and they had three sons.

And he did not love her.

He couldn't. Love was an alien affection, a luxury reserved for the unscarred and the innocent, and he was neither. The events of the last thirty years had shriveled his heart, leaving only a fraction of it free of scar tissue, and that sore, tender area was fleeting and ephemeral.

And filled with Rosa.

But the last thirty years were more important than faded emotions, and he could read all those years in her eyes. Every time Collier gazed into them, he saw everything that happened to him, to her, to all of their friends, to everything they had believed and held precious Before. It meant that he saw, in a glance, what he'd survived, what anyone could survive and where the journey takes them, in this case to a mountain home draped in the cool nights of October out of the sounds of guns and screams.

There is a kind of love in that.

And she did not love him, that he knew. Her heart had started out more fragile than his and it was now a smoldering cinder. But she respected and admired him, both excellent substitutes, and she genuinely loved their sons as mothers usually love their children. Usually.

He gathered her to him, in the candle light her body insubstantial, already half in the fairy world. "Let's go home," he said.

1.4

Yesterday Evening

"Is everyone all right?"

Stupid question.

Cass and Slickie didn't bother to respond but lay gasping under the cover of a honeysuckle bower. Price sympathized. A five- or six-mile run through the woods tested the stamina of even the youngest and strongest, which is why Price hadn't relied on it. He'd let sheer terror motivate him, instead.

Price leaned against the side of the bower to get his own gasping under control while slapping at his clothes to get as much of the dirt and thistle and crap off him as possible. Looked like he'd managed to drag along half the underbrush he and the kids had crashed through as they fled. He was torn up, scoured and gouged and filthy. One of the reasons these woods were so secure was their difficulty. Sometimes, that was a detriment.

Like when you're running for your life from a bunch of masked crazy people.

Price moved to the corner of the bower and cautiously peered through the opening. He had a clear view down the slope from here, at least in terms of angle. There was a lot of vegetation blocking the view but that was an advantage: it would slow down any pursuers; would tear them up as much as he was torn up; the swaying and breaking of branches and the cursing and yelping would give them away. It was late, shadows forming but not enough to obscure his vision and he squatted, peering hard down the line of the slope. Satisfied, or, at least, not duly alarmed, he turned back to the kids. "To repeat, are you okay?"

"Yes," Cass wheezed. Slickie just nodded, but sat up, indicating his wind was back. "Uncle P," he said, "what the hell was that?"

"An ambush," Price replied mildly. "Your first, I believe."

"But," Cass spluttered, proof her wind was also back, "those guys were dressed like the Faceless!"

"That's because they *were* the Faceless," Price kept the mild tone, "Led by none other than the commander of the Faceless, Major Rickard Lawless."

They both went stark white. "I see you appreciate the gravity of that news. Good. So why don't the two of you tell me who you talked to yesterday?"

The white faces took on blank looks. Cass, though, immediately turned red, proof she realized his implications. "We didn't tell anybody!" she snapped, mortally offended.

"And I didn't ask that question," Price pointed out, "I asked who you talked to."

That took some of the offense off Cass's face. "Well …" she thought, "Dad, of course."

"And Mom," Slickie added.

"I figured that," Price said dryly, "Who else did you tell you were doing the run today?"

"We didn't have to tell anybody," Cass snorted, "It's our week."

Hmm. Good point. The Stump Run rotated among the youngsters, teams of two circulating through the six stumps scattered about the Valley, from Lexington up through Waynesboro. It was fairly safe duty because the city boys wanted them some popskull; the swill that the regime passed off as whiskey was hardly worth the queue. Popskull was cheaper too, costing a couple of pieces of something relatively precious readily attainable from the many abandoned houses and stores still untouched by looters. And no monthly quota: if you had the gold or diamonds or porcelain, you could come out every afternoon and order up your three jars. And it was safe: no one saw each other. The city boys knew to come back to the stump an hour after they'd made their yodel, even a pathetic one. Any sooner, and there was a good chance they'd get an arrow in the throat, which was significantly worse than a throatful of popskull, so the time limits were scrupulously observed. If they found their payment instead of popskull was still inside the stump, well and good, try again tomorrow; but that never happened because the teams made the switch quickly and then melted back into the woods, not bothering to see who their customers were. All around, safe.

Except for today.

"All right." Price moved off this line of inquiry. "Who'd you tell I was going with you?"

Cass threw out exasperated hands. "No one! We didn't even know until you rode out with us this morning!" Slickie nodded in confirmation.

Hmm. Another good point. He'd joined the run as a last minute thing, primarily because he was tired of office work. Wasn't his style. Yes, necessary, required, because his far flung empire (chuckle) needed managing: books to balance, lucre to count, recalcitrant gangsters to discipline. But a few weeks of administering his far-flung empire from a chair in his main office – located in an obscure corner of an old, musty warehouse in the back of the old Sydney-Hampden College – made him antsy. Had to get out. Had to go do something. Anything. Even something as low level as a stump run.

So he'd got up, pushed the chair back, stretched, walked into the main area where his angels were sorting jewelry, said, "See y'all later," grabbed his horse and headed out. 'No particular place to go,' as Pap used to sing whenever they got into his old rust bucket Ford and set off to do some business. Price hadn't told the angels where he was going because, as Pap used to say, "Doan let anyone know where ya headed,' and, frankly, he'd had no idea, simply that he had to get away from ledgers and valuations and streams of people coming in to give intelligence reports or cause problems. At first, he'd thought he'd head up to New Market and visit one of his satellite warehouses, the very same warehouse from which he'd done Col Leideig's bidding, an irony he privately enjoyed but that no one else knew about because, well, no one else was alive from those days. Every time he showed up there, he expected the good Colonel's irate ghost to leap gibbering out of some closet and wail, "You killed me, Price!"

Well, yeah, Colonel, because you tried to kill me first. Now I'm running your old business. Cute, huh?

But going there would mean another few days of ledgers and snitches and he needed to do some real work, see some real people, so he'd turned the horse west and, yesterday evening, trotted into the Dinwiddie's yard, hidden behind the remnants of another old musty warehouse in the back of another old college, Sweet Briar. Old musty warehouses in decaying colleges were excellent hideouts because colleges were the last places anybody wanted to loot these days. All they had anymore was books, and the number of people who could read diminished every year, so there was no market.

Didn't take long for things to go straight to hell, did it?

All of which meant ... even *he* hadn't known he was going to the Dinwiddies until yesterday. And, until this morning, he hadn't known he was going on the stump run. Last night, he and the Dinwiddies had enjoyed several rounds of Homer's particularly excellent brand of popskull well past the time Cass and Slickie went off to bed. Somewhere about the crack of dawn, the kids woke him up from a wondrous drunken sleep as they saddled horses right outside Price's window, grumbling the whole time about the twenty-five miles to Buena Vista where the Stump was located. Price's war years had given him the gift of instant wakefulness at any disturbance of his drunken slumber, so he'd gotten up and invited himself along, Pap's ancient wisdom urging him on, and followed the kids through the back trails and ridges to the woods near Buena Vista where the Stump waited.

Where the Faceless waited.

"Okay," he said, "scratch that. I don't know how they knew where I was going, but it's obviously not anything you guys did." He paused. If you wrong 'bout sumpin', Pap always said, you say so. Right away. More ancient wisdom, but this kind wouldn't get him killed. He hoped. "Sorry to give you that impression."

"You think this was about you?" Slickie asked before his crazy sister could go off on Price for daring to think ill of her.

"With due modesty," Price said, peering out again, "I can't think of any other reason such firepower would be waiting for us. Those guys operate on a whole different level."

"But, why you?" Cass interrupted because, really, why you? Left unsaid: you're a pissant.

Indeed.

"Kill the head, the body falls," Price said, simply, and considered moving out of the bower and into the open to get a better view. Dude. No. Stupid.

"But!" Cass was incredulous. "We're not doing anything!"

Of course they were, but Price knew what she meant: they weren't doing anything big enough to attract this kind of interest. Indeed, they weren't doing anything much bigger than what several other gangs did, scattered from North Carolina to wherever was still inhabitable out past Nebraska: buncha yokels getting together for a little larceny and smuggling, bribing an official here, doing a favor there and filling the gaps that the People's Republic woefully left in food and comfort. As a result, people ate better than they did under the Five Year Plans and had coal to warm their houses and medicines to cure their ills .
…

… did, didn't they? He frowned. "Yeah, we are," he said, grimly. "Better than they can."

They absorbed that in silence. "So what are we going to do?" Slickie asked.

"First, we're going to get out of here."

"Uhm," Slickie interjected.

"Second," Price continued, ignoring him, "we're going to find out what rat bastard gave us up."

"Uh …"

"And *how* they gave us up," he concluded, grimly. Because, really, how the hell did they pull this off? Best Price could figure, someone had been following him ever since he left the warehouse. So, why didn't they simply kill him somewhere along the route?

Really, why?

"Uncle P!" Slickie hissed as he grabbed Price's arm, an action that would usually get the grabber a separated shoulder, but this was Slickie who was not prone to dramatic movements. "I smell smoke!"

Price stared at him for a moment and then took in a

deep breath. Yes, smoke. He turned back to the slope and scrutinized the tree line. Yep, there, wisps of it threading through the woods. Coming their way.

"Sonofabitch," Price swore, then looked at Slickie. "Looks like your little popskull fire lit off good."

"Shouldna made it up here so fast," Slickie, crouched next to Price in the bower entrance, whispered.

"Why not? It's up-slope." Price measured the distance to the first tendrils. "We should go now," he said, and wiggled his way to the entrance. Standing up, he caught his foot on a loose vine and pitched forward. "Sonofa ..."

Dien Bien Phu.

The bower and the ground in front of it shredded as a thousand bullets from the tree line systematically ripped the place apart. "Shit!" Price screamed as he dove head first back through the bower entrance, pulling the stunned Slickie and Cass along with him and slamming them into the bottom of a little trench running down the middle of it and falling on top of them. "Shit!" he reiterated.

The bower became a rainstorm of leaves and twigs as the bullets took it down, inch by inch, the buzz of angry hornets flying micro inches over Price's body. He flattened himself as much as he could without squashing the kids, but he was seconds away from bullets skittering along his spine. All the Faceless needed to do was continue erasing the bower bit by bit.

The firing stopped.

"Uncle P?" Cass's quavering voice in his ear.

"Quiet!" he snipped. "They're coming."

"What do we—" Fear taking her over.

"I'll tell you what we do!" He snapped louder. "We're getting the hell out of here, and we're getting out of here alive. But you do what I say. First, shut up! Second, follow me!" He crawled across their bodies, ignoring their whimpering, reached the wall of honeysuckle at the back, whipped out his trench knife, and began cutting his way through.

Cut and crawl. Silent, urgent, because the Faceless were coming.

This honeysuckle hedge ran along a rivulet that would probably be full of water next month but was dry now, thank God. Following along it, Price cut and crawled, leaving just enough room to slip through because they needed the cover. Because the Faceless were coming.

Cut, crawl, agony, thirst, gasp but keep that under your breath because one loud noise and they were dead …

… and they were at the end.

Price viciously slashed through the last bit of vine and kicked himself through, ensuring that no vines gripped him on the way out. Even more viciously, he reached back and yanked both Slickie and Cass through and next to him, sweat pouring off their red and mottled faces, almost passing out as they did everything to suppress their loud panting.

Price rolled to his knees and peered hard along what was left of the rivulet. It sloped up to an open field, a series of boulders marking a ridge line about twenty yards beyond it.

Price pointed at the boulders. "Run. Now."

1.5

Later Evening

"So you knew that guy?"

Collier peered over his ear of corn at his oldest son. "Yes, I knew him."

Second shook his head. "Wow. Just wow."

Collier put the ear down and glared. "What does that mean?"

The twins, Art and Bart, popped eyes at each other over their own corn, then at their elder brother sitting across from them. Almost on command, they dropped their ears and sat back to enjoy the show.

Evelyn, sitting opposite Collier, frowned. "Collier," she warned.

"No, no." He waved her down. "I'd really like to know what that means. Please." He made a gesture at Second, which was a title more than a name. He was the second John Rashkil, the first having disappeared somewhere near Manassas when Breakout happened, at least as far as Collier could piece together. *That* John Rashkil had been a tough, old school, old-style cop ("Not a cop. An agent," he'd correct), relentless and fearless, who'd fought a one-man war to restore civilization in the DC area until he was overrun. A hero, a man of principle and honor, who loved his wife, his son, and his country. Second did not live up to the name. Just didn't.

A terrible thing to think about one's own child, Collier

knew, but facts speak for themselves. The fuck of it was: Second was very much like Collier, who'd spent his own childhood fighting with John over every stupid thing imaginable and getting into trouble in school and the neighborhood until, finally, got his stupid ass sent to Fishburne. Perhaps Second was John's revenge. Collier could picture John sitting on a cloud somewhere and laughing himself silly. If Fishburne still existed, Collier would have already shipped Second's stupid ass right on down there. The place had saved Collier's life, figuratively and literally, since he'd been there when the Event happened. Second would benefit from a stay there, also figuratively and literally. Collier wouldn't end up breaking his neck.

Realizing he'd stepped in it – again – Second mumbled, "I don't mean nothin'," into his plate.

"Oh, no, no," Collier said with solicitude, "You obviously meant something. There's obviously something on your mind. Please," Collier waved a solicitous hand, "elaborate."

Second didn't respond, simply stared at his plate.

"Let me help you out." Collier kept the solicitous tone. "You are under the impression that my knowing this person has brought trouble to our doorstep. Or something to that effect." A pause. "Right?"

"Collier," Evelyn warned again.

"I didn't say that." Mumble.

"Didn't have to. In fact," Collier wiped his mouth with a napkin, "we can take this a step further and lay bare your main issue … that your Dad, me, is running an illegal church. And now, the Directorate has come." Third pause. "Right?"

Second glared at him, combat full on his face. "The church IS illegal!"

Could have heard a pin drop. Certainly heard Evelyn

drop her fork as she glared at her oldest son. "You will APOLOGIZE!" she yelled, the fire blazing in her eyes.

Ordinarily, Collier would sit back and let Evelyn eviscerate Second because she was very good at it. But this required direct intervention. "Evelyn," he said quietly, raising a hand, and she stopped, but the fire remained.

Second, of course, did not know when to shut up. "But it IS illegal!" he insisted. "It's a crime against the State!" A wild gesture at Collier. "That makes us all criminals. We'll all go to the camps!"

"Oh, no, Second," Collier responded softly. "Not you. Just me, your mother, and your brothers. They won't take you. You've proven yourself a loyal subject."

Second went white at that, stood up, his jaw working but speechless, then kicked his chair back and stormed out, slamming the front door so hard that the candles, even the precious oil lamp, flickered. The twins, open mouthed, watched this whole thing, then looked at each other and, reaching silent agreement in their secret twin language, got up and followed their brother out the front door.

"That was a bit harsh," Evelyn said, but her tone indicated she agreed with the sentiment.

"I know," Collier said, "And I'm regretting it now, but that kid needs to wake up."

"How can he?" she said. "When all his friends are getting appointments to State academies while he can't even attend school—"

"Because his Dad is a proscribed person." Collier finished it for her. And frowned.

"I am, too," she said, irritably. "You know what I mean. The kids don't know anything."

True. The children of the Breakout generation only knew that the world was a scary place, with portions of the country still off limits, skeletons everywhere, towns and cities and skyscrapers and malls all moldering and collapsed and haunted, a nightmare landscape underscored by stories from dads and moms about death and murder and genocide, while the State heroically proclaimed that it could end the nightmare if 'you young people would simply put yourself in our hands.' Not your parents' hands, not your family's.

Not even God's.

He sighed. "You're right. They don't. We didn't either. I fought my Dad on everything. I'm sure you fought yours, too."

"I was a good girl," she said, tonelessly, and got up and collected the unfinished dinner. The food would go into salvaged Mason jars and old Tupperware and would appear as some other concoction tomorrow night, because food was too precious these days to allow a family huff to ruin it.

"I know," he said. And he did. The scars on her soul came later. "But I think we've failed to get our point across."

"What point?" She scraped stewed tomatoes off the twins' dishes and into a silver bowl salvaged from an old mansion at the bottom of the hill.

"That the only person you can rely on is yourself." He got up and grabbed plates, piling the remaining food into another dish.

"So you can't rely on me?" An angry strike of fork on dish.

"Don't start an unnecessary fight because you know what I mean."

She did and the color in her cheeks faded. "That's one point. What are some others we failed to pass on?"

"Well, that the State hates freedom. Which is why the State hates the Church."

They were both silent as they gathered food into one

place and Collier had to admit it looked tasty, the beginnings of an excellent stew. Waste not, want not.

"We have explained it, all of it, already," she said, after a moment.

Yes, they had drilled and cajoled and expressed these points to the kids on hundreds of thousands of occasions. At home, in church, while working in the hills. "In one ear."

"Not the twins."

"Hmm," Collier grunted. That might be true, but Collier wasn't sure if the twins' actually accepted his teachings or merely acted as if they did, a function of their secretiveness. The twins lived in their own symbiotic world. They gave tacit acknowledgment of Collier and Evelyn in a manner that looked suspiciously like humoring. They treated Second the same way, so who knows what they really thought. But at least they did not challenge him.

Evelyn and he converged on the farm sink with the various dishes and Collier grabbed the tin bucket (also liberated from the same mansion), and headed out to the well. An almost quarter moon provided sufficient light for him to make his familiar way from the back door to the pump. No sign of Second, but the twins were obviously in the barn, judging by the fooling-around noises. Collier almost called out to them to knock it off, but forget it. Enough authority for one night.

He dragged the full bucket back inside – each passing year made this job harder and harder – and set it by the sink and the two of them washed up. Many traditional family roles had reverted to 19th Century standards since the Event, but Collier did not regard women as servants. Rosa had taught him that. Besides, Evelyn worked as hard as he did.

"So are we in danger?"

"We're always in danger," Collier replied absently as he scrubbed up more lye soap. Lye soap. My God, how things have devolved. "Remember Joy?" he asked.

She turned to him, surprised. "Do I look unhappy to you?"

"No, no," Collier laughed, "I mean the dishwashing liquid, Joy."

"Oh," she said. "Oh, yeah, in the yellow bottle, right?"

"Yep. Squeeze a little on a rag. Suds a poppin'."

"Uhm," she said, looking at her lye-reddened hands ruefully. "I think we used Dawn."

"Dawn, yeah." Collier wrung out his cloth then moved on the pans. "It had universal applications. My Dad used it to make bug spray."

"Huh?"

"He'd mix garlic and mineral oil in a spray bottle, add some Dawn, and then spray down his garden with it. Drove the bugs off."

"That'd drive off people, too. Garlic, umm," she savored. "It would be nice to have some."

"Can we grow it here?"

"I don't know," she said, flipping a towel at the dishes. "I think it needs more warmth. Besides, where would we get seeds?"

"We could order a pizza and scrape it off the top."

She laughed. "Domino's, or Pizza Hut?"

"Papa John's. A Hawaiian pizza."

She wrinkled her brow. "What's that?"

"Pineapple and ham slices."

She rendered judgment. "Eww."

Collier chuckled. "It was actually pretty good. It was Dad's favorite. He'd order two and then grab a couple of scary movies and there was Friday night."

"CDs," she said, wistfully. "VCRs."

"Electricity."

They said nothing but stopped drying and regarded each other. "Do you see why they don't understand us?" she whispered.

Yes, he did. He and Evelyn were children of Oz, where you rubbed a lamp and food appeared in refrigerators and there was ice cream and milkshakes and home delivery of piping hot pizzas and Marvel comic books and Saturday morning cartoons and warm houses in winter, cool ones in summer, and lights at night. And there was a future, one you could choose. Be an astronaut. Be a doctor. "By the waters of Babylon, we lay down and wept," he whispered.

"Don't you see?" She placed a hand on his shoulder. "They hear us talk about these things and they want them, too. And their only hope of getting them is through the State. Their friends down in town, the ones with parents in the Party, get better food. They get to learn things. They even get oil."

This was not new. They had both, long ago, realized they were competing against Mammon. "I know," he said. I know I've lost, he did not say. But I will not go down without a fight.

"Are we in danger?" she repeated.

He was quiet for a moment. "Yes," he said.

1.6

Last Night

Nightmare.

The moon was not quite quarter, its light dim, diffused by the trees, everything striped in silver and black and Price could not see. Running was murder, Price's face and hands ripped to pieces by thorns and blackberry and low hanging larch and sharp juniper needles. His lungs burned, his knees and ankles ached from the dips and troughs he had missed in the dark and one wrong step would mean a twisted and/or broken ankle but keep going, keep going.

Cass and Slickie, gasping at his heels, were better able to keep up, but they didn't have Price's woods sense and suffered more from the punishing terrain than he. Too much time on horses and the remnants of the old highways and smooth trails. How many times had he told them and everyone else to get off the roads and walk the uncut paths, learn the ridgelines and how the land fell, the folds of it, feel it underfoot and gain a rapport with it. Because you never knew when you would have to run like hell through it.

Speaking of horses ... got to get to theirs.

They'd left them hidden in a copse of trees at the bottom of the first ridge that fronted the hidden trail, which wound up the mountain and through the woods to the Stump. A good two hours' walk, which should be cut in half by their speed. That is, if they were still on the trail, but they weren't: Price had forced them into the tree line, keeping the boulders off to his right so they weren't making a direct approach to them because that would get them killed. Because the Faceless were still with them.

Behind them, maybe a hundred, two hundred yards, but still there, sticking to Price like blackflies following a mule, not quite gaining but never getting far enough away that Price could dash for the boulders and then slip down the mountainside to the horses and escape.

How are the Faceless still with them?

Price couldn't say. Obviously, they had expertise, but tracking down fugitives in the night-time mountains – mountains that the Faceless shouldn't know – was a rare-enough talent well before the Event, much less now. So someone in that pursuing pack of wolves was familiar with the area. Familiar with the Stump. And familiar with Price. Okay, pretty much had reached that conclusion earlier and, given the circumstances, Price assumed it was someone who was also a master of surveillance because Price hadn't picked up a whiff, and Price was whiff sensitive. "Watch your back, boy," Papa always exhorted, and meant far more than wariness of the hovering knife. Look for people who are far too interested in you. He had. And saw no one.

Was he losing his touch?

"Watch it!" Price suddenly whispered fiercely as he felt the ground disappear under him. He leaped, praying he'd judged the depth of this sudden decline accurately as he landed hard, collapsing his legs and doing a rather undignified break fall to his side. "*Oof!*"

"*Oof!*" repeated twice as Cass and Slickie followed his lead and landed on either side of him. Fortunately, not on top of him. Red flickered up and down Price's legs and back and, for half a second, he was afraid he'd broken something. No, just his oldster body registering a protest. "You two okay?" he hissed.

Affirmative gasps were the only answer, and Price watched as their moon-striped bodies sat up and began brushing themselves. Price looked around. They had dropped into a depression, very steep, and through some trick of the moon, fairly well-lit; Price noted the clay-riddled walls, occasional boulders and tree roots protruding from them, running in the direction they wanted to go. Risky, because of the light, but it offered a route that would keep them below eye level for a bit.

Unless the Faceless had night vision.

"Uncle P!" Cass wheezed and Price shook his head no. He knew what she wanted: to rest a minute, catch their breaths, settle their aching limbs.

Can't. The Faceless were coming.

"Let's go," he snapped and was on his red-flickering feet and hurtling down the ditch, Cass's "But!" desperate in his ears but there was no time, no time. Catch your breath when we escape this, Cass. If we escape this.

Because the Faceless had night vision.

Only thing that made sense. No one was guiding them. There weren't that many people left in the world, much less this area, who could lead the Faceless on a leisurely pursuit of Price over this terrain. Two of such rare people, Cass and Slickie, were right alongside. The next two best candidates were Cass and Slickie's parents and, while Price did not put anything past anyone anymore, that was so unlikely as to be downright laughable. Which meant night vision.

Where did the Faceless get night vision?

Sure, lots of night vision units were lying around ripe for the pickin'. There were still plenty of unlooted Radio Shacks across the country where one could help oneself to all kinds of cool stuff, from computers to radios to night vision scopes. Toys, to be sure, but they still worked. And then there's the hundreds of abandoned military bases still dotting the countryside with pallet loads of night vision units stacked up to the ceilings of their unlooted warehouses. Who would get first crack at them but the State?

But how do you power them?

They'd had night vision in the Blues but rarely used them because batteries were hard to find and no one knew how to fix the units once they broke. Science goes right out the window when the Dark Ages descend. If someone did have batteries, they could be recharged, but that required electricity and there was precious little of that. Only the elites had it.

Like the Faceless.

Grimly, Price lurched forward, keeping his eyes about four feet ahead to watch for tripping hazards. Don't fall; stay up; keep going. After a few minutes, a red hot coal formed in Price's side, a stitch, but he ignored it. Would rather suffer from that then get stitched by a machine gun.

A machine gun. Price could really stand a machine gun about now.

Would even things up. The Faceless, obviously, had an armory manned by a couple of guys (or gals. Let's not be sexist, old boy) who knew how to maintain those things. They, also, must have at least one guy (gal) who knew how to make bullets because they'd sprayed them rather indiscriminately back there. That indicated an unlimited supply ... or a real desire to put Mamma Price's little boy into a grave. Price didn't think he rated this much attention, so lots of available bullets.

Price had machine guns, but not in a place he could readily get to them. His were cached because the last thing a happy-go-lucky smuggler such as he wanted to do was to get caught with one. That was instant death, not only for the smuggler but for everybody in a ten-mile radius. The State took a very dim view of weapons capable of challenging them and, although they knew a lot of guns were still out there (especially among ex-Blues), they didn't make an issue of it unless they showed up. It was okay for smugglers and other enemies of the State to kill each other with clubs and knives and crossbows, but let someone pop off a round … scorched earth, the burning of towns and houses followed by wholesale executions to rival anything that Breakout had done. Not worth it. So the guns remained stored and safely away, in case of an emergency.

Would the present situation qualify?

Despite his short breath, Price had to chuckle because yes, yes it did. But his weapons caches were rather far from here, and digging them up and pulling things out of cosmoline and praying that the bullets were still viable would take up a little more time than the Faceless would give him …

"Uncle P!" Cass's gasp in his ears.

"We can't stop!" he gasped back. "They're still with us!"

And they were. He couldn't see them, couldn't even hear them but there was a disturbance in the force. Birds behind them and off to the side, lifted from their roosts, screeched their annoyance. Small animals skittered out of the way, creating an unprecedented racket, and wild dogs barked. That meant something big was in the area, and not a bear. Something a lot meaner and more dangerous than that.

"Uncle P!" once more in his ear.

"Dammit, Cass!" he yelped a little louder than he intended. "We can't stop!" And he sped up,

And Slickie's hand seized his shoulder, almost lifting him off the ground. Doubly surprised by Slickie's strength and that the kid was stopping a perfectly good attempt to escape death, Price lost his footing and went tumbling into the sand and clay that lined the bottom of this ditch. "Are you crazy?" he said as he whirled around and faced the two idiots.

"We're going the wrong way, Uncle P!" Cass's harsh whisper in his ear.

"What?" Price responded, immediately intrigued. He'd been heading generally north, generally in the direction of the horses, and was confident enough in his sense of direction that he'd kept a proper heading. But maybe these two kids knew this area better than he thought.

The two of them had collapsed beside him, their expressions of pain clear in the moonlight, and the grasping of their sides clues that they, too, suffered from stitches. While they fought for enough breath to make their explanations intelligible, Price scrutinized their branch-torn faces. The kids were scared to death. Not that he could blame them; this was probably the first true life-and-death situation they had ever faced in their lives, not counting some smuggler-generated danger, or Homer's wrath.

"That way!" Cass could finally form words as she pointed over the lip of the ditch eastwards. "There's a cave!"

"A cave?" Price looked at Slickie, who nodded in confirmation. Price dismissed it. "Cave won't do us any good. We'll be trapped." And he gathered his legs under him.

"Runs through the mountain." More gasps. "All the way to the bottom."

"What?"

"Like a chimney," Slickie explained, his own breath somewhat restored. "It's tight, but doable. Ends up close to the horses."

"How do you know?"

Cass was annoyed. "You always told us to find escape routes, so we found this one. We checked it out. It works!"

"Well," Price said, standing up but keeping his head below the lip. Didn't want to get imaged. "That's good, but right now," he pointed down the ditch, "we've got a straight shot at the horses. We keep our heads down and they won't see us. Besides, this is going to get us there a lot faster than crawling through a cave. And getting stuck in it." And he squared on the ditch.

"But Uncle P!" Cass, frantic, pulled at him and Price shook her off ...

... and heard it.

An undertone, unnatural, in the air. It was familiar somehow, but Price could not place it.

"What's that?" Cass, hearing it, too, asked.

Price held up a finger. The undertone had a rhythm to it and it was growing louder by the second. No longer undertone, it was a blatant, overt assault on the night and the natural sounds of a mountain forest ...

... *whupwhupwhupwhup* ...

"Oh shit!" Price groaned as the Blackhawk helicopter burst over the trees on the west side of the ditch and careened along the line of it, slapping the air with its blades and jinking right and left as it flew. It slowed and hovered about fifty yards up, the sounds of winged demons drowning out everything, the hurricane whipping the trees back and forth and sand into their eyes. Suddenly it went incandescent as a searchlight snapped on and flooded the ditch, blinding them, even though the light was still far away.

"What is THAT?" Cass shrieked in sheer terror, forgetting that such a shriek was like a beacon to the pursuing Faceless. Not that Price could blame her. She had never seen an aircraft of any kind actually flying. The wrecks of them, yes, pictures and stories told by veterans, sure, but a dragon was legend until it showed above your town, roaring and flapping its wings and breathing fire.

"Death," Price said. He whirled on Slickie and seized the lapels of his jacket. "The cave! Now!"

Slickie, mesmerized by the Blackhawk now quartering the ditch front, stared uncomprehendingly at Price for a moment before he snapped out of it, yanked himself free and scrambled up the ditch side directly opposite. "Come on!" he shouted and waved them up.

Cass was a mouse in the serpent's eye, helpless, paralyzed, as the searchlight waved and pulsed and flipped around the ditch, slowly reaching out to her standing dead in the middle of it, waiting to be eaten. Price grabbed the back of her coat and hauled her up the ditch side, unmindful of the telltale signs they were leaving for the Faceless. Screw the Faceless. Had bigger problems.

He pushed her in the direction Slickie had gone. "Run!"

1.7

Midnight

Nightmare.

Worse than the previous one.

These woods became thicker, downright impenetrable, with every known species of thorn and briar growing exactly at head height, ripping Price's face to pieces, assisted by every single larch and pine and oak along the way whose pointed branches were positioned exactly at eye height. How he had not blinded himself, he did not know.

And a dragon stalked them.

The Blackhawk made ovals around them, flying to either side of their line of escape and crossed their T well ahead, containing them within a search area that narrowed with every pass. Its pattern completed behind them, it hovered and flipped on its great searchlight, close enough that the forest in front of Price was well lit and he avoided the worst of the tree spears reaching for his face.

Mostly.

It had taken Price a bit to figure out what the Blackhawk was doing, but as it tightened its grid, it became apparent: the pilot was taking directions from the pursuing Faceless. Obviously, the Faceless had found the spot in the ditch where the three of them had entered the woods, obviously guided there by Cass's screams. Should have a word with her about that. Later.

If there was a later …

The smashed branches and shredded clothing and skin Price and the kids had left behind in their headlong flight marked a clear path for the Faceless to follow. The saving grace was that these woods were also impeding the Faceless. But there were more of the Faceless than there were of Price, which meant they could spread out and find easier ways through the woods and catch up and begin flanking.

And they had a dragon.

That it flew in ovals then hovered and waited, told Price a couple of things. First, the Faceless didn't have radios, otherwise the Blackhawk wouldn't have to keep going back to get an adjusted heading. Made sense: no repeaters or antennae in these mountains anymore, at least ones that worked, their metals and generators long since scavenged. And second, the hover told Price exactly where the Faceless were. And how far ahead he was.

And that he was losing ground.

"How. Much. Farther?" he wheezed at Slickie's back. The kid didn't bother answering, didn't even bother turning around but bulled ahead, taking the brunt of the thorns and damage.

That far, huh?

Cass was right behind Price, mostly because he had a death grip on her coat and dragged her along. She was a gibbering mass of terror, especially as the helicopter narrowed and narrowed and drew closer and closer …

They were running out of time.

Either time or forest. Price wasn't sure which would end first. The tree cover was keeping them out of the Blackhawk's sight for now, but forests had an annoying habit of disappearing quite suddenly. All they had to do was reach a clearing at exactly the same time the pilot wheeled over and there they'd be, caught and blinded by the searchlight, and there they'd be, cut in half by the M60 mounted in the door.

The gunner wouldn't even need night vision.

Price didn't think the Faceless needed them, either, at least, not anymore. Night vision would actually be a detriment in this operation because the helicopter's searchlight would overwhelm the units. No, the Faceless were tracking them by skill alone, which brought him back to his recent oft-asked question as to who was providing that skill. Had to be someone like Price; one of those rare young'uns who had learned the way of wood and dale at the hard hands of Pap and Granny and the cousins and uncles who ran the Stump business out of Farmville. Someone who had survived the Flus and the plagues and the zombies and warfare and death. Who had been recruited by the Faceless and was now leading this mission.

Which was stupid – this mission, that is – because the Faceless simply didn't bother with pissants like Price. They were big time, the personal assassination squad of General Kant himself, small in number and elite in action, a rare, rare group of people in a world that had a rarity of people to begin with. Kant used them to take out rivals, the troublesome leaders popping up here and there in the Mexican Territories, in the Dead Lands, and the Northern California Republics. The Faceless were based in the State's capital, Fredericksburg, which was close enough to Farmville that Price had made it a point to familiarize himself with the unit and its leaders, like Lawless. But that had been mere precaution. Price, in a million years, never figured the Faceless would be set loose on him.

With a helicopter.

In the midst of headlong flight, Price still shook his head in amazement. A helicopter. Talk about a precious resource. Yeah, planes and helicopters still flew because there were still enough pilots around to crew them and teach others how to fly, but, again, that was a small, elite group, its talents not wasted on pissants. Nor was fuel wasted on pissants. Nobody knew how to refine aircraft fuel anymore, so the gas came out of existing stocks and there wasn't a lot of that. One thing the Event had taught everyone was that fuel broke down, and if there wasn't more fuel being made, then the viable stores of it shrank each year, becoming more and more precious. That's why cars, the few that existed, had devolved into coal-burning monstrosities so incredibly inefficient that most of the Party officials authorized their use preferred horses. A helicopter certainly couldn't run on coal. And, heck, there was maintenance, which had to be tough these days: no mechanics, no parts. The Blackhawk had to be a real bitch to keep flying.

And yet, here it was.

Why?

What the hell had Price done to attract this level of expensive, rare, and deadly, attention?

Should probably spend some time over the next few days figuring that out.

"How. Much. Farther?"

Again, Slickie didn't answer and Price fumed. Must insist the kid give him ballpark so Price could calculate how much longer he had to live and Price gathered breath to do so when Slickie stopped cold. Price almost piled into his back. "Man!" Price snapped, recovered his balance and pulled Cass to him, "Give some warning!"

Slickie said nothing but canted his head at the helicopter's *thwupthwupthwup* from somewhere to their left. Uh oh. The helicopter was hovering. Had it spotted them?

Suddenly, the woods exploded in searing light as the searchlight popped on and they were dead, dead, and

Price braced for thousands of 7.62 rounds to eviscerate him. Any moment now ... but nothing. Straining, Price located the center of the searchlight, which was quite some distance from them and focused on something else, some feature rather difficult to make out through the trees and underbrush and bright light ...

A cliff face.

"We're here," Slickie whispered.

"We're where?"

"The ledge that leads to the cave entrance." Turning abruptly, Slickie reached past Price and seized Cass, yanking her forward. "Snap out of it!" he hissed at her and shook her roughly.

"Okay, okay!" Cass yelled, grabbing at his hands. "You're killing me!"

"Would you two keep it down?" Price shushed. "There's some crazy people trying to kill us."

That quieted them and Price stood back to let the two of them evaluate the current situation. "Well?" he said, impatient, after a moment. Need to hurry this along, young'uns. Crazy people are trying to kill us.

"We can't figure out what the helicopter is doing," Cass whispered, panic in her voice.

Price let out a long breath and fixed an eye on the bright searchlight wavering back and forth. "I'll tell you what it's doing, it's looking for us. The pilot has figured out we are headed for this cliff and he's going to do everything he can to keep us from climbing it. So, the question is, where is this cave entrance and can we reach it before the helicopter drifts over this way and holds us here while the Faceless amble on up?"

Slickie glanced back at him and then at the helicopter and made a disgusted sound and stepped boldly up to the rocks, reached up at some handholds, hauled up the side and rolled over a ledge Price hadn't noticed. In seconds, his hand popped down and made impatient gestures at Cass, who grasped his arm and pulled herself up and over. Price didn't wait for assistance but ran at the cliff, his momentum taking him halfway up the side and he scrambled at protrusions until he cleared the ledge's lip and launched himself onto it.

They were exposed.

Price gasped. They were on a flat ledge of rock about six feet wide and hard up against another cliff face. There was no cover. There was no place to hide. And the helicopter was right there. Lighting up the whole area. Pinning them.

"Uhm," Price said. "This ain't good."

Slickie said nothing but stood up in the full light, a suicidal move Price had never thought the kid capable of, and ran almost headlong at the right corner ...

... and disappeared.

"Huh?" Price was taken aback. Especially when Cass rolled to her feet and pushed her head at the same location, which looked like a presage to bashing her brains all over the wall, and disappeared, too.

Price blinked. He looked at the helicopter. The center of the searchlight had yet to focus on this ledge, which was why the gunner hadn't spotted them yet. Don't give him the opportunity. Jumping to his feet, he ran at the same corner, convinced he did not possess the magic key that would cause the rock to open and reveal the Door to Narnia or wherever. At the last second, sure he was about to break his face against rock, Price saw that the cliff folded here and what looked like a solid wall was actually a break wide enough for him to slide past. Next thing he knew, he was standing in shadow, the cliff draping the top of a cave.

"Nice," he said.

"This way," Cass's whisper came out of the dark and

he moved in her direction. He ran into her outstretched hand and grabbed hold. "Lead on," he said.

They might stand a chance, after all, Price decided. If the helicopter didn't mark the cave entrance. If the Faceless didn't find it.

If.

1.8

The Morning

Nightmare. Of a completely different nature.

The best analogy Price could make was that of creeping through a miles-long clammy stone sarcophagus, one so tight that, at times, it was a struggle to move an inch. Any moment now he'd get stuck tight, and spend the rest of a severely shortened life jammed inside an itty bitty stone funnel, his screams echoing through the mountain into emptiness. A black, endless emptiness.

"How the hell do you guys know where you're going?" he frantically whispered to his front.

"It only goes one way." A frantic whisper back from Cass.

Down. That much he could figure out. The slope was about 10-15 degrees, the angle causing him to jam his palms like air brakes into the grit-covered stone floor whenever the funnel widened out enough to release his shoulders. Those were the better times; at least he wasn't being squeezed in the stomach of a stone anaconda.

"How'd you guys find this thing?" he groused at one particularly thin portion of the tunnel where it felt as if his head was being pressed into a vise.

"We saw water running out of the bottom," Cass said.

"Where?"

"At the bottom!" she answered, irritated. "Where it empties out at the bottom of the ridge."

Price thought about that. "So, you saw water pouring out of a hole in the base of a wall, and you decided to go inside it?" A pause. "And climb it? All the way back to the cliff ledge?"

She didn't answer because, yeah, put in those terms, sure sounded like a stupid thing to do. And it was. That it had resulted in the discovery of a fortuitous channel through the mountain allowing them to escape the dragon and its minions didn't change the initial fact that it was a stupid thing to do. They could have blithely stumbled into a den of rattlesnakes or cougars, or got lost in a vast cavern twisting and turning endlessly in the bowels of the earth. Price didn't know if it was a decision made by the impetuousness of youth, or by a lack of judgment. They often intertwined, but one was outgrown, the other was a character flaw. He might have to re-evaluate these two …

Hey, what had she said? Water running out of the bottom?

Hmm.

Price didn't know much about caves. The Shenandoah Valley was rife with them, some of the better ones serving as tourist attractions back when tourists existed. But Price had ignored them because they didn't figure into this business; at least, Pap had never employed them. And, besides, they gave Price the willies. Sure, they could serve as good hiding places for gold bars and other precious items that a wily survivor of the war needed in order to buy a small army of smugglers and quietly take over a three-county area around Farmville. But they were obvious hiding places, and Price didn't want thieves intent on his wealth to have an easy time of it.

So Price did not know what it meant that the bottom entrance of this cave – or chimney, which was the better word – had water pouring out of it, but he could guess. It implied that water entered the top of it, the one now well behind his feet. And enough water to flow through this hole and empty at the bottom … for that matter, enough water to carve a chimney through this ridge all the way down to the bottom … was a lot of water, indeed.

He sure hoped it didn't rain.

He also sure hoped they got to the end of this wormhole soon because Price was discovering a latent claustrophobia. Of course, stick anybody down a hole barely wide enough to wriggle shoulders through and claustrophobia would develop. Immediately. He'd heard horror stories of premature burials, people mistakenly buried alive rousing themselves and slamming their hands into the satin-lined top of their coffins. Or stone sarcophagi. Price now understood their panic; the reason he didn't succumb to it was knowing there was a way out.

Allegedly.

"How much farther?" he said as he pulled himself through a particularly tight section of the cave, silently thanking God when it widened enough that he could take a full breath. No one answered.

So keep going, following the sound of grunts and gasps and quick intakes of breath, making the occasional rest stop to recover from the strains of extricating oneself from a four-inch tomb, and then go again. Minutes became hours, became years. Maybe this *was* a premature burial, because it certainly felt like he was stuck in a coffin …

Wham!

A hammer of air busted him right in the butt, a sudden blast of pressure that actually drove him a few inches forward as it smacked his eardrums silly. "What the hell?" he might have yelled but didn't know if he actually did because he couldn't hear a thing. He felt Cass's feet scrambling against his hands so, apparently, she had suffered the same effect.

Oh, God, was it raining, and there was now a mountain of water rushing at him, displacing the air and changing the pressure?

Wham! Again! With the same results …

Not rain.

Grenades.

The Faceless were tossing grenades down the hole.

Price had hoped the hidden nature of the cave had caused the Faceless to pass on by and climb up the cliff face to the top of the ridge in the mistaken belief Price had gone that way. But it was a forlorn hope because the Faceless were good and their dragon would have told them no one had scaled the cliff or had reached the top. Instead, they'd cast about until they discovered the cave and now they were throwing grenades inside.

Apparently, Price and the kids had crawled far enough down this hole that the shrapnel couldn't reach them, but the grenades still had an effect. Eventually, the Faceless would get curious about that effect and either change their fusing, allowing the grenades to explode at a deeper depth, or send some skinny guy down the hole where he could roll grenades farther along the tunnel, right into Price's feet. That'd have an even worse effect.

Or maybe they'd pour a few gallons of gasoline down the hole, lighting it and sucking out all the air.

"Move!" Price shouted, not caring whether the Faceless heard him or not. He reached forward and grabbed Cass's spasming legs and pushed hard, smacking her on the calf harder to snap her out of it. She got the message because her feet immediately scrambled for purchase, and caught Price's fingers against the stone floor, causing him to yelp in pain. But, no time for that, no time, go, get moving because …

Wham! Another damn grenade!

Price wasn't sure if this one had a bigger yield or was

closer because the air slam actually hurt him. Whatever. Let's go.

The crawl changed its nature from a wearying loss of time and skin layers into a terrifying scramble to put as much distance as possible between themselves and the grenades. At places wide enough, Price tried to turn his head and look back to spot the monsters in pursuit, but that was wasted effort. It was too blasted dark to see anything but the blast of a grenade, and if he could see that he was dead a second later. In the following ten (twenty, one million) minutes, only two more explosions rang through the tunnel, but that was enough to spur all of them to greater efforts. Price marveled at the speed with which he pressed through impossibly thin areas of the tunnel. There was something to be said for panic. It focused the effort.

Crawl, crawl, pull, try to look back, crawl and crawl and crawl and a light.

A light.

Price stopped, confused, because he could now see Cass's boots doing the fandango in front of his eyes as she scrambled along. Oh no, he thought, the Faceless are on top of us, or a burning stream of gasoline is but, no. Not fire.

Dawn.

With a whoop Price simply couldn't contain, he fandangoed right behind Cass and, moments, hours, later, tumbled out of the sarcophagus and into a pile of water and stone and the dawn's early light. Light. Air. Freedom.

"Oh God," he groaned.

Cass, to his right, groaned back, "Let's not do that again."

"Agreed." Slickie, to his left.

Price lay there trying to recover strength and breath and all the other things that people not prematurely buried in stone coffins enjoyed. It would be very nice to lie here for the rest of the morning, but there were other considerations. Faceless ones.

Price sat up. The air was gray and still and cool, a typical mountain pre-dawn in these hyeah parts. That meant Price had been awake for about twenty-four hours straight, a rather eventful time filled with assassins and dragons and chimney crawls and he should be exhausted and collapse right here for a necessary twelve hours of sleep but the one thing he had learned from the war, you sleep when you are safe.

And they weren't safe.

Price looked around. They were up against a moldy, green-tinged rock face with a much larger cave hole set about three feet above. Again, why would anyone think it was a good idea to crawl into that scum-smeared, nasty opening?

Damn kids.

He looked at them, beaten up and tired; their faces slack and pale and filthy with dust and blood and bruises and their eyes glazed and half-closed and maybe he should let them sleep. "Get up," he ordered. "Now."

They didn't move, didn't even twitch. "Get up," he ordered again. "Or die."

"Sounds like a good idea," Cass mumbled.

Price kicked her. Hard. Right in the butt. "Ow!" she yelled. Price stepped over her and kicked Slickie just as hard, getting the same reaction.

"Get up now. Or die."

They did, rubbing their Price-induced bruises and bitching that he'd be the one to kill them but he ignored that and examined the area. They were behind a screen of trees and bushes – thank God for small favors because they were hidden from view. "Where are we?" he asked the still bitching kids.

"The horses are over there," Slickie made a gesture in a vague southerly direction and then resumed rubbing his sore rear.

"How far?"

"About a mile," he answered, keeping his feet somewhat unsteadily. Price looked at him. Wow, the kid looked bad. But, rest when you're safe.

"Go get them, then." Price chin-gestured along the same vague direction Slickie had pointed. The kid's eyebrows raised in some surprise at Price's brusqueness but too bad, too bad. Price was too damn tired to be nice. Slickie hesitated, glanced at his sister and spun about to push through the tree screen. Good. Price relaxed internally. Soon they'd have their mounts and could get out of here ...

Wait.

"As you were!" Price, instinctively falling into an old Army command, shouted at Slickie's retreating form.

Very old Army, because all Slickie did, was turn around, confused. "What?"

"Come back," Price said and waved him in. Puzzled, Slickie did so, exchanging looks with his sister, who had sat back down. "It's no problem, Uncle P," he said, "I can make it to the horses ..."

"... where there's an ambush waiting for us," Price interrupted. Slickie started at that and cocked a head at Price.

"Best I can figure," Price explained, "we were followed. I was followed," he corrected. "So they know where the horses are and expect us to retrieve them, especially after losing us back up the ridge." He thumbed in that direction. "And it won't take them long to realize we survived their little grenade attack—"

"So that's what that was," Cass muttered.

"and even less time to figure out where that little

tunnel empties out." He flipped a finger at the entrance. "So, no horses."

"You mean." Cass was incredulous. "We gotta walk back home?"

Price nodded.

"Oh!' She flopped over in exasperation. "It's twenty miles!"

"Yep," Price agreed. "So you can stay here if you want. Say hello to Major Lawless for me, will ya?" and he stepped through the tree screen, pushing past Slickie.

It took a few steps before Price heard her teenage "Humph!" and sotto voce imprecations that Price figured addressed his lineage as she stamped along behind him, a quieter Slickie taking up the rear. He grinned inwardly but kept his line, moving through the trees which thinned quickly as they descended the slight decline. When we're safe, young'un, I'll let you sleep for a week.

It was getting lighter off to his left and Price examined the horizon, broken by ridge and mountain and forest. Sunrise in about thirty minutes, so best not to be in this thinly wooded area when that happened. Price peered ahead. The slope was mostly scree and shrub for about hundred yards then began a rise to what might be a low pass in the two hills at the front. Probably a mile or so to that point, and then they could skirt the woods and ridge, using the trees and shadows as cover until they broke out of the mountains south of Buena Vista and made their way to Sweet Briar.

Where another ambush waited.

Price set his jaw. Deal with that as it came up. Deal with this now. Need to get to the woods over there before the sun—

THWOPTHWOPTHWOPTHWOP!!!

The helicopter burst around the left side of the ridge line so shocking and sudden that all three of them fell to the ground as if it had rammed them, the craft cocking to the right and so low Price could see the gunner in the open doorway hanging there by a safety line and careening the M60 around. The gunner apparently hadn't spotted them yet because the helicopter came around sharp and headed back toward the ridge at almost the exact spot the cave exit was located. Cass was screaming, Slickie so pale he was albino, and Price was paralyzed; all he could do was follow the helicopter as it stove up near the rock wall, slowly spun about ...

And the gunner had them.

Things happened instantly and simultaneously. Price saw the gunner charge the M60 and lean it out for a steady shot at the same moment he grabbed Cass in one hand and Slickie in the other and hurled both of them off the line of the barrel and then pitched himself forward.

BRRRRRRRRRRRRRR!

The 60 sang, just sang, its death song different than the *ThwopThwop* of the helicopter blades, a sweet dirge, a requiem, as it reached for him, the bullets ripping the trees and dirt and rocks and sending smaller shrapnel versions of themselves in all directions but the line of it, the center of it, was coming for him.

Price dove.

The stream passed his boot heels, pulverizing the rocks and sand covering the ground and rocketing them into the bottom of his shoes and pants and stinging his legs like a thousand hornets. He hit his shoulder and rolled, gasping with the pain as he somersaulted to a semblance of standing and yelled, "Scatter!" to the kids and did not wait but ran straight where his nose pointed, right at the sunrise. He noted with satisfaction that Cass and Slickie broke left and right so at least they'd listened to him ... or blind fear pushed them along their own noses. Now, let's see who this helicopter is after.

Why, him, of course.

The helicopter wheeled off its line and swerved on Price's, the action whipping it side to side so the gunner had to grab the line for dear life. He was yelling something, probably telling the pilot to knock it the hell off and stabilize and Price screeched to a halt, digging his heels and turning sharply to the right ... and saw Slickie, all elbows and knees, running in that direction. A turn to the left and Cass in the same mode and Price knew if he cut either way then he would bring both kids under the same gun so ...

He stood still, right where he was.

Slowly Price turned and watched as the helicopter settled and nosed down and moved in line with him. The gunner, actually grinning, lowered the barrel and Price mentally saluted a long, fun life, filled with a lot more adventure than most people got (and a lot more death and pain than he'd been initially promised) and, given his chosen lifestyle, living a lot longer than he should have and, really, what's the complaint? He looked the gunner in the eye, raised his middle finger in another salute, and braced.

Gunfire.

But not an M60.

Price was momentarily confused. Had the gunner eschewed the 60 for a 16? Because that's what it sounded like, the low-frequency *ratatatat* of one on full auto. More than one, actually, so, what, the pilot decided to get in on this, too? But, no, the gunner still gripped the 60, but was ducking his head and moving the barrel frantically off to the left. There were sparks all over the helicopter, and the pilot was whipping it right and left, throwing the gunner all over the place so, no, they weren't shooting at him. Someone was shooting at the helicopter.

What the hell?

Price was so baffled he began having silly thoughts, like why would the Faceless take on the helicopter? Were they so desperate to take the credit for the kill they'd shoot up one of their own? Well, of course not, so this meant only one thing.

The cavalry had arrived.

The sound of the helicopter's engine changed and black smoke poured out of the housing below the rotors. The gunner whipped the M60 all over the place and fired wildly from ground to sky, probably more intent on dodging the incoming fire than engaging the attackers. The pilot, though, had had enough; the helicopter wheeled over, the entire frame vibrating, and scooted off to the ridge with a broken roar that telegraphed a wounded engine and whipped around the cliff, trailing thick black smoke.

It was instantly, and oddly, silent.

Price stood there, rather amazed by recent events. He turned and watched as the sun peeped above the mountain line, no doubt as astonished as Price. He should be dead. He should be Swiss cheese, not even recognizable as a human being. But, he was standing there, enjoying a fall sunrise.

"Price!' A voice called from somewhere off to his left. "Get your ass moving!"

Price knew that voice. Homer Dinwiddie.

"Cass, Slickie!" a woman's voice screamed. "On me!"

Zoe Dinwiddie.

The cavalry.

Price broke, beelining straight for the voices, not caring which one he got to first. Turned out to be Homer, who emerged from a thicket, a still smoking M16 in one hand and frantically waving Price to him with the other. Price zipped past him and Homer took the rear, watching for trouble as he pointed along a small game trail cutting through the brush. Price ran for it, ducking under branches and thorns with Homer on his heels. About a hundred yards along, they careened into Zoe and Cass and Slickie and the whole group, one behind the other, ran the trail until they were back in the shadows of the ridge, the sun not high enough yet to dispel the shadows. No one spoke, just ran, knowing they were making enough noise through the brake to alert the Faceless; heck, loud enough to bring the helicopter back. But no shots rang out, no Faceless called for them to halt, no helicopter roared overhead, and they kept on this heading until the trail suddenly dipped, the steepness of it sending Price stumbling but he stayed up and the trail emptied into a hollow where the horses stood.

And a body lay on the ground.

"The guy was hiding near the horses," Homer explained succinctly as he, in a single movement, mounted his horse from a run. Price, a bit less agile, paused and found stirrups and hauled himself up, looking at the body. White guy, 30s, scraggly, with a rather large knife wound across his throat. "I don't know him," he said.

"Me neither," Homer confirmed and whipped the horse around. The others had also mounted and were lining up behind Homer, the kids looking at the body with curiosity. That's about it. They were too numb for any other reaction. Zoe took up the rear, covering the trail with her rifle.

"Where'd you get the hardware?" Price asked.

She merely looked at him. Yes, he answered her mentally, it is a stupid question.

"Let's go," Homer said and urged his horse along another trail skirting the ridge.

"Where to?" Price asked.

"Someplace safe."

And they were gone.

1.9

This Evening, Late

The cabin was far back in the mountains that ran along the old West Virginia border, probably about thirty miles from where all the fun had started yesterday Price guessed, but wasn't sure. He had fallen dead asleep in the saddle about five minutes after they took off, not waking up until the convoy had entered the clearing around the cabin and, even then, he had given it a mere once-over before numbly falling – more than dismounting – out of the saddle, clomping up the steps, then collapsing into an old rocking chair on the porch and instantly falling dead asleep again. He'd woken up a few hours later, joints locked by fatigue and cold and rocking-chair posture, and took a painful look around.

Nice place.

Price figured it was a vacation cabin once used by the DC elite to get away from all the stresses and strains of telling the peasants what to do because, man, keeping the peasants in line was such hard work that all those gol'durned muckity-mucks had to buy a sissy little cabin (with my gol'durn taxes) up hyeah so they could sashay 'round like they wuz folks … at least, according to Pap, who put on quite the show when he got hisself all riled up and, in a spectacular display of southern vernacular, listed what was wrong with the country. Hilarious. And, given events, damned accurate.

Price had a pretty good memory of the Twin Towers attack and the subsequent Event, and had to give Pap credit for accurately predicting that the self-regarding Federal bureaucracy would eff things up so far out of kilter that the country – and the world – would collapse. "Gol'durned pointyheads shoulda kilt that gol'durned Bin Laden," which he pronounced 'laden' "years ago. Gol'durned pointyheads shoulda known them Kaydas was gonna pull sumpin' like this!" A reference to the Event. "Pointyheads screwin' up everythin' with that gol'durn quarreltine." The quarantine. The world wars. The War here. And now Price was sitting on a cabin porch once owned by gol' durned pointyheads, hiding from gol'durned assassins that the gol'durned pointyheads, through acts of omission and commission, birthed.

Maybe he should pay Pap a visit and tell him how right he was.

Price shook his head. No, not gonna do that. After all this time, he still hadn't gone home; specifically, the ramshackle Craftsman house on the outskirts of Farmville where his mom had dumped him to the tender ministrations of Pap and Granny when she took her meth-head self off to the cities and the streets and the pimps. Price did not remember her and didn't bother trying to because his grandparents were parents enough; good ones, who railed and disciplined him into a somewhat productive human being, if one considered the smuggler life productive, which turned out to be an excellent skill set for these times. Pap had been hard and Granny harder but he loved them both and there was simply no way he was going to walk inside that house and find their intertwined bones on their rusted iron bed, a tattered and motheaten sheet barely covering the remains. Sure, he'd passed the house numerous times, but all he did was stand a moment at the bottom of the driveway and then move on. He wanted to remember them as vibrant and gigantic and alive. Alive.

"You need this," Homer said and shoved a glass into his hand.

The fumes alone made Price's head swim. "You sure?" Price asked as Homer settled in a chair next to him, Zoe on the one next to Homer, and the kids on the porch steps. "I think I need my head clear."

"Don't think it makes much difference now," Homer said but did shove a slice of corn bread in Price's hand, which should mitigate the effects. Some.

The smell of cornbread smeared with currant jelly made Price's head swim even more and he practically crammed the entire slice down his throat. Manna, especially for someone who had not eaten in at least twenty-four hours or more. Price took a swig of the popskull to stave off choking, which made him choke.

The kids giggled and, as Zoe lit a few candles, giggled even more as Price's currant-and-crumb smeared face became illuminated. He licked his fingers and then held out his hand and made dog panting noises. Zoe gave him another slice and he ate it with a bit more dignity but made sure to smack his lips rudely. "Excellent," he said.

Zoe smiled and gave him a cloth and Price wiped his mouth into a semblance of cleanliness, took another drink and then looked at Homer and said, "You've got the floor."

"When the kids didn't make it back by sunset we figured something was up," he said. "Figured y'all were in trouble, big trouble, so we responded big." He patted the M16 draped across his knee.

"I guess it's rather pointless for me to ask how long you've had those," Price said, flatly.

"About as long as you've had yours."

Touché, Price thought. "Difference is," he responded,

taking another sip, "mine are safely hidden away, not in close proximity where some overzealous cadre or commissar could find them and then kill me and my entire family." He raised significant eyebrows at the kids.

"Lots of good hiding places at the college."

"Indeed." Price nodded himself into another sip. "Good enough that you could, from time to time, pull them out and clean them and ensure the ammo was still good." He paused. "Right?"

Homer said nothing for a moment because he knew this was a violation of Price's gang rules. "Bet you're glad we did," he said softly.

Touché.

Because he was. And he was pretty sure all of his gang rules had been overcome by recent events so, let's move on. Price made a gesture to move on.

"We let Tat and Little John know what was happening and told 'em to spread the alarm," Homer continued, "and we came up."

"How'd you know where we were?"

"We didn't," he said, "We knew where the kids staged the horses, so we went there. It was past midnight when we arrived and the horses were still there, so we knew right then something had definitely gone wrong." Zoe's intake of breath punctuated that. "So we started looking around and we found that guy sleeping nearby."

"Question him?"

"No," Homer said, shortly. "Killed 'im."

Lost opportunity, Price thought, because he would love to know who the guy was, where he came from, and how the eff did he know where Price's HQ was, much less *who* Price was. But, dead was a good consolation prize.

"We stayed there 'cause it was too dark to go up to the Stump and we figured if y'all were okay you'd be by soon enough. Or we could collect your bodies later," said grimly, accompanied by another Zoe breath. "Saw the helicopter, ran up, you know the rest," he ended the tale.

Price nodded. He did. He let the words settle as the moon rose and added silver to the candle orange. "Your kids did good," Price said.

Homer nodded. "I thought they would. I thought you'd keep 'em safe, too."

There, the mutual compliments and gratitude expressed in the sparse manner of these times. No need for effusiveness anymore. Being alive was heroic enough.

Both Cass and Slickie had perked up at this and beamed at each other but Price noted the dark look crossing Zoe's face. Mama Bear's cubs had been in danger and Mama Bear didn't like it. Price supposed it was a Mom thing. Even Granny had fretted when Price went out with Pap. 'Course, Granny had never shown up at some spot o' trouble wheeling an M16 and taking on dragons. He looked at Zoe with great respect. Soldier. "You both did good, too."

Homer responded by holding out his glass and they clinked and Zoe clinked and even the kids did and they drank. Cass ended up coughing up half of what she swallowed but no one laughed because popskull was an acquired taste, and this was a somber moment.

"All right," Price said, as the moment settled. "Do you have any idea what's going on?"

Homer shook his head. "No. I'm as surprised by all this as you."

There was a bit of accusation in that but Price brushed it off. It was, actually, all their jobs to keep all their ears open. "Did we miss a payment somewhere?"

"Not on our end."

Again, the accusation, and this time Price bristled. "Not on mine, either. Even paid a little extra this month because we're coming up on autumn deliveries." People wanted their popskull and dope and black market food before the snows flew. Made the lonely winter months a little easier to bear. And the cadres and commissars wanted their cut, too, because it made their risk a little easier to bear. So, that wasn't it.

Homer raised an eyebrow. "What about the others?"

Hmm. Price mentally went through the region chiefs, the ones he trusted: F for Freddie, Sally June, Beau, Squint … and Homer … and the ones he tolerated: Inez, Rodger Dodger … and Homer. Funny the guy who recently saved his life made it to both lists. That might have something to do with how they met. Homer and his gang of housebreakers had tried to find Price's rumored gold and, during one of those efforts, Price and his gang had trapped them in a cul de sac all set to end them when Homer proposed joining forces. Turned out to be a lucrative arrangement, although Price suspected it was Zoe's presence alongside Homer in the cul de sac and the very real prospect of her getting ended that had motivated the guy.

Zoe had been in a slave camp after Breakout until Homer and his gang had busted the place up and she had clung to him with ferocity, the same way she clung to her kids, and Homer had clung back. Homer had never done anything since to cause Price to move him permanently into the Do Not Trust ledger, but no one who'd been forced into a subordinate position ever cherished the demotion.

Price reviewed the list a couple of more times and then shook his head. "I think we're wasting our time if we look at this as a business glitch. As I mentioned to your kids, the Faceless are a whole new level of crap." He sipped some more. "And I have no idea why they're here."

Homer took his own sip. "Trying to kill you, I'd say."

"And us," Cass piped up. Zoe shushed her.

"I don't think so," Price said, "because they could have done that anywhere from Farmville to Buena Vista. That guy you killed," Price left the reprimand in his voice, "had to be on me that whole time, otherwise the Faceless would never know where I was going. By the way, did you find anything on him?" Like a radio?

Homer shrugged. "Didn't search him."

Price frowned. "You didn't?"

"No." Homer glowered at him. "We were a little more concerned about finding our kids. And then the helicopter showed up."

Okay. Fine. Don't belabor the point although, boy, would be real nice to have that radio, if there was one. Other points were more important. "For the sake of theoretical argument," Price said as he raised a hand, "let's mull the implications." He counted down fingers with the other hand. "One, my HQ at Farmville, and no doubt yours at Sweet Briar, are compromised."

Homer spat off the porch. "Figured that."

"Number two." Price pressed the appropriate finger. "The Faceless knew the Stump and the procedure."

"So someone sold us out!" Cass yelped.

"Number three." Another finger pressed as Price ignored the outburst. "The Faceless didn't acquire all this knowledge in an afternoon."

All of them looked at him blankly, except Zoe, who flushed red with anger. "So they've been here a long time."

Price saluted her with the pressed fingers. "And, last," Price counted off the fourth finger, "they had no intention of killing me. At least, not at first."

Homer cocked a puzzled head. "How you figure that?"

"Because Rickard put something called the Bismarck

Sapphire in the bag. And, if I am any judge of jewelry – and I am – that is one valuable piece of equipment. Which would make my conviction for violation of the Antiquities Act, something Rickard specifically cited, by the way, absolutely assured."

Homer's face screwed up in disbelief. "But, that's stupid."

"Yes, it is."

"Why go through all that trouble?" Homer continued his disbelief. "Easy enough to just shoot you as a smuggler."

"Yes, it is," Price replied, letting Homer's doubts make his argument for him.

Homer sputtered in confusion and Zoe looked at him for a second and then said, "Something else is going on. Something real big."

"Give the lady a cigar," Price said and would have, if he had any. Man, a cigar would be excellent. The last one he smoked was, what, back at Pemberton when he'd warned Rashkil about what was coming? The last good one, anyway. Funny how cigars popped up at the worst of moments.

The silence grew and Price sipped a bit more, enjoying the trickle of hot liquid down his stomach. Not a cigar, but'll work.

"So what are we going to do?" Slickie asked.

"Nothing," Price said.

The kids gasped but the adults remained quiet. Price elaborated, "We do nothing for now, at least not anything the Faceless will notice. They don't know where we are or what we're doing. Let's leave them in the dark for a few days. Let's not leave our people in the dark, though." He looked at Homer. "Alert everyone else, but tell them to stand by."

Homer nodded.

He slapped the cabin porch rail with his hand. "Who knows about this place?"

"Us."

"Good. Let's keep it that way until we know who the rat bastard is. This," another rail slap, "is HQ now. For both of us."

Homer's face showed he didn't like that and Price almost laughed out loud. Getting a little possessive, comrade? What would the State say about that?

Price took a long, medicinal swig of the murderous popskull and traced the lava flow all the way down to his navel. Apparently, it had been a rather impressive pull because the others looked at him like he was crazy, Cass giggling over it.

"We need to get some sleep," Price said, giving in to the numbness stealing over him. He waved the glass at the kids. "Especially you two." He paused. "Because I've got a job for both of you. Jobs," he corrected.

Both Cass and Slickie lit up at that and exchanged excited glances. Homer and Zoe exchanged worried ones. As they should. Because what Price had in mind for the kids was not good.

Not good at all.

D. KRAUSS

Part II: Loosed the Fateful Lightning

2.1

Whittaker

It had taken Whittaker two days to find the steam car, which was surprising; you'd think it was enough of a novelty that everyone would be talking about it. But Whittaker's cadre pals had been strangely tight-lipped:

"Hey, Joachim, how's it hanging?"

"Hi, Ben, what brings you to town?"

"Well, I heard there's a steam car running around. Think I'd like to see that!"

And Joachim walked away.

About five others did, too, or warned him off with fingers pressed to lips, so, that evening, Whittaker had slipped back into the stalls or houses of the finger-pressers and found out the car was garaged in Stephens City, in an old railroad yard up Marlboro Rd that also served as the cadre's headquarters. Or did, before Major Deavers had commandeered the place and thrown them out. Right after showing up from the Strasburg office. Right before visiting Collier.

Hence the tight-lippedness: the Directorate had surprised everyone. And no one, so far, knew why they were here.

Disturbing. On many levels.

First, why set up a Directorate cell here? The main Directorate office was down in Staunton, a presence sufficient enough to cast a shadow over the entire Lower

Valley. The mere threat of their interest was enough to keep most of the cadre and non-Party members in line. No one wanted to do anything that would result in a Directorate squad suddenly riding into Kernstown, breaking into houses, and dragging hapless workers off into the night, never to be heard from again, as had happened a few times when the Party first established its authority. Cadre and workers inclined to conduct illegal activities, such as eating more than your monthly designated caloric intake, had learned discretion: do just enough to fulfill a need but not to rouse official ire. The winked-at, tolerated, and downright ignored pursuits would gradually disappear as the Party slowly transformed society into the Utopia their doctrine insisted was inevitable ... Whittaker actually kept a straight face at that thought. But they were a long way from that point, so Deavers and his minions popping up like this set everyone on edge.

Second, why stop to see Collier first?

Very disturbing. Very.

Because it meant the Directorate, whether the office in Staunton or the HQ in Fredericksburg, knew who Collier was. And if they knew who he was then they also knew about the church, which was proscribed because it was exactly the kind of activity not winked-at, tolerated, or downright ignored; was, instead, the very kind of activity that made Directorate officers conduct midnight raids and drag people off never to be heard from again, especially the pastor of said church.

Yet ...

Deavers did not haul Collier away. He did not haul anyone away. It looks like he drove up the mountain spouting steam and sparks and scaring the bejesus out of cattle and horses simply to have a conversation, and then drove down the mountain and into the compound, ejecting the cadre in the process. So, Deavers was not working with cadre, not even the commissar. Which meant he did not trust the cadre or the commissar. Which meant neither the cadre nor the commissar could trust anyone else.

Hence, the tight-lippedness.

Shaking his head slightly, Ben sipped the chicory crap that passed for coffee these days and gazed down the street at the compound's gate. He was a couple of blocks away on the porch of a co-op that specialized in corn and cabbage, and since Ben was known as a supplier of both (and other things), his presence here was legit. It was, after all, cabbage season, and there were quotas to fulfill or commissars would get fired and cadres disciplined, so cabbage suppliers, especially an affable, fun guy like Ben, were always welcome. For a bit.

Right at the moment Ben was trying to calculate how long a "bit" actually was as Tweedledum and Tweedledee, two of the dumbest State troopers assigned to this area, slid around the corner of the condos across the street and aimed right at him, slapping their truncheons against their jodhpurs and fixing Ben with the fish-eye. Ben smiled and saluted them while inwardly sighing. Some things never changed ... before the Event, after the Event, a black guy got the bad eye from the cops. "Good morning, comrades!" Ben expressed a cheeriness he did not actually feel.

The shorter of the pair, Tweedledum, a red-faced redneck obviously in love with his truncheon and Brownshirt get-up, cast a suspicious face at him. "Whachew doin' hyeah, boy?"

"Coordinating," Ben said, cheerily, his head almost exploding. "We have many units, produced by the heroic efforts of our brother farmers, to deliver to the cities."

It was to laugh. There were barely enough "units" to keep Kernstown fed, much less the parasites manning the government offices in Fredericksburg. But this was the language that kept Ben out of the hoosegow; in earlier times, expressions such as "Nawsuh, or Yassuh" served the same purpose. A slow burn formed in his stomach, and not from the crappy coffee.

"Well, yew been 'coordinating,'" Tweedledee, Tweedledum's gap-toothed one-white-browed inbred partner, made air quotes, "for a coupla days now."

The problem with being one of the few black men still alive in the entire Western Hemisphere, at least, as far as Ben knew; (there'd been no information about the black Caribbean countries in decades) was the notice one attracted, especially from a couple of crackers who'd been propelled into positions of power more by the dearth of anyone else capable of doing the job than any true competence. A golden opportunity for two losers who, pre-Event, would have ended up meth cookers and fifty-year alumni of a West Virginia State prison, but who could now indulge every racist Klan precept their slope-headed daddies had taught them, under the guise of enforcing the law. Or, more accurately, Party regs.

"Yes, sir." Gawd, Ben hated himself right now. "We have to ensure we do not disrupt the elegant schedule of wagons and horse teams that the State in its wisdom has already established." Ben scratched his head absently. "Sometimes I'm not sure I'm up to the task."

Gawd, he hated himself right now.

The two Klansmen smiled broadly because this is what they knew, this is what they believed, the inadequacy of the mongrel races. Ben wouldn't be surprised if they gave a white power salute right now. 'Yeah, no doubt," Dee sniggered at Dum, "but if you hyeah, you loafing, and that's an offense against the State." And he slapped the truncheon with more enthusiasm.

Ben figured it was time for his Stepin Fetchit voice and a lot of "Lawdy Lawdy's" when he noticed a couple of guys walking down the middle of the street from the direction of the compound. Two white guys – of course – wearing what looked like farmer getups, plaid shorts and overalls and clodhopper boots, but they were also sporting high – and – tights, and farmers around here kept their hair loose and long or shaved it all off because there was no time or money for haircuts. Only military guys had the time and scrip.

Or Directorate troops.

Dum and Dee had leaned into him with wolfish grins, prepared to "tich" him sumpin' about State regulations when they noted his intense gaze and both turned to see what had caught Ben's interest. They blanched, exchanged worried looks, and then scuttled away. Fast.

Bingo.

Ben turned in his seat and grabbed a clipboard hanging on the wall, then stood up and scooted into the shadows. Taylor, the cadre manager behind the counter, blinked at him and at the approaching Directorates and beat a hasty retreat through the back door. Pretending to write down something, Ben watched the troops approach, holding his breath, but they didn't even glance at him as they stepped through the intersection and made for the street running next to the co-op. Ben slipped behind the counter and followed Taylor's exit into the storage area. Place used to be some kind of honey store and there were lots of shelves and nooks and crannies and Taylor was nowhere in sight. Good.

Ben jogged to the back loading docks and cautiously looked out. The two were walking along the street, probably heading into town. Maybe he should see if they did. There were a lot of wrecked trucks and trailers scattered throughout the back parking lot which no one had bothered to clear out, even though they were a real pain for the wagons coming up to load or unload produce. But they were an asset when Taylor opened the warehouse at night for the wagon loads of stuff he wasn't supposed to have, and Ben now used them to his own advantage, slipping along the rusted hulks until he had a good view of the Directorates' route.

They didn't turn toward town. They kept going on.

Puzzled, Ben stayed with them, moving from one set of wreckage and abandoned warehouse to the other, staying about a hundred yards behind the pair. They didn't seem like they were in a hurry, and didn't seem tail conscious, either, so Ben closed the distance a bit, but was cautious, cutting around the far sides of buildings and remaining in place until he was sure neither of the two would catch him in their peripheral vision. He crouch-ran through the back of a set of storage buildings fronting the remains of another parking lot bordered by piles of metal that must be the skeletons of house trailers until he reached the end of them and peered around …

… and almost had a heart attack. One of the Ds was standing in the middle of the road, arms crossed, looking back at him.

Well, not exactly, he was actually staring back along the road, but a slight glance in Ben's direction and he'd be made. Easing back into the wreckage, Ben put as much of the twisted metal between him and the D's scrutiny as he could, then froze. Good thing because right then the D flicked his head in Ben's direction, probably catching the motion, and scrutinized the area for a good five minutes before going back to the road. Fortunately there were a lot of birds flitting around and the D probably thought that was it.

Not tail conscious, huh?

Ben mentally slapped himself and took in as much of

the terrain as his now limited view allowed. He was on the edge of an overgrown field that bordered both the road and the parking lot. There were buildings on the far side of the field; the remains of a series of townhouses that had collapsed into themselves over the years. They'd been upscale places before the Event, but were now ruins, punctuated by a still intact asphalt circle at the far end. A road ninety-degreed right before the townhouses, leading into town. Ben was pretty sure that's where the other D went, but why split up here? This was an odd place to do a tail check, especially since their destination was obvious.

There was a low whistle from the area of the townhouses that Ben would have dismissed as one of the flitting birds except that the road D dropped his arms, took another hard look around the area, and then turned and vanished in the whistle's direction. Ben waited the appropriate minutes and then dashed into the line of brush bordering the field and followed it until he reached the corner. Going prone, he eased an eye around a mimosa tree in enough time to see the D disappear below the road's crest. Hurrying along the shoulder, Ben made it to the high point of the road and then crawled along until he could see over.

The D was at the end of the townhouse ruins and moving steadily into the circle at the end when he suddenly angled off to the right and headed toward a big patch of woods. Puzzled, Ben waited until the D entered the tree line and then he sprinted along the shoulder until he reached the first set of ruins. He'd been exposed the whole way and was pretty sure they'd spotted him and he braced, certain he was going to end up in a Directorate interrogation cell in the next hour but no one came out of the woods shooting at him. Ben wasn't sure what to do or where to go. It didn't look like the Ds were headed into town as he'd first thought because this was a fairly tough way to get there. These woods were thick and served as a better place to hide from people than taking a leisurely stroll.

Or hide things.

Hmm.

Creeping along the wreckage and not making any sudden movements that would catch attention, Ben worked his way to the middle of the townhouses, where he had a better view of the woods. As he was thinking about moving to a remarkably intact wall across from him, he heard some odd sounds coming from the tree line. What was that? Sounded like branches snapping, something big moving and …

… horses neighing.

Startled, Ben watched as a couple of horses, ridden by the Ds who were now armed with rifles, broke the northern perimeter of the woods and headed into the fields, taking a northeasterly line. Ben shifted up to the wall and other vantage spots and watched until the horses disappeared from view in the brush and woods, which didn't take long because it was thick out there. Obviously, these guys didn't want to be followed to wherever they were headed.

Now, ain't that interesting?

Ben waited a half hour as the sun dipped in the west and then dashed into the woods from which the Ds had staged. If they'd gone through all this trouble, it was a certainty they weren't coming back anytime soon and Ben had time. It took him about ten minutes more to find what amounted to a corral built among the trees, with a hastily constructed shed right next to it.

What the hell?

Cautiously, he opened the shed and noted riding tack and water bottles and extra changes of clothes. No weapons, so the Ds took the ones available.

Guys have been here a week. Now when did they have the time to put all this together?

Bewildered, Ben stepped back and carefully closed the shed door then spent considerable time erasing his boot prints and any other signs of trespass. Obviously, the Ds intended to use this place a few more times, otherwise why the infrastructure? Problem was, Ben did not have any means to follow the Ds from here and find out what they were up to.

But he knew someone who did.

2.2

Washburn

Washburn lay on a rock outcropping that topped one of the smaller mountains ringing the Kernstown area. To the casual observer, he looked like an odd break in the scenary. To a more alert observer, he'd still be an odd break in the rocks, downright invisible, as long as he remained still. Not a problem. He'd learned to be still and invisible many decades ago and had perfected both skills over the subsequent years. Looking at him, most would find that hard to believe because he was huge, well over 6'5," and tipping toward 300 pounds, remarkable in these days of food shortages, with most of it muscle ... most; he did have fat rings here and there, an inevitability of middle age.

Couple all that with a cascade of black wiry hair that blurred into a massive beard and he should stick out like a grizzly bear, especially on top of a rock. But he didn't. And that made his observations of the little Directorate group down there easy.

Or, at least, surreptitious.

When Ben had contacted him and told about the horses in the woods, Washburn had been certain it was a one-time event, the Directorate taking an excess of precaution to conduct a surveillance they didn't wish to telegraph, and that probably due more to the nature of the organization than any need for secrecy; they liked all that cloak and dagger stuff. Washburn had long ago learned that most such efforts were a waste of energy because people didn't see anything. Nothing. At all. Even when it happened right in front of their faces. Animals did, and stalking them so he and his brothers and parents could eat, had taught him the importance of stillness and invisibility, which had served him well after Breakout. Dozens – hundreds – of times he'd waited, hidden in brush and leaves, for the thugs to come stumbling out of whatever house they had just looted, covered with the blood of the woman they had just raped and skinned, and then he rose from the ground, a devil, a wolf, a bear, and severed them. Severed.

For you, my love. For ours.

So he'd been initially scornful of Ben's insistence, because Ben was excitable and a criminal and a sellout, who had spent the Event years and the Breakout years and the war years switching allegiances between Red and Blue and ingratiating himself with one faction or the other, while Washburn roamed woods and mountains avoiding all of the factions until they came too close and they took and took and took. Not Ben himself, of course; he was a city boy and soft but he'd lent comfort and aid and Washburn could not help believing that one of those who had gotten to his wife and children, safe behind woods and mountain, had the energy to do so because of some comfort and aid that Ben and others like him had provided. Washburn didn't believe that back then because he didn't know Ben during those years, did not know him until joining Pastor Rashkil's church, but he believed it now because Ben had told him his story because Ben could not shut up and thought he had a brilliant tale of survival and playing one against the other and all Washburn could see was his wife's naked and headless body strung up from the cabin rafters and the heads of his children lined up on the sink and, Ben, how much did you contribute to that?

One day, when the Lord told him to, Washburn was going to kill Ben.

But not today, Lord, not today because it looked like Ben had been on to something.

Washburn had gone to the woods in the dark hours and had found the resting horses and cached supplies, which the Directorate had installed with an air of secrecy far above any institutional imperative. He'd decided to follow the Ds and see what secret thing they were doing. It had been difficult. Washburn did not dare follow them directly because a horse trailing behind two other horses would be noticed so he had set a hide where he could observe the Ds as they traveled until they were out of sight, then set another hide at the spot they fell out of view and waited there for a day and a night until they passed by again and then another hide and another and, this way, he knew their route, where they went with secrecy and urgency every other day:

Here. Right here. The old Kernstown battlefield.

Battlefields were everywhere in the Shenandoah Valley. It was a warred land, from the Shawnee and the Seneca to the English and the French and then the English and the Americans and the Americans and the Americans and the Americans until the wars piled on top of each other and the blood was so thick Washburn could not tell one war from the other. But he knew the warriors because they all spoke to him as he walked the forests and the mountains, singing their death chants and soul songs, all of them entwined in the land. The Lord gave Washburn the gift of hearing them. This particular battlefield was from the war for the slaves, the southern armies overrunning the northern armies here only to lose their lives and their cause in Pennsylvania. Back in the days

Before, this was a tourist attraction so the free and prosperous people of a nation that had lost its soul could come here and stand on bloodied ground and imagine they were one with the souls beneath them, but they weren't. They had no soul that could speak to the souls beneath them and so the Death came on the breeze and they died in millions in their soulless cities and streets, leaving behind soulless monsters, the ones that came for Washburn's family.

Rage overtook him. Some warrior souls down there in the holy ground raised spectral hands in warning and Washburn gritted his teeth to keep from shaking. Stop it. Get control. Remain still. Remain invisible. He breathed, breathed, and said a prayer to the Lord thanking Him and asking for the power to remain still and invisible. Your gifts, Lord, yours.

The Directorate agents had ridden their horses through the creek that bordered the old brick house set under the oaks and sycamores, thick and ponderous, marking the yard of the man who had owned these lands before the wars had come to him. Smart, because the creek was heavily wooded and underbrushed, even at this late time of the season, and the agents would be undetectable to anyone looking for them, unless someone had already spotted their emergence from the creek on two previous occasions, that same someone now on top of the small hill behind the crumbling house from which northerners or southerners or Shawnee had launched attacks and counterattacks in the centuries before. The agents had paused at a clearing past the creek and scrutinized the area, their eyes passing over Washburn several times but he had remained still. They had then ridden their horses up to the collapsed bricks and porch of the old house and tied up outside the part of it still standing, one of the Ds staying with the horses, watchful (although he did not see the shade of the man who had owned the house standing next to him, incensed), while the other D had gone inside. Why? Washburn had mouthed to the warriors but they had merely waved spectral hands of patience so Washburn was still and invisible and patient.

And was rewarded.

The agent came out of the house and slid more than walked out of the sagging portal where the door once stood, eliciting some comments from his partner, the two of them chuckling as they remounted, pushing the old gibbering ghost out of their way, and making for the creek. No need for care, they had already checked the area and hadn't been here long enough for anyone to notice them. The need now was haste and they made the creek and its almost-tunnel of interlinking branches and brush and were gone.

Washburn remained, seeing if anyone else left the house even though the ghost warriors threw beckoning arms urging him forward as the old man stood by the once magnificent porch and fumed. Ghosts could be fickle, so Washburn waited until the sun dipped lower and then he dropped off the rocks and snuck down to the house. He paused beside the one intact wall and shrank against the brick work, the old man ghost coming around a corner and imploring him to do something about this mess. "The Lord awaits you," Washburn whispered to him but the man was more in love with his pain than his potential rest. The warriors cackled. They would never seek rest. They loved the blood.

Well past the time any persons lurking inside would have given themselves away, Washburn crept around the bricks and carefully entered. The sun was almost gone now and the light was dim and he waited for his eyes to adjust until he could see the disturbance of boots in the dust and rubble of a once magnificent stone floor. He followed the lines of disturbance to the intact wall, sunlight choosing that moment to stream in the broken window frame and illuminate the brickwork. One brick was out of line. Washburn walked over to it and examined the space for a tell, like a piece of rock or a string laid across the brickface to alert someone that it had been disturbed since the last time it was moved, but nothing. Washburn snorted. "Amateurs," he said, and the warriors snorted back and he pulled and the brick came out. He fished out a leather bag inside.

Empty.

So, the agents had collected whatever their spy had left them – a note, a map, some stolen papers, whatever – and had left nothing in return. No gold. No jewelry. Not even scrip. Which meant their spy was the worst kind possible: a true believer, not a mercenary. Doing it for God and country or, in this case, for the godless who had stolen this country. A fanatic.

A problem.

Washburn frowned. He'd been prepared to spend a couple of days on top of the rock waiting for the spy but there was no point. The spy would not come back to this dead drop until he, or she, had something to pass. The agents would continue servicing it every other day until something showed up which they would collect and take back to their Major, and they would not leave anything for the spy until the Major ordered them to do so, and then not until they had placed a signal somewhere alerting the spy to come get it.

In other words, it was pointless for him to wait.

"What do I do?" he asked the warriors, but they merely shrugged. The old man gibbered.

Washburn replaced the bag and the brick and left.

2.3

Collier

"… and this you must always remember," Collier drew in a breath, preparatory to his last point, "regardless of where we find ourselves, we are always found."

Silence in the sanctuary, a flickering of candles in the drafts that the log walls enclosing this place simply could not block. The fifty or so people sitting here and over there and standing in other places didn't move for a good thirty seconds or so, and then bent forward and got to their feet and quietly milled about, quietly talking as they gathered shawls and cloaks and their dangerous Bibles and meandered to the door. No singing. Voices carry. No loud talk or "Hallelujah brother!" either, for the same reason. "Good one, Pastor." "Thank you, Pastor." "Pastor, do you really believe that sin is overcome?" The whispered comments of the ones who made it a point to speak to him as they passed through snuffing candles which dimmed the dim light even more, a necessary precaution because candles were like a lightning flash off the dark mountainside, so no door came open until the only illumination was the little spirit light Collier kept on his rough pulpit, the same spirit light he'd been carrying since Pemberton. "Thank you, Annabelle." "You're welcome, Christian." "Most definitely, Xavier, but I'll be happy to elaborate next week."

The shuffling toward the door continued and, by twos

and fours, the congregation slipped out to make their separate, safe ways home. In this same manner they came here, at the end of the day, at dusk, making separate, safe ways up trail and rill and path by twos and fours until they crossed the ridge line and slipped into the sanctuary and took accustomed places on log benches still perfumed and sticky with sap, sitting for the hour or two that Collier taught his lesson until it was time to go back home. Silent, careful, like the first Christians, hungry for a message, aware that hunger could get them killed.

Collier saw the last person out and latched the door and walked back to the pulpit shivering as a particularly cold draft made its way into his jacket. Winter was coming, and the hard days with it, and each year he tolerated it a little less. Getting old, of course, an old he could not afford and did not expect, as was the case of every person ever born. But, it was worse now because things were so much worse now than during most other times in history, even the Dark Ages, which was the first time civilization had disappeared. But this recent disappearance, caused by Event and Breakout and war, was more egregious because a level had been reached, a point of comfort and technology and sophistication unmatched during Roman and Renaissance and other enlightenments. These late days, this 21st Century, was the culmination of the ages, the end of history, the maturation of the race … and it all collapsed into the dust heap of history in the same ignominious way of Goths pounding on gates and Northmen burning monasteries.

Collier looked down at his Bible. In all that time, there was only one consistency.

God, that is the search for, the understanding of, the railing against. Because, even now, even as pastor of this hick backwoods church serving a hick backwoods and rapidly deteriorating congregation, Collier had doubts.

About this calling, about his efforts, about the existence of God.

Yes, it was oddly fortuitous the way this Bible, the one that had belonged to Dad, had fallen into his hands: delivered by a crazy guy in the middle of a wrecked house on the eve of the Blue's defeat. And after losing so much, the war, his country, his family, his friends …

… Rosa …

… he still had it. During those first days of his escape from Pemberton and the search for Rosa, he'd forget about it until he'd rummage through his backpack looking for something else and there it was. Often, by a campfire on a hillside in Pennsylvania roasting squirrel and crying out, "Rosa, where are you?", he would study Dad's cramped handwriting in the margins, often unable to make out the words but the gist of it, the sense of it, came through. Which was this: Dad thought God was crazy.

Well, not in those words; that was Collier's summary, but Dad considered God standoffish, aloof, aware of us and worried about us but like a grandparent watching wayward grandchildren mess things up. And allowing them to do so. Because God was gracious and a gentlemen and let us make our mistakes and maybe, one day, we would wake up and go, "Man, have I messed up!" and we would walk winding roads and find ourselves at the end of a country lane beholding a great white farmhouse and God would step out and see us there and run to us and say "Welcome!" and kill the fatted calf.

Something like that.

Collier was certain he did not have the same sense of it that Dad did. Dad's notes were incomplete and hard to figure and Dad seemed mystically drawn to God as He Was, God's Essence, Personhood, whatever, and cared little for the everyday implications and applications. Dad sought the God Of Time and Space, and mused about time and how it did not work for us in the same way it did for God and how the Considerations of God were so far above anything we could conceive that what we thought of as His indifference, His downright cruelty, was an aspect of God that had nothing to do with us but everything to do with the structure of the Universe, with the very particles of it and the interactions of dimensions and powers of which we had no clue.

Something like that.

And Collier knew he was not drawn to God in the same way, was barely convinced that the God Dad sought was the real one because Collier's world was pain and misery and death and outrage, more evidence that God did not exist or was far more indifferent than even Dad had believed. Yet, here Collier was, a pastor of a church, something neither he nor Dad would have ever predicted, teaching the doctrines of God's Love and Salvation, things he questioned, to a congregation of people who accepted the lessons without question. Collier should not be doing this. He did not want to do this. But he did it.

Compulsion.

There was something beating against the walls of his heart that forced him, after a day of hard, physical labor, to make his weary way up the mountain trails to this slapdash drafty log church hidden in a cove to protect him and the congregation from the arrests and re-education and executions that belief of any kind, from witchcraft to Sufism, invoked because the State would have no other God before it, and then open Dad's Bible and teach. Not teach. Render his opinion, which wasn't the same thing. But it was taken as Gospel and his authority unquestioned and they came back and brought others and they listened silently and were a community, a church, a congregation of the Lord's.

He was a complete fake. He did not believe what he

was saying. But he was compelled to say it. He was no servant of God. But he was serving.

His family noticed. Evelyn read the confliction in his soul and applied her own balm of Gilead, not sure what the source of his pain actually was but knew it had to do with a service forced on him (like the war had been forced on him, first by the Event and then the Reds and the State). Certainly Second noticed, his rebellion a reaction, whether conscious or not, to the hypocrisy Collier wore on his sleeve because teenagers had a radar for hypocrisy and a cruelty of expectation that made them judge, jury, and executioner of every adult, especially a parent, imbued with it. How many times had teenaged Collier challenged Dad over his perceived hypocrisies, and gotten himself sent to Fishburne for his pains. The twins knew it, too, but they did not challenge, merely retreated further into their twin world where no one other than them was allowed.

But there was an actual core of truth within Collier's conflict, the source of the compulsion to open Dad's Bible and struggle with what could be truth, should be. It was the conviction that Collier himself mattered. Evelyn mattered. The twins and Second did, too. All of them, every single human, mattered. Not according to the State or cadres or commissars or democracies of any kind that lumped everyone into a mass of greater good, as defined by the monsters and tyrants that had wrested control from each mattering person, but according to this God. This elusive God of grace – maybe. Of judgment, most definitely; this God said that you matter, Collier. And God was the Only One saying that. And it was the only thing Collier believed.

Someone cleared a throat.

Collier looked up and squinted, the interior of the church nothing but shadow on shadow, the feeble spirit light catching a corner here and there. But it was enough for him to see two figures sitting there, one at each end of the same pew. Ben and Washburn.

"What do you have?" Collier asked.

Ben shifted forward in his seat. "Two of the Directorate guys have got some kind of espionage thing going."

Collier smirked, an expression lost in the dark. "I'd expect no less."

"This is pretty elaborate," Ben explained. "They're hiding horses in an old townhouse ruin and then taking them out cross country from Stephens City, into the woods. I couldn't follow them so I told Wash," a nod of the head at the mountain man, "and he followed them for a few days and found they were servicing a dead drop at the Kernstown battlefield house."

Collier looked at Washburn, who nodded and then gave a sideways glance at Ben that, even in this light, was murderous. Collier frowned. Geez, you'd think after all these years of terrible things that race hatred would be the least of someone's motives. "That's the old plantation house ruin on the west side of Kernstown, right?"

Washburn nodded. "And they didn't leave anything there."

Collier knew enough about tradecraft to get the implications. "So," he said, softly, "there's someone deep cover in the community."

"Looks that way," Ben confirmed.

Again Washburn gave Ben the snake-eye but Collier couldn't worry about that. "What makes us worthy of that?"

Ben leaned forward and spread his hands to encompass the church. "Well, this!"

"No," Collier said. "This," he mimicked Ben's motion, "is easily crushed. Shoot a couple of us. Jail a couple of us. When they take me off to the camps this time, just leave me there. Burn the place to the ground, even. What the Ds are doing now is well above what's necessary."

"Well, what then?"

"I don't know." And he didn't. He was genuinely clueless. He had no idea why the Directorate would be going to all this trouble, but it had to be something big to require this much effort. But there was nothing here that big. Yes, there was smuggling and a group of former Blues and patriots who, in their hearts, yearned for the America of their youth, but that was simply in their hearts and no one was acting on that, so there was no need to crush it.

Was there?

Collier shook his head. I don't know. Rosa would know. Rosa would have smelled out any nascent uprising weeks ago, before Deavers even showed.

Rosa.

Collier shook her away. She was not here. He had to make do with the material available. "We need to find out."

"How?" Ben's exasperation was evident, Washburn's contempt of him even more so and Collier wondered how Ben couldn't see it. Maybe he did and had learned, long ago, to ignore it, a tactic black people had used before the Event and made more critical these days, when there were so few black people left, Ben and Felicia being the only two he knew about. Collier putting Ben and Washburn on the same mission might help ameliorate that. Or make it worse.

"Washburn." Collier turned to him. "How difficult would it be to keep the dead drop under surveillance?"

Washburn's shrug was evident in the dark. "Could do it."

"Would you, then?"

Washburn sat like a stone for a moment, then nodded.

"Good," Collier's tone was flat. "Let me know what you need. We'll get it delivered to you, just tell us where."

"Won't need nothin'," Washburn growled.

"All right." No need to belabor it. "Ben, how many Directorate agents are there at the compound?"

"Three," Ben answered.

"Deavers and his two crewmen, right?"

Ben nodded.

"What are the cadre and the commissar doing?"

"Keeping their heads down."

Collier chuckled humorlessly. "I'll bet. I'll bet they're nowhere around the compound. Is anybody?"

"A couple of troopers. Real winners. But they don't like the agents and make themselves scarce whenever they appear." Ben sounded puzzled. Where you going with this, Collier?

I'll tell you, Ben. "I want you to search Deavers's office."

Collier could imagine both sets of eyebrows arching, one in consternation, the other in amusement. "You're kidding me, right?" Ben, consternated, replied.

"No, I'm not. Washburn," Collier gestured at the big shadow, "could be up there for weeks before we know anything. By then, it might be too late."

"I'm not exactly a break-in artist, Pastor."

"I get that," Collier acknowledged, "but you're most familiar with the area. You even know Winchester." Left unsaid was the bravery and skill necessary for that knowledge. Winchester was a horror, a ghost town haunted by old Breakout thugs still contagious with a form of Phase 2 that no one could survive, making the town an ideal place to stash priceless items being moved up and down the Valley, like old paintings and jewelry.

For those brave enough and skillful enough to do so. Like Ben.

"But I … I don't do that stuff anymore."

"But you did. And you did a lot of intelligence work during the war." Collier noted Washburn's irritated shift. "And those are skills we need again."

"But … a break-in?"

"Yes." Collier stepped around the pulpit, bringing the spirit light with him, and down to the pew, standing where he could see both of them. "And you'll have to do it in a way that Deavers doesn't notice."

Ben looked at him with incredulity. "Now how do I do that?"

"Figure it out," Washburn rumbled from Collier's left. "You did it before." A pause. "You did a lot of things before."

Both Collier and Ben looked at Washburn, both puzzled by the vehemence in his voice. "What's with you?" Ben asked.

"Nothin's 'with' me." Collier could hear the air quotes in Washburn's voice. "We've got a job to do and you don't need to pussy out."

Ben was stunned. "I'm not pussying out!" he yelped. "I don't want us to get caught!"

"You mean 'you,' doncha?" The vehemence remained in Washburn's voice. "You don't want *you* to get caught."

"*I* don't want him to get caught, either," Collier interrupted softly, "I don't want any of us to get caught. But." And he shifted toward the bewildered Ben. "If we don't get some idea of why Deavers is *really* here, then we'll all be caught. All of us." He let that sink in. "Ben, you won't get caught, if you take your normal care, do your normal good job." He nodded at the door. "I'll leave the details to you. But it needs to be done. Fast."

It took a moment for Ben to realize he'd been

dismissed and he slowly got to his feet, hesitant, giving Collier a look of uncertainty and then Washburn one of hurt. Washburn sat quietly, staring off. Ben shifted, then, without looking back, left.

Collier let a minute go by, then looked at Washburn. "What's going on with you?"

Washburn canted his head toward Ben's empty seat. "He's not one of us."

Collier let out a long, slow breath. "I never had much to do with that race thing, Washburn, even less these days."

Washburn waved an impatient hand. "No, no, I don't mean his color. He's not of the Spirit."

"Pardon me?"

"He does not share the Spirit. His soul is dark, lightless. You can't trust him."

Collier was taken aback. Washburn had a long streak of mysticism in him, but this was ... odd. "Think you need to explain that to me."

"No, I don't, Pastor, because you have the Spirit and you know it in others and you know it ain't in him."

Collier caught an inkling. "Because he doesn't believe, you mean?"

"Well, that." Washburn raised a conciliatory hand, "But there's others that don't, like Felicia, but they have the Spirit. I see it hover around her. But Ben, Ben is out for himself. Always was."

The light went on in Collier's head. "Ah," he said. "Because of his war time activity. Because he worked both sides. Is that what you mean?"

Washburn said nothing.

"You could hold that against him, but everyone back then did what they could to get by. And I can assure you, without going into the details, that Ben did more service for us," the Blues, "than he did them." No need to say who that was.

"But doing one good thing for them meant disaster," Washburn said with bitterness.

Collier cocked his head. That sounded specific. "What do you mean?"

"Never mind." Washburn let out a short, exasperated breath, then stood, regarding Collier. "You needn't worry. I will do my job. I am a servant of this Church." And he bowed his head with some reverence.

It was as close to a promise that Washburn would not allow his animosity toward Ben to interfere with either of their duties as the big man was willing to say, and Collier reached across and dropped a hand on Washburn's shoulder. "I know you will, Washburn. I rely on you." He paused. "Do you actually see the Spirit?"

Washburn met his eyes. "Everywhere," he whispered and silently, for such a big man, left.

Disturbing, that.

Collier stood for a moment, more to gather his thoughts than let Washburn increase the distance. How much of what Washburn said was actual or metaphor, Collier was not sure. If enough time went by, one became the other, and then there was no line between delusion and belief. It was something that Collier himself had to guard against, and he was fairly certain his doubts held all that in check. Washburn had no such doubts. The man had spent decades alone roaming the cathedral of the Valley, and such direct contact with nature made even the hardest man spiritual. At what point that turned into psychosis, Collier did not know. At what point that made a man a saint, he knew even less. Maybe Washburn had the touch of God.

Or madness.

Collier bowed his head. If that was madness, it made Washburn a better pastor than Collier could ever be.

Washburn had no doubts. He saw God. But so did Mohammed, and here we are.

Collier sighed and looked around. Best that a man of doubts struggles with the nature of existence, and the nature of God. The Certain drove airplanes into sides of buildings and threw plagues to the wind and set up Utopian, murderous regimes. The Doubtful let life play out.

Keep on eye on Washburn, then. He may not let things play out.

Quietly, Collier snuffed out the spirit light and let the moon fill the darkness and then walked silently up the aisle to not disturb the Spirit that Washburn saw and pulled the door to him ...

... and the twins tumbled at his feet.

Collier looked at them, saying nothing. Right at the door, were they? "What did you hear?" he asked, quietly.

"Um, nothing, nothing!" they both chorused as they disentangled feet and arms and swarmed upward, a mirrored image of flustered boy. "We came to tell you supper was ready," Bart added, lamely.

"Uh huh," Collier said as he shooed them back and then closed the door. "So let's go have supper then. And, boys," he said as they whirled to run ahead of him, "whatever it was that you didn't hear." They both stopped and looked at him, worried. "Make sure it stays unheard."

2.4

Slickie and Cass

Cass hunkered in a corner of the old railroad station in the center of Staunton, shivering and trying to find a way out of the wind. No luck; the wind was demonic, seeking her out no matter where she crouched. Dang, but it had gotten cold the last couple of days. Of course. Uncle P sends her out on a big-time mission and it gets big-time cold.

She shivered again, but not from the cold. This *was* a big-time mission that was big-time dangerous, over-the-top dangerous, and Cass now wished she hadn't shown such enthusiasm to be up and at 'em. As soon as Uncle P told them what he wanted, Mom had been stricken, Dad had looked concerned, but her? Naah, not "I'll do anything!" Cass! Nope, jump right up there and right into it and here she was, right into it. Boy, was she.

"You are too impetuous," Tat, exasperated and frustrated, slapping the jodo sticks out of her hands and then throwing her around the mat about ten times for good measure before he finally walked away, shaking his head and throwing his own sticks into a corner of the barn. "I am not!" she'd shrieked and leaped at him and got her ass royally kicked. But that was okay. She had learned from it. She would never be as good as Tat, of course; he'd been taught by his father, some guy assigned to the Japanese embassy in DC, who'd been taught by *his* father, and father before all the way back to samurai times, if she credited his stories. Sometimes she did. Today, she didn't.

"Was your dad actually a samurai?" she asked him.

Tat, huddled against a wall a few feet away and hidden inside cloak and hood, clucked and then whispered harshly, "Silence! We don't want to attract attention."

She fumed at that because there was no one's attention to attract because no one else was stupid enough to be hanging out in the ruins of an old railroad station while an ice wind tried to turn them into a popsicle ... popsicles. Ummmm. She'd had one once, when Dad had brought in an old freezer and Cass had worked on it and actually got it running with power from one of the mill engines and Dad had said, "You're gonna love this," and he'd put cherry juice deep inside and it froze enough that Cass could actually bite into it. Heaven. "We used to have this stuff all the time," Homer said.

Which was so unfair.

She didn't get to have popsicles and Snickers bars (at least, ones that weren't so old they were chocolate bricks infused with ptomaine) or Nintendo or comic books (except the ones the boys down the hollow drew and those were obscene) and a car and a prom and a boyfriend (well, she could get a boyfriend if she wanted to but there wouldn't be a prom). All because she'd been born after all that ...

"No," Tat said.

"What?"

"My dad was not a samurai. We are descended from samurai." And he went silent inside his hood.

"Same thing," she said.

The hood turned and Tat's sharp, angled features confronted her. So alien. To think, there were entire islands and continents of people who looked like that; at least, before the wars. No one knew if they were still there or not. Not even Tat knew.

"It is not the same thing," he said, quietly. "To be descended is not to be. You are descended from Americans, but you are not one."

Cass's dander went up. Dander. What exactly was that, anyway? Dad, who used the phrase all the time, didn't know. "I am TOO an American!"

Tat shook his head. "No, you are not. There are no more Americans." He turned away from her. "They are all gone."

Cass was prepared to argue how wrong that was because she and Slickie and her entire family, even Price's gang, were all Americans but, maybe Tat had a point. Americans wouldn't have allowed the Ruskies (as Little John called them) to take over and make everyone their slaves. Not that she considered herself a slave, but she was definitely an outlaw, and what kind of system thought that, if you grew more food than they said, you should go to prison? Couldn't have more clothes than the State said and Cass would really like to have a nice pair of dress shoes like the ones Mom kept hidden in a back closet and, every once in a while, put on and paraded in front of Dad, to his great applause. Couldn't read the books that Mom and Dad kept hidden in the shuttered Sweet Briar library, the Ray Bradburys and Philip K. Dicks and Tolkiens and Dickens and, oh, oh, so many good books! Even the ones in Greek and Latin that Dad taught her to read because his parents had taught those languages at Liberty University which was a series of burned out ruins now. University! To go to one! A real one! Not the indoctrination camps laughingly called colleges. To have a car, a real working one. How many times had Cass stumbled on the rusted hulk of a Ford or Toyota back in the woods and had taken her tools to the engines and broken them down and saw how everything fit and knew she could get it to work if she could get some oil and gasoline, both of which were exclusively reserved for elite Party units ... like the Faceless, apparently. The best she could hope for was a jury-rigged steam car but the State would throw her in jail for building it.

So, yeah, she wasn't an American. But she wanted to be.

She sighed and threw her head back and took in the blustery sky. It was cloudy but blue showed here and there as the wind tore the clouds apart and threw more cold at her and, any other day, she would be running through the woods loving the sharp stab of it because the fields were brown and the woods were shedding and the deep snows were nigh, so run now while you can. Hiding against a wall in a town was simply the waste of a good, last day of autumn.

At least it wasn't a bad town. Cass preferred the woods and mountains but if she had to go into a place of buildings and streets and surly people, this was at least interesting. Staunton had ridden the last decades of war and death fairly much intact, with the exception of a smashed building here and there that had succumbed to either neglect or deliberate attack. Draft Gangs had roamed the streets from time to time but Staunton had fared better than other Valley towns, such as Harrisonburg, which was a burned out ruin and an actual impediment to travel. Charlottesville was in better shape but it was on the other side of the mountains and passage across those in winter was impossible, a situation that benefitted Price's gang because it allowed them to roam pretty much at will between Harrisonburg and here. But not IN here, at least not at will, because all the main State regional headquarters were here.

Which was why she and Tat were here.

It was somewhat of a pretty town, all brick and old

style architecture like the 1800s or something, and the streets were weird and curved and cut back on each other and that was actually excellent because there were lots of places to hide and she and Slickie had spent a couple of days mapping the place in their minds as they circled the State buildings scattered here and there around the area of the ruined station, focusing especially on the Directorate HQ located at the end of a narrow street – more an alley – two blocks away, Tat trailing them both as security.

Not that they needed it. Cass thought Lexington, the town she was most familiar with, was more dangerous than this place because the cadre and troopers there were more alert. The ones here were downright asleep. Even the Directorate troops walked around in a trance and she and Slickie had moved among them with ease. There were lots of other workers moving in and out and Cass and Slickie made themselves part of the faceless proletariat in town to address some bureaucratic requirement or another. Everyone here was part of the State or needing something from the State so why should the troopers concern themselves? After all, this was the center of everything.

Geez, Fredericksburg must be downright in a coma.

"You ever been to Fredericksburg?" she asked Tat.

"A few times," Tat's hood said.

"Really?" Intrigued, Cass shifted to where she could look at him. "What did you go there for? To see the General?"

The alien eyes blinked at her. "No. Before."

"Oh."

Before. Before the old world ended. "Why'd you go there?"

The cloak shrugged. "It was what you did back then. You visited towns. My father liked the onion rings that a little restaurant in the middle of town cooked so we would go there for that. It was a very pretty town, very old, had a battlefield from the Civil War there."

"I thought all the fighting was around Richmond."

"Not that civil war. The first one."

Oh, right, there had been a civil war before the one that brought the Reds to power. "What's an onion ring?"

Tat actually smiled at that and leaned forward to explain when there was a low whistle from the direction of the overgrown tracks. Quickly Tat was on his feet, the tanto in his hand, and was at the far corner, peering around. Cass had rolled to her feet and took out her jodos, watching his back for a clue as to how this would go. Tat straightened out and waved her down and made his own sharp whistle. After a moment, Slickie came around the far corner with Tat and they both slipped down the wall to where she was. She kept an eye on the street on her side for a moment, then said, "Clear."

Slickie sat against the wall and splayed his feet. "Whew," he said, "I'm hot." He wiped the sweat from his brow.

"Hot?" Cass looked at him like he was crazy. "It's freezing out here!" and she hugged herself in demonstration.

"Well I haven't been sitting on my ass," he snapped.

Cass was about to snap back that if he hadn't taken so damn long then she wouldn't have been sitting around long enough to freeze her ass off but Tat raised a hand. "Stop," he ordered and Cass glared at him, but shut up. Tat then turned to Slickie. "Talk."

"There's a way in," he said and leaned forward, tapping the concrete pad they were on. "An old skylight on the end of one of the buildings. It's not secured."

"How do you know?" Tat asked.

"I went up there and checked."

"In daylight?" Cass was incredulous. "Are you

crazy?"

Slickie looked at her with annoyance. "No one saw me. They're all trying to stay out of the wind." And he pointedly glanced at her as she braced against the corner.

Cass was all prepared to let him know that she might be cold but always kept her eyes open when Tat made the point for her. "Do not underestimate the Directorate," he warned. "They are better trained than most. Better motivated."

"Not from what I've seen," Slickie muttered.

"Then you will die," Tat said shortly and squatted down in front of Slickie and fixed him with the death stare.

Slickie froze and so did Cass because the death stare strongly indicated Tat was pissed off enough by something stupid they'd said or done that he felt the need to teach a lesson, which usually involved a fairly severe Tat beating that left no marks but plenty of pain. Oh, lordy, not here. Their screams would draw even the sleepiest trooper.

Apparently, Tat concluded the same thing because his blood red death face subsided and the eyes went from yellow fire to his calm brown. "Okay," Slickie said, holding up placating hands.

"Okay," Tat agreed and sat back. Cass sent up a small prayer of thanks.

"So how are we doing this?" she asked, relieved to move the discussion along.

"Same way we've done it before," Tat said to her. Which was: she'd go to the front of the building with a cart and sell corn to the guards and whoever else will buy it. Stay there as long as she could while Tat lurked around the back of the building ready to cut throats as Slickie made the slick moves that had earned him the nickname: get in, grab stuff, get out. Signal from Tat and she extricated herself from the amorous intentions of the guards and they went separate ways and met up later at Dad's and split the take and had a party. Like they'd done a hundred times already.

A hundred times.

She frowned. Do not underestimate the Directorate. "Should we try something else?"

They both looked at her in surprise. "Like what?" Slickie asked.

She shrugged. "I don't know. Maybe ... start a fire somewhere or something." She made a helpless gesture.

"What's with you?" Slickie sneered. "You scared or something?"

"No!" More helpless gestures. "It's just ... we've done that lots of times. What if the Directorate is on to it?"

Tat sat back, thoughtful as Slickie tried to ridicule her but Tat's attitude brought him up short. He turned almost into a statue as he considered then, slowly, shook his head. "I think it will be all right," he said, finally.

Cass met his eyes and he nodded encouragement and, okay, if Tat thinks it will be all right then it will be all right.

She hoped.

2.5

Slickie

He loved this.

It was dark now, the sun had dropped and clouds rolled in smothering the afterglow and it was colder, making this the perfect time and conditions, and Slickie was a shadow within a shadow in the back of the yellow brick building that served as the Directorate's regional headquarters. He squatted behind sacks and sacks of smelly garbage that the Directorate, and apparently everyone else in a six block area, tossed back here. Someone was probably responsible for dragging it all away on some kind of schedule but that hadn't been done in quite some time … or the Directorates were messy people. Good thing, because this assured no one was going to bother him.

He glanced back and located Tat's slight form hidden behind an old car and giggled to himself. Tat was going to have to deal with the smell and the rats while Slickie ran around having a good time, so the sooner we get this show on the road, Tat old pal, the sooner Slickie's good time commenced …

There.

Tat had waved a hand, visible against the red brick of the opposite building. All clear. Slickie broke cover and, three steps and a jump later, he was on a ledge protruding from what was once a loading dock on the second floor.

He wondered why someone would build a second-floor loading dock. Had there been some kind of elevator here once? Who knows? Who cares?

Slickie had already done this route in daytime and was confident enough to run it in the dark, heck, even blindfolded. It was almost a total blackout now so he might as well *be* blindfolded but this was all in his favor: he knew where he was going and no one would see him, absolutely no one. The moon was no factor and the clouds took care of the stars. The only light around the area was reflections from some candles in some apartment building across the street, and the torches of the infrequent patrols, none of which looked up, none of which stepped behind the buildings even to pee. Slickie was invulnerable.

In about five minutes, he was hiding behind an old piece of vent located across the roof from the skylight. He could simply stroll over and do this thing but Slickie was a professional, proud to be called a professional and a professional did not stroll anywhere; a professional was disciplined and always checked. Always. He sat for a count to one hundred, but nothing moved, no sounds reached him, and he judged it safe. Slickie dropped to his stomach and low crawled to the skylight. Seemed silly: if no one had seen him walking across the roof in daylight, what're the chances of someone seeing him now? But, professional. Besides, there was an apartment building across the street and there were a couple of candles in random windows which meant people were home and people home here were likely to be cadre, maybe even Directorate, although Slickie bet most of the Directorate people lived right inside the building he was crawling across.

Which will make this even more fun.

Suppressing another giggle, Slickie reached the skylight and slowly poked an eye over its edge. Pitch black down there, which he expected because it had looked like an attic when he'd checked it earlier. He felt around the edge to the hinges he'd loosened and, slowly, carefully, lifted the skylight and moved it off the cutout. Noisy, yes, because this thing was rusty and creaky but he'd timed his movements with the wind roar and didn't think it was noticeable. He took a moment to catch his breath because this thing was heavy and he ran his hand across it, wondering how it had remained intact all these years. Good thing it had; otherwise there'd have been a leak and someone would have come up here and replaced it with a metal plate and Slickie would be entering the building through some side window into a room he couldn't scope. He'd been surprised before doing that, stepping on a bed and the stomach of its resident who swiped a blade at him as Slickie danced out of the way, grabbed some coins off the bureau, and ran like hell.

That had been fun, but a fun he'd prefer to avoid this time around.

Slickie reached into the backpack and pulled out the rope. In seconds, he had it secured to one of the metal crossbeams supporting the skylight, tested it, and then slowly lowered it until he felt slack. Testing it a few more times, Slickie located one of the pre-tied loops and saddled his foot, then the other, down down down and was standing on the floor. He breathed slowly and listened for running feet coming up this way. Nothing.

Reaching back into his pack, Slickie grasped the packet and pulled it out, unzipping the top and grasping one of the sticks in there. Placing a black cloth over it, he snapped the stick.

Ghost light.

Slickie couldn't help marveling at the glow stick, as Dad called them. They were a fantastic bit of pre-Event science. Wizardry. "We used them for Halloween," Dad had said, an old children's holiday about monsters that had fallen out of favor. Imagine, a marvel like this used as a kid's toy. The people before the Event were downright geniuses. People today weren't, because no one knew how to make these things anymore and existing ones were now as precious as diamonds, at least in his line of work. As rare as the few working flashlights Slickie had and, one day, they wouldn't be working anymore and Slickie would be forced to use flint and steel and punk light to work his way around in the dark. "Medieval burglary," Dad had joked, and Slickie got the reference.

The green light glowed inside the black cloth and Slickie pulled back a corner so he could look around. Lots of boxes and crates piled here and there and covered with dust and tarps. A sewing dummy in front of one set of boxes made Slickie's heart skip a beat because it looked like a person standing there … uh oh, a small window set in the eave. Hastily, Slickie doused the light with the cloth because the last thing he needed was someone looking up and start screaming about ghosts in the attic. After a minute, he cautiously exposed a small corner and looked around again, eyeing the dummy to see if it had moved. Might be a real ghost in the attic.

Slickie scrutinized the boxes. They'd been up here for decades, maybe since the 1800s, and could harbor some very rare, very precious items like old cloth and patterns, if the sewing dummy was any clue. The ladies would go crazy. Farm dresses and blouses and other simple patterns that even the clumsiest of seamstresses and tailors could handle were quite in vogue. Mighty tempting. But that's not why he was here:

"What am I looking for?" he'd asked Uncle P.

"Documents."

"Where will they be?"

"In an office. The commander's office. And they'll be

locked up."

"Where's the office?"

"It should be on the top floor."

"Really, Uncle P? Wouldn't the commander be on the first floor so he doesn't have to climb stairs?"

"Top floor discourages visitors."

Which made sense, and which made Slickie grateful for the skylight because he was already on the top floor … well, once he dropped out of the attic. He cast a small beam of the glow stick around and spotted a folded attic ladder. Slickie moved to it and put his ear to the floor. Nothing. Fumbling around the edge, he located a latch and pulled it while keeping a death grip on the ladder. Wouldn't do for it to smash into some passing guard. Slowly he lowered it, praying no one was down there but, why worry? No lights, so how would they see?

Slickie ducked his head in and out of the opening looking for any lamps or candles or other indications that he'd attracted attention. Nothing. He flashed the glow stick. A hallway, rather short, with what looked like a right turn about ten feet away and a couple of doors at this end, probably utility closets. He climbed down the ladder and paused for a moment, listening for sounds of approach, but, hooray hooray, nothing. Looked like he'd pulled this off. Still, if some idler came boppin' along and found the ladder down, then alarms would be sounded so, quietly as he could, he raised it, wincing at the inevitable creaks of the metal hinges while making sure the pull-down strap was in reach. Might have to make a hasty exit.

Now, which way?

Slickie closed his eyes and counted to sixty to invoke night vision. When he opened them, the turn was easier to spot and he slid along the wall until he could peer around it. Ha, it was like looking down a well. All right. He pulled back a corner of the cloth and let some of the glow stick escape and made out a hallway, with doors on both sides of it, running down to a window at the far end. Good start, but which door?

Sliding along the wall, Slickie came to the first door, an old fashioned wooden one with a glass panel, and he flashed it with the glow stick: A...N...N, ESQ. Obviously, some letters were missing and Slickie wondered what it meant but doubted it was a Directorate title. A dead office, the ghost of someone's name still there. The next four doors, two on each side, had nothing on them and Slickie was frustrated. If something didn't give him a clue, he'd have to go back and search every single office, even the dead ones.

Bingo. Plaque over the middle door: Commander.

Easing up to it, Slickie tried the doorknob but it was locked. He knelt and flashed the key hole. Easy peasy. Two picks inserted, jiggle it a bit and click!

Open.

The door squeaked as Slickie carefully pushed it, and he looked nervously up and down the hallway but no weaving lights and alarmed voices so he slipped around and closed the squeaky door and locked the knob behind him, in case there was an actual diligent security guard going around checking doors. He flashed the interior. All right, two desks on the right and left facing each other, ink blotters and pads of paper and inkstands on each, as well as old fashioned In and Out boxes. A typewriter covered a separate stand next to the desk on the right and Slickie wondered if it worked or was mere decoration. Were they getting ribbons from some old stockpile? A row of chairs ranged the same wall as the entrance door and there was a window in the far wall opposite him but the curtains were pulled, thank God.

Okay, if this was where the clerks and visitors sat waiting for the commander, where was the commander's desk? Slickie walked to the middle of the room and stood between the desks then flashed the room again. Ah, there, a recess on the left. Slickie walked up to it and saw a door. Knob was locked but easy peasy and he went inside.

Bingo.

The commander's office.

Slickie shook his head in admiration. Uncle P knew his business, which was why he's in charge. That, and the rumors of gold bars stashed somewhere, and his tendency to stab anybody that crossed him, and that he'd outwitted Dad in some kind of deal years ago and Dad, who wasn't stupid, thought it better to work for the devil than have the devil mad at him … all right, all right.

A real big picture window graced the alcove wall and Slickie frowned because it's curtains were open, a little glow of light coming from below. Slickie walked over and risked a quick look see. The window topped the main street five stories below and a couple of torches down there marked the troopers at the entrance. The torches wavered and moved about and that probably meant Cass was down there selling them corn and flirting and generally keeping them distracted. He smiled. Good girl.

He scrutinized the room, flashing the stick to get a picture. The commander's desk, a big wooden slab about the size of a barn door, elaborately carved and heavy and elevated and designed to intimidate, dominated. A huge leather chair, also designed to intimidate, canted carelessly to one side. Come to see this guy and there was no doubt who was in charge. Slickie noted several drawers in the desk but only one of them with a keyhole. Okay, that's a possibility, but there was a filing cabinet against the left wall, a metal one with filigree and brass knobs and keyholes for each drawer so that's a possibility, too …

… and a safe on the floor against the right wall,

tucked in next to the desk.

Bingo.

Slickie pushed the chair back a bit and squatted in front of the safe to get a better view. A dial combination safe.

Crap.

No one used combination safes, no one. No one knew the combinations. All these safes had been manufactured before the Event and, unless someone had the combination to begin with, there was no way to figure them out.

Had the combination to begin with …

Hoping against hope, Slickie opened the drawers and rummaged through them quickly: account ledgers, handwritten personnel listings (might be good to know but not his mission so forget it), proposed schedules … nothing. Okay, check the locked middle drawer. Slickie carefully set the glow stick where he could see and applied the lock picks and had the drawer open in mere seconds. A manual, a printed one: Operational Procedures. Wow, this might be worth something. He took it and a black book filled with names and addresses out. All the names were women so wonder what *this* is about, huh? He put it back because the commander would immediately notice its absence. The manual, not so much. Random scraps of paper here and there with a meaningless word or two on them and nothing else.

Nothing else.

Frustrated, Slickie slipped the manual into his backpack and relocked the drawer and sat back and concluded this mission over. He had not found the documents Uncle P wanted so it was a failed mission. Oh, he knew where they were, in the safe on his right, but he had no way of getting in there short of a stick of dynamite which would definitely attract attention. He glanced at the safe, which mocked him in the green light, and saw that the dial was set at zero.

Zero.

Something nagged him about that. He didn't know a lot about combination safes but knew that zero was important. Wasn't zero the last number dialed, the one that allowed the safe to open?

No. Way.

Carefully, holding his breath to not move the dial even a micron, Slickie grabbed the handle and turned it.

And it opened.

No. Way.

Slickie sat back, stunned, This had to be a trick. Had to be. There must be a rattlesnake coiled up inside or a bomb or poison gas set to go off when he reached inside because there was no way the commander of the regional Directorate office would be so stupid as to leave his safe in the unlocked position. Unless he was in a hurry to get out of here. Slickie flashed on the black book. Must have had a date.

Chuckling, Slickie shook the glow stick out of the cloth and laid it on the floor where he could see inside the safe. Papers and folders...

"Look through the stuff that's dated the past three months," Uncle P had said.

Which should be the papers on top. Carefully, he pulled them out. The first one was dated a week ago and had a Fredericksburg heading, a listing of scheduled inspections by the Directorate Secretary. Slickie mused. Was that important? Maybe to the commander but, unless Uncle P was planning an ambush, not so much to us. Pushing it aside, Slickie found a brown envelope with a broken wax seal and flipped it open and pulled out the top paper. It had the hammer-and-sickle logo of the State and General Kant's letterhead underneath and was completely in typed code.

Crap.

But there was another paper in the envelope and Slickie pulled it out. It was pen and ink and looked very much like a decipher of the letter, so Slickie began to read it.

And went completely pale.

Thump thump thump...

Someone was coming down the hall.

"Shit!" Slickie muttered, still shocked by the cipher's content, and he stuffed both papers and the envelope into the side pocket of his backpack, doused the glow stick with the cloth, and closed the safe and threw the handle and debated whether to spin the dial but decided to leave it at zero.

Thumpity thumpity thumpity ...

More than one set of footsteps and they were at the outer office and someone was inserting a key and there were voices and he was dead. There was no way he could make it out of here before the door swung open. Looking around wildly, Slickie noted a dark shape against the wall. A couch. He rushed to the end of it and scrunched, making himself as small as possible as the outer office door swung open.

"...they are more trouble than they're worth," the smarmy, irritated voice of a middle aged man was saying.

"Yes, Colonel," a squeaky ferret voice.

If Slickie was a good judge of voices, and he was, then the Directorate commander and his toady had just come in to do some work. With an uninvited guest hiding next to the couch.

Squeezed into as little a person as possible, Slickie panicked as sudden, rather bright oil light flooded in from the office door. Nothing but the best for our boys. Sounds of a key in the alcove door and Slickie blessed himself for locking it as the door swung open and the two sets of boots tromped in.

"This is what I'm thinking," the Colonel's voice said as he placed the light on the desk and illuminated the entire room; all the Colonel had to do was look up and see the odd dwarf shape at the end of his couch and Slickie was dead. The Colonel, though, was intent on other things as he pushed the chair absently out of his way (thank God he was so sloppy he didn't remember how he'd left it) and pulled open some of the desk drawers. "We'll put Lawless right here, in the guest suite on the third floor."

Lawless? Ice ran down Slickie's spine.

"And I want the rest of those Faceless assholes over at the hospitality rooms at the end of the street. Tell 'em we've got no other room."

"Yes, sir."

"And I want to know every time one of those Faceless bastards pays a visit to Lawless and vice versa. You understand me, corporal?"

Gulp. "Yes, sir!"

"Now, where's that list ..." Sounds of rummaging through papers.

List. The ice down Slickie's spine turned to a glacier. You mean, the list that Slickie, moments ago, lifted from your safe, Colonel? A fact you are going to discover moments from now and then raise the alarm because there's a thief, a thief! Yep, Slickie was dead.

"Ah!" The Colonel said with relief. "Here it is." The Colonel's relief didn't even half match Slickie's.

He heard the sound of movement and then a finger tapping paper. "You see these addresses, Corporal? That's where I want those effin' bastards, but stagger them. I don't want them next to each other. And before you assign it, you run your ass over there and tell the guys next to each room that I want eyes on at all times. Tell Lieutenant Cadgers he's in charge of that and tell him if he misses one guy I'll have his balls for breakfast. Got that?"

"Yes, sir!" A querulous reply and Slickie almost felt sorry for the little dweeb.

"And if you fuck this up, Corporal, I'll have your balls for breakfast."

"Yes, sir!"

Yep, definitely felt sorry for him.

"Now," the Colonel said as he slammed the drawer shut and rattled some other papers. "Let's go entertain that bastard Lawless." And there were sounds of feet and the chair moving and relief flooded through Slickie because they were about to leave and terror flooded through him because Lawless was here, right here.

Which meant he had to get to and through the attic and back on the street in the next five minutes because Cass was out there, exposed. To Lawless. C'mon, c'mon, leave already...

Shouting, distant, but sudden and urgent.

Slickie froze, listening, trying to locate it but it sounded like it was coming from the stairway. The Faceless pouring up the stairs in search of him. Oh no.

"What the hell?" The Colonel, halfway out the door, had stopped.

"I think it's outside, Colonel," the corporal said, and relief flooded through Slickie because, whew, no Faceless stormed the hallway and he was almost free ...

... until the Colonel and the corporal both walked past him and toward the window.

Why they didn't see him, Slickie had no idea. The oil lamp the corporal carried had probably blinded them, but they were now pressed against the window a mere six feet away. Slickie risked a look. The Colonel was as big a bull as his voice and attitude indicated and he was in full brown Directorate officer uniform, replete with a garrison cap, while the corporal was as dweeby as Slickie imagined and dressed in green utilities.

"What the fuck is going on down there?" the Colonel said as he pressed his face against the glass and folded his hands on either side of his face to block out the light. "Don't you ever clean these fucking windows, Corporal?"

"I'll get right on that, sir," the corporal, standing back a bit, said. Slickie had to give the guy silent kudos. He knew how not to get killed.

"What are they doing …" the Colonel said.

There was high-pitched screaming. A girl's screaming. Cass.

Oh shit oh shit oh shit …

As full-blown terror gripped Slickie, the Colonel laughed. "Look at that fucking Lawless down there!" he roared. "Already entertaining himself with the local talent!" and he pressed and shifted to get a better look.

Move. Now.

Slickie unfolded and slid as silent as a cobra across the side of the couch and along the front. Halfway down it, he gained his feet and moved to a crouch and looked back …

The Colonel still leaned against the window, thoroughly enjoying himself. The corporal looked straight at Slickie, the oil lamp reflecting back in the window glass. Apparently, the corporal had seen Slickie's reflected movement.

Their eyes met. Slickie braced for cries and bullets, but no; the corporal remained still. They held each other's gaze for a moment, and then Slickie put his finger to his lips.

The corporal gave a slight nod and moved back to the window, setting the lamp in such a way it blinded any peripheral vision.

Slickie, gone, to the right and out the outer door, flashing a quick glow-stick but the hall was empty, thank God, so move, move! On silent feet, he fled down the hall and around the corner and pulled the ladder down and scrambled up and pulled it back, not caring how much noise he made and was up the skylight and across the roof as the keen of a young girl filled the air.

Cass. Hang on! I'm coming.

2.6

Cass

Cart, check. Roasted corn, check. Slit cloak revealing a little too much leg, check, And a hood to help mask her features, check.

Little Red Effin' Ride Me Hood, she was. My, what big eyes you've got, trooper. The better to see your jail-bait body, little girl.

What, exactly, was jail bait, anyway?

She shrugged and pushed the cart through a particularly rough portion of broken asphalt laughingly called a street that paralleled the Directorate's headquarters. Best she could figure, there used to be age restrictions on dating or getting married or pregnant or something, but years of war and the subsequent population reduction had thrown all that out the window. Now, only the strength and orneriness of one's father and brothers protected a girl's virtue. From what Cass had heard about some of the hill people 'round hyeah, even that was no guarantee. Add the Directorate's insistence that every woman in America justifies their continued drain on resources by either working themselves to death or becoming pregnant, young girls had much incentive to give up that virtue at the first opportunity. A baby earned more rations, leading some families to farm out daughters about a day after their first period and give the resultant babies to the State Ministry of Education in exchange for large bundles of scrip. Daughter or two dropping a kid every nine months, and a family could live well, or, at least, better. Men in light blue Ministry uniforms came by, threw the babies in the back of their carts and off they went, returning nine months later for the next load. What happened to the babies? Who knows. A labor camp or factory, or the Army. Or the Faceless.

She shivered. Thank God her father and brother were ornery.

Speaking of which ...

Cass paused at the corner of the alley that ran beside the Directorate building and surreptitiously peered down it until she located an odd pile of clothes propped in a corner - Tat set against a yellow brick building. Thank God; made it easier to spot him in the dark. Tat acknowledged her presence with a flutter of the clothes and she stopped pretend-primping and futzed with the cart, moving around it like she was trying to fix something while keeping an eye on the pile of Tat clothes.

It was colder than earlier, something she did not appreciate, and wondered if it might be a good idea to suggest they run these operations in spring and summer only. Winter sucked. Okay, it wasn't actually winter yet, at least according to the people who still kept track of days and dates, but it might as well be. She threw a gimlet eye at the clouds racing overhead, ones so contrary they teased a star or two and then covered it right back up. Laughing at her, they were. You think this is bad, little girl, wait until we bring the snows.

The snows.

She shivered again thinking about it. Brutal snows, locking them deep in the hollows and creek sides of the Valley, ensuring no movement, no visits, and no food. If a family didn't put up enough supplies against those months, then their starved bodies appeared the next thaw with evidence of cannibalism among them. If a family didn't know how to hunt, same result, although even the best of hunters had a hard time tracking the deer and elk in the cold months. Six-foot drifts hindered movement and the wolves competed, often wiping out a herd before hunters could reach them. Dad said the wolves were new; the only predators before the Event were coyotes, the occasional black bears and, of course, people. There hadn't been elk back then, either, only deer, most of which got slaughtered running into the hordes of cars racing up and down Skyline Drive.

The world was getting colder, Dad said. The summers were getting shorter, the winters, longer. Slickie had read a book about the Revolutionary War – the one that had made America before the Event unmade America – and the winter back then had been so bad that whole rivers froze. Cass hoped things wouldn't reach that point. She'd never go outside.

Thank God Dad had plenty of food stored up.

Cass took solace in that. Dad also made sure they'd get through the winter in relative comfort with sacks of coal and stacks of firewood to keep the stoves lit. Cass spent most of the time huddled against them while Slickie razzed her as he bounded outside in minimum winter garb to hunt deer or run an operation, leaving the door wide open as he left. "Close it, you bastard!" she'd scream and Mom would admonish her about language while Dad burst out laughing as she stomped across the floor and slammed the door herself, throwing the bolt so the jackass couldn't get back inside. Hope he froze to death … well, at least grew an icicle down his nose.

Sometimes she hated her brother. But not today.

Tat's arm was straight up against the brick, a spear of a shadow rising above his pile of ragged clothes. Showtime. Uneasy, she looked around, halfway sure this old gag had worn itself out, and then pushed the cart up and around the corner. "Roast corn!" she yipped, "Roast corn!"

There was no such thing as trade in this brave new world of Utopian socialism that the Reds had instituted after their defeat of the counter-revolutionary and reactionary Blues (oh, boy, almost busted out laughing here). Each from his abilities, each according to his need, as explained in pamphlets and the harangues of local political officers so, technically, she was not supposed to be offering up any products on an individual basis. Cadres distributed all production from a centralized system of gathering and determination in which everyone got plenty to eat, plenty of clothes, plenty of radios and TVs and Cadillacs and computers ...

This time she did laugh out loud.

Because it did not work. It would never work. Instead of admitting that, though, the cadres allowed a certain amount of supplemental capitalist activity for items considered critical. Like food.

"Over here, girl!" The first customer, er, comrade, standing in the doorway of a small building with a huge overhang, smoking a cigarette, called out as soon as she turned the corner. She zeroed on the glowing tip and trundled the cart over. "How many?" she asked.

The cadre, an older man sporting the uniform and badge of a transportation unit and a permanently sour expression, held up five fingers. "Okay," she said, "what you got?"

The man offered an unopened pack of State cigarettes. "Ugh," Cass responded, "that won't get you a niblet."

"Yeah?" the man became instantly belligerent. "What if I just take them then and throw you the pack, anyway?"

"I'll scream," she replied, mildly. The man stopped his ominous steps forward and scowled at her. A young girl alone in a city street was fair game these days, especially with platoons of desperate nubiles seeking to get pregnant, but a nubile that screamed in terror or protest was going to attract a lot of attention, most of it violent, from other cadres who felt cheated out of an opportunity. After all, in a chain of rapists, someone always wanted to be first. "So treat a girl right," she added, to calm the air. "It may help you out later." And she gave him a lewd wink.

The old man guffawed and reached into a side pocket and produced another pack of cigarettes, shiny and still cellophane wrapped. Marlboro's. Pre-event. Probably stale as crap but the boxes alone were valuable. Cass's eyes rounded as avarice gripped her. "Do you have more of those?"

"Maybe." The man leered. "What will it buy me?"

Cass snapped back to attention. "Right now," she said, opening the cart and reaching inside, "five ears of corn." And she deposited them, still warm and steaming a bit (courtesy of one of Tat's pals who lived in some old deaf school on top of the hill), on top of the cart. "Later … we'll see," and she winked lewdly again as the man dropped the pack and gathered the ears.

"How long you gonna be out here, girl?"

"Until I'm done. So why don't you keep an eye on me?" and she pushed the cart away, making sure she stuck out her rear end and wiggled it enough to keep the man's interest as she headed toward the Directorate building.

You're such a whore.

She giggled at that because the things she had to do to keep an op safe would make Mom blush. Which is why she never told her, and why Mom never asked. If there was anyone who had recognized the new realities of this world it was Mom, but, like many of her generation, she was conflicted by the values of the old. Not that she let it paralyze her, as many of her peers did, but occasionally Mom would grow wistful and nostalgic about things like television shows and movies and musical groups, all from Jupiter, as far as Cass was concerned. Dad and Mom sometimes reminisced over those things and a lot of it sounded so great and wonderful that Cass halfway suspected they were exaggerating. But it also made her sad, first for Mom and a world now lost, second for Cass and a world never known and, judging by the way things were going, would never know. Cass's world moved backward; the Dark Ages they currently inhabited were becoming darker.

Cass knew about the Dark Ages because Dad knew about it and he knew about it because his parents were actual professors of medieval life and had taught him Latin and Anglo Saxon. Dad, in turn, had taught her enough she could read a lot of the texts herself, the old tales of Homer (gee, I wonder who Dad was named after?) and Ulysses and Beowulf. As exciting as they were, the world they inhabited was anarchic and ruled by might. Strong men with swords and armies determined who lived and died. How was that any different than now?

"Hey, baby, watcha peddlin'?"

This time a couple of troopers, stamping their feet and huddling by a little fire grate in front of the Directorate building, waved her over. With a backward glance at her first admirer, she steered the cart in their direction, pulling up short of the grate and saying, "Corn!" With a flourish, she opened the top, letting the aroma serve as advertisement.

"Uhm, uhm, uhm," The trooper on the left, a guy so sloppy even his tucked uniform shirt was riding up his sides, stood over the cart and took in a deep breath. He then leaned forward and sniffed at Cass's neck. "That sure smells good."

"Oh, you!" Cass giggled and play-slapped at him and cast a backward glance and, yep, old sour guy was stomping this way. Start some crap. Attract a crowd. That's how this worked.

The other trooper was obviously more hungry than anything because he reached into the cart and rummaged around. "Now, now," Cass said and slapped at him with a lot more than playfulness, "You gotta trade for it first."

"How 'bout I don't run you in for illegal peddling?" the guy, skinny and mean-faced, glared at her and dug some more.

"Do you hear this?" she pleaded at neck-sniffer. "He wants to steal from a poor, defenseless girl!" And she took an exaggerated pose of helplessness.

"Hey, Sam." Neck-sniffer straightened up and waved at his pal. "Give the girl a break, will ya?"

"You give her a break," Sam snarled and grabbed an ear and peeled it back and turned to the fire grate, ready to warm it up even more.

"He's stealing my food!" Cass wailed right as Sour Face stepped up.

"What do you think you're doing, man?" The old guy grabbed Sam by the lapels.

"Hey!" Neck-sniffer now had to defend his pal and his post. "Lay off!" And he grabbed Sour Face's arm.

Perfect.

Cass stepped back and couldn't help a little grin. This was escalating nicely. Soon blows would be struck and other troopers and cadre would come running to see what the fuss was all about and all of their attention would be on the growing scrum and the cute little girl who needed a hero because she was going to choose someone out of the crowd on whom to bestow her charms and no one would give a crap what was going on in the alley and the back and the roof of the building itself. Eventually, the pile of clothes that was Tat would appear on the street and scratch its head in puzzlement, and Cass would huffily cart away with a dismissive word, the scrum too busy to even notice her or, if some elements of it wished to take her charms, then a slap with a jodo stick or one of Tat's blades would make short work of that. Even as she surveyed the growing chaotic scene, she heard feet running in her direction; this was going exactly as she wanted.

"What's going on here?" The bellow of someone who sounded as though he was in charge. Oh boy, an officer has joined the fray. Stepping back for a better view, she craned her neck past the pushing and shoving cadre.

And her blood ran cold.

"Stand down!" The tall, very thin man's green eyes blazed in the many torches and lamps that had been brought to bear. Scary enough, especially with those thin eyebrows, but what made him more terrifying were the two Faceless flanking him.

And the squad of masked Faceless standing behind him.

Apparently, enough members of the riot knew who Green Eyes was, or knew who the Faceless were, to make them break off and even a couple to flee down the street, including Sour Face. Her hero. The Faceless didn't pursue but looked on impassively while, in the most unfortunate of moves, the scrum parted so that Cass was face to face with Green Eyes.

Those eyes bore down on her. "What are you doing here?"

"She's selling vegetables!" Sam yelled as he pointed a finger at her.

"And that ain't all she's selling!" Neck-sniffer added his own accusation, with his own finger point.

Green Eyes glared at the two of them and pushed

them aside and was there, right in front of Cass. "Do you have a peddler's license?" he snarled. Those laser-like eyes struck Cass dumb, unable to even shake her head. That voice. She knew that voice.

Green Eyes held up a lecturing finger and focused on her. "It is a major violation of State directives to trade in State merchandise without prior approval of cadre transportation and produce committees! Such activity is a threat to State security and can be prosecuted as tre—" He stopped and his eyes narrowed. "Don't I know you?"

Of course he did. They'd met a few weeks ago. Don't you remember me, Major Lawless, commander of the Faceless? You tried to kill me.

And, in seconds, would try to kill her again. Or worse, take her prisoner.

So, here she was, in the middle of enemy territory, in front of the main enemy's regional headquarters, no less, surrounded by the *crème de la crème* of the enemy, themselves supported by lesser enemies like troopers and cadre, about to be taken into custody by one of the most fearsome enemies she'd ever encountered. What to do?

What any little girl threatened by a gang of men would do … stand back and scream.

She did.

Piercing, spine-shattering screams, the kind little girls made when terrified or under attack, the kind of screams that triggered something atavistic in men within earshot: there's a damsel in distress or a damsel to rape so, whichever inclination moved you, come running.

They did.

Doors flew open and windows did, too, and lamps and candles and torches stuck out here and there as lots of people yelled, "What's going on? What's all the noise?" and feet hit the street and pounded in their direction. The immediate enemies – Sam and Neck-Sniffer and Major

Lawless – grabbed their ears because a shrieking girl was an annoying sound. So let's add to the confusion, "Lucifer!" she screamed. "The devil! God and his angels!"

Which, by State standards, meant she was completely insane. And the last thing with which any grown man wanted to tangle was an insane little girl.

The immediates, suddenly wary, took backward steps right at the moment the on-rushers reached them and it was a collision of varying interests, from those genuinely concerned to those who were hoping to get in on the action, and everyone was thrown off balance. Except her.

Now.

Pushing the cart hard, Cass bowled over Sam and Neck-Sniffer at the same time she spun the jodo sticks in both hands and drove them behind her as hard as she could, feeling with satisfaction as the two people back there doubled over with respective *"Oofs!"* of pain. Spinning on the balls of her feet, she racked the shins of two other people causing them to scream and dance out of the way and there was an opening through the crowd and she made for it …

"You!"

The shout was like a grab at her coat and she had to turn and look. Major Lawless, tall and murderous in the torch light, his eyes ablaze, his mouth cruel and open, pointed a finger at her. "You!" he shouted again and reached to his side and pulled out a pistol. The Faceless beside him whipped small machine guns from behind their backs.

Seconds away from a massacre. Starting with her.

Hands grabbed her shoulders from the front and she brought the jodo sticks down ferociously on elbows and forearms and there were screams and she was released but she was not out of the way and she glanced back in horror as gun barrels came to bear and she was going to die horribly right here in the street. Oh no oh no, Slickie go, please go get away and tell Dad and Mom what happened to me …

The Faceless's eyes, visible above their baklavas, suddenly widened and they screamed in pain and spun around as their guns canted right and left and fired into the crowd, one barely missing Major Lawless. Cass glimpsed blades sticking out of their backs and upper shoulders. Tat's blades.

"Sonofabitch!" Lawless roared and wheeled about, firing behind him, presumably at Tat, who Cass could not see and she doubted Lawless could, either. Tat was gone after buying her the seconds she needed so get moving, girl!

Whipping the sticks right and left, she drove off the last two crowd members who were either too stupid to get out of the way or too stupid to realize what was going on and she pelted down the street and cut up the first alley she found and then over a wall and go, go, hearing Lawless shouting, "Secure the building!" meaning the Directorate building as he finally figured out what was really going on here.

Slickie, please, get away.

Tat, please, get away.

Cass, please, get away.

2.7

Whittaker

Had to be a trap. Had to be.

Ben was hiding in a corner of an abandoned building next to the old cadre compound – 'old' in the sense that Deavers had run them out – and not liking what he saw, which was … nothing. Not a thing. The compound, dark and silent, had all the appearance of being empty. Which made no sense at all: the Directorate couldn't be that sloppy, that careless.

So, had to be a trap.

Ben frowned. What more perfect way to set up the church than catch one of its members breaking into a classified compound intent on stealing State secrets? That's all Deavers would need to march a squadron up to Bluemont and round up everybody and send them off to the camps, thereby shutting down dissent for the next hundred years or so. Except there was no Directorate squadron here. Not even a platoon. Just three guys.

Made no sense. At all.

Any Directorate guy half his salt ought to know that a Directorate compound was a prime target and would take precautions. There should be guards, lights, patrols, dogs, heck, maybe even mines. But this place was a ghost town.

Maybe that was the point.

In a little town like this in a little area like the northern Valley, there was no need for physical precautions. The reputation of the Directorate sufficed. Anyone stupid enough to break in would be found, days later, nailed to a barn door skinned alive, while their family would never be found. So Deavers wasn't worried about it.

Yet, Deavers knew Collier. And should, therefore, be wary.

Ben knew Collier, too, but not the way Deavers did. Ben knew about the Ghosts, knew the legends that everyone knew. Ben had heard that the pastor of the new church in the mountains above Bluemont was an honest-to-God Ghost, had the tattoo and everything, and he'd gone to see. After seeing, he had to join, even if his own religious beliefs were somewhat unclear.

Because Ben, like the Ghosts, was willing to die for freedom. Ben was a Blue.

Okay, yeah, he'd never worn a Blue uniform and, yeah, sure, he'd treated with the enemy back during the war, but he had to: the community relied on his information and trade goods and sometimes that required dealing with the devil. But Ben fought for the Blues all the same, carrying information and intelligence to their units in the Valley and on the outskirts of the quarantined zone. He identified Red units setting up ambushes on the still viable Interstate 81 and passed that information to those Blues still running supplies to the Ghosts and others holding the line above the Potomac. No one knew his name, no one gave him credit, but he was as much a part of it as Collier, because no other country in the world except America believed in him. Him, Ben Whittaker, son of Leslie and May, insurance agents and entrepreneurs who were the first in their families to go to college and who had told Ben, over and over, that no other country in the world would give a black man the chance to rise in two generations from sharecropper to business professional. No other country in the world had fought a war with itself to free the black man and, yes, there were still people who hated a black man because he was black and all those people were Reds because Reds believed a man needed to be under another man's thumb but the Blues, the Blues, they believed a man stands on his own.

Ben stood on his own.

When the Event occurred and the Zone Camps were set up across the Manassas line, his parents sent him there to sell goods to the guards and the Zoners languishing inside because they were the Blues ... well, not yet. The labels "Blue" and "Red" were still a few years off but they *were* Americans, fellow citizens of the United States or what was left of it, especially as the factions broke into open warfare and one military unit after another vied to take over, promoting their own candidate as President until "Who's the President this week?" turned into a running joke, the punchline always, "You are!" Some of those Army units were simply bent on taking over but others wanted to preserve the Constitution and those were the ones Ben worked for, proving himself so valuable that their commanders protected him from the Draft Gangs.

And then the Reds showed up.

The enemy was clear and stark and obvious and Ben fought them. In the midst of them, ingratiating himself and doing favors and acquiring goods, he noted their numbers and dispositions and patrol lines and tactics and took it all to the Blues and was absolutely sure, absolutely certain, those Red bastards would be defeated ... and then the Ghosts were betrayed. And Ben had lost.

Temporarily.

Because, if there was a principle instilled by his parents, it was this: never give up. Ever. Especially for what's right. The Blues were right. The Reds were not. Collier was a Blue, in the most legendary category of Blue, and he still fought. He had organized the church and the congregation and they were an invisible force in the entire Lower Valley, people who kept the faith and the vision and opposed the State in a quiet manner and spread hope, spread knowledge, over time and over space, and Ben had heard of this and made his way up the mountain and made Collier his leader.

And Deavers knew Collier, knew he was a Ghost because Deavers was a Ghost, and they knew each other's capabilities and could not underestimate each other, could not. So this was a trap. It would destroy Collier. It would destroy the church. And Ben.

He hesitated. If he did this and the trap sprung and they were lost then hope was lost and the State wins, the Reds win and the light of freedom throughout the world blinks out. That was far more important than any disappointment Collier might feel over Ben's refusal to move. The greater good outweighed the personal. He could not be the instrument of Collier's destruction. He should leave.

"You're pussying out."

Washburn's words rang in his head and he burned. Pussying out, you redneck asshole? I'm saving us!

Or was he pussying out?

Ben sighed, long and silent. He'd faced possible traps before and he'd learned from those instances that the best way to find out if it was, indeed, a trap was to spring it.

So, spring it.

Peeking around the corner, Ben surveilled the compound one more time to ensure there was no light or movement then dashed to a corner fence post where the chain link sagged. Yanking on it, he located the stake and, using his favorite old crowbar, strangely free of rust after all these years, pried it out of the ground. The link was now loose enough for him to pull up the bottom skirt and, propping it with the crowbar, scurry underneath. He rushed for the corner of the main building, or what he thought was the main building, judging by the comings and goings of the agents. No shots rang out, no shouts, either. So far, so good.

Now what?

Well, he supposed he could simply stroll around the front of the building and open the door and waltz on in and casually look around until he found Deavers's office and then spend a few hours rummaging through it, if no one objected, of course. While that would be ideal, Ben didn't think it was the smartest way to go. Let's keep the surreptitious nature of this whole goat rope surreptitious and find a safer way inside.

Maintaining a crouch, Ben crept along the back of the building. It was a giant railroad shed, all tin and rust with some inexpert repairs made here and there over the years by the cadres, probably to keep the building from falling down. There was a lot of trash in the yard, stuff that threatened to trip him up or advertise his presence so he picked his way carefully because it was dark and cloudy and the wind shifted things in a dangerous way and, after about three days, he cleared the corner of an extension and could see ...

He could see.

Ben froze.

There was a light in a back window throwing beams over this part of the yard. It was weak light, no more than a couple of candles, which is why he didn't see it from around the corner. It meant someone was there. Thirty years ago, people left lights on willy nilly whether they were home or not but leave a candle unattended now, burn the house down. So, someone's awake.

Ben figured it was Deavers sitting in bed and reading. The two agents had left the compound about the time it was getting dark and had not come back in the three hours

Ben had lain there watching. Enjoying themselves downtown, or off on another spy mission. So, this was the bossman, and a guy like Deavers would put his office in a part of the building that had no windows and his sleeping quarters in a part that did because bedrooms needed a view. So all Ben had to do was wait for the candle to go out and Deavers to fall asleep and he had the run of the place, provided the two agents didn't come stumbling back.

Quietly, Ben settled on the ground, pulling his coat tighter against the wind and waited. And waited. And waited.

This was getting ridiculous. C'mon, Deavers, go to sleep already. What's so interesting? *Das Kapital*? Maybe he wasn't reading at all. Maybe he was entertaining.

Well, wouldn't that be something? Smiling a bit lecherously, Ben headed toward the window.

The light, weak as it was, made it easier to navigate the hazards and Ben crouched underneath the ledge a few moments later. He inched up the wall until he could place one eye in the corner of the glass.

The candles sat on either side of a desk, illuminating the man sitting there with his back to Ben. The man wore a robe of some kind, probably to keep warm since it was a chilly night and a tin building like this couldn't keep out the drafts. Ben couldn't tell if he wore a uniform or not, but he assumed this was Major Deavers. The man hunched over the desk, which had numerous papers and books scattered across the front of it, writing on one piece of paper while consulting another laid next to it. He used an actual ball point pen and Ben had to admire that. Those were pretty scarce, working ones, that is. Ben kept a box of them as rewards for his contacts.

So, this was not a bedroom after all, but an office, an office with a window. And the Major had his back to it.

Sumpin' ain't right.

If Deavers was a run-of-the mill cadre guy, Ben wouldn't worry, but Deavers was a Directorate major, a former Blue, a former Ghost for that matter, and who, according to Collier, was no slouch. This, though, was slouchy and Ben looked around, sure the candles had been set to lure him to this location where the other two agents could grab him. But, no one there. And, given the mess in the yard, there was no way they could approach without him hearing. So what is this? Is the guy so sure of himself, so comfortable, that he can afford laxity? Ben didn't know, so he settled in to watch for a while until he did know.

After what had to be an hour, Deavers sat up straight, stretched luxuriously, then stood. He stared down at his papers for a moment then absently reached into a pocket of the thick robe (velour? Man, the guy was living large) and pulled out a pipe. He examined it and then pulled out a red plastic bag from the same pocket, opened it, and scooped the pipe. Ben's mouth watered. Tobacco, and probably the good stuff. Deavers fished around in his robe again and grabbed something like a spoon and worked the tobacco in the pipe bowl, replaced the spoon, reached over and picked up a candle, and nonchalantly walked around the desk and to the right and out of sight.

Leaving the papers on his desk, next to a lit candle.

Had to be a trap.

It was too inviting not to be. An unguarded desk right in front of a casement window that was begging Ben to jimmy it, slide over the transom and onto the floor and be right there. Right at the moment he reached the desk, a net would fall on him or the hounds would be loosed or Deavers would leap around the corner yelling, "Aha!"

Ben waited. And waited. Deavers did not return.

Spring the trap.

It took Ben a few more minutes than he anticipated to caterpillar his way across the transom and onto the floor because the window frame was rusty and sharp and took about nine layers of his skin as he got through. Shouldn't be too difficult identifying what black man this came from, sir (or black woman. Like you, Felicia, he chuckled to himself). The crank had stuck halfway and he had to squeeze through a narrower opening than he wanted, grunting and scraping and sure he was waking up everyone in Stephens City. Stifling his gasps, he lay there, fully exposed to anyone who might happen back to finish the night's work. But Deavers did not appear.

Cautiously, Ben gathered his feet and tiptoed past the desk to where Deavers had gone. It was a long hallway broken up by partitions that dimly disappeared in the distance, probably the offices that the cadre and Commissar used when they had possession of the place. Far down there was a glimmer of light, probably Deavers and his candle. Ben could not tell what he was doing but figured he was smoking and maybe eating a snack from what served as the cantina and would be ambling back this way in the next few moments to finish up the night's work.

You've got maybe five minutes to find and search Deavers' office, bucko. Which, fortuitously, appeared to be the very office in which he was standing.

Ben ducked back and slipped around the desk to Deavers's chair, careful not to move it and thereby alert the Major that someone had been here in his absence. He needed to go through every drawer and maybe that cabinet on the left until he found something that explained Deavers's presence in the Valley but every search had a starting point so let's begin right here, with the documents Deavers had been working on and had left so conveniently illuminated and open right here for Ben's prying eyes. Looking around wildly for the expected trap, Ben stepped up and peered at the documents.

And gasped.

He read them again. And gasped again.

Ben did not have a photographic memory. He'd never be able to reproduce this word for word. But he got more than the gist of it and made sure to memorize the dates and names because that was going to be critical. Too bad he could not take the documents, but then they'd know we know and things might happen faster than we wanted. It'd be nice, too, to show Collier the proof of what he reported because no one would believe this. No one. He wasn't sure he believed it himself.

Trap? Of a different nature?

Ben considered. It had been way too easy to get this information, almost like Deavers wanted him to have it. Suspicious, Ben narrowed his eyes and waited for Deavers to come around the corner and urge him to get on with it. C'mon, you got what you need, black man, what do you want, a medal? But, no Deavers. Which meant nothing; guy could be cheering him on from a distance. What to do?

Tell Collier.

It was just as hard going out as it had been going in and Ben was sure he no longer had any skin on his stomach. He clanked something metal when he landed on the ground and that was it, someone heard that, had to, so he hastily pulled the window and jimmied the handle closed and took a quick look to be sure there was no one descending on him and then made his way back along the building. Harder to do so going back because the candle glow no longer illuminated the way. Besides, he was in a hurry.

Ben reached the other end of the extension and did a quick look around and then hastily ran to the fence, locating the propped-up section more by guess than skill and slid under and turned back to grab the crowbar …

… and stared straight at Deavers standing at the end of the building quietly puffing his pipe. And staring straight back at Ben.

There was nothing Ben could do and he braced for the bullet or arrow to take him in the chest. And braced. And braced some more. Deavers simply stood there, puffing, watching him, no weapon in his hand, and not reaching for one. There was no sound of rushing feet, either. It was just the two of them, Directorate Major and treasonous spy, regarding each other, sharing a moment.

After that moment, Ben pulled the crowbar to himself, stretched the chain link back out, and stood up in full view. Deavers watched, maybe even gave Ben a slight nod. Ben took a tentative step back, turned and melted into the darkness.

2.8

Collier

Someone pounded on the door.

Years ago, when Collier was young, dumb, and full of … well, you know, he'd have leaped from the bed fully armed and ready for combat. But now, all he did was lie there confused.

"Collier?" Evelyn whispered to him, fear lacing her voice.

"I'm awake," he said, which kickstarted everything and he rolled quickly and silently to his feet and padded around the bed, reaching into a corner and grabbing the baseball bat. Used to grab an M16 or a .45, but he was proscribed and subject to random searches by any passing trooper or cadre (and now, any passing Directorate agent) and if they stumbled over a random rifle or two they'd shoot him. And Evelyn. And the kids, so bat would have to do. For now.

He stepped into the doorway. The house wasn't all that big but it was long and Collier's bedroom was straight across from the front door so he was looking straight at it, but it was black as pitch and he couldn't see anything. The front door flanked two picture windows, discernible as lighter squares against the night, but not enough to show anything. And then suddenly it was.

"Dad?" Second blundered out of his bedroom rubbing his eyes and waving an oil lamp around. Dammit!

Collier's night vision was gone. And Collier's position was now revealed to anyone looking through either of the picture windows.

"Shut that light out!" Collier hissed.

"Wha— Dad?" Second turned to him confused and Collier rushed him, snapping the lamp switch around and killing the light while roughly pushing Second back into the room. "Stay here!" he ordered. "And shut up!" he added as a protest mounted to Second's lips. Kid didn't react well to situations, did he?

By that time, the opposite door had opened but the twins had the presence of mind not to bring out a light or say anything, two shadows bobbing in the doorway, their eyes so wide Collier could actually see them. "Stay there," he ordered, not so roughly and the two of them did. Thank God someone listened.

Whoever was at the door had stopped knocking, no doubt alerted by idiot Second's light. Collier peered at the windows but there were no torches out there illuminating soldiers crowding the frames. That's encouraging. More encouraging, the door was not off its hinges allowing cadre to pour in and begin tossing everything around. Even a robber gang would have been inside by now so it was probably just one or two persons pounding on his door after midnight on a night so cold it might as well be winter already. Could be some traveler seeking shelter, and wasn't that his Christian duty? Collier gripped the bat. Depends on the traveler.

Collier moved quickly down the hall, the bat at the ready. Halfway down, he called out, "Who is it?"

There was some shuffling next to him and Collier, startled, stopped and looked and there was Evelyn, armed with a machete. More shuffling behind her and Collier guessed it was Second who didn't listen, just didn't listen, but he took comfort from the kid being there, anyway. Be nice to have someone else in the upcoming fight; if anything, could use him as a distraction. "Who is it?" he asked again.

Something stirred at the door and there was a kind of scratching, and Collier swore he heard a whisper. "What?" he called.

The whisper, more urgent now, came clear. "It's Ben!"

Collier may no longer have the soldier reflexes but he could still realize implications, and if Ben was at his door on a cold midnight, then he'd discovered something critical. "Everybody get back!" he snarled and glared both Evelyn and Second away. He then opened the door and stepped out. "This way," he said to the dark shape huddled against the door jamb and strode through the dark, Ben beside him, until they reached the barn. Pulling the latch, he urged Ben inside and then followed, closing the door behind them. "Hold on," he said and fumbled around on the bench until he located the steel and struck it at the tinder box until he got a flame and then lit a candle. The light filled the room and Collier scrutinized the smaller man. Ben looked as if he had run miles through thorn bushes and scree and a gauntlet of very angry ladies carrying roller pins. His clothes were torn in many places, he was bleeding here and there, and one eye was swollen like someone had socked him. "You look like crap," Collier observed.

"Gee, thanks," Ben said, grinning despite his obvious distress.

Collier pointed at the eye. "How'd that happen?"

"It's hard getting up here at night," Ben replied, gingerly touching the swollen area. "Especially on a skittish horse."

Despite the gravity, Collier chuckled. "Wait here," he said and went outside. He came back a moment later with a cup of well water. Ben took it gratefully, downing the entire amount in one gulp. "Wait here," Collier said again and went to the house, which was lit now by a couple of candles. "I need some bandages, some salve, and a big drinking cup," he said brusquely as he entered and Evelyn got up immediately and gathered stuff because she realized the implications of things, too.

Not so Second.

"Dad, what's going on?"

Said with the belligerence and petulance that had marked adolescence since Abraham's time, an echo of Collier's own teenage belligerence and petulance and Collier simply didn't have time for this. No time at all. Collier raised an impatient hand to his son, who stood candlelit at the beginning of the long hall, arms crossed, the twins hovering behind him and ducking between his shoulders to get a view. "Look, I need you guys to go back to bed. I know, I know." A wave of the impatient hand. "You can't sleep, but you don't have to. I just need you out of the way for now. And." He raised an emphatic finger to cut off Second's protest. "I *will* tell you what's going on. In the morning." And he dropped the hand in emphasis.

The twins looked at each other and backed off, heading to their bedroom. Second maintained his stance for moments past propriety, letting Dad know what he thought of all this, but then dropped his arms and stomped off, slamming his door in further emphasis. Collier inwardly sighed. Kids.

He turned and Evelyn was at the door with the gathered supplies laid inside a large porcelain bowl, including a couple of corn muffins from dinner and a determined look on her face, so Collier didn't bother protesting. He led the way out the door, stopping halfway to take the bowl and cup and headed to the well, filling both. He entered the barn, where Evelyn had Ben sitting on a stool while she examined his injuries, clucking the whole time as Ben looked at her with amusement. "Where's your horse?" Collier asked.

"He's tied up over by your drive."

Collier nodded, setting the filled bowl and cup next to Evelyn, who slapped Ben's hand away from the water. "Yes'm," Ben said soberly and Collier laughed as he headed back out.

He located the horse by sound because it was very unhappy and tossing its head as Collier took the halter and pulled more than led the damn stubborn thing into the barn, where it finally realized a human was doing it a favor and almost eagerly headed toward Flicka's stall, something the big roan horse, Collier's favorite, did not appreciate so Collier dragged the horse to the open stall next to Evelyn's horse, Ginger, a pale quarter horse that loved everyone and nickered a welcome as Ben's horse went inside. Collier unsaddled it and examined the cuts on its flank and shook his head and grabbed the horse salve and applied it to the cuts he could see as the horse remained amazingly docile, happy with the hay, Collier supposed. After all this time, he still didn't know that much about horses. He'd not grown up with them. The only horse from his youth was a Ford Mustang.

But he did know when a horse was rode hard. "You damn near killed that one," Collier observed as he came back to the table. Evelyn was wrapping a cloth around Ben's wrist, which looked swollen so probably sprained, confirmed by Ben's wincing as she tightened it. Ben's eye glistened with the aloe salve that Evelyn made from her house plants, a very effective antibiotic. Nature is a wonderful thing.

"Had to get here," Ben replied, eying the nearby corn muffins but, warned by Evelyn's look, restraining the impulse.

Collier pulled up a work table and balanced his rear on the edge of it and could not help thinking how this scene was so 19th Century, not 21st; at least, not in keeping with all the progress everyone presumed the future would bring. By now, Collier should be living on the moon and shuttling back and forth to his job at the robotics plant in the Arctic. Instead, he was living on a wilderness mountaintop, the wind and wolves howling as he and the missus attended wounds and horses by candlelight. The only things missing were the Indians.

Which, if he thought about it, weren't missing at all.

"Okay," Collier said.

Ben looked askance at Evelyn and raised a querying eyebrow. "It's all right," Collier assured.

Ben nodded and took in a deep breath and said, "They're coming for us. But it's a trap."

Evelyn didn't bat an eye, kept wrapping Ben's arm, but Collier saw her shoulders stiffen. "Okay," he said, evenly, "They usually are and it usually is, but tell me the specifics."

"There was a letter on Deavers's desk. Just laying out there in the open. It was coded, but the cipher was right next to it. I saw Deavers working on it."

Collier frowned. "Pardon?"

"Yeah. He was right there, his back to the window I was peeking through, and then he got up and walked out and the window was a piece of cake and I read everything a second later." He looked at Collier, incredulity still on his face.

Collier frowned deeper. "So he wanted you to see it."

"Not only wanted me to," Ben said, flexing his arm to test the bandage and nodding thanks at Evelyn, "verified I saw it. Looked right at me when I left the compound."

"You sure?"

"Dead on sure."

"Hmm," Collier made a noncommittal sound but his shields had gone up.

Evelyn looked at them both, worried. "Why would he do that?"

"Depends on what the letter said." Collier nodded at Ben.

"It was direct from General Kant's desk. It ordered raids on every co-op, every independent farm, every trade center from Kernstown through Strasburg. Every manager and assistant manager was to be executed on the spot, their families arrested, any sons over eighteen to also be executed, and the rest of them sent to the labor camps. Any girls from 14-19 were to be sent to the education centers. All buildings were to be burned, all livestock and produce confiscated and sent to holding centers near Fredericksburg." Ben stopped.

Evelyn had gone white. "Oh my God," she breathed.

Collier said nothing, let the silence build for a few minutes. "That's," he finally said, "ridiculous."

Ben looked like he'd been slapped. "I'm telling you what it said!"

Collier raised a hand in placation. "I don't doubt that's what you read. But even you think it's a set-up."

"Well, yeah, I mean, Deavers wanted me to see it. Doesn't mean it's not true."

"But," from placating to dismissive, "it's ridiculous. Why in the world would they do this?"

"It said something about Kant wanting to make examples of counter-revolutionary forces impeding the glorious revolution … crap like that." Ben said, disgusted.

"By slaughtering the very people he needs to impose the glorious revolution? That's stupid." Collier shook his head. "It makes no sense."

"When did anything the Reds do make sense?" Ben challenged.

Good point. The Reds were brutal and cruel and murderous … but all of their actions had followed a logic. Granted, a flawed logic, based on a flawed ideology, but logical, all the same. "I'm not buying it," he concluded. "There's something else going on."

Ben made a helpless gesture. "Like what?"

Good question. What would be the purpose of Deavers faking a letter like that and ensuring one of Collier's guys got an eyeful? Draw them out? Make them run around like chickens without heads so Deavers could easily identify the congregation, round them up, and then remove their heads for real?

But, for that to work, Ben would have to think he got away with it. Ben had just told them, though, he DIDN'T get away with it.

"Sonofabitch," Collier whispered.

Alarmed, Evelyn whirled on him. "Have you figured it out?"

"No. I'm calling Deavers what he is."

She frowned. "That doesn't help. He may be, but we can't ignore this."

"We have no idea if it's true or not."

"We can't afford to act like it isn't!" She raised a finger.

Another good point, dammit. She was right: they couldn't afford to ignore this, even though the whole thing was too over-the-top for him to believe. But remember, bud, no one had believed Caldwell was a traitor, either. And look what happened.

Look what happened.

"When's this s'posed to happen?" he asked Ben.

"Next week."

"Next week!" Evelyn's voice rose, "Next week? How?"

"They're sending troops," Ben said, "Army." He

paused. "And Directorate. They'll be arriving any day."

Collier simply nodded. Imminent disaster was an old friend. Evelyn, for a moment, appeared to panic, but then shook her head and swallowed hard. "Oh my God," she said again, but quietly this time.

Because, now, despite the fearsome news, they had a marker, a way to tell if it was true or not: troops showing up. Now, whether that was testament to the pending slaughter, Collier still wasn't sure. Could be nothing more than planned maneuvers and Deavers, aware of them, had planted the false story to smoke the church out. Pretty devious. Pretty far sighted and smart and well thought out … and that wasn't Deavers. Guy flowed with the current; he didn't make long-range plans. He did what the long-range planners told him to do. Until it got too hot: then he sidled away.

Maybe things were getting too hot.

"Scapegoats," he whispered.

Evelyn furrowed her brows. "What do you mean?"

Collier settled back and mused for a moment and then said: "The State is failing. They can't feed people. They can't do anything right. We're living in the Middle Ages. The country is breaking up, turning into a series of feudal regions run by overlords and criminal gangs and … people like us. The General is losing his grip on the areas he still controls because his cadres are so corrupt they're no different from the gangs. But that can't be his fault, oh no." Collier's voice turned bitter. "Not his beloved Marxism. That's pure and wonderful. So it must be saboteurs. Capitalists." He paused. "Blues." He looked both of them in the eye. "So he needs to regain control, with the only tools a crackpot dictator has. Fear. Terror. Murder."

"But," Evelyn looked perplexed. "That won't work. It'll make things worse."

"Yes," Collier agreed, "But no one will dare blame him or Marxism. They will, instead, enthusiastically search out the Whites and the kulaks."

"Huh?" Evelyn was confused. "Aren't we all white?" She caught Ben's rising objection. "Most of us anyway."

Ben raised a palm. "No offense taken." Slight sarcasm. Slight.

Evelyn *moued* at him. "You know what I meant."

Ben gave her a slightly sarcastic salute.

"I don't mean race," Collier said to her, gently. Not a whole lot of people had the benefit of an excellent Fishburne education. "The Whites were the faction fighting against the Bolsheviks during the Russian Civil War. The kulaks were the prosperous farmers in Russia that Stalin starved to death because he wanted to confiscate their property. Both were blamed at the time for Communism's failure. It's the same story here. And once this pogrom begins," he checked to see if they knew the word. Apparently, they did. "Survivors, and anyone wanting to ingratiate themselves will hunt down anyone who disagrees with Kant for any reason. Us, for instance."

"But we're not a co-op," Ben pointed out.

"True," Collier agreed, "we're not. We're something worse: a church, the opiate of the people. And we have several members who work at those co-ops and centers. Once this starts, it won't end there. We'll be denounced. We'll join the murdered and the enslaved."

"So you believe me?" Ben said, relief in his voice.

Collier immediately shattered that relief. "No. It's a trap."

Ben was thoroughly confused now. "But, you just said you believe me!"

"I believe that you read what was on Deavers' desk, and that's what it said. But, it's still a trap."

Ben sighed and threw out a bandaged hand. "That's

what I've been thinking. He wants us to try and warn everybody so they can catch us."

Collier shook his head. "No. He wouldn't have let you know he saw you, if that was the case. It's something far more diabolical than that. It's a Hobson's choice."

"What do you mean?" Evelyn asked.

"Deavers is a guy who plays both sides. He goes with the winner but always leaves himself an out in case the loser doesn't lose. So, that's what he's doing. He's not sure if Kant can pull this off, so he's giving us a chance to warn everyone. That way, Deavers won't be tried as a war criminal when it fails, or … he knows it's going to work and he's giving us a chance to clear out."

Evelyn was puzzled. "Why would he do that?"

"So no one will give him any trouble."

They were both quiet for a moment absorbing this, but then Ben shook his head. "That sounds … implausible."

"Which part?" Collier replied, "That he's warning us, or that he's getting us out of the way?"

"Both of them," Ben said and, without waiting for the go-ahead, went on, "If Kant is sending in extra troops, then why would he lose? And why would Deavers want us to clear out? We get purged, his problems are solved. I mean," Ben shifted where he could look Collier in the eye, "why else would Kant send a guy you know?"

"Because," Collier replied, patiently, "Kant doesn't know that Deavers plays both sides. He sent Deavers because Kant thinks he knows me well enough to neutralize any response."

"But what if Kant DOES know that?" Ben countered. "What if he's counting on it, in fact?"

So, that's what it's like to have your surety challenged, Collier thought, almost chuckling. How many times had he challenged Caldwell and Jonesy and Rosa …

… Rosa …

Annoying, it must have been, except, nine times out of ten, he'd been right.

Was he still right?

"I think something else is going on," Ben persisted, "We're not seeing it."

"Like what?" Collier asked, unable to keep some annoyance out of his own voice.

Ben shook an exasperated head. "I don't know."

"Okay." Collier put it to rest. "Then we go with what we know. At least, what we think we know."

"It's what we don't know that bothers me," Ben muttered.

"And perhaps Washburn will come up with that." There was an edge to Collier's voice, to the point that Evelyn laid a warning hand on his wrist. "Sorry," Collier said, "Don't mean to sound ungrateful or anything, you've done an outstanding job. But, we're out of time."

"So what do you want me to do?" Ben asked, some edge in his own voice.

"Rest," Collier said. "Let your horse rest. Then, at dawn, go get the others and tell them to come here."

Ben nodded, the exhaustion overwhelming him now and he slumped in the seat. Evelyn walked to the back of the barn and in minutes had a pallet made up from an old sleeping bag and hay. "This should keep you warm," she said and guided Ben over to it. As he sagged on the edge of it, too weary to even lay down yet, she placed the corn muffins and the candle on a metal sheet kept on a nearby shelf to prevent accidental fires. She then gathered Collier and firmly pushed him out the barn door.

"No more talk," she ordered. "He needs to recover."

"Yes, ma'am." Collier gave her a mock, but respectful bow.

She grinned a bit, the starlight highlighting her face and Collier gathered it and kissed her gently on the lips.

"It'll be all right."

She grasped his hands, the warmth of her palms pulsing through the night chill. "Will it? Because, what if all this is just to kill you?"

He was surprised at that. "Lots of effort for something easily done by one guy with a knife."

"Kill you," she repeated, "Then kill us all."

The chill climbed his spine, not all of it due to weather. Kill him. Kill the church. Kill the soul.

Kill what's left of America.

A shuffling sound off to the side of the house and Collier, now in a heightened state of alert, broke from her and headed toward it, ready for combat. But the shuffling stopped, immediately replaced by a scraping sound as a twin-sized figure, momentarily illuminated by an interior candle, crawled into the window with someone twin-sized leaning out helping it.

"Damn kids!" he muttered and took combat steps in that direction but Evelyn yanked him back.

"Leave it," she said. "There's enough fighting already."

He paused. She's right.

The cold wind blew. He shivered and led her inside.

2.9

Price

"Dinner!" Price shouted as he cleared the door hauling a gill net filled with pigeons he'd trapped, followed immediately with a louder shout of, "Good God!"

Cass, Slickie and Tat were piled in the middle of the cabin room, all three of them looking like they had run for eight days straight without a gulp of water, a moment's sleep, or a bite to eat. Zoe and Homer stood over them frenzied, half-panicked, like the kids were at death's door. They sure looked like they were at death's door.

"Good God!" he said again and leaped into the pile with every intention of helping but Zoe pushed him away with a curt, "They're fine!" and took over all ministrations, even glaring her husband away.

"What happened?" Price asked, standing over the mess of clothes and blood and exhaustion that used to be kids and Tat.

Zoe whirled on him. "What happened?" she yelled. "You sent them out!" and she turned back to her charges. Both Price and Homer exchanged glances, exchanged shrugs, and decided to make themselves useful elsewhere. Price scooped the net of pigeons off the floor, not worried about the blood because, Holy Hannah, the kids were making bigger pools, and headed out, Homer right behind him.

"What happened?" Price asked but Homer said

nothing, silently head-gestured to follow and led Price and his catch around the corner of the cabin to a table under a tree. Price dumped the net there as Homer went into a small shed nearby and emerged with two hatchets and a couple of filet knives. "I'll help you with these," he said. "The kids could stand some food."

"You're telling me," Price said and the two of them began dressing the pigeons. Too bad they weren't doves, but those had become scarcer over the years as their hardier, ghetto-wise cousins muscled in. Still good to eat, though. Squab for the masses. "So, you get anything out of them yet?

Homer shook his head. "Not much. Something about the Faceless chasing them all the way through Stuart's Draft before they got away. Slickie may have some good info, but I can't say what."

"Stuart's Draft, huh?" Price shook pigeon entrails off his hand. It was a nothing place, a speck in the road between Staunton and Waynesboro. Price didn't know much about it. Inez and Rodger Dodger ran the area and Price received a not insubstantial cut from their efforts, but it was, at best, an outlier about which Price couldn't care less. He couldn't care less about Inez and Rodger, either. Inez had made attempts on Price's gold until he'd slapped her down, and Rodger ... the guy was a toad. Stuart's Draft wasn't even the locus; Inez and Rodger overlapped the area and traded responsibility based on whoever had something going in Waynesboro. It was actually closer to Homer's territory than anyone's, and even *he* didn't have much to do with the place.

So what the hell are the Faceless doing there? "What do you know about it?"

"Stuart's Draft? Not a lot." Homer was dressing the last of the pigeons as he tested the smoker he'd lit sometime during the process. "Good place to hide. Lots of trails and roads meet around there, so it's a good place for an ambush, too." And he raised eyebrows at Price.

"For us, or against us?"

"Both."

"Hmm," Price grunted as he palmed the smoker lid to judge the heat and popped the lid and piled pigeon carcasses. Homer opened the bottom and threw in some hickory branches and bellowed the fire and the smoke rose, a sweet savor in the nostrils … of God, of mortals, of anyone, and, by tonight, they'd have a pigeon feast. Maybe the kids would be articulate by then, and Price could find out how much trouble he faced.

A lot, he bet.

"Can you get a message off to Squint?" Price asked, "Tell him to scout around the Draft?"

"Sure," Homer savored the smoke, "he'll probably want to know why."

"No, he won't," Price corrected, "He'll just do it."

"Uh huh," Homer's doubt evident. "What about Inez and Rodger?"

"No, because they'll want to know why."

Homer chuckled appreciatively at that. No love lost between them. "Anyone else?"

Price considered. "Yeah. Sally and Beau." They were farther east and north than Stuart's Draft, but Price had other reasons for getting them ready.

Homer nodded, reserving comment because he knew Price had a good relationship with those two. Of course he did: Sally had been Price's on-again off-again girlfriend in high school, pre-Event. Beau had been his best friend in high school … well, the times Price went. That Beau ended up with Sally was okay. He trusted them with his life. And with other things.

Homer and Price stood quietly, allowing the smoker to offset the chill wind that had sprung up and letting enough of a decent interval go by for Zoe to do her thing. And calm down. "Shall we?" Price said, gesturing at the house. They both went up the stairs and into the cabin.

The kids sat on the upholstered bench, side by side and supporting each other, but looking like kids again. Man, that Zoe, miracle worker.

Tat sat on the floor, shirt off, revealing the body art that gave him the nickname: a lot of Japanese mythological figures; at least, Price assumed they were. He didn't know a Japanese god from a samurai, but it all looked intimidating. Wasn't tatting up something the old Yakuza did? At least they did in the movies Price saw before the Event, but Tat's father was a diplomat, or something like that, and you'd think Yakuza involvement would be frowned upon among highfalutin' Japanese royalty. But, hey, who knows? Maybe they're like the Mafia and their presence is winked at. Price didn't know enough to say, but Tat was ferocious, a warrior-monk, and that's good enough. All the Japanese were fierce fighters. Look what they did to the North Koreans and the Chinese during the wars. That's why Japan was a radioactive wasteland now. Tat could very well be the last Japanese in the world. That would have made Pap happy. He fought them on Okinawa and had nothing good to say about Asians, let alone Japanese.

Pap, Tat's a good 'un.

Price grabbed a small stool and set it before Tat and hunched down until they were eye-to-eye and raised a brow in query.

"Faceless," Tat said, "They're in Staunton now."

Okay, so they were flanked. Price nodded and kept his questioning look. "We lost them outside Waynesboro," Tat responded.

Eyebrow remained raised.

"We cut through the mountains down to Mills Creek,

followed that to the end," said Tat laconically, but Price inwardly whistled. Good God that was a rough way to go. Especially in the cold. "Then we used the old North Fork Road to the Tye, followed that down to the valley, got here."

Even rougher way to go so, uh uh, definitely not followed. Even a West Virginny hillbilly would have a tough time on that trail.

"You did that in five days," Price said, in admiration. Man. Would have taken a platoon of Rangers two weeks.

"Lost the horses," Tat added.

Cass jerked at that with a grimace of sorrow, and Price felt for her. The relationship man had with horses had been revitalized in the last few decades, and no one liked to see a horse die. Especially those that saved your life.

"All right," Price said and turned to her. God, she had been through hell. And he was willing to bet half his gold stash that it had done something to her. The exposure and deprivation and physical assault she'd just been through were bad enough; add to that her second pursuit in less than a month by a bunch of professional assassins and she'd been altered. Had to be. At the very least, she was no longer a little girl. Price felt a pang of familiarity. Childhood is over when the monsters turn out real.

"They recognized me," she said, a sob on the edge of her voice as she quick-glared at Tat and then Slickie in a half-stupor next to her. Price frowned. What's this? Does she blame them? "That guy in charge of the Faceless—"

"Major Lawless?"

"Yeah, him." She shifted restlessly and gave another glare at the other two and, really, what's going on? Was she still being a little girl and finding someone, anyone, to blame? He looked at the pools of terror embedded in her eyes and realized no, the little girl was long gone.

"How?"

She threw her hands out. "Because we did the same thing we always did!" and she drew back, miserable.

Price turned another questioning look at Tat. "We used the corn cart," he said, toneless. "In retrospect, that may not have been wise."

"I TOLD you not to do it!" Cass, exasperated, looked at Tat with accusing eyes.

Okay.

"Cass." Price, gentle, calming. "We're in unknown territory here. There's something bigger going on than we all knew—"

At that point, Slickie leaned forward and wordlessly handed him a piece of oil cloth torn from some other cloth, probably a tarp, then, just as wordlessly, sat back, the war so clear on his face that, for a moment, it was twenty years ago and Price was hustling up and down the Valley gunning Reds and other gangs, a little piece of him dying with each combat. Know how you feel, kid.

Price unwrapped the cloth. Inside was a brown envelope, dirty but intact and folded in half. He unfolded it and looked at the wax seal. An official envelope, this, and he fumbled inside and pulled out two pieces of paper, the one from Kant, the other the handwritten translation. He read. "Holy shit," he said, after a moment.

"What is it?" Homer asked.

Price read out loud: "'Before Polar Star can initiate, it is imperative that you detain the persons listed in this directive, and that you ensure they are unable to activate any counter-revolutionary columns which they lead or with which they are in contact. You must NOT, repeat, MUST NOT, conduct these detentions as anything other than a standard round-up. Please utilize whatever subterfuge or ruse you deem necessary to make these detentions appear to be the normal response of Directorate personnel to violations of the law.'" He paused. "Then there's a list of names. A lot of 'em."

"Look on the back," Slickie rasped.

Price flipped it over. The names were not in any particular order … Ah. There. About halfway down. "Price, Henry. Farmville, Virginia."

It was quiet. For a moment.

"You brought them down on us," Zoe whispered.

"Zoe …" Homer warned.

"You …" she had gathered breath to repeat the accusation.

"… brought them down on us, yeah, yeah," and Price waved that away. Puh-leeze. Weren't all of them in the same business? He gave her a look of utter scorn and she blushed beet red. She definitely wanted to go all Mama Bear on him because of what he had done to her kids but that would be somewhat illogical, given the world today, and their roles in it. "What's this Polar Star?" he asked Slickie.

"I don't know," Slickie replied, his voice so rough that Price wondered if he'd caught something in the mountains. Great. Another epidemic of hill fever, coming up. "The Colonel came in, along with his gofer, before I had a chance to finish looking through his safe."

"Okay," Price comforted because Slickie looked guilty about that. "You did good. This is a lot more than I expected. All of you," he waved the cloth to include Cass and Tat, "did great. I am very impressed."

Zoe's lips tightened and Price expected another salvo but the kids and Tat sat up straighter, their eyes shining, looking like great weights had dropped from their respective shoulders. Really must learn to give more praise, Price reminded himself for the millionth time.

"Well," he said, rattling the translation paper, "let's go with what we know. Whatever this Polar Star is, it must have been in the works for quite a while because it took a bit to get this list together ... took a bit just to find me, much less everyone else—" He frowned.

List of names. Something nagged at him. He pulled the paper open and studied it intently, flipping it over to read the names on the back, and when he came to the last one, he visibly started and said, "Holy shit!"

"What?" Cass asked, impatient.

Price ignored her and flipped it back over to the front and read it again and then read the back again. Four times through before the nagging little thing in his head suddenly turned into a bright, neon light. "Holy shit," he breathed.

"What?" Not only Cass but Slickie and Homer.

"These." He held the paper up to them. "These people. They're Ghosts."

Cass was puzzled. "You mean ... they're dead?"

"Not those kind of ghosts. *The* Ghosts. Of the Blue Army."

"What?" Zoe was incredulous. "How do you know that? And why are you on the list, then? You weren't a Ghost." A little bit of snark at that last part.

"No, I wasn't," Price acknowledged, noting the snark. "But I was there."

"There where?" Zoe upped the snark.

Price went silent and hard. A little vein pulsed in his temple, his color up and his already big eyes widened even more as the thunderstorm gathered. The others shrank involuntarily because this was Murder Price, the one who ran the gang, ruthless, no quarter asked, no quarter given. "What I am about to tell you," he said, the murder clear in his eyes, "is not known by any other person. Except one. So if I hear this story anywhere, I'll know it was one of you, and I will kill all of you." He let that sit there. "All. Of. You."

There was no challenge. They knew his capability. If

all of them rose as one right now and attacked, they may get him. But not all of them would survive it.

He let that sink in and then said, "I was the guy who warned the Ghosts about Caldwell."

He might as well have said "I found Bigfoot," or "I started Breakout," because how the Ghosts figured out that they were betrayed and surrounded was the stuff of tin foil hat speculation, even to this day. It was a rather incredible claim to make.

So incredible, that Homer snorted derision. Price simply looked at him. And that was enough.

"Holy moly," Homer said, instantly a believer. Jaws unanimously dropped around the room signaled the others were, too.

Zoe finally broke the silence. "But how do you know that's," she gestured at the paper, "a list of the Ghosts? You don't know who they are."

"I knew who a couple of them were," he explained. "Especially this last one, who is the only person who knows, other than you five now, that I warned them." He turned the list over and read: "Rashkil, Collier John."

2.10

Washburn

Cold. Hungry. But not bored.

Washburn hunched as tightly to the outcropping as he could, trying to squeeze out of the wind that was doing everything possible to turn him into an icicle. It was going to be a bad winter. It had already snowed in the upper peaks and there was an edge to the wind that foretold ice and cold and bleak, dark days. The winters had been getting worse over the last ten years, cutting the growing season shorter and shorter, and today it felt more like middle December than middle November. Next Thursday was traditional Thanksgiving, although the State had turned it into Gratitude Day when everyone was supposed to thank General Kant for his bounty. Washburn sniggered at that. Yeah, bounty: horse feed oatmeal; blocks of cheese so hard an ax was needed to cut them; and bread half made up of sawdust. Praise Kant.

No. Praise God.

Washburn cast an eye across the blasted land and wondered how long the whip of the Lord would scour them. We are deserving of your wrath, Lord, this I know, but how long, how long? Washburn watched souls flit across the field moaning and clutching at their heads trying to tear out the lit coal dropped inside their skulls and was moved to pity because many of them were victims of their own ignorance and the lies of false shepherds, and Washburn was not so hard hearted to think they all deserved it. But, they had made the bed they lie in, and the whip of the Lord flayed us all.

There was no one righteous. No one. Righteousness wasn't possible in mortal man, but there should be a striving after it. If the people showed the Lord that they were willing, were straining to be His children, then He would pity them because the Lord of Being knows the limitations of humans. We cannot overcome the sin within us. But we can acknowledge it.

Collier preached the message that human flaws were so overwhelming God should not give us the time of day but God was moved from His own essence and, despite our stink, our offense, He gave us a seat in Heaven. Washburn approved. He could not stand the mealy-mouthed, straw-spine preachers who'd helmed every single church in the world before the Event, all of them simpering and effete and proclaiming how lovely we were and we must love each other and prove how loving we are to God. And fire rained down from Heaven and the cities are tombs and ants nest in the eye sockets of those preachers. They did not know God. God is robust. God is manly. He had no time for softness. Look at the land below and tell me different.

Look at it.

Nothing but a winter desert. The dead wandered it for their forty – or four hundred – years, weeping and tearing their robes. The grass and undergrowth had already died and the trees dropped their cover and all was skeleton and ghost.

Maybe I should go home.

Washburn considered that. It had been four days and nights and this was the fifth dawn and no one had come to the house except the two agents making their daily check, taking nothing in, bringing nothing out. He wondered if it was mere activity, a reason to justify riding around the countryside on spirited horses and laughing and goofing off, which was so much better than filing reports. They knew Washburn was there and were putting on a show. Their informant had already been warned and a new drop site established and was serviced by agents Washburn did not know and this was all a joke. So how did they find out? How did they know that odd fold in the rocks was actually a man watching them?

Ben.

Washburn stirred, the anger warming him. Of course, Ben, the man who played both sides, whose honor was limited to what benefitted him, who spun his own plots and counterplots. Bearing false witness, feet running to trouble, a man who delighted in controversy for the sake of it alone, who enriched himself by dividing others and who did not have the touch of God in his soul but the touch of avarice. All through the war years he had cozied to the godless and laughed with the soulless while God's people starved and wearied. Judas, Benedict Arnold, his treason murdered hundreds.

Murdered.

The images raced past his eyes: Washburn coming back to the cabin at a dawn similar to this one with the deer across his shoulders and saw the head of his wife being kicked around the yard by two Breakout monsters while another one sodomized his daughter and another finished eviscerating his son, beside the already eviscerated and headless bodies of his two other sons.

He'd strung all four of the monsters up from a tree, pulling out their lower intestines and leaving them there for the coyotes to finish. He'd tried to bring his daughter back but she died in sections, shock on her face, accusation in her eyes and Washburn had burned the cabin with his family's bodies insides and went into the woods and the mountains and began killing people. Everyone. Anyone. Red, Blue, Breakout thug, civilian, it did not matter. He did not fall sick, which he saw as favor from God, and so the people, filled with sin and rape and murder, fell before his blades and he was the righteous arm of the Lord and he'd scythed and culled and winnowed the unrighteous.

And one day the Lord told him to stop.

It was a winter day, a true winter, years ago and he had brought his rifle to bear on a young soldier with Blue markings, trudging along a trail on the side of Short Mountain, head down, weary, beaten, probably some former local finding his way home and Washburn's trigger finger tightened and then he was told not to shoot. There was no more need. So he'd trudged his own way down the mountains and sat on a bench on a street of the reconstituting Kernstown as locals and newly-arrived Reds eyed him warily but he did not budge, just sat, just listened. That's how he heard about Ben. And the church tucked away in a ridgeline above Bluemont. So he went there. And stayed.

Let's not go home. Let's go see the preacher.

Washburn gathered himself to roll off the ridge and into a little saddle below it that would hide him while he did last minute checks to ensure no one counter-watched. For purposes Washburn could not articulate, he needed to see Collier and become reassured that the voice of God whispering in Washburn's ear (and the souls that flitted before his eyes) were real, were manifestations of God's favor. Collier believed such things were imaginings, but God's imaginings, so he didn't call Washburn crazy, only sought to clarify what Washburn saw. He could reassure the mountain man that it was not torment but a gift, a cooling oil when the rage volcanoed in Washburn's veins. And because Ben had played him for a fool, it was time for medicine.

Something moved.

Washburn froze, blinking his eyes clear and then fixing a stare to ensure it was true movement and not a soul drifting across the field. That was one annoying drawback of God's visions: sometimes he had to sort them out. But no, this was real movement, not a phantom. On the edge of the woods bordering the battlefield, about ten yards from the old house, branches shook and not from the wind. This was a bear or a deer about to step into a clearing and if he were hunting, he would bring up the rifle slowly so his own movement was not noticed and he would drop the bear and sling it and bring it home for his Papa and Mama and his brothers and sisters and they would eat for four or five days while Papa loudly proclaimed he now felt good enough to head down the mountain and find some work and get them some money so the kids could have shoes and food but Papa would be at the still an hour later and in a stupor five minutes after that and Washburn would go out again and find food. Or it was a Red or a Blue or a thug breaking cover to violate the sacred grounds of his children's graves while seeking more death and Washburn would oblige them. But Washburn was not hunting to keep his brothers alive, and he was not dispensing justice in the name of his children, so he did nothing as the bear or deer broke through.

He wished he had.

Because it wasn't an animal or a Blue or a thug; it was a person, and Washburn knew him.

"No," he whispered to the wind and the ghosts gathering below to chorus the sudden grief and pain and shock overwhelming him. No. It could not be. He was seeing this wrong. His true eyesight was altered by the devil, the Eternal Enemy fogging what he saw. The person ducked quickly into the house, giving Washburn, at best, a mere glimpse and at this distance, he may have been fooled, may have been deceived by the devil's own lies. But there, the person running for the tree line and made a backward glance and there was no mistaking him.

"Can't be." Washburn denied the evidence of his own eyes as the ghosts gibbered and pointed and implored and demanded he accept what he saw. He would not. Eyes played tricks, ghosts. Your presence proved that. Washburn had to be sure before he leveled accusations, before he took the appropriate action. The ghosts looked at each other and nodded and turned, as one group, and pointed at the house.

It took Washburn about an hour because it was still day and he was visible and he was more than half-convinced that this was a trap. The agents hid in the woods with rifles trained. They had sent out the person to make Washburn throw caution to the wind and come charging across the field and they would drop him. To test that, Washburn stood full and tall and terrible in the doorway to draw the fire but no shots rang out. He went inside and pulled out the brick and the paper there and read it. "No," he whispered.

Because Washburn had seen correctly.

He slipped the note into his pocket, replaced the brick, and, trailed by the wailing ghosts, left.

2.11

Whittaker

Ben slipped around the corner of the cadre distribution warehouse at the south end of Kernstown and stopped dead. "What the hell?" he muttered.

Washburn sat on a bench across the road, slumped, staring at the ground beneath his feet. "What the hell?" Ben said again, more astounded than anything because he'd spent the day dashing back and forth between Kernstown and Stephens City dropping signals so the others would know about the meeting tonight and he'd had to keep running back to see if Washburn had posted the counter signal or not because the guy was supposed to be surveilling the drop house and Holy Hannah, bud, it was a real pain running back and forth checking signals without getting caught so what are you doing, you hillbilly oaf?

Really, what was he doing?

Alarmed, Ben stepped back onto the porch of the distribution center from which he'd signaled Felicia and looked wildly about, expecting cadre and troopers or maybe Directorate to pour up the street smashing everything and seizing everyone and carting them off to the camps. Washburn was bait; they'd already collected him and were dangling him in the hopes of attracting other counter-revolutionaries or … Washburn wasn't bait, was simply Washburn, and out here all exposed on a cold

November day which was odd, odd behavior, even for a known weirdo like him, so the cadres were curious and waited to pounce on anyone who approached, because approaching Washburn themselves was a dangerous proposition even when Washburn was in a good mood so grab the black guy and demand to know what's going on and, you know, I just don't need this right now.

You're being stupid, Ben.

He frowned. Yes, he was. As much as he didn't like the old hillbilly racist, the guy would never let himself get caught, even by the Faceless. He would put up a glorious fight that would send fireworks and flares up for miles around and Ben would have heard about it and be nowhere near here. And no cadres cared enough about Washburn or, for that matter, some black guy, to leave the comfort of a pot-belly stove and moonshine to inquire. So something else was going on and it had to be very bad for Washburn to abandon his surveillance and sit moping in the middle of Kernstown on a cold might-as-well-be-winter day.

Taking one more look up and down the street, Ben slowly walked over and sat down at the other end of the bench, eyeing Washburn the entire time. "What are you doing?" Ben hissed.

Washburn didn't stir. "Nothin'," was all he said.

Ben looked up and down the street again for cadre or troopers or curious civilians wondering what the hell were two guys doing on a bench during the best work hours of the day – as designated by the State – and leaned into him. "Why aren't you watching the house?"

"Don't need to," Washburn's same toneless response.

Ben eyes widened. "You know who the informant is?"

Washburn said nothing but slowly turned his head and looked at Ben, a look of such sorrow, such grief, that Ben was instantly chilled, and not from the weather. "Good

Christ," he whispered.

"Don't blaspheme," Washburn replied but without rancor, more like a reflex.

Ben scooted closer, almost hip to hip, and whispered, "Who is it?"

Washburn looked at him. "That ain't for you."

Ben *tsked* annoyance. He wanted to know. "Tell me and I'll pass it on to Collier."

"I'll do it myself," Washburn said, "at tonight's meeting."

Drat. "You saw my signal?"

"No."

Ben furrowed a brow. 'Then how do you know about the meeting?"

Washburn said nothing but returned to staring at his shoes.

Another chill up his spine not weather related. "Good Christ," Ben said, ignoring Washburn's reaction. "Are we compromised?"

Washburn slowly turned his head and fixed Ben with a murderous stare. "We been compromised for a long time."

Ben cocked a confused head. "What? You mean me?"

Washburn kept the murderous stare, a pulse pounding in his temple.

Ben, open-mouthed with astonishment yelled, "I'm not the spy!"

"I know that!" Washburn hissed him down but was still intent, still violent.

Ben was now completely baffled and completely alarmed because it looked like Washburn was going to beat the hell out of him any second, which would definitely draw the troopers. "Then what the hell are you talking about, man? You think because I'm black, I'm some kind of sellout?" The chill up Ben's spine turned into rage from the pit of his stomach. "Listen, you cracker asshole, ain't no one more loyal to Collier than me. Not even you!" Ben's own pulse flared against his temple.

"It ain't 'cause you're black," said with so much conviction that Ben instantly knew it was true, "It's 'cause of what you did."

Whew, but then back to full-on bafflement. Ben threw out exasperated hands. "What did I do?"

"You … brought them down on me." And Washburn turned and fell into a grief so profound that Ben could not help feeling the sorrow himself.

He put a hand on Washburn's shoulder and the grief transmitted through it. and down Ben's own arm. like a physical thing. Ben was shocked. He'd had his own gut-tearing, heart-stopping moments of grief these last few decades: when Winchester succumbed to Phase 2 and everyone Ben knew, everyone, died. Horribly. His efforts to save the Blues had ended in the Blues defeat and he'd had to keep pretending he was a Red supporter as all his hopes collapsed … but this was worse than that. "Tell me," he whispered.

"They came out of the dark," Washburn whispered back, "They took my wife and my children and what they did …"

"Who?" Ben asked. "Who came out of the dark?"

"The Break Outs."

Ben nodded. "I know. My parents died from Phase 2. You can't even go into Winchester anymore because of them." He paused, suddenly puzzled. "What's that got to do with me?"

"You helped them."

"Helped them?" Still baffled. "I didn't help the Break Outs! No one did."

"You laughed with the enemy, traded goods with them, encouraged them, made them your friends."

"What are you talking about?"

Washburn made a gesture at the street. "The enemy."

Ben had no idea what this crazy coonskin-wearing peckerhead was talking about … and then he did. "The Reds." He saw confirmation in Washburn's eyes. "You're talking about the Reds." From baffled to genuinely perplexed. "What the fuck do they have to do with the Break Out thugs?"

Washburn's eyes raged and reddened in power and righteousness, lightning flashing from them, almost. "They are of the same!" Washburn raised a righteous finger to the cold, merciless skies. "The Spirit abandoned them, they are empty vessels. Empty! The dark fills them and crushes the land and the Lord," an emphatic point of the same finger, "chastises us, blasts us with the breath from His own nostrils and we are left broken and torn! Broken!" More frenzied sky pointing. "And torn!"

Ben couldn't believe what he was hearing. He knew the guy was crazy but … "Man, you are in desperate need of some good meds."

Washburn dropped the sky finger's arm around Ben's shoulders and pulled him tight, a vise-like grip that left Ben helpless. "You are not of the Spirit!" Washburn hissed and Ben felt a thud and a tearing that didn't really hurt but took his air away. Just away. He could not breathe, his head suddenly screamed with a roaring, blackening onrush of darkness, and he was confused and instantly sleepy and there was something very, very wrong … he looked down at Washburn's other hand jammed against his lower rib cage and the handle of the Bowie knife pulsing there and covered in blood and Washburn's hand working it in, shoving it here and there and then it came clear to Ben that Washburn was cutting his heart in half, severing all the arteries, a quick knife-kill that a hunter used on a wounded animal.

Wounded, And dead.

"Die now," Washburn whispered.

2.12

Cass

So tired, to the point she was completely numb. Or maybe she was just cold.

Cass braced against a corner of the building that sheltered her from the wind but God it was still too cold. And she was hungry. And, yes, she was tired. And pissed off.

Why does this keep happening to me?

Simple, she answered herself as she pulled the long cloak tighter and turtled inside it, you keep doing what Uncle P asks. Take this letter, the one Homer wrote in such an advanced Greek script that Cass could read only a smidgen of it, and deliver it to that guy Collar and get the hell back here but don't go anywhere near the guy yourself; instead, find somebody in Kernstown who knows him.

"Where's Kernstown?"

"Don't worry, Little John knows the way and he's going with you and that should be enough to keep you safe but if anyone stops you and asks what the letter is you act all retarded and go 'Pretty writing!'…"

… and Slickie thought that was funny, yelling out, "She won't have to act!" and she'd slugged him, and Uncle P frowned at them both and reiterated, "You go full retard. Got it?"

"And what's Slickie going to do?" she flamed because

he was still laughing and it's not fair, not fair, that she has to go off in the middle of a godforsaken winter to some godforsaken town to find some godforsaken old guy that Price knew a thousand years ago.

"He'll be doing something else." And Uncle P had held up the list of names.

God.

She glanced down the street where Little John was fussing with the horses in front of the co-op that had food and cots for travelers who were willing to do some work. Even in this failing light, she could see him keeping a worried eye on her. She almost laughed. Little John was such a Boy Scout ... what *was* a Boy Scout, anyway? She didn't know but Mom used that term derisively for Little John and anyone else Mom deemed a goody-goody and it fit because he *was* a goody-goody, had actually fought Dad for a while until the Reds showed up and Little John hated them more than he hated smugglers and so changed sides. He was such a Boy Scout that Dad had no suspicion of any conflicting loyalties because Little John's word was his bond. But he was so much a Boy Scout, keeping her under so much surveillance, that she sometimes wondered how she was going to do her job.

Since he's busy with the horses, maybe now would be a good time to slip away. Maybe this time she'd get lucky and find that Collar guy.

They hadn't had a lot of luck so far. Cass had broached the name obliquely at a couple of the cadre centers south of this place and was met with askance and a request that she leave. Now. A couple of times, she saw a cadre she had offended speaking to a passing trooper and pointing at her and she had hastily left the area while Little John lingered to take care of any followers. There were no followers, so the Boy Scout was doing his job, which was why he was so intent on her right now, but his kind of scrutiny was like a spotlight on her and she wondered if maybe they had already blown it.

Which, given Uncle P's urgency on this matter, would be tragic.

Cass was not sure she understood the issues. Obviously, the gang was in big trouble when assassins usually relegated to high-level missions were chasing pissants like Uncle P and her around the countryside with helicopters (helicopters!), an escalation that even she knew was overkill. What had they done to deserve such attention? It had something to do with this Polar Star thing, but not even Uncle P knew what that was. All everyone could conclude was that it was bad. Very bad.

So maybe she should find out what this Polar Star is.

How? was the first question. She couldn't very well use a corn cart to break into some Directorate office (was there one around here?) anymore, now that even troopers were on to that trick. She didn't know who around here would have information about it, anyway. She doubted cadres would be trusted with a secret so important that the Faceless guarded it. But if that guy Collar was on the list, then something was going to happen around here, so someone around here knew what that was. The problem was finding that someone. Perhaps she should start with this guy Collar.

Sighing, she gave Little John the signal that she was about to go make some inquiries and he gave her a worried 'Okay' signal back and she sympathized. It was getting late in a world limited to daylight. Candles were too weak and oil too precious, so the days had devolved into a medieval work schedule of sunup to sundown, which was shortened as the year progressed. Cass had minutes left before sundown and the natural curfew it imposed. Someone out walking the streets after dark was obviously up to no good, and she would attract trooper attention and detention and discussion which, given the nature of that organization, would mean she'd be kept in a back closet for a couple of years until they tired of her and then slit her throat and tossed her off a cliff. Best to be off the street in the next half hour, then. Better to be on her way back home but she had a job to do, and she wasn't going to disappoint Uncle P.

She stepped around the corner and scrutinized the street but it looked like the few remaining buildings had already closed for the day. She could see someone locking a door across the way, which was a laugh in the heroic People's Republic of Peace and Buggery, as Homer called it. Wasn't everything in your store the property of the people, comrade? She grinned and kept it on her face because it made her look vapid and empty and mentally challenged, which was the only plausible reason she was out wandering the streets. Wouldn't stop the troopers from appropriating her charms for the next two years, though, so let's get going.

She looked at the building next to her and was surprised to see light through the window. All right, let's give this one the old college try … what *was* a college try, anyway? Homer should stop saying things that no longer have any relevance. Keeping the smile fixed, she climbed the steps and pushed through the double wooden doors that looked like they'd once belonged to a barn. No more glass, so everyone improvised. "Hello!" she said brightly as she cleared the threshold.

A man standing in front of a long wooden counter piled high with candles – ah, that explained why he was still open – turned and gazed at her in complete surprise. He was actually fat, something you didn't see much these days, and bald and wearing a green apron and checkered shirt of good quality and Mom would recognize him as a store clerk from her childhood and Cass was immediately on guard because a man of prosperity these days was a man of the State. "What are you doing here, girl?" the man asked.

"Mommy said we need candles," she giggled and began humming tonelessly and looking around and hoped she was conveying the empty-headedness that would keep her out of jail.

Apparently, she was convincing because the man got an "Oh' look on his face, followed by a sympathetic expression. "Well, hon," he said, "we're about to close."

She dropped into a pout and stared at the floor and put tears in her voice. "Mommy will be mad at me."

"All right, all right," the man said hastily and wiped his hands nervously and threw them at the candle display. "You can have some of these. What have you got?" Meaning what did she have to trade.

"Scrip!" she said triumphantly pulling out a handful of the useless papers and waving them around, dropping a few in the process and dancing excitedly.

"Great," the guy said under his breath and it was all she could do to keep from laughing. The last thing this guy needed was a simpleton crying in the streets that a cadre distributor wouldn't take official scrip. She held the papers out as the guy irritably bagged a few candles and shoved them at her, taking the scrip with the same irritation.

"Thank you, comrade!" she said brightly and tucked the bag into one of the numerous pockets badly sewn to her cloak. "My mommy also wants me to say hi to someone!" she added, in the same bright tone as she fished into another pocket and brought out a closed fist.

"Yeah?" the guy had already turned from her putting the scrip away. "Who's that?"

"His name is Collier Rashkil," she answered, her tone no longer bright but subdued. "Do you know where I can say hi to him?" And she opened her palm to reveal the gold ring there.

She might as well have slapped the guy, he reacted so strongly, turning so red his bald head changed color and his eyes widened as he stepped back. "What the hell is this?" he said, nervously.

"Mommy said I should give this to him," and she looked at the ring mournfully. "But I don't know where he is." She then looked at him brightly. "Can you tell me?"

The guy's eyes were fastened on the ring because this was something far more valuable than scrip. "I ... uh, can take that to him," and he moved toward her.

As he reached out, she snatched her hand away. "Where?" she said in her dangerous voice and the guy realized her entire stance had changed and she was as dangerous as she now sounded and he was in reach. "Uh," he said with growing fright and backed away but she stayed with him. "Where?" she demanded.

"Look ... I don't want any trouble," he said as he hit the counter, trapped, and about to die.

"Where?" she demanded louder, and with more menace.

"I don't know! He's somewhere near Bluemont!" he whined, trying to move right or left and out of her reach but she wouldn't let him. "But I know someone who knows!"

She raised menacing eyebrows.

"Ben!" the guy was almost crying. "His name is Ben!"

"Where do I find this Ben?" A bit of a press with the fist against his chest.

"You can't miss him. He's the only black guy in town."

The guy was sweating death by now and Cass decided to be merciful. Patting his chest, she opened his top pocket and slipped the ring inside it. She backed off and walked to the door while keeping an eye on him. "Thanks, mister," she said, "And thanks for the candles." She added as she tapped the bag and turned toward the door, almost giggling as the guy sagged with relief. "Oh, one more thing," she said turning back and enjoying the sudden terror. "If someone follows me, I'll tell them you've got that ring." And she winked and stepped outside.

That should guarantee silence.

She stopped on the street and gave Little John the all clear, and then frowned. All right, I'm looking for a black guy. Problem is, no one's out running around, much less a black guy. The sun was almost down and the clouds were coming in and candles were showing up here and there in windows of apartments on top of the co-ops and soon troopers would be roaming the street looking for people like you-know-who so maybe call it a night, go help Little John with the horses, plan on looking for a black guy tomorrow. Right now, she could stand a sandwich. Even some oatmeal.

She looked at Little John who was standing there in a what-are-you-doing stance and okay, okay and she glanced in the other direction and saw two guys at the far end of the street sitting on a bench and huddled together, probably trying to stay warm.

Man, one of those guys looks black.

Stepping off quickly, she gave Little John the "hold on" signal and briskly headed toward the bench, humming and smiling in the most vapid way she could. Head on a swivel, she kept a lookout for the troopers and was halfway to the bench in moments.

Yep, definitely a black guy sitting there and that's gotta be Ben – please, please – and her heart quickened because, oh boy, this was it, but the guy sitting next to Ben ... hmm. Bear of a guy, big as Little John, maybe bigger, looked dangerous, and he'd made her the moment she walked out of the coop and had kept an eye on her the whole way down and that wasn't good. Ben didn't stir at all but this guy was hyper-aware.

She slowed. She stopped. Something was wrong.

The big guy had Ben in what amounted to a death grip, shoulder across the black guy's back and yanked hard against him, the other arm actually inside Ben's coat. What's going on here, some kind of weird old guy perv thing? She took an uncertain step back.

"Can I help you, girl?" The big man called, like a bear calling from a distant hill.

"Um ..." Think fast, Cass. Interrupting a couple of gay guys may not be the best of moves, but when else would she have a chance to talk to Ben? "Is he all right?" She pointed at Ben.

"He's ... passed out. Has a drug problem. I'm making sure he doesn't fall in the street and get sent to a camp."

"Oh." That actually made sense and she was relieved she was not interrupting something untoward. Or, more untoward. "Is he Ben?"

The bear's eyebrows rose and a weird light came into his eyes. "He is. How do you know him?" A pause. "Because I don't know you."

Fair enough. "I don't know him," she conceded. "I need to deliver something to a friend of his."

"I'm a friend of his," the bear said, and the weird light in his eyes danced.

"What's your name?" Cass asked, hoping against hope that the Bear was Collier and she could get out of this increasingly weird town.

"What's yours?" the guy countered.

"Victoria," she answered without hesitation which is the way to give a false name.

"I'm Washburn."

Drat. She shook her head. "You're not the friend."

"Then tell me the friend's name."

"It's …" and she stopped before naming Rashkil. Washburn could say, "Oh yeah! Good pal of mine and Ben's. Hand it over." Let's see if he actually knows him. "The guy used to be a Ghost."

"Collier Rashkil," Washburn said with no hesitation. "You are looking for Collier Rashkil. Why are you looking for him?"

"I have a letter for him."

"From who?"

"An old friend of his." She hesitated. "Another Ghost."

Washburn appraised her, the lights in his eyes going in and out and Cass wondered what kind of drugs this guy was on. She'd heard about people who had stolen gobs and gobs of old drugs and kept using them long past their expiration date and how crazy they became as a result and these two guys sure fit the bill. Washburn flicked his attention to Ben and frowned. "I am going to see Collier tonight. I can take your letter."

Relief flooded through her. "Can you really?" Oh, man, perfect, her mission was done and she could get off this street with its weird drug users and out of this town and get back home where everything was normal.

Ha.

"Here," she said, casually taking the envelope out of a cloak pocket and holding it close to herself and shaking the end of it at the Bear. Take it, man.

He didn't. "Put it on the end of the bench," Washburn ordered.

She blinked at him. "In this wind? It'll blow away. Just take it," and she shook the envelope at him again.

"If I let him go," he nose-pointed at the comatose guy in his arms. "He'll fall and the troopers will be all over us. Put it in his pocket." Nose point at Ben's jacket.

202

She frowned and looked up and down the street but not a trooper in sight. Still, if the guy did fall over, she'd have to help lift him back. "Oh, all right," she groused and moved forward, stabbing at the coat pocket with the envelope. Snapped closed, of course, and, irritably, she grabbed it with her other hand and pulled it to her …

… and saw Washburn's hand wrapped around a knife hilt, the blade buried deep in Ben's side, and all the blood.

The blood.

"You shouldn't have done that," Bear Man said quietly and let go of the hilt and grabbed her wrist with a blood-dripping hand like a vise.

She screamed.

Given the situation, not the best thing to do. Troopers would come running and find the letter and her false story and she was dead, but she was dead if this Bear Monster got hold of her any tighter and the scream had the effect of freezing Washburn for enough seconds for her to reach in her cloak with the letter-encumbered hand, exchange the letter for the jodo stick, and bring it savagely across Bear Monster's hand.

Washburn let go, grunting in pain, but he was on his feet like lightning, pushing the obviously dead body of Ben hard enough it crashed into her waist and forced her stumbling back and Bear Man had seized her by both shoulders, the white weird light in his eyes dancing and spinning with insanity.

She screamed again.

He clamped a hand over her mouth and wrapped his other arm around her waist and lifted her off her feet. He hauled her across the sidewalk and into an alley between the two buildings and it was dusk when everything was obscured and maybe people were leaning out of windows and squinting toward all that noise but all they could see was some kind of tussle and a pile of something lying on the street before the bench and no one was going to come running unless they clearly knew what was happening. Didn't want to get caught up in some cadre or trooper action. And no troopers were running this way going, "Stop! In the name of the State!" or whatever those bozos yelled which was actually a relief because knowing them, they would like to spend an hour or two raping her before they let Bear Man kill her.

So stop screaming and start fighting.

Her jodo hand was still free and she stabbed it as hard as she could into Washburn's ear, once, twice, and he rocked and finally dropped her and staggered back on the third strike and she bounced her head off the gravel and was scrambling to get to her feet before Washburn could recover when a locomotive hit the guy at about 500 miles per hour.

Little John.

Both of the big men went flying through the air, the momentum of a guy Little John's size enough to carry Washburn off his feet, the two of them punching and growling and kicking at each other and it was a tornado of giant hands and feet and overcoats and Cass could not tell who was who but she better figure it out quick.

Leaping to her feet, Cass charged at the scrum and saw that Washburn had Little John in a strangle hold and was doing everything he could to snap his neck and Cass fished out her other jodo and brought both of them down as hard as she could on top of Washburn's head. "*Ack!*" he yelped and loosened his grip enough that John could take a breath and Cass slapped and slapped at Washburn's face until he flung John at her, driving her back hard against the wall. "*Oof!*" she gasped as John collapsed at her feet and Bear Man, the terrible death light in his eyes downright glowing, reached for her.

And John came roaring up from the ground and drove

his knife deep into Bear Man's throat.

Washburn made a whimpering sound, clawing at the blade but John had pressed it all the way through the back of his neck and there was nothing to do but watch the bear sink to his knees, his eyes bulging and his open throat trying to find air or seal itself around the blade so it could then get air and he was making weird little wheezing sounds and he was on his side shuddering and convulsing.

"Die, you sonofabitch," John, sitting with his legs splayed, said to the bear.

He did. Slowly, gagging around spouts of blood.

Cass watched for a few seconds and then leaned over and vomited.

Again and again.

What did you expect? She'd seen two people murdered in the last two minutes or so. Little John had the decency to hold her hair back as she emptied all the food she had eaten in the last four days all over the ground. "It's all right," he kept murmuring but she knew it wasn't. They were in an alley of a strange town at sunset with a body in front of them and another in the street so guess who was going to get arrested any moment?

"Don't move!" a woman hissed.

Cass turned from the disgusting mess she had made and looked. A small figure wielding a big sword stood over her, the blade hovering inches from her head. Cass shrank but the blade stayed with her. John shifted but the woman braced and said, "You move and I'll cut her head off!" and the blade whistled expertly next to Cass's neck. They both froze.

"What the FUCK did you kill Washburn for?" the woman glared at them with murder in her own brown, almond-shaped eyes. She was an older black woman and Cass couldn't help marveling at her extraordinary hair, which sat on her head like a black dandelion. She wanted to reach out and touch it but would lose her head if she twitched. The woman's small, heart-shaped mouth was drawn back in rage indicating how ready she was to cut them both in half and it looked like there was nothing Cass could do to prevent that.

Except tell the truth.

"Washburn murdered Ben," she said quietly, softly. Do not stir the beast.

"What?" The black woman's eyes glowed red with her rage and the blade flicked at Cass's neck and she felt one of her hair strands part. Man, this thing was sharp. "He did," she repeated, just as quietly. "He stabbed Ben in the heart, I think. He was going to kill me, too, but Little John," a careful nod at the still frozen man, "saved me." Another careful nod out the alley at the body in front of the bench. "Go look."

The woman glared at her and furrowed her brow and took a quick glance out the alley and gasped then reached down and, with amazing strength from such a little woman, yanked Cass to her feet and pulled her around and swept the blade so that the sharp edge was braced against Cass's back. "You move," she warned John, "and I'll open her like a watermelon." John raised surrender hands and stayed where he was; the woman pushed Cass out the alley and next to the body and it was all Cass could do not to begin retching again.

"Motherfucker," the woman whispered as she stared at the knife still stuck in Ben's side, apparently recognizing it. She dragged Cass back into the alley and slammed her into the wall next to the still-surrendered John and drew back the blade, which looked like some old cavalry sword, and aimed it right at Cass's heart. "What are you two doing here?"

"I've got a letter for Collier Rashkil," Cass said quickly, her own arms raised in surrender. "I was supposed to give it to Ben but Washburn killed him and tried to take it from me."

"What's this letter?" Vicious jab stopping micro-inches from her cloak.

"It's from another Ghost!" Cass said frantically, expecting the blade to plunge deep into her heart any second.

"We're not your enemies," John said from his sitting position. "We're here to help."

"Help?" The woman slashed at John, forcing him to flatten against the wall even tighter, if that was possible. "You call this help?" and she slapped Washburn's body with the flat of the sword.

A paper fell out of his jacket and onto the ground.

Quick as a snake, the woman snatched it up as she placed the blade back against Cass's breast. "This the letter?" she asked and began reading it, the setting sun throwing enough light directly down the alley she could do so easily, and Cass knew she was dead.

The woman reacted like she'd been hit by lightning. "What the FUCK?" she yelped and read the letter again. "WHAT THE FUCK, WASHBURN!" This time a full out scream. "You fucking traitor!" and in one motion, she decapitated the corpse, skillfully avoiding Little John's still throat-stuck blade as she did so.

Cass wanted to vomit again because she had no doubt her own head would be rolling down the alley in a moment but there were shouts and the sounds of running feet converging on their position and the woman whirled and looked at them both. "Let's go!" she yelled and pelted out the back of the alley toward the setting sun.

Didn't have to tell her, or Little John, twice.

2.13

Collier

"Where's Felicia?" Collier asked.

The others looked at each other and back at him and shrugged. "Where's Washburn? And Ben?" Eulen added his own questions.

Collier shook his head. "I wasn't all that certain those two would make it tonight, but I expected Felicia. I guess that means Ben didn't get a message to her."

"I saw the signal," Darra said.

"And, obviously, so did I," Eulen added.

Collier frowned. What this meant, he couldn't say. The longer nights made travel more difficult. A couple of sudden squalls this past week, one of them an actual sleet storm, had made the trails up the ridge that much more treacherous. But it was also likely that Felicia had been intercepted by Deavers. Or was sick. Or simply decided not to come.

"We'll go on without her, then," he decided. "We can always back brief everyone."

Eulen spread his hands. "Sure that's wise? If this is something that requires a decision, we should have everyone."

"I know," Collier conceded, "but we have run out of time."

That was ominous enough to raise Darra's eyebrow and shoot a concerned look at Eulen, who pursed equally concerned lips. "What have we run out of time for?" Darra asked.

Collier was quiet for a moment. "Saving our friends. Saving ourselves."

"Are you speaking about salvation? Is this a missionary call?" Eulen, somewhat flippant, which Collier understood. Anything to relieve the tension.

"No. This is a war call."

Both sat back in almost a coordinated movement that would be funny in other circumstances, but not now. Eulen gestured. "Perhaps you should get on with it."

Collier did. "Ben has discovered that the State intends to round up the co-ops and butcher them as scapegoats for the State's many, many failures." He stopped, awaiting their reaction.

"Good God," Eulen breathed. Darra had merely gone white.

"This is to begin soon. Immediately." Collier paused. "Tomorrow."

Eulen was first to challenge the intelligence. "How did Ben find this out?"

"I wish he was here to tell you," Collier replied, "but I'm satisfied it's legitimate." He paused. "You should know there's a complication. Deavers caught Ben gathering the information."

Gasps from both of them. "What?" "Is that why he's absent?" "Is he dead?"

"No," Collier said patiently, "He's not dead, otherwise, how would either of you know about this meeting?" Collier almost smiled as they both realized that. "*Why* he's not here, I can't say, but Deavers made sure Ben knew he'd been caught, and did nothing to prevent Ben from leaving with the information."

"So it's a trap," Eulen concluded.

"Yes."

"Worse," Darra offered, "it's a lie designed to trap us."

Collier shook his head. "I don't think it's a lie. The order for the purge was on Kant's letterhead. The Directorate is devious but that's a degree of planning well beyond normal."

"So why would Deavers let Ben get away with the info?" Eulen challenged.

"I have a theory." And Collier gave them the Hobson's choice.

The two sat there considering it. "What should we do?" Darra asked, softly.

"We cannot let our people die," Collier said.

Eulen gave him a baleful look. "How do you know they're going to? This has 'set-up' written all over it."

"Yes." Collier agreed. "It does. And it is. But we can't afford to ignore it. We cannot let our people die." Collier emphasized that last part.

Eulen kept the baleful look. "So you're calling for war."

"I think I already intimated that."

Darra sat forward. "Why don't we withdraw, instead?"

"We could do that," Collier agreed, "save the church, our immediate families, some of the outliers. But we couldn't save everyone, and a lot of people we like and have supported will pay the price." He leaned forward to meet Darra. "Are you willing to live with that?"

Darra frowned. "I'm not a coward," he said, stiffly. "But it's stupid to go to war when you're outnumbered. And outgunned."

"And outmaneuvered," Eulen added.

"And out of time." Collier put on the finishing stroke. "But no one is ever ready for war. No one. I guarantee you Kant will not be ready for our response."

Eulen was skeptical. "And how do you guarantee that?"

"I have … resources," Collier almost whispered that.

"What kind of resources?" Darra didn't whisper. "Unless you've got a nuke squirreled away somewhere, we're going to be in trouble."

Collier said nothing for a moment. "A long time ago," he said, quietly, "I was given a map showing where some very valuable art treasures were buried. Doesn't matter how I got the map." He stopped the question rising to Darra's lips. "It came to me. Along with a few other things." Collier was silent for a moment, then continued. "This was after the battle for Pemberton, after the Blues lost the war. Things were in flux and I managed to parlay the art into quite a substantial cache of weapons, before the Reds consolidated power. State-of-the-art weapons." And he stopped.

Darra's eyebrows rose. "So you're telling me that you've got a nuke?" said with incredulity.

"No, that would be foolish," Collier said. "No one knows how to handle those anymore. I do have weapons and ammunition."

Darra gave him a sideways glance. "Rifles? Machine guns?"

Collier nodded. "RPGs, Claymores, even artillery and anti-aircraft."

Darra was hammer struck. "Why didn't you tell us this before?" he spluttered.

"Need to know," was all Collier said and he gazed full at Eulen.

Momentarily puzzled, Darra furrowed brows at the old man, and then it came clear. "You knew!"

Eulen said nothing, keeping his eyes fixed on the table. "But!" Darra was in full-blown spluttering mode now. "Why … how … why didn't you tell the rest of us?" That last thrown at Collier.

"Again, need to know. Eulen has the background for

this." And he left it at that.

"I have a bit of a background, too," Darra said sarcastically.

"Yes, I know." Collier was patient. "You did your war time and you did it well. But others did more." A nod at Eulen. "Even more than the two of us put together."

Darra turned and regarded the old man. "One day, you're going to have to tell me your war stories. And I'll tell you mine and we'll see. But I ask you now, do we have the resources," air quotes "to handle the Directorate?"

"We do," was all the old man said.

"And are they close enough we can break them out quickly?"

Eulen nodded. "Yes. If we start tonight."

"Tonight?" Darra's eyes popped and he looked at Collier wildly. "Tonight?"

"We have no time," Collier spoke softly.

Darra was still wild-eyed. "Do we have the people for this?"

Neither of them responded.

Darra looked between them and then threw his hands up. "Great. Just great. We're committing suicide!"

"No one is ever ready for war," Collier repeated in the shocked silence …

… which was broken by a commotion outside, shouts and yells and running feet. Instantly, Collier stood and drew his old bayonet, Eulen a half second behind him pulled out a short cudgel. "They're on us!" Darra shouted as he leaped back, wielding his own blades.

The door burst open with such force that the candles fluttered, creating a strobe effect, and Collier crouched into combat stance as four-or-five people came stumbling across the threshold. "Call 'em off!" Felicia, in the middle of that group, shouted.

It took Collier a few seconds to realize that the two guards he always posted for these meetings were engaged with two strangers, a big man and a little girl, blade to blade and club to club and Felicia was vouching for them. "Back off!" Collier ordered the guards and they looked at him and then at their antagonists and broke contact, weapons still ready. The two strangers, exhausted and cut and bleeding, stopped fighting but stayed ready. Everything remained tableau as Felicia frantically waved Collier down. "It's okay," Collier reassured the guards, "You did good. Go on back now," and he gestured at the door.

They hesitated but Collier urged them and, after satisfying themselves that Collier and the rest were armed and ready to resume the fight, should it be necessary, they slipped out, but not before glaring the two strangers back a step or two. "Drop your weapons," Collier ordered the strangers, "No one's going to hurt you here."

"Drop yours first," the big man countered.

"This is my territory," Collier retorted, "so you comply."

The big man frowned and was about to say something but the girl placed a hand on his arm. "Stand down," she said and put away her two sticks, which she seemed to know how to handle. The man stared at her a second and, with a sigh, sheathed the blades. The girl nodded at Collier.

"Felicia?" Collier turned to her for an explanation.

The black woman leaned against the table, her eyes downcast and her face wreathed in sorrow. "Ben is dead," she said tonelessly, even as an electric shock ran through the others. "Washburn killed him."

Darra and Eulen shouted simultaneously, "What!" as Collier sat down wearily.

"These two," Felicia waved at the strangers, "killed

Washburn." As Eulen and Darra grew instantly murderous, she added, "Washburn was trying to kill them."

"It's true," the girl said, in a small voice.

Collier cocked a head at Felicia but said nothing. She took in a big breath. "Washburn is the traitor."

Eulen and Darra jumped forward brandishing their weapons, which caused Felicia to raise her sword defensively and the big man to reach for his blades but the girl did nothing. Smart one, Collier concluded. Collier raised a hand to stop the pending fight. "How do you know?" he asked Felicia.

"He had this on him." And she took a paper from her coat and handed it to Collier.

It was a handwritten note. It read that Collier was having a meeting with the committee. Tonight. It said where the meeting would be, in grid coordinates, and who would be there. And it listed every member of the church and where they lived.

And Washburn did not write it. Collier knew who did.

He sat quietly, reading and re-reading, as time stood still and implications washed over him and a grief he had not felt since … since Pemberton, gripped his heart. Oh no. No. I cannot bear this.

"Collier?" Eulen said, concern in his voice.

After a few years, Collier looked up. "It's a note that was to be delivered to Deavers. It told about this meeting and who would be here."

The others gasped. "What?" Alarmed, Darra looked at the door, expecting the Directorate to crash through at any moment but then realized the note had not been sent. He sat down, deflated. "Washburn?" Darra shook his head, incredulous. "Washburn?"

"Yes," was all Collier said. He looked at the two strangers. "Why are you here?"

"We brought you a letter," the girl said, hastily, and pulled out an envelope and shook it at Collier. "We weren't supposed to actually bring it to you. We were supposed to find someone who knew you and give it to them and that guy was Ben but, when I found him, Washburn had just killed him and he tried to kill me and Little John," a nervous wave of the paper at the big man, "saved me from him and then … her," a glance at Felicia, "… and …"

Collier stopped her with a look. "Who is the letter from?"

"Henry Price."

Collier's face remained impassive as he whirled through time and space and was back in the barracks, twenty years ago, little guy with big eyes dressed in fatigues standing near Collier's hammock and asking, "You gonna shoot me, Sarge?"

And everything that happened after.

"Give it to me," Collier said as he reached out a hand.

"Um." She was hesitant. "It's in Greek."

"Greek?" Darra asked.

"Yes. See, if we got caught …"

Collier waved that away. "I don't read Greek. What does it say?"

"I … know some of it," the girl hedged, "but my Dad wrote it and his Greek is so much better than mine."

"What does it say?"

She took in a breath but Eulen held out a palm. "I read Greek. Give it to me," he said. As everyone looked at him, he added, "What? I went to school before the gummint effed it all up. Even in Down Holler by God Kentucky, we had good schoolin'. You had to learn either Latin or Greek. Most people took Latin but I had to be different. I was good at Greek, which, of course is why I got assigned to Latin America, but, you know how that goes," and he waved a hand at Collier to underscore the universal incompetence of all government organizations, pre- and post-Event, but Collier was suffering from multiple hammer blows and he said nothing. The girl shifted, glanced at Collier then handed the envelope to Eulen who broke the seal and shook the paper out and read it, taking his time.

"First of all," Eulen finally said, "it's a greeting from this guy Price, who reminds you of your past association," Collier was stone-faced, "and how surprised he was to learn that you're still alive and nearby—"

Collier interrupted, "Where is Price?"

"Farmville," the girl responded immediately, ignoring the glare from her big companion. "But he's in hiding right now because we were attacked—"

"One story at a time," Collier stopped her and nodded at Eulen.

The old man continued, "The State is planning some kind of action," exchange of glances around the table that the girl caught, "and they've tracked down all the surviving Ghosts and intend to eliminate them before this action, whatever it is, begins."

"Holy shit!" Darra interrupted now. "So that's why Deavers is here!" He gave Collier a stunned look.

"So it would seem," Collier replied, successfully keeping his voice level.

"This changes everything," Darra added.

"I know."

"Who's Deavers?" the girl asked but Collier ignored her and gestured at Eulen.

"Price is contacting those remaining Ghosts …"

"Wait." Collier held up a hand. "Price knows where the Ghosts are?" And he looked at the girl.

"Yes," she said. "We have a list." She stopped but the silence grew and she realized more explanation was necessary. "My brother, Slickie, got it out of a Directorate colonel's safe—"

"Slickie?" Eulen cut in. "Your parents named him Slickie?"

The girl's face flamed. "It's a nickname. His name is Homer, after my Dad."

"And what's yours?"

"Cass."

"Short for Cassandra?" She nodded, and Eulen chuckled. "Your dad is a classicist."

"He's a smuggler," she corrected.

"Where is this list?" Collier interjected, impatient. He pointed at the envelope. "Did you include it?"

"No," Cass said. "Price kept it."

Hope danced on the edge of his heart. "Can you remember the names on it?"

"No," she replied and the hope collapsed. "I didn't read it."

Eulen rattled the letter to get everyone back on track. "Price says he sent this boy Slickie," an apologetic nod at Cass, "out to contact the Ghosts, but it will take a while because they're everywhere. Price hopes you don't mind but he's going to tell the remaining Ghosts where you are —"

"Deavers was a Ghost!" Felicia reminded them with a hint of panic in her voice.

"Yes," Collier said, "but I doubt he'd be on a list of survivors to be killed."

"Let's hope," Felicia muttered and Collier ignored her. "How many names on this list?" he asked Cass.

"I think about forty."

Collier's heart stilled. Forty. So, there was a chance. He flipped a hand at Eulen.

"He wants you to take precautions and hopes you will treat his couriers well." Cass and Little John exchanged glances of relief. "And he is willing to consider anything you decide to do." Eulen stopped.

"That all?"

"He wants to know if you still have those cigars."

Collier couldn't help chuckling at that, even though his heart was empty. "Everyone sit," he ordered and Felicia sheathed her sword and did so and the couriers, after a moment, found chairs and pulled them up, but kept a defensive distance. Collier admired that.

He was reflective for a moment, and then looked at the couriers. "Tell me about this attack."

Cass's brows furrowed for a moment. "Oh. We were making a delivery," bit of an eye roll that Collier found amusing, "when we were attacked by the Faceless."

Felicia's mouth fell open. "What?"

"With a helicopter," she added.

The other three buzzed among themselves but Collier said nothing, waiting for their panic to subside. "Why?"

She shrugged. "I guess because Price's name is on that list, too." She looked at Collier. "But he was never a Ghost. Right?"

"He was close enough," Collier replied, then bowed his head, thoughtful as the others settled and waited for him. After a bit, Collier looked at the couriers and Felicia. "The State intends to massacre the co-ops and their families in the Valley. I'm sure that includes Farmville, too."

"We're at Sweet Briar," Cass said, then "Ouch!" as Little John elbowed her viciously.

"Sweet Briar, then. This massacre will start soon. Like tomorrow." He saw Felicia's eyes widen and he turned to her. "Ben found this out. Deavers let him find it. Deavers did that so we would dither trying to figure out what Deavers was up to and, if Washburn's note," he said, with no irony, as he tapped the paper with his finger, "had been delivered, we'd all be dead right now." He looked slowly around the table as they realized the implications and other eyes widened and nervous looks shot at the door. "So, there is no further discussion. There is no other path." He paused. "We are going to war."

Silence around the table.

Collier let it sit for a moment, and then looked at Cass. "Here is the message you take to Price. War is on us. Gather your army. Gather your weapons. Come to Burnt Church."

"The burnt church?" Her voice was quavery.

"No. Burnt Church. It's a place. Find it." And his tone advised she would not receive any further information.

"And tell him," he said, as he stood and removed his jacket and slowly rolled up his sleeve, "that he has earned this." And he turned his arm to the available light and they saw the tattoo. Of a ghost. Armed with an M-16.

All of them stared. It was legend.

And a call to arms.

"Go," Collier said, rolling his sleeve down. "All of you."

Eulen and Darra exchanged glances, held Collier's eyes for a moment, and left. Felicia stood up, tears in her eyes, and waved at the couriers. "What do I do with them?"

"Fresh horses. Provisions. Then point them on their way," he toned.

Felicia nodded and gestured irritably at them. "Let's go."

"But …" the girl protested, "We're exhausted. We need food and sleep." The big man next to her nodded in support.

"You eat on the way. You sleep in the saddle. Otherwise, your family is dead." He let that sink in.

The girl paled but the man did not, merely sighed in

acceptance and nudged the girl and they stood, the girl bewildered but Felicia determined; the big man nodded a salute to Collier and they were gone.

Collier sat quietly watching the candles and the sparks flying upward. He gathered the letter and the note and put them in his pocket and knew what he had to do.

2.14

Collier

"Are you okay?" Evelyn was in the kitchen, her hands clutching a towel and water dripping from her hands, the worried expression on her face evidence of how anxious she had been for his return. Collier stood inside the door a moment, ensured it was closed and latched behind him and then could no longer keep the grief and rage off his face. "No," he said.

She clucked and moved forward and gathered him and then ushered him to the table and lit a few more candles and brought him cold chicken and corn and the first of the preserved peaches and a glass of homemade beer and she fussed at him to eat but he just sat there. Just sat.

She became afraid.

"Where are the boys?" he asked.

"In their rooms. Supposedly studying." She tried adding a bit of levity but he didn't react.

"Second, too?"

"Yes."

He stood. "Tell him to meet me in the barn."

Her face wrinkled with concern. "Why, Collier?"

"I have something very important for him to do."

"What is it?"

"He needs to carry a message to someone."

"What message?"

He looked at her. "A message. And I need it carried by

someone I trust."

Suspicion replaced the concern. "You've never trusted him with a mission before."

"Then it's about time I started."

She regarded him. "What's going on, Collier?"

He swayed on his feet, the grief almost too much, too much, and her hand went to her mouth. "Oh, God!" she whispered.

"Yes," he said, regaining control, "oh, God. We are undone. I need you to gather everything, quietly, while I'm talking to Second. Don't cry. Don't scream. Don't alarm the twins. But get everything."

She was now completely white and trembling but she nodded through her hand and turned and headed toward the back and Collier spun and headed out the door. A sliver moon gave enough illumination to see, even at midnight with clouds scuttling by and hiding the winter stars. Winter, the end of things, the death of things, how fitting. Last time everything died, it had been spring and there had been false hopes. No such delusions now.

Collier unlatched the barn and was greeted by the nickers of the horses who presumed the entry of a human meant food and Collier grabbed an oil lamp and struck his iron until he had a spark and lit it and the soft light filled the space. Corn oil, the only lamp fuel on the market, and, even then, not much available because corn was food, so candles provided most lighting; lamp oil of any kind was a luxury and a composter didn't make that much in scrip to buy it but a smuggler did and Collier's compost deliveries always had something extra in the bottom of the wagon, usually corn, and that got him a few ounces of oil that he stored up for those nights when he needed to do something important in the dark. Like now.

Collier turned up the wick for maximum light, wrinkling his nose at the burnt popcorn smell (a wave of nostalgia, movie theaters and late night VHS fests with Dad), and opened one of the stalls and led the filly out and grabbed a saddle. He was attaching the halter when the door opened and the wind fluttered the lamp. Collier looked over. Second stood in the opening, blinking. "Dad?"

Collier ignored him, finished the halter and bridle, checked everything and left the horse. He walked over and hit Second as hard as he could in the mouth.

"*Errf*!" Second shrieked as he almost toppled back outside but Collier had him by the coat lapel and flung him into the barn, the filly shying away and he drove a fist deep into Second's stomach and then slapped him and slapped him and slapped until the boy was a quivering, pleading mass at Collier's feet. Stumbling a bit and gasping with the effort, Collier seized Second and threw him into a sitting position on a bale of hay.

"Dad!" Second was crying and spluttering through his ravaged face. "What'd I do?"

Collier reached into his pocket and threw the note into his face. "You wrote this."

Wallowing around the bale and threatening to up-end it, Second glanced drunkenly at the paper lying at his feet, then stopped and centered on the clear handwriting indicting him from the page. And said nothing.

"Do you understand," Collier said evenly, "that, if this had been delivered, I and everyone in the church would now be dead, your mother would be raped and murdered, and the twins would be on their way to labor camps?"

"That wouldn't have happened," Second leaned over and spat blood to the side. "Only you. They promised."

"And you believed them."

"Yes!" and Second came halfway up, the rage and defiance in his eyes. "Because they're not criminals!"

Tableau. Father and son, opponents, enemies, traitors,

in each other's eyes. The waves of hate coming from his oldest son staggered Collier and he felt his knees and resolve weakening. History tilted down several paths and who was he to defy the future because the future belongs to the children and the new order and your day and your beliefs have passed and God is dead and has abandoned you and your own father had his time and his world is gone, gone and yours took over and now there is a new way and a new time and it is your son's.

Absalom, Absalom, my son, my son.

Second, sensing his weakness, took a belligerent step forward. Collier drew a pistol and placed it against his son's head. Second fell to his knees. "You have a gun," he said in disbelief.

"A pistol," Collier corrected. "A .45 automatic. Carried it in the war. When I was fighting for our freedom. When I was a Ghost." He looked down the barrel into the terrified eyes of his son. "I am going to give you a choice you did not give me. You can live. Or you can die. Right here." Collier cocked the pistol and Second began crying. "Shut up. Here is your choice ... you get on that horse and ride away and never come back. Ever. Or I shoot you." He paused. "You have thirty seconds."

"I don't have my stuff," Second sobbed.

"I'm sure your new masters will be happy to supply you. Twenty seconds."

"What about Mom?"

"She thinks you're going on a mission for me. I'll keep that fiction going for as long as I can. Ten seconds."

Second's eyes suddenly cleared and he stared up the barrel, cold and ugly. "You won't shoot me."

Collier snapped the barrel against Second's head, driving him back with a yelp of pain. He leveled the barrel right at his son's face and steadied it, his finger around the trigger, and began a slow squeeze as the pulse pounded in his temple and his eyes turned combat red and here was the enemy, the enemy with his son's face, his boy, his baby laughing in the sunlight and chasing leaves and snowflakes and learning to ride and read and hunt and fish and you are not my son, you are not …

"All right!" Second shouted and rolled over with his hands in front of his face and crabbed toward the horse. "Don't shoot me! Don't shoot!" and refused to look at his dad, he mounted the horse, kicked it and was out the barn door and gone.

Collier walked to the entrance and saw him round the corner of the house on the heading for Kernstown which would probably take him two or three hours in the dark which was fine. They would be long gone by then. His son looked back once and their eyes met. Collier saw loathing. He hoped his son saw mourning.

Evelyn waited on the porch, framed by the now brightly lit house. She had followed her son's hurried departure around the house and then looked at her husband standing there, dead, in the barn. "Why are you armed?" she called.

"Just in case," he said and holstered the pistol.

"Do we wait for Second?" she asked across the yard.

"No," he responded across a thousand mile gulf, "he'll meet us." He held up a hand. "Five minutes."

She nodded and went back inside. Collier saw the twins running here and there dragging bags and sacks and letting out an occasional yip of protest over what they were doing, but Evelyn would not brook that and they would be ready or else. Collier went back inside and took the two other horses and the two mules out and saddled and bridled and packed and led the train into the yard and waved Bart, who was standing on the porch round-eyed, to him. "Pack," he said and handed the lead reins to him and went back inside the barn. He picked the note off the floor, noting there was blood on it now, and lit it in the still burning lamp. He then threw it on the bale and waited until it was caught, then stepped outside.

Evelyn had mounted, the twins on each mule, leaving the front horse for him. He walked around and checked the pack webbing and approved. The boys did good. The boys were silent, questioning, but, in their odd twin way, refusing to speak to anyone but each other. Collier looked at the house and the smoke gathering in the front door. He looked past the trees at the peaks here and there and saw the blooms of firelight here and there. He walked around and grabbed the reins off the horse's head.

"You remembered the book, right?" he asked Evelyn, and her immediate glare of offense told him it was a stupid question. She knew how important Dad's book – now stained and dog eared and the back cover missing – was. He nodded an apology, then took the reins and led the train away.

Part III: Terrible Swift Sword

3.1

The Season of Fear

It's not possible to be this exhausted and still be alive, Cass decided. Perhaps she was dead, but her soul refused to leave her rotting body until it got a good night's sleep. And, after three nights and almost two full days in the saddle, her body was completely rotten. And stiff. And a raging mass of pain from the top of her head to the bottom of her feet.

You can sleep in the saddle, Collier had said.

That called for a snort of disgust but she barely had enough spit to wet her throat, much less express herself. In her haste to get them mounted and gone, that girl Felicia hadn't supplied them with any canteens. "Go. Just go! Get water on the way!" and she'd slapped the horses and off they went, down a midnight trail. Yeah, 'get water on the way,' like 'sleep in the saddle.' They'd found a few streams but the water was dark and ugly and Little John had turned up a nose. They had better luck at a big river Little John said was the Shenandoah which, wow, Cass didn't realize it flowed all the way up here, and drank their fill and then followed the bank looking for a bridge but, when they got to one, trucks were crossing it. Actual, honest to God trucks, the gasoline kind, and Cass had stood there marveling because there had to be hundreds of them, one right after the other, and she did not know such wealth was possible but Little John had pulled her back into the woods and said, "They're Directorate," and the wonder evaporated and fear replaced it. It began raining and Little John said they had to swim across before the river swelled and they went back upstream and found a relatively calm spot but the water was freezing and the horses balky and it was a struggle and Cass didn't want to see a river ever again.

Except right now. She was dying of thirst, so, please, God, help us find a river. Or an ocean. She didn't care if it was salt; she would drink it until it came out her ears. And then die.

She looked back at Little John, slumped over his poor horse which was poorer than Cass's poor horse because it carried John. Bet the guy's lost a few pounds since this thing started. Not that you could see it. She would have giggled but she had no more strength.

He must have felt her regard because, wearily, he lifted his head and looked at her with bloodshot eyes and then held up two fingers. Two more hours until they were home. Or, at least, the cabin. Two more hours. Don't die until then.

By the time the horses broke through the last bit of cover and stood in the clearing next to the cabin, she was asleep in the saddle. She didn't remember too much other than Dad carrying her into the cabin as Mom fussed and hovered alongside and there was some water at some point like sweet nectar and she heard Price and Little John talking for a bit and she was in a bed. A bed. And asleep.

But, no more.

"'Bout time you woke up," Price said.

"I'm not awake," she said from deep within her pillow and deep within a dream about a river that would not quit.

"That wasn't an observation."

Cass blew out a long, long breath and came out of a long, long well of darkness and warmth and peace. Let me sleep, God, let me sleep and opened an eye and there was Price, sitting in a chair next to her bed. "It's not polite to watch a lady sleep."

"You're no lady. You're my niece."

She would have thrown a pillow at him but that was an expenditure of energy beyond her desire and she merely frowned. "Go away," she said.

"Only if you get up," he said, "We have business."

"I'll get up, but I'm not happy about it."

"Okay," Price said and ruffled her hair, something she would have protested but it felt welcoming and appreciative and she grinned. "There's coffee," he said as he pushed up and headed toward the door.

"Sure there is," she said and contemplated the pillow and five more minutes of sleeping on it.

"Yes, there is. The real stuff," he said and slipped out.

Her eyes popped open and she sat up and took in a noseful and, my God, coffee, the perfume of life. She threw the blankets off, noting that (a) it was cold and (b) she was wearing an old pair of woolen pajamas (please let Mom have changed me, please) so the cold didn't matter and she padded to the door and down the loft's ladder and through the main room and into the kitchen and was slapped to a stop by a wall of aroma. "Oh my God," she said. Coffee and eggs and some kind of meat, maybe pork or wild boar, who cares, it's meat and there was a plate of it piled high before an empty chair at a table where Price and Mom and Dad and Little John were already shoveling it in and she almost did not feel the rawness and pain of marathon horseback riding – almost – as she winced her way into the chair, dangerously tipping it in her haste but it stayed balanced, and she fell to.

"Take it easy," Dad ordered and he poured her a cup

of heaven from a steaming iron coffee pot and Cass could not help swooning over the black liquid. "Secret stash," Dad said, winking and pushing the tin cup her way. "Probably stale."

Who cares? The aroma was unbelievable.

She grasped the cup, burning her hands, and wanted to slurp but it was too hot so she sipped and burned her lips but who cares? Her body cried out with the joy of it. "My God," she whispered and the others laughed and she did not care.

Life returned as she ate and sipped. Even Little John lost his thousand-yard stare and smiled. Cass looked out the window and saw it was morning. "How long was I out?" she asked.

"Overnight," Dad responded.

"That's it?" she said around a biscuit. A biscuit! Made of real flour! Wow!

"The resilience of youth," Mom said and winked at Dad and they both smiled and even beamed at Little John who winked at her and this was a feast.

A feast.

She stopped eating. "What's going on?"

They all stopped the false joviality and the atmosphere turned suddenly grim. "We're leaving," Price said.

"Going to Burnt Church?" she said with some dread. Oh no. How many more days in the saddle?

"Maybe," Price responded, "but not yet." Confirming glance at Little John, who must have given him the Cliff Notes – what were Cliff Notes, anyway? – of what happened at Collier's. "And maybe not at all."

"Why not?"

"I'm not sure we want to get involved in this war," he concluded, "More scrapple?" He sliced at the blob of so-called meat.

"Aren't we already involved in it?" she asked,

debating the wisdom of eating ground-up hog snout. Eh, smelled good, so yeah.

"No."

She gave him an incredulous look. "Huh? Didn't we get chased by Faceless goons? With a helicopter? Didn't we break into Directorate offices? Isn't that pretty much a declaration of war, something that could get us all shot?" She saw Mom suddenly cringe. "Sorry," she said to her and then looked around the room. "Where's Slickie?"

"Still on a mission," Price said blandly while ignoring Zoe's glower at him, "and that mission could very well mean whether we, indeed, sit this one out or not."

She blinked. "How?"

"Because others will come to Rashkils's aid. And we can avoid the whole thing."

She put down her fork because she had suddenly lost her appetite. "We can't do that."

Price looked at her mildly. "We certainly can."

She looked at the others and saw more mild expressions, even from Little John. "But, this is war!"

"Yes," Dad said, "it is. And I've seen war. We've seen war." A nod at Price. "And it is not romantic and heroic. It is awful. To be avoided, if we can."

"But they've declared war on us!"

"Hence," Price said as he buttered – butter! – a biscuit, "the reason we're leaving." He pointed the butter knife at her. "Eat up. This is the last of the supplies here. Everything else has already been shipped."

"Well, how is that going to stop them?"

"If they can't find us, then they can't wage war on us."

Cass frowned and took a breath. "So, we're running away."

"Tactical retreat," Price said, taking a bite, "It sounds better."

"It's still running away." Cass sat back, crossing her arms. "And deserting an ally."

The table went still and they all looked at her, Mom's face more distressed than the menfolk. Cass understood that. Women suffered more in war than men, who only died their own deaths but women died theirs and everyone else's. "Cass," Mom said, "we're not deserting our friends or family or the people we know. We are protecting them."

"If we don't fight them, then they'll come for us," she declared. "And we won't be able to protect anyone."

"Cass!" Mom was sharp. "You're too young to understand this. We have already made the decision. We're leaving, we're not fighting, especially for a group of people we don't even know!" And now it was her turn to sit back, arms crossed, her eyes blazing.

And afraid.

Cass jolted a bit inside because there was very little that Mom was afraid of – mad at, scornful of, oh yeah, but afraid? Perhaps Cass didn't quite understand what was going on and should meekly duck her head and say okay. But there was something inherently, basically, wrong with all this. She looked Price full in the face. "He showed us, you know."

'He, being who, showed you what, darling?" Price said nonchalantly licking his fingers.

"Rashkil. And, the tattoo."

She didn't have to explain what tattoo. Everyone knew it. It was as sacred a symbol as a cross used to be. People who had put one on and tried to pass themselves off as Ghosts got it torn or burned right off their arms. "And he said you had earned it." Spoken as an accusation.

Because if a Ghost said that you had earned the right to wear the tattoo, then you were brother. You were soldier. You were blood.

And you don't run out on blood.

Price had a pulse in his temple and his gigantic eyes narrowed to slits and Cass knew she had stepped in it but she swallowed hard and held and accused him with her eyes. "We. Are. Not. Abandoning. Them!" Price stabbed the table with each word. "We are regrouping. We are gathering our resources and people and centralizing so we can protect each other."

"But not Rashkil."

"Rashkil can take care of himself. That's one thing I know."

"So," she said triumphantly, "you ARE abandoning him!"

A heartbeat or two passed and Cass was sure Price was about to slap her across the room. With Mom and Dad's approval. Little John was still too busy eating. So when Price shoved his chair back violently, his brow murderous, she couldn't help cringing. "This conversation is over!" Price barked and stood and stomped out.

Dad looked at her with raised eyebrows, shook his head and followed Price. Mom sat there, stricken. "Cass," she said plaintively.

"Mom!" and she hated the way she sounded, like some pouty little teenage girl mad that she had to go to bed early, because this wasn't some little snit fit, this was their very soul.

"Cass," Mom's voice dropped and was laced with such grief that Cass knew she could not win this. Could not. "I cannot lose you," Mom was whispering now, "I cannot lose your brother. None of you."

"Mom," was all Cass could say, and there, done.

"Good biscuits!" Little John said, sopping up the last of the butter.

Oh, God, another horse ride. My aching back.

"So where are we going?" Cass could not keep the petulance out of her voice.

"A convocation." Little John, beside her, tightened the last of the buckles around the mules, which didn't like the loads on their backs and let him know with brays that split the morning. "Shut up!" Little John said and actually slugged one mule in the mouth.

"What's a convocation?" Cass asked, glowering at the mule. She felt like punching something herself.

"Everyone's coming together. Everyone."

Cass cocked an eyebrow, amazed. "You mean … everyone? Like, the whole gang?"

"Even the affiliates." Little John said, giving one last tug and baleful look at the complaining mule.

"Where?"

"Beau and Sally's, at Raines Tavern."

Beau and Sally. Huh. She'd met them once before, back when she was about ten and Uncle P had taken her and the rest of the family north into the woods and waters of Brier's Creek because Beau and Sally had another kid and he wanted to personally deliver a bottle of real champagne. They'd ended up staying for three days celebrating. She'd liked it up there, isolated and woodsy and private, a paradise, and she got the impression there was some past history between Price and Beau and Sally, something before the Event. She'd asked Tat and he'd said that Sally used to be Price's girlfriend in high school.

High school. What a concept.

It had been a pleasant time and she felt her spirits lift remembering it, even though this visit was nothing but a bug-out. "Is Tat going to be there?" she asked Little John.

He shrugged. "He went with Slickie."

"Where?"

He gave her the snake eye. "On a mission," he said

and pulled on the pack once more and walked away.

"*Hmph!*" she snorted and pulled at her own pack with a little more energy than the horse, the one Felicia had given her, thought necessary and it gave her a reproachful look. "Sorry," she said and stroked it affectionately. "Think I'll call you Ghost."

Be a good reminder of how all this got started.

She glared at Price, up there at the front of the column conferring with Homer and Little John, all of them waving their arms around like they were saying something important. You need a good reminder. You don't walk away from a pal.

You don't.

She sighed and ran her fingers through Ghost's mane and knew there was nothing she could do. Pout and throw a fit, yeah yeah, make her feel better but the adults had decided and that was that. She was "too young to understand." Well, is there an age requirement before knowing that you stand by your friends and fight, if necessary? How many times had she and Slickie, even when mad at each other for some dumb brother-sister thing, fought bullies and poachers and cousins who gave them a hard time? Admittedly, those fights didn't involve machine guns and rockets and ...

... helicopters.

She frowned. She blinked. That sound ...

The others suddenly stopped their pointing around and froze, eyes widening, as the air beat and thrummed with the same death wings she and Slickie and Price had fled what felt like a thousand years ago but here, again, now.

Cass screamed.

No one heard it, not even Cass, because two helicopters blasted over the tree line. Two, roaring and canting and smoking and drowning the world with their death wings so loud no other sounds were possible. Her screams and the screams of bucking, wild-eyed horses and shouting adults running around and pointing at the helicopters were all drowned by the death wings.

The helicopters crossed in front of each other and then X'd back over the ridge line behind the cabin and almost went sideways X'ing back in front of each other again as they leveled and lined up …

… weapons.

Smoke and fire spat from some kind of carriages sticking out like blunted wings on the helicopter's sides. Streaks of smoke reached for her.

The cabin evaporated in fire and smoke, and shredded wood and glass spewed death fragments all around her. The woods behind her did the same. She did not. Nor did the convoy. The dragons had missed them.

On this pass.

As the dragons roared overhead and made another X to come back and finish the job, she saw Price on his rearing horse waving his hat and shouting something she could not hear. Mom and Dad were fighting their own horses for control and Mom's and her's eyes met for a split second and Mom mouthed something as her horse turned her out of sight and then Little John was near her, his mouth against her ear and she could hear him verbalize what Mom had mouthed. "Run!"

She mounted. She kicked. She ran.

3.2

The Season of Death

The branches tore at her as the horse lurched and stumbled through them and she was tossed in the saddle, all her old bruises and muscle tears renewed but she did not care, did not feel them because she was running for her life. The one benefit of terror: it left you numb.

The helicopters didn't appear to be following her specifically, but they crisscrossed the sky above her so they must have a bead on the rest of the group fleeing in the same general direction as she was, north by north-east, toward the deeper mountains and woods that should hide them from the relentless air search.

And relentless attack.

Every few minutes or so, she heard the thrum of machine-gun fire as the helicopters sprayed the trees, and the whoosh of rockets as they blew other trees to hell. Only once since the pursuit began did bullets kick up near her and those were mostly high up, cutting branches and leaves that rained down. Because of that, she'd concluded the specific target was one of the others riding off to her right, which was odd because she'd been the last one in line so how did someone get over there? She guessed that normal lines of travel get blurred when everyone is panicking and scattered, running for their lives.

Speaking of running … where, specifically, was she running to?

Well, on this heading, she'd eventually hit the old Lexington Road, a mess of wrecked asphalt and stone piles left by the various avalanches the mountains threw at it from time to time. Despite that, it was still a viable way over the mountains and was the road she and Slickie and Price had used when they did the Stump Run a thousand lifetimes ago. Problem was, even the dimmest of helicopter pilots would notice it and, the moment she popped out of the woods, there he'd be, lining up his guns and rockets and grinning before evaporating her.

Maybe she shouldn't go over the mountains. But, where else was there?

She pulled on Ghost's reins, the horse rearing a bit as it slid to a stop. They were in a thin patch of woods, which made her nervous. The helicopters could easily spot her, but she had a decent view of the surroundings from here and she needed to get her bearings. Besides, the helicopters were far off to the left busy shooting at somebody. Please don't let it be Mom or Dad.

Mom and Dad, where are you?

Her breath caught in a sob as she spun Ghost about in an effort to get the horse under control. She needed her parents to come flying up the side of this knoll, seize Ghost's reins and pull her to a safe place free of rockets and aerial machine guns and then stroke her hair and tell her everything was going to be all right. Mom and Dad had always been there, always a presence in the middle of this dangerous life, always saving her. They'd taught her to ride and fight (well, Tat had actually done that but he worked for Dad) and run scams by acting stupid or sexy or innocent as the play required. They'd taught her how to live in this world of murder and kidnap and starvation and labor camps and oppression. She was daughter to a man and woman who had forged an alliance with Price and his gang to stand defiant against a state that sought their bodies, their lives, their prosperity. In a land not free, they roamed mountains and trails and laughed and played and she and Slickie were loved and protected. Dad taught her to read dead languages that told the history of the world and Mom taught her that a woman can survive anything, even the rape camps Dad had saved her from, and that a woman, a man, everyone, should cling ferociously to the spark of life within them and never, ever give up.

"Do not give up, Cass."

Mom's whisper in the wind and she spun the horse about, straining to see Mom or Dad rushing to her rescue, but they were not there and she heard the tone of the helicopters change and that meant they were swinging back her way and Mom, I will never give up, never.

Plunging over the side of the knoll, Cass broke into a protective screen of oak and chestnut right at the moment the helicopter burst over, hiding her so successfully that the crew didn't bother to spray the area. She took a deep breath and patted Ghost's neck to calm her and noted a little rill falling down the slope. It formed a natural dip, low enough to get her through the shrubs and thorn branches while still maintaining the thick limbs overhead. Grateful there were still enough leaves on the trees to help hide her, she picked her way, the rill growing as she descended, until the knoll bottomed out and ran into what she first thought was a wall but then realized was the berm of a bridge covering the rill that now drained into a large stream.

The Buffalo River.

With a gasp she urged Ghost forward as she realized exactly where she was: this bridge was part of the old Lexington road, one of the few bridges still standing, probably because it was more banked-up material than crossbeam and trestle, and there was an intact water pipe underneath that carried the rill over to the Buffalo River, which did not cross the mountains but wandered off into the woods generally eastward until it hit the Lexington Road again …

… not that far from Raines Tavern.

Now she knew where she was going.

She pulled the horse's nose up and kicked her a bit to get up the bridge's slope and cross the broken asphalt and then they'd slide down the other side and pick up the river and, by nightfall, be at Raines Tavern and safety…

Voices. Coming from the road.

Hastily, she pulled Ghost back around and slid to the bottom of the bridge and she jumped off and tied the horse and scrambled back up the side until she was about three feet from the top and listened. Yep, men's voices, some laughing and calling and sounding like they were having a good time. Slowly, one inch at a time, she peeked over the top of the road. At first, she couldn't see anything but piles of broken asphalt. The voices resolved further to the right so she pulled herself up until she could see down the decline.

There, about a hundred yards away, in the middle of the intact portion of the road, a truck. A real truck, the kind that runs on gasoline, one of those marvelous things from a dead past, the back of it covered with some kind of tarp or cloth. Twenty Faceless stood around it.

Her heart stopped. She was dead.

Thirty or so seconds passed without her being shredded by rifle fire, and she realized they hadn't spotted her yet, so she scrutinized them. The Faceless had congregated around what looked like some kind of cooking stove set on the ground behind the truck and were grab-assing, apparently enjoying the hell out of themselves. Well, of course. They were waiting for the helicopters to drive Price and her parents and yours truly right into their waiting arms and this was fun and games

because they'd get to execute traitors while eating
barbecue. As if to underscore that, one of the helicopters
appeared in the sky farther past the truck, silhouetted
against the blue for a moment before it whirled back in
the direction it came. The Faceless all cheered at that as
Cass went cold. My God, this is a trap. She had to warn
the others.

One of the Faceless stepped away from the cooking
crowd, looked right at her, called something and waved
her over. Lunch, Cass.

That couldn't be right and Cass almost had a heart
attack when someone, no more than eight feet in front of
her but obscured by the asphalt pile, called, "On our way."
Two Faceless carrying rifles sauntered down the road to
the cookout, Cass sure they would turn around at any
moment to investigate that wildly beating bass drum her
heart played. Staying still long enough to make sure there
weren't any more Faceless lurking there, she quietly slid
down the berm until she was back with Ghost.

Oh. My. God.

She took in deep breaths to quell the panic rising from
her throat and into a scream that would undo her. They
were going to die. All of them. There was no way to cross
the road without getting caught. There was no way back
up the hill without helicopters gunning her down. And
there was no way she could stay here; eventually some
Faceless will cast an idle glance over the side. She had to
get out of here. She had to warn the others.

Had to find a way out.

She looked at the water pipe under the bridge, then
scrambled over the rocks and peered down its length.
There was daylight coming from the other side so it was
clear, but the pipe was too small and cluttered to get
Ghost through it. Okay, there it is, a way out but,
unfortunately, a horseless one. Rest of the way on foot,

she inwardly groaned, but hunted traitors can't be chosers. "Gonna miss you," she whispered to the horse as she stepped back onto the bank and grimaced because, man, the leaves were popping loud like firecrackers, they were so dry.

Dry.

Warn the others.

She grabbed her pack and some food and a canteen off Ghost and dropped it all near the water pipe. She quickly climbed part way up the hill, making sure to stay out of sight of the Faceless enjoying their feast, and gathered as many twigs and dry leaves as she could and piled them near the base of a dead tree. Striking her tinder until there was a spark, she touched it to the pile and blew and blew until there was smoke and a little flame and she applied it to a couple of other leaf piles and the fire got going and so did she.

Sliding back down, she reached the now alarmed horse. "Go," she whispered and slapped it hard on the rump and the horse, snorting at the growing smell of smoke, bolted along the base of the hill and disappeared into the brush. Please be okay, she prayed.

She grabbed her equipment and secured it and pulled herself into the pipe and crouch-crawled along. Nasty in here, and she was suddenly worried about snakes or foxes or something else equally noxious as she made her way underneath the highway. Took longer than she thought and was harder than she thought and she was gasping for air by the time she reached the end, having scraped her hands and knees raw on dirty surfaces that would probably give her lockjaw or something. Grasping the edge of the pipe, she peered out, wondering if the guards up there were still down at the cook stove eating their food.

No.

Shouts, lots of them, coming from the road but not directly overhead so no one directly above her. Yet. Stepping out gingerly, she flattened against the berm and peered upward. More shouts, growing louder, and she was dead but no, no, they seem far enough away. Nothing ventured, nothing gained, and she took about six steps out and turned, bold, ready to face whatever happened.

The smoke against the sky, quite a bit of it, grew thicker and more volatile as she watched and she almost gave out a whoop of joy because, Holy Hannah, you talk about a smoke signal! The shouting Faceless ran up the other side of the road to see what was going on. While their attention was so misdirected, and before the helicopters came back to see what the fuss was about, let's remove ourselves from the immediate vicinity.

She ran up the stream until she was swallowed by the woods.

3.3

The Season of Thanks

"Don't move," someone said quietly as something hard shoved into the back of her head, probably by the same someone speaking quietly.

"I couldn't if I wanted to," Cass muttered with the last of her strength. She didn't have enough to turn her head out of the mud and see who was shoving what into her skull. Wouldn't do any good because the Faceless wore masks and who else could it be?

"Well, that'll save me the trouble of shooting you and then having to explain it to my Dad," the voice, that of a young man, said cheerily while the object remained steadily against her head.

Explain it to your Dad?

Despite her desire to simply lay here for the rest of her life, which, given the threat just made, was probably measured in minutes, Cass summoned the lost strength and turned her head and rubbed mud out of her eyes until she could squint enough to make him out. Not Faceless; at least, he wasn't wearing the black mask, nor anything else resembling a uniform: old jeans and a plaid shirt with a hunter's vest covering it, no hat unless she counted the mop of black curls crowning his fresh blue-eyed face grinning at her over the barrel of a bolt-action rifle.

"Who's your Dad?" she asked, hoping to satisfy her curiosity before she died.

"Who's yours?" he challenged, still cheerful but still ready to blow her brains out.

"Homer Dinwiddie," she said and watched the electric change in the kid's face.

"Oh my God!" he said as the barrel withdrew and the young man stooped down and hoisted her up by her shoulders, so he was pretty strong, too, and not bad looking and he said, "Cass! I didn't recognize you! My Dad's Beau Armee! I'm Junior!"

"Didn't recognize you, either," she whispered, "You've grown a bit." And she passed out.

"Here, drink this," someone said and shoved a bottle against her lips and she almost died because it was popskull and the fumes alone could peel flesh at fifty feet and she choked and cried and knocked it away and yelped, "Good God!" to a round of general, appreciative laughter.

She sat up, instantly regretting it because of the dizziness and she would have lain down again but somebody had to pay for that prank and her vision was blurry, so she rubbed her eyes while demanding, "Who's the wise guy?"

"I am!" said a familiarly cheerful voice and she followed it through the filmy afternoon sunlight ... oh, it was filmy because some gauze curtains were covering a couple of windows cut into the side of a metal building ... and was suddenly having double vision. There was Junior Armee sitting on a stool grinning at her next to Junior Armee sitting on a trunk grinning at her ... wait, the Junior on the trunk was an older version.

Older version held the popskull bottle in one hand while sticking out the other hand in greeting, "Hi, Cass, remember me? I'm Beau. My son," a nod at younger version, "dragged you in here and, well, welcome!" And he offered the bottle.

"No thanks," she said, shuddering. "I don't want to pass out. Again."

Beau chuckled appreciatively and took his own swig and offered it to Junior who matched his swig and they both looked at each other in mutual appreciation and gave mutual burps.

"That's disgusting!" she said amid their laughter and couldn't help laughing herself and looked down at herself and noted she was in completely different clothes. "Hey!" she yelled. "Who changed me?" And she looked accusingly at Junior.

"I did, honey," said a husky woman's voice as a cold cloth suddenly materialized against her brow. Startled, she looked into the blazing blue eyes of a big blonde woman with way too much hair and bones and strength and personality. "So don't you fret. These two heathens," a flick of the cloth at the men, "didn't see nothin'. Just your Mom and I did." And she nodded behind Cass.

Cass spun through the thick blankets on the cot and saw Mom sitting on another cot next to her. "Mom!" she cried and leaped into her arms.

"It's all right, it's all right," Mom soothed and stroked her hair.

"Everything's going to be okay," added Dad and she looked up and he was standing over them and there was a group hug and Cass couldn't help it, she began to cry. Such a girl thing to do and she was instantly mad at herself but the look in Mom's eyes made her not care. "I thought you guys were dead," she sobbed.

"Did you set the fire?" Dad asked and she nodded. He patted her on the shoulder. "That saved us."

"Say'd a bunch uh us," a grouchy, old timer voice added and Cass looked up to see the sourest old man in the universe, his face all sucked into itself and crowned by the baldest head in the universe. "Squint!" she squealed and jumped into his arms because he was gruff and cantankerous and she loved him.

"Now, now, little girl!" he protested but took her in and hugged her and called her honey and darling and others, including Price, stood at the end of the cot. "You did real good," Uncle P pronounced, "That fire not only warned us all but masked us from the helicopters, too. Far as we know, they're still up there trying to find us." He dropped a hand on her shoulder. "You bought us some time," and she couldn't help feeling proud.

"Are you okay?" Mom, being Mom, was hovering. "Are you hurt?"

She shook her head. "No. Tired. Hungry. And thirsty. But," she added quickly pointing at the bottle Beau still held, "not for that."

"Ha!" the husky blonde, who had to be Sally, chortled and pointed at a double door at the end of the metal building, "Then come on out, all a ya's, 'cause dinner's ready and we got lots to eat and talk about." And she spun and stomped out, followed by her husband and son and the rest of them, Cass folding into the group.

The door opened onto a big courtyard surrounded by large trees that provided a massive screen. Here and there were large piles of metal that took Cass a few minutes to recognize as old trucks with trailers, the kind that used to run up and down the old interstates. The trucks served as barricades around several farm tables set in the middle of the courtyard brightly lit by the afternoon sun. Sitting at and around the tables was an army.

Cass stopped, somewhat surprised. A hundred, two hundred people at a minimum, all of them armed, most with the traditional bows and swords and clubs, but lots of others were carrying guns, which was dangerous. At least, that's what she'd always been told. Get caught with a gun and you and your entire family were instantly wiped out.

Given recent events, was that any longer a consideration?

The tables were piled high with food, lots of food, far more than Cass had ever seen in any one location, save for the breakfast she'd had with Mom and Dad and Little John … when? "How long was I out?" she asked Mom, who was walking beside her.

"Overnight," Mom said as she took her elbow and guided her to one of the farther tables that still had some empty spaces. So, let's figure this out … Junior found her in the afternoon after the night she had spent running along the Buffalo River until reaching the Lexington Road and then southeast to the Raines Tavern roads … so, two days since that breakfast. Which explained why she was starving. Which was why the offerings on the table now commanded her attention.

Because, wow. Wow. The meat alone, piled high and sizzling and replenished by guys running platters of it from big iron cookers ringing the picnic area: venison, wild pig, chicken and other fowls, but, unbelievably, steak and hamburgers, too. Tomatoes, sliced and piled high, along with steaming buckets of corn and greens and … mashed potatoes? Her jaw dropped. Where in the devil did they get fresh vegetables this late in the season? Look, even potato salad! "Where'd you get the mayonnaise?" she asked with wonder.

Mom smiled but said nothing and pushed her into a seat flanked by Little John and Dad. Little John immediately slapped a plate overflowing with everything, including the much-admired potato salad, in front of her then slapped her on the back with his ham hands, almost killing her. "Good to see you again, kid!" he bellowed as he fell to a whole turkey leg. "Thanks," she said, trying to get her breath back, and then did her own falling to.

Oh my God, what a feast.

She demolished the potato salad in seconds and the half chicken and the steak – steak! – and went to a second plate with less meat this time but more potato salad and as many green things she could get on there, including spinach and chard and there were pumpkins – pumpkins! – candied and in pies and whole turkeys with drumsticks and more and more was brought and someone down in the middle began singing:

Praise Him from Whom All Blessings Flow
Praise Him All Creatures Here Below

which others here and there echoed. It was an odd song, different from the ones Mom sang about living some vida loca and a mambo number five. Dreadful stuff, that, even though Mom insisted those were the best songs before the Event ... which sometimes made Cass grateful for the Event. She preferred Dad's music, when he broke out his banjo and sang what he said were old folk songs about things blowing in the wind and where all the flowers had gone. "What's that they're singing?" she asked Little John around a mouthful of candied yams.

"A hymn," he said around his own mouthful.

"Him who?"

Little John choked a laugh. "No. Hymn: H-Y-M-N. A song about God."

God? Cass was familiar with the concept but God was not a major subject of discussion in the house. She listened to the hymn, which didn't catch on although a few others kept it going, and looked at all the food and the people gathered to enjoy it, and asked, "Is this Thanksgiving?"

Dad, next to her, shrugged and said, "Might as well be," and went back to his deer meat.

Again, Thanksgiving was not a subject thoroughly

discussed in their household but Mom and Dad would sometimes reminisce about family gatherings with real grandparents and real cousins at real farm houses set in sylvan glades but Mom was not that enthusiastic about those memories or the holiday, a proscribed one, because of what came after. Still, Cass was drawn to the concept and decided that this, right now, was the actual holiday.

She looked around. She knew most of the people here, or, at least, had seen them once or twice in her life. Those at her table were part of Dad's group, from the outliers who did shadowy things in distant places like Clifton Forge (where Dad said he had first formed the gang) to the more immediates like Little John and his pals. The next table over was Price's gang, the ones in charge of all the other gangs, and Cass exchanged waves with Sweet Pea, Price's administrator or secretary or whatever title one chose, but she was most definitely the Keeper of the Secrets. Sweet Pea was cheerful and charming and Cass figured that's why she had the nickname. But she was also quite deadly, so she could just as easily have been called Poison Ivy. One more table over was Squint and his boisterous, mountain-man gang that ran things all the way from far-off Luisa to the borders of the Armee's territory. She blew Squint a kiss and, not only got one from him in return, but from a couple of his leering lieutenants, too, and she stuck out her tongue at them and deliberately turned around so she wouldn't hear them laughing and faced the Armee's and immediately caught the eye of Junior who saluted her with a glass of (no doubt) popskull, and she felt all warm at that.

She looked up at golden sunlight filtering through the protective trees and it was a warmer day than it should be, given how late in the year it was, or maybe it was all the barbecue pits driving off the chill, and the companionship and the joviality and this … was family. Family.

"Where's Slickie?" she asked, suddenly.

"Due back any day," Mom responded but she could not keep the worry out of her voice and Cass frowned and was about to press for more details when a ringing sound brought her up short. She looked around.

Price stood under the limb of an oak tree that still had its leaves, a metal triangle suspended from it and some guy clanging it with a spoon. "All right," Price said, when everyone had turned to him, "we've got a few things to discuss while you're finishing up your meals." He nodded at the ringer who stopped, thank God, guy was giving her a headache, and Price stepped to a middle location where everyone could see him and waited for the last of the hubbub to die down.

"First, let's all thank the Armees and Squint and F for Freddie," here a goofy looking guy with a deliberately greased shock of hair formed over his forehead like a ship's prow, turned from one of the pits and waved, "for putting on this fine send-off feast."

"Send-off?" Cass asked Mom as the crowd, some of them getting to their feet, stood and cheered and made good natured insults that F for Freddie and the others returned good-naturedly.

"Wait," Mom shushed her and Cass made an exasperated sound but complied.

Price seemed to hear her question. "And it IS our big send-off." He paused, looking grim to match the sudden mood change. "Y'all know what's going on," he resumed, "Y'all know how much I wanted to keep us out of this war, but I can't." His eyes caught hers for a moment and she felt some satisfaction, although it was nothing to crow about. "War is upon us."

The crowd went from grim to worried and there wasn't a sound, not even the clink of silverware, as everyone waited for him. Price looked down at the ground, sadly shaking his head. "A lot of you have been in wars. You know what this will be like." Serious murmurs of agreement from the older ones. "And that's why we're all here now, not as separate gangs and groups loosely working together for our mutual benefit," some sardonic chuckle at that, especially from Squint's group, "but as a fighting force. To defend what's ours." Dramatic pause. "An army."

Cass could not help goosebumps at that … cut short by a very loud, very obvious snort of derision from some table she could not see. "An army?" the snorter cackled, to gasps from some, "More like a squad."

Price had turned in the direction of the snort. "Gotta start somewhere, Rodger."

Ah. Rodger. Must be Rodger Dodger, the guy working the Lynchburg area along with that woman, Inez something. Dad didn't like Rodger very much even though he was real good at siphoning off cadre supplies.

"Well," Rodger Dodger said as he stood up where Cass could see him now, affable and smiling and everyone's friend. Alarm bells sounded in her head. "I count," Roger Dodger made exaggerated counting motions with his finger, "little less than two hundred of us. Some of them kids. To take on the cadres? The troopers? The Directorate?" and he cocked a ridiculing smile at Price.

"Don't forget the Faceless," Price added mildly and a shock wave ran through the clearing, wiping Rodger Dodger's smile off his face. "Yes," Price said to the rest of the gathering, "the Faceless. They're here, as some of you know. And after us."

Rodger Dodger glowered. "After you, you mean."

Price shrugged. "Me. You. All of us. That's what happens in war."

Rodger Dodger threw up his hands. "Great. So we've

got *them* to contend with, too. How do you propose we do this?"

A half-smile formed on Price's face. "The way we've always done, RD. By being smarter than them." That earned him a rousing cheer from practically all the tables except Rodger Dodger's and the one next to it, where a very unhappy little Spanish-looking woman sat. Must be Inez.

Rodger Dodger would not be cowed. "Even greater!" And he raised two hands clasped together like a boxing champion. "Yay, us! So we'll march out there with our weapons," here he flourished a bowie knife, "cheek to cheek and asshole to asshole with our bows and arrows and spears and clubs and get mowed down." That sobered the crowd and Rodger Dodger gave Price an exaggerated stare. "They've got helicopters, too, so I'm hearing."

"Yep!" Price said jovially, "They sure do. You'd think there wouldn't be enough pilots and mechanics still left alive to man them, but, apparently, there are. But, that's okay," he assured the increasingly concerned crowd, "we've got countermeasures. Like RPGs." A wave of surprise ran through the crowd, including Cass, because even she knew what those were. "LAW rockets." She wasn't sure what those were but it had the word "rockets" in it, so must be good. "M-60s. M4s. Grenades. And all the ammunition we need."

By this time, there was a general roar of confusion as the gangs turned and looked at each other in amazement and Dad leaned into Mom and said, "And the artillery. Don't forget that," and they winked at each other.

Cass zeroed on them. "What? What?" but they turned back to Price and a skeptical Rodger Dodger. "Yeah?" he shouted over the crowd. "Where's all that?"

"Nearby," Price said and he turned and nodded to someone behind Cass. She, like everyone else in the clearing, turned to follow the nod and saw a craggy boot of a leather-faced old guy, a *real* old guy, someone who had to be an adult before the Event, and she knew immediately who he was: Grampop Armee. And she knew immediately everything was going to be all right.

"All y'all shut up!" Grampop bellowed in a parade ground voice. He'd been Airborne and fought in Vietnam, which Cass understood to mean he was legendary, and tough and kind and merciless and gracious and the guy you wanted on your side, supposedly the guy who taught his son Beau and friends how to *be* a gang and who now lived like a hermit somewhere on Brier's Creek. "And line yerselves up by gang!" Grampop bellowed louder, if that was possible, "'cause y'all are coming with me. Now!"

At that, chairs overturned and plates fell off tables as people stumbled all over themselves to form chaotic little squares of shuffling, roiling scrums next to their respective areas. Grampop sneered and yelled and cursed and walked to a little trail off to the right of the clearing. "Where we going?" Rodger Dodger's voice above the fray.

"To arm up!" Grampop yelled back and stepped off.

The army followed.

3.4

The Season of Betrayal

"Where. Are. We. Going?" Cass puffed. She was regretting the three plates of food now.

"I. Don't. Know," Mom puffed back, probably filled with similar regrets because this trek through the hills behind Raines Tavern felt like a death march as the woods closed and thorn bushes and ivy, the only things that seemed to thrive in winter, tore at them. With no discernible trail, Cass could not figure out how Grampop, way up there at the top of the parade, had any idea where he was going. Maybe the old coot had finally snapped and they were *really* on a death march. But Price was up there, too, looking confident, and Dad marched along like he had a goal, as did everyone else that she could see up and down the line, so bear it.

She had much to bear. Almost immediately after queuing into the woods, they came to the banks of a little creek which Cass figured was Brier's. Should be renamed Briar's, she had joked to herself as thorn bushes tried to disrobe her. But, after about thirty minutes of slogging along the swampy creek side, she was no longer in a joking mood because of the welts along her exposed arms and face from the branches whipped back at her by the careless people immediately in front, Mom. Another thirty minutes and she was growing concerned because it was getting dark. The sun touched the tops of distant trees that became more detailed as the parade hit rise after rise and skirted fields, actual fields, which indicated agriculture, which indicated people and their cadres, and she was nervous as well as concerned because how could this motley group go unnoticed? She kept glancing upward for helicopters.

But apparently she was the only one so concerned because they kept moving, in a somewhat festive mood, although many of the marchers looked like they, too, regretted the big meal, especially the ones who'd overindulged the popskull. A couple of times, she'd craned ahead hoping to see if Junior was seriously affected, but she couldn't spot him. Dad had once told her about the previous civil war between pretty much all the people who lived in Virginia and all the ones who lived in Pennsylvania and there had been hijinks and hilarity when the war first got started because both sides believed they would defeat the other in a matter of hours. The Virginians and the Pennsylvanians had to fight each other with one-shot rifles and hand-to-hand, so how could they figure it would be over in a day? Took more than a day simply to *reach* each other, for goodness' sake. With the weapons available now, the helicopters and the machine guns, how much longer would *this* war go on and how many of these jovial people would survive it? She could now appreciate Price's hesitance, although she couldn't understand his reluctance to back up a friend.

Maybe they were getting helicopters and machine guns, too.

But, she doubted it. If they were walking up the side of a boggy creek to arm up, then it was probably with a better class of spears or longbows. There were no forges up here, no factories. There were no forges or factories anywhere, for that matter, except in exclusive State enclaves into which the State had managed to throw the few people left who had mechanical skills or the knack to learn them, and from which the steam cars and electricity mills came. But those were poor substitutes for the real things, the sleek cars of Mustang and Pontiac and the big transport trucks that carried ice cream – ice cream! – for thousands of miles at two or three hundred miles per hour. Dad had said they'd even been to the moon, but Cass didn't buy that. If that was so, why wasn't someone up there signaling them nightly?

So where'd the Faceless helicopters come from, then?

That, she couldn't figure out, but from what everyone else was saying, they were old models that some person, or persons, still knew how to fly. Scary, on the one hand, that someone could still fly them, but encouraging, on the other, because there couldn't be that many left. So the chances of them getting rocketed along this path were pretty slim, unless the two helicopters that had chased them from the cabin stumbled across the marchers about now. It wouldn't matter then if those were the last two helicopters on earth; they were all dead.

She looked up for the dozenth time and scanned for aerial attack, and noticed the head of the column had made a right turn off the creek and filed into an open field. So, they'd arrived at wherever they were headed, huh? Or were they beginning another phase of this death march? Nope, must be their destination because the head of the column had bunched around a set of low bluffs lined by trees.

It took about twenty minutes for her part of the parade to reach the glob of people and she had to spread out along the sides until she could see. The glob formed a semicircle around Price and Grampop who stood in front of the bluffs, which looked like nothing more than a sudden rise of clay and limestone out of the otherwise flat ground. The buzz grew along the lines of "Now what?"

and "What are we doing here?" which Grampop let go for a few minutes until he cut it off with, "I need five strong people from each group!"

Uh oh, a call for volunteers, which guaranteed an almost simultaneous step backward by the whole crowd, because if there was one class of people who never volunteered, it was housebreakers and smugglers. But they weren't being asked to storm a hill or take a castle or something and curiosity was rampant and, slowly, a trickle at a time, some big guys, and some big women, and some of both not so big, filtered forward. Cass saw Sally and Beau step up with enthusiasm, which indicated they knew what this was about. That made sense because Grampop was their Grampop, or Dad, or something, and Junior stepped forward, too, and that was all she needed and she almost beat Little John to the line. She looked back and saw Mom smiling at her while glancing at Junior a little way ahead and her ears flamed. Couldn't get anything past Mom.

Grampop looked them over, his gaze lingering on Junior and they beamed at each other, and then he pointed at some brush and fallen logs jammed up against the bluffs and said, "Move those."

Oh no, physical labor, and the group let out a collective groan but they had stepped forward so, let's do this. Cass was smart enough to stay more to the back of the big guys who got to the pile first but still had to pull some stuff and stack it off to the side at Grampop's direction. She did manage to work herself next to Junior and shared some branch hauling with him, getting an appraising look from him that made her heart beat a little faster.

You strumpet.

She laughed inwardly at that word, one of Dad's fun ones, but managed to keep next to Junior as Grampop shooed them all irritably out of the way and approached what looked like a long canvas drop of some kind suspended from the top of the bluff. It was the color of clay and limestone and very hard to spot, especially with this light, and Cass realized this was clever camouflage. Hiding what?

With a flourish, Grampop pulled one end of the canvas and walked it back until it folded in half and she could see what it hid: a cave. Not a real one; it looked too smooth and she figured it had been dug into the bluffs by somebody, probably Grampop and the broadly grinning Price standing behind him. "Get back," Grampop ordered as he pulled a torch out of some recess and used his tinder to light it. From its light, Cass could see that the cave went back quite a ways, smooth walls and ceiling, although the floor looked muddy.

"All right!" Grampa waved the torch at the volunteers. "We're going in there single file!" And he stooped, torch and all, and headed down the passage, immediately swallowed up, only the torch light showing his location.

Looking at each other and back at the now very interested mob, the twenty or so of them shrugged and lined up and Cass made sure she was behind Junior. "What's in there?" she whispered.

"You'll see!" he grinned and went on.

Yep, homemade cave because, other than the annoyingly muddy floor, it was easy going and there were no bats, thank God. It was a straight line, too, because the torch was visible ahead of them and Cass kept pace, enjoying the incidental (and deliberate) contact she made with Junior's back. He seemed to be enjoying it, too. After about ten minutes of this touchy-feely game, the torch light ahead suddenly flared and expanded and she crossed a threshold into a large clay chamber that Grampop walked around, lighting torches stuck in the walls until it was fairly bright in there, revealing …

Crates, stacks and stacks of them. Some were very long, others short, and all covered with a tarp of one kind or another. Some of the tarps had fallen off and she could see stenciling here and there: long strings of numbers and letters with "Lot Number" followed by additional numbers and words. Grenade, Fragmentation; Grenade, Smoke (Red); Rifle, M14; Ammunition …

"My God," she whispered, awestruck.

"Yeah!" Junior giggled, "Isn't this great?" and she almost made some snide comment about boys and toys but this was … this was …

… a miracle.

"Start haulin'," Grampop ordered.

Given the configuration of the room, only two of them at a time could pull one of the heavy crates off the stack and struggle with it down the tunnel. She made sure her partner was Junior but she still had a hard time with each crate, especially the ones marked "Ammunition" which, although shorter, were a lot heavier, and Junior wasn't that much more help because he wasn't Little John who, apparently, could haul a crate by himself.

Junior and she bumped along, catching each other's shins every once in a while and turning into enemies by the time they exited the cave, where they met Price directing the chain gang to stack the crates depending on size: the longer ones to the left, the shorter ones to the right. Then, back again for the next load. Back and forth drop a crate, back and forth drop a crate, bumping and getting into other haulers' ways and, after what had to be an hour, Grampop came down the tunnel as they were going back for their four thousandth crate and pushed them out. "Finally!" she groused and the mean look from Junior confirmed he shared that sentiment.

Guess their love affair was over. Before it even got off

the ground.

Irritably, she located Mom more or less at the same spot as before and flounced over, to Mom's amusement, all set to kick Mom if she said anything but superseded by Price yelling, "Line up!" Price gestured toward the long crates and she shuffled over with everyone else who formed a gaggle there. Price handed out crowbars to the people at the front and she faded back because she had done enough work, thank you very much. "Open 'em up!" Price ordered, followed by movement and the sound of wood and nails pried open and gasps of admiration, and now she wished she had stayed up front.

"This is how this is going to work!" Price shouted at the scrum surging forward for a better look, effectively halting the rush as more light flooded the area. Cass glimpsed Grampop walking around lighting torches, a good idea because the sun was now on the horizon, visible through the distant tree line at the creek. "You grab yourself a weapon, whatever takes your fancy, however many you want ... don't worry, there's plenty," apparently a response to a question, "and then go over to the other side," a point off to the left, "and get the ammunition for it. Make sure you get the *right* ammunition," he added to some general laughter and Cass frowned. How would you know?

In the ensuing shoving, someone stepped on her ankle. "Ow!" she said to the guy rushing past her and he turned and smirked and kept going, following right behind Rodger Dodger, intent on making sure he was first and got the best choice, the bastard. That guy and his gang were all over the boxes grabbing whatever before Cass even got to look inside the first set.

Wow.

There were long rifles, like the kind she had seen in pictures of US soldiers, and shorter ones and very long tubes with triggers slung below them and several crates marked "Kalashnikov" that were very popular because everyone grabbed those but they looked heavy and Cass searched for smaller –and lighter – weapons.

She came across one box that had really cute guns in them that could almost be pistols but they looked more substantial than that. She picked one up. "What's this?" she asked a guy at the next box over, one of Price's guys, Carter something, a good friend of the Winthrop's, if she remembered him correctly. He looked up. "An MP5 9 millimeter," Carter said.

Cass was impressed by his knowledge, but had to ask, "How do you know?"

Carter shrugged. "That's what it says on the box." He pointed at the cover leaning against it.

She immediately felt stupid and lowered her estimation of the guy's intelligence and his knowledge of women and clucked her annoyance but she liked the little MP5 so she grabbed it and saw canvas containers in one corner of the crate and she grabbed one and unsnapped the metal button covering it and found three long things in it with springs in the middle. Oh, yeah, she'd seen pictures of these. They were called 'magazines' and the bullets went in there and then got slapped into the rifle with great violence, if what she'd seen was correct. She examined the MP5 and saw an opening that appeared to be the right size for the magazines so she grabbed a couple more of the canvases and, feeling pretty smug, headed toward the ammo crates. On the way, she spotted a box filled with pistols, "Glock 9mm," written on it and she grabbed one because it was small and lethal looking and she made sure to grab some matching magazines out of that same box.

"Perfect!" a familiar voice crowed and she turned to receive accolades and an apology for earlier behavior from Junior but his back was turned to her and his praise was for a long rifle, which had a scope and a bolt on the side, that he was holding aloft. Grampop, standing a little ways away, nodded in approval. "One shot, one kill," Grampop said.

Hmpf.

She tossed her head and weaved her way through the next set of crates and stopped short because these were filled with grenades and her eyes rounded. Oh no, don't want any of these, very dangerous, but Little John was standing there and he noticed her hesitation. "Take these," he said, handing her two. "In fact, take a lot more." And he began shoveling grenades at her.

"I don't want them!" she protested.

"Yes, you do!" he insisted.

"They're too heavy!" more protest but he ignored that and stuffed them in her coat pockets and, when she stepped out of his reach, threw a canvas belt at her with a lot of pockets. "Use that!" he barked. "Put your clips in there, too."

She was puzzled. "Clips?"

He wagged a finger at the magazines. "Those."

"I thought these were called magazines."

"Clips, magazines, whatever, just put them in the holders. You'll thank me later." And he went back to collecting grenades.

She slipped on the belt and had to admit it distributed the weight of grenade and clip ... er, magazine ... better but she sure wasn't going to admit that. It even had a little hook for the MP5 and, when she attached it, had to admit, she looked like a badass.

Now, if she only knew how to use this stuff.

"Over here, all y'all!"

Cass looked up. Grampop was standing in front of the cave and making big gestures at the milling groups of people. She walked over and stood with a group of about twenty, all carrying rifles and some of the long tubes.

"Quick OJT on your rifles!" he announced and, while Cass was trying to puzzle out those letters, Grampop held up an M16. "This is a rifle, not a gun. One is for shooting, one is for fun!" and he grinned evilly and Cass was left even more bewildered as Grampop held up one of the magazines.

"Y'all should have at least one of these. It's a magazine, not a clip. Summa y'all have them old M1s. Good rifles, but they have clips and they load different and I'll show ya after I show these."

He dumped some bullets into his hand and showed everyone how to put them in the magazine, then showed them the receptacle on his rifle. "Front of the bullet goes to the front of the rifle. You want the bullet going out this end." He tapped the barrel. "Make sure the magazine is seated. This is the charging handle. You pull it back, let it go, and you're in business. This is the selector." A point of a finger. "Keep it on safe until you want to shoot someone, then select … get it? ... semi- or full-automatic. I recommend semi until you get a better feel. All right?"

He looked around with satisfaction and Cass realized that was all the training she was going to get.

"You might want to get some bullets for that thing," Grampop said, grinning at her. "Nine millimeter, over there. You clip people, gather round," and he turned away.

Cass wandered around the ammo boxes until she found a crate marked "9mm" and then took a few boxes of it, trying to keep her weight balanced but, boy, all this was getting heavy. How'd soldiers march miles and miles weighed down with all this stuff and food and water and a tent and shovel and clothes? War wasn't dangerous; it was exhausting.

She took out some rounds and fooled with a magazine

until she figured out how they went in and then slapped the magazine into the MP5 and now where's that charger handle?

A hand suddenly covered the top of the gun ... er, rifle ... and firmly pushed the barrel down. "Whoa there, Cass," said a cheerful Junior, "make sure that's on safe before you shoot somebody!"

"What?" she asked, genuinely puzzled, so he showed her the switch on the side with the many-bullets logo and the three-bullets one and the no-bullets, then showed her the slap handle on the top, different from the pull-back charge handle that Grampop had demonstrated and he told her never point the gun ... machine gun, not a rifle ... at anyone unless she intended to shred them. "Now, here's something cool." And he showed her a fold-out stock attached to the side of it.

"How do you know all this?" she asked, forgetting that she was mad at him.

"Grampop!" he said brightly.

"So you've known about this stash all along?"

"Yep!" More brightness. "Came out here once a month and cleaned them with him."

Now that was cool. "What's that?" she asked, pointing at his rifle ... a real rifle ... slung from his shoulder,

He whipped it off his shoulder and wrapped the sling around his arm and had the rifle up and pointing at the sky in about a half second. "The M24," he said with love in his voice. "War tested, mother approved." And he unwrapped and re-slung and smiled at her and she, definitely, was no longer mad.

"Here," he said, pulling a grenade out of his coat pocket, "Let me show you how these work." He turned and headed back to where Grampop was teaching some guys how to use some tube thing that he called an M72. "Gramps!" Junior called, hefting the grenade, "Can I demonstrate?"

"Be my guest," Grampop said and waved everyone away.

Still grinning, Junior walked past Grampop, showed everyone the grenade, pulled what looked like a pin on the handle, then pulled a ring on the side and flung the grenade over the bluffs into the tree and dropped to his stomach. "Get down!" he yelled which was unnecessary because, when everyone saw him hit the ground, they followed suit, or at least crouched down, which was Cass's response. Cass instinctively covered her ears, but that wasn't enough to completely drown out the *crack!* of the exploding grenade, the sharp flash of light, and tree limbs spiraling into the air and out of sight.

And the cheers.

She stood up and applauded along with everyone else as Grampop and Junior beamed at each other and she was downright in love.

"Having fun?" a voice called out over the laughter, and it was an accusing voice. Everyone, suddenly quiet, turned and there was Price, who stood off to the right of Grampop, a black box next to him. "Enjoying yourselves?" Price repeated and they all caught the underlying tone and looked at each other sheepishly.

"I know, I know," Price said, "it's all fun and games until someone loses an eye. Or, in this case, when we lose half of you," a wave at the now silent crowd, "the very first time we engage the Directorate troops. Because, they know what they're doing. We'll learn as we go along. And it'll be painful. We'll have to make up losses, Quite a few losses." He slapped the box. "With this." And he reached into the crate and pulled out a gold bar.

Gasps of admiration and wonder. A gold bar, an actual gold bar. Which meant …

"Yep," Price said, hefting the obviously heavy bar in

one hand. "This is the much-rumored, half-legendary Farmville gold. Or, at least, what's left of it. I won't tell you how I got it, but will say that it all started not too far from here, in New Market." A grim look crossed his face. "And a lot of trouble went into its acquisition and hiding. And a lot of it went to the acquisition and hiding of the weapons you now hold. And all that remains is three bars. Three. Out of ten. The gold built us. It made us family."

Price held the gold aloft. "So you're probably wondering why I'm showing you this. Simple: it's not about us getting rich. Never was. It was about survival. Y'all have your gangs and you do well smuggling and stealing and tweaking the State's nose, but that was so your kids could eat. So you could even have kids. So you could be free." Price held the bar out to them. "And with this, we'll remain free ..."

"Wanna bet?" a voice called out from the back, along with the new metallic sound of lots of bolts on lots of rifles being released. Confused, Cass and everybody else turned around to see what was going on.

Rodger Dodger.

He and his gang, along with Inez's gang, had ringed the rest of the group and had their newly acquired weapons leveled at everyone. "What the heck?" said someone near the group and Rodger Dodger grinned at the voice. "What the heck!" he emphasized and moved the barrel of his rifle threateningly. "You move. You die."

Frozen, Cass watched with horror as several rifles rose in response and Inez's gang raised theirs and there was the sound of safeties being clicked and this was going to be a massacre, when Price yelled, "Stand down!" and his gang, those still with him, hesitated.

"So," Price said calmly, the gold bar still in his hand, "it WAS you." His glance flew over to Inez. "But you, Inez? Figured you were better than this."

"It's just business, Price," she snarled but Cass could see the wound in her eyes.

Price nodded, still calm. How could he be so calm? Cass was on the verge of panic. "That's right, business," Price agreed. "You did take a couple of runs at me when I first showed up, didn'ja? How'd that work out?"

Inez said nothing, her lips tightening. "Not well," Price reminded her, "so, instead of fighting me, you threw in. And now you throw in with this guy?" and he pointed a mocking finger at Rodger Dodger.

"Just give us the gold, Price," Inez said angrily and raised her machine gun as a hostile murmur ran through the crowd.

"You want it?" Price said and casually let it drop with a *clang*! back through the top of the box. "Come get it. But, I have to ask, how do you expect to get away?" He let his eyes run significantly over the growingly restless crowd.

Good question, Cass thought, because now she was full-on angry and she had a machine gun, too, and grenades and a pistol and if this is where the war starts, and it starts against our own people, traitors all, then so be it. Inez, thoroughly alarmed now because she could do the math and add up all the angry eyes facing her, turned to Rodger Dodger and hissed, "Thought you said this would be okay!"

Rodger smiled mildly at her. "Oh, it will be," he said and he was too calm, too sure of himself, and Cass's alarm rose again. Rodger looked across the crowd at Price, smiled broadly, and then held up some small black-looking plastic thing. He pressed it and there was an odd sound, a beep, and a light glowed on the device and he held it up high where everyone could see. "You're fucked!" he called across to Price.

Cass didn't know what to expect and, apparently,

neither did Inez, who looked at Rodger with confusion, and neither did Price, who ducked like he expected an explosion of some kind. Seemed reasonable, because who knows what a plastic beeping box will do? But, there was no explosion and Rodger laughed as Price stood back up. "Nothing that easy, Price, old boy," and he gestured behind him.

Where there was this sound ...

Everyone stared at the far tree line and fields and swamps leading back to Raines Tavern, dark and shadowed in the afterglow of an autumn sunset. A rumbling came from there, distant and disturbing because it was unfamiliar but not quite, not quite, because Cass had recently heard this sound before...

Trucks.

Lots of trucks.

She spun and looked at Junior with terror, a feeling he and everyone else reciprocated because they all, whether they had ever heard the sound a fleet of big trucks or not, realized what it was. Directorate trucks. Coming for them. Cass spun back and saw, just above the far horizon, just above the ridges, a couple of blinking lights, coming fast.

The helicopters.

"Mom!" Cass shrieked and there was pandemonium as others shrieked differing words in exactly the same way and people ran to and fro, chickens without heads, except for Rodger Dodger and his gang, all of whom had taken a couple of steps back and now trained their weapons not only on their former hostages but on Inez and her gang, too. "What are you doing?" she yelled at him.

"It's just business, girl," he said, loud enough that Cass could hear him over the chaos, and she watched as Inez almost fell down in her shock and Rodger Dodger threw his head back and laughed and laughed ...

… until a crossbow bolt suddenly burst out the front of his neck, blood and liquid spewing everywhere.

"*Urp!*" was all Rodger could say as his eyes almost blew out of his sockets as he clasped at the bolt and began the oddest dance trying to remove it. Two of his gang members on either side suddenly lurched as additional bolts smacked one in the back and the other high on the shoulder and they went down, and the rest of Rodger's gang whirled to confront whoever was attacking them and Inez and her gang took that opportunity to attack and the whole area exploded into gunfire and stabbing and clubbing and more bolts hit more targets and Cass saw Tat leap over a rock and envelop one of Rodger's gangsters, his knives slashing and cutting and she knew who'd fired the bolts.

"Slickie!" she screamed and jumped up where he could see her, wherever he was, and another gangster drawing a bead on her screamed as a bolt took him in the upper leg and she had the MP5 in her hand, like a giant pistol, and she slapped the charge handle and pulled the trigger but nothing happened and, oh, yeah, safety, and she clicked it to the many bullets.

And riddled the guy with many bullets.

The machine pistol tried to get away from her, rise right over the top of her head and flip her over and she had to wrestle it back down but the guy was a blood fountain and as parts of him flew off and he went down, shocked and dying. And Cass stood there, shocked, and leaned over and vomited because she had killed a man so easily, with no effort. Not like slapping someone silly with her trusty jodo sticks; no that was skill, but this was simply murder. Death came so easily with these guns.

Death came so easily.

Others were shooting, some the remaining members of Rodger Dodger's traitorous gang resolving their dispute with Inez's no-longer-a-traitor gang toe-to-toe and eviscerating each other with machine gun fire and eviscerating others behind and in front and then there was a line of red bullets ripping into them from the side and Cass looked and it was Tat, armed with a seized machine gun and he turned that spray of bullets on Inez's people, too, and death came easily.

She could not see Slickie but two more bolts *thwunked* into bodies to her right and left and she looked and saw that two of Inez's gang members had been ready to shoot her and they now writhed around Slickie's bolts.

"Run!" Tat screamed at her and changed magazines, shooting again, driving what was left of the traitor gangs and the not-so-traitor gangs away from her, the thrum of his rifle finishing off who was left ...

... as the thrum of helicopter blades grew louder.

She looked up. The blinking lights were higher in the sky but she could see the shape of the helicopters and they were lined up on her, drawing a bead on her, all their guns and rockets aimed right at her, and there was no place to run, Tat's urges to the contrary, because you cannot outrun a death that came so easily. A *whoosh* and she made fists and braced for the rockets to evaporate her, but the rocket was going the wrong way, over her head and streaking toward the helicopter on the left. She watched, fascinated, as the smoke exhaust with the tiny fire point in front met the helicopter head on and turned it into a fireball, white sparks and fireworks all over the sky and the fire helicopter spun on itself and crashed into the ground.

She turned around to where Grampop stood on top of the bluff as he tossed away a long tube-like thing with what looked like a basket on top of it, while Junior, standing next to him, had an identical long tube balanced on his shoulder and peered through what looked like a scope next to the basket thing. Some smoke and what looked like a spear leaped from the end of the tube and *whoosh*! fire and smoke and it was over her head and she turned to watch it as the smoke trail corkscrewed and zeroed on the remaining and now-frantically canting helicopter doing everything it could to avoid the little fire point but no luck and it collapsed in another fireball.

She watched as Grampop and Junior shook hands and jumped from the bluff, landing in the middle of a roiling group of people scrambling to grasp as many more weapons and boxes of ammunition as they could. She took a step their way to help when she was seized from behind and she screamed bringing the machine pistol around but Tat blocked her, and there was Slickie, grabbing her by the other shoulder and steering her through the crowds and bodies and shouting, "Run! Run!" and had pointed her back to the creek where a long line of people scattered and flowed and ran for their lives to the distant trees as Tat kept looking fearfully off to their left. She looked. Winks of light randomly from the far horizon and the buzzing of bees around her and she realized someone was shooting at them. The Directorate. Off their trucks and racing this way.

So she ran.

How they kept together she did not know but it was Tat and Slickie and Cass racing parallel to the oncoming Directorate for the creek, almost as if they were one person, the Tacassie, and they hit the swampy area next to the creek and leaped as one into the water and waded across and it was dark but someone was shooting fireworks so they could see well enough and they were up the next bank and in the middle of a corn field already stripped except for stalks that tripped her and tore at her arms but she stayed with the other two and there were Mom and Dad joining them and they ran.

They ran.

3.5

The Season of Flight

It was about seventy miles, give or take. Back in the old days, when there were cars and interstates and gas stations, it was about a two-hour trip. Why anyone back then would make such a trip, well, that's a question. Perhaps there were relatives to visit, some obscure antique store to patronize, or maybe simple curiosity about back roads and a Virginia rarely seen, but it wasn't a route normally taken.

Desperation made it one.

The running crowd pulled her along, good thing because she wasted energy and speed constantly turning around to see what was behind them. Not much, at least from what the murky twilight revealed but she did get flashes of battle going on back at the bluffs. She didn't think the Directorate had reached that far yet, so it had to be gang members intent on loot versus gang members intent on vengeance. How stupid, lingering in a well-lit area that drew the enemy – the real enemy – like murderous moths. She was too far away to see much detail, but the lacing of bright, sharp lines like lasers (what were lasers, anyway?) with the slight delay before the *bapbapbapbapbapbap*! of machine guns reached her ears told her all she needed to know: war was here.

War was here.

The relatively flat fields petered out quickly into thick woods and she was glad for that because the trees hid the hundred, hundred and fifty, people running madly away from the war behind them, the clink of metal weapons and ammo belts defining the size of this undisciplined mob linked by fear and the desire to get away, small pockets of mutual support chained together here and there to keep the group cohesive – Cass and her immediate family forming one link, ringed by their gang members mixed in with the Armee's and their cohorts to one side (relief to see Junior and Grampop, laden with more tubes, side by side), F for Freddie's gang in front and Squint and the mountain men leading, Uncle Price in the middle front and turning his head to consult with Squint as they ran. Glimpses of all these people were enough to reassure her, and she put her head down and became part of the fleeing herd.

They crossed a berm and all tumbled down its short length to a flat area that was once a road and here the group piled into each other as Uncle P and Squint held a hurried conference and there were arms pointing north and then Uncle P making hurried assignments: "You two! Take your groups either side of the road as flankers! You guys, spread those heavy weapons through the group and be ready to defend,"…things like that.

"We're rear guard!" Little John said as he grabbed her by the shoulders and whipped her around. "Gotta keep watch on everything behind us! If you see lights, hear trucks, you let us know!"

"It's Directorate, right?" she asked him, pulling hard on his coat lapel.

"And Faceless," he added, grimly, and turned and the group surged as she almost died right there in fright. Major Lawless was after them. He would find them. They could not escape. But she pulled herself out of it and surged along with the rest.

It was Tat and Slickie and her at the very rear and they ran with heads on a swivel, looking for the glimmer of truck lights or listening for the sounds of engines and shouts and bracing for the sweep of rifle fire taking them all in the back. There was no breath or time for talk and crying; only running. The quarter moon manifested as the twilight died and it was a cold, crisp autumn night, weeks from winter; the stars brightened and swept over them and they had enough light to see the old, old, road as a suggestion in the dark bounded by the woods and berm and further defined by persons running along it.

Within ten minutes, they all piled up again at another intersection, the asphalt long gone but two deeps ruts showed the passage of carts and horses in the years since cars died. Another quick conference between the leaders and they angled on a new heading with the same assignments and she watched and watched behind them, seeing nothing, but that did not matter. Death followed. The hours flew past as the road flew past, and the moon crept up to watch them.

After about thirty minutes of this, a stitch formed on her right side, a red hot knife stabbing into her stomach and cutting her air; her running became a stumble and she gasped with it. She was slowing but no, no, death followed and she cast terror glances behind as she limped-ran alongside her brother who, wordlessly, tucked a hand under her arm to act as a crutch. She gave him sideways grateful looks and more terror looks behind.

An hour, maybe two, and they all came to a screeching stop at a wood-lined lane, an ancient one, probably in exactly the same condition as it was during that war between Virginia and Pennsylvania a thousand years ago. Consternation swept through the group because this path was too beat up and rutted and trashed to be useful ... but the lane widened a few hundred yards on and emptied into a bigger road stretching in the moonlight off to the northwest, which appeared to be the direction they were going. The bigger road was a nicer road, still intact.

One trucks could use.

Cass didn't care. She collapsed or, more accurately, was lowered to the ground by Slickie, who was the one who actually collapsed as "Rest!" came down the line in whispers, followed by "No fires! No noise! Load your weapons but quietly. Drink!" A canteen or something was passed to her and she would have greedily drained the whole thing but Tat beside her looked in need so she took enough to kill the dryness and passed it on and sat, numb and gasping, until her breath came under control and the pang of the stitch subsided.

"Are you all right?" Mom, shaking her out of her stupor a year, a day, later, but it probably was just ten minutes or so.

"Mom, where are we?" she asked.

Mom gave her another canteen and this time she drank it all. "Not far from Sprouses Corner," Mom replied which was unhelpful because Cass did not know where that was.

"Where are we going?"

"Burnt Church." And Mom was gone.

Up, up, and the mob stepped carefully along the civil war path until they could see the better road, the death one. It would be suicide to go that way and they didn't. Well, sort of they didn't: they slipped onto a wide trail in the woods paralleling the nice road, the bases and frames of long-ago electric towers interspersed along the way, the metal skeletons of their wreckage fallen here and there – those not hauled away by scavengers – and that was good because the metal meant no trucks could come this way. But they could still ride the parallel road, glimpsed occasionally in the distance through the woods and fields, so this was dangerous still.

Their pace became a jog because speed was important, at least, speed enough to keep ahead of the trucks that were coming. Of course they were coming. The Faceless were tracking them. Lawless stood on knolls and his devil eyes pierced the dark and he saw their frantic prints in the mud and he pointed a clawed hand and the demons, the blank-faced demons, cackled and dropped their hound noses to the earth and followed. Followed.

The moon rose higher. The stars wheeled.

The metal skeleton trail emptied abruptly into a field and, in single file and crouched, they followed a wood line away from the moonlit road, a knife against their throat, and curved about a pleasant valley with no more trail but woods, thick and impenetrable and slowing them down. They could not go this way anymore. They had to use the knife-throat road.

"Run!"

And they did, on the road, a lumbering, limping run as best they could because they had no other choice, this was the way, this was the only open way, and the moon showed them and mocked them and death was following so they ran. Cass became a stitch, one sharp red hot pain from her ribs to the top of her head, her feet numb stumps and after an hour or a day or maybe a minute, she stopped. Because she could not go on.

She fumbled at the ammo belt and its heavy grenades and magazines and machine pistol because this was slowing her down and if she could get rid of it, she would fly. Fly, over the road and the woods and through the welcoming sky and back home, to Sweet Briar and the bed and books and comfort that awaited. "Come home," all of that whispered and she tugged at the belt.

A hand seized her hand. "C'mon, Cass," a voice in her ear. Dad.

"I can't, Daddy," she said back.

"Yes, you can," he countered and pulled her hand away and she looked at him to say Daddy she was just too tired and wanted to be a good girl and lay down right here and go to sleep and would you tell me a story Daddy, of ancient gods and heroes and do it in those weird, dead languages that you know but then she heard it …

… a rumbling.

It was not quite at the level of hearing. It was more underneath, a disturbance in the beauty and stillness of an autumn night, an intrusion, still a great distance behind her but if you lay down here and sleep, little girl, the demons will eat you.

She got up. She ran.

It was a race, then, between the flesh eaters behind and the safety of mountain and wood ahead. The moon watched, laughing and casting just enough light so that the demons could follow the helpless as they fled, and made bets with the cold stars. She listened to their banter and the passing of gold coins and souls between them as the bets followed the odds because there was no other way to go and the demons behind them knew it and they were faster in their chariots than the helpless were on their feet and it was inevitable but she ran anyway.

They all did.

Sometime well after midnight, when the stars had grown tired of watching and the moon had gone onto other matters and the only light was the pale gleam of the Milky Way, they came to a ghost town, one of the dead ones killed by Phase 2 and murder and war, the few intact buildings standing silently like old skulls, no lights, no sound, and, cautiously they filtered through, leaving ghosts and their pointing fingers behind. "Run fast!" "Fast!" almost a scream which was stupid in the silence because the demons could hear from miles away and it was a dead run on the road north into another ghost town and Cass did it because she would not be eaten and, suddenly, a sharp leaving of the road and a plunge down an embankment, half of them falling flat on their faces, Cass included, but without losing a step she was back on her feet and then behind some building and onto another trail of raised earth stitched with the iron bones of those old railroads, fabled and mythological, the fossils of their passing laid out in straight lines across the country and right beside another road – really a trail running through the woods – to their right. And they kept running fast, much more difficult now with the scrap metal rails and the remnants of cross ties grabbing at them and she did not know how many times she fell and got up fell and got up and how many times the road to their right disappeared from view only to reappear up ahead, a guide, a showing of the way. At some point that she could not remember, they left the railroad and cut to the right and were back on the road and their running turned into a march, a walk, grateful for it, grateful for it and, as the sky turned lighter and the dawn approached, they filed off the road to either side of a rickety bridge crossing a river and they all, all, fell down into a deep sleep. Somebody may have posted guards but she did not care.

"Cass," someone whispered, "wake up."

She did, but did not want to, because her dreams of home and fields and dancing in sunlight and butterflies, no worries, no fear, and who wanted to leave that? She opened her eyes and could see nothing because the sunlight blasted her vision and a headache blasted her head and waves of ache and exhaustion roared up her back and legs and paralyzed her and she did not want to get up or stand up or move for the next few years and she groaned. "Shush!" The someone took on Mom's frantic voice and Cass's vision gathered itself and it *was* Mom, squatted next to her in some high weeds, and looking off. Fearful. "We've got to go!"

Fearful.

Cass moved, her body screaming at her stupidity but survival instincts told it to knock it off and she got to her knees and reeled but Mom held her up. "Drink this, quickly," Mom's fearful whisper and Cass took the canteen and a big swallow that choked her but she suppressed it with tears down her cheeks and all the time Mom was looking off, the fear in her eyes. "Take these!" a couple of pills that she equally choked down. "Eat this!" Some bar of crap wrapped in paper that looked twenty years old and almost choking her and it was godawful but she felt a 'thank you!' rise from her stomach. "Let's go!"

She half-crawled, following Mom's feet through the tall grass and the bright cool sunlight and breeze, the fear contagious, keeping her quiet; movement around her, other trolls through the grass, and the way was easy despite the underbrush because it was a slope and they were on the banks of the river, a sluggish brown stream fairly wide and, as it turned out, hip deep with cold water and Cass looked curiously at the bridge next to them as she slogged through the current. Why not use that? Why get all wet and chilled and risk drowning? As she stepped through, doing her best not to trip on the slippery rocks, she saw knots of others emerge from the weeds and woods, some she recognized, like Slickie and Tat, and some she didn't, fearful looks on all their faces as they quietly plunged in, holding their weapons out of the water and perhaps she should do the same thing so she lifted her ammo belt high.

Made the other side and a climb up the bank that was painful and aching and why won't they let her sleep a few more hours, good God, what was it, mid-morning? They had been running all night and a girl needs her sleep ...

All hell broke loose.

Fire and explosions and death all at one moment and she screamed and ran up the bank, just ran, sure red hot bullets or explosions would rip her apart but nothing seemed to be coming her way; it was all across the river. "Run!" Mom and thousands of others screamed and she really did not have to be told that, thank you very much, and she pelted up the bank and over the crest and into the woods, risking one look back. She saw, for an instant, Price standing on the road on this side of the river frantically gesturing at somebody to his right and there, on a rise on the other side of the river, distant so she shouldn't know who it was but recognized him anyway: Major Lawless.

She ran.

Woods skirted an overgrown field and she plunged through the border line, hesitant about which way to go but Mom was behind her pushing her hard. "Run!" Mom screamed and Cass pumped her legs straight on, fear the best analgesic because all of her hurts and exhaustion were gone, gone ...

Armageddon.

A powerful hand slapped her in the back and she flew through the air and she was going to yell at Mom about pushing her so hard but Mom was right beside her flying through the same air and both of them slammed into the ground as the roar of the explosion overwhelmed them and something covered the sun. Mom was on her feet, dragging her up and they both careened into the woods but not before Cass looked back and saw a gigantic fire cloud filled with debris and bridge parts somersaulting through the air rising and rising above the river …

They'd blown up the bridge.

Relief flooded through her as debris rained down, threatening to crush her but she didn't care because someone had the intelligence to sever the road and prevent the demon hordes from using their trucks to chase them. Now, they were all equal, all on foot, and there was a chance.

A chance.

So she ran lightly, like a faun through the forest, avoiding the trips and traps of woods and brush and she could see the shadow figures of Mom and many others to her right and left and front also running lightly, the chance spurring them all and she could have burst out laughing but no, not appropriate, so she celebrated with springy step instead. Another one of those mythic railroad lines suddenly appeared and they all made for it because springy steps could fly over broken rail and crossbeam far easier than wood and branch and besides, they could see the pointer road, the one leading north, off to their right again so go this way. The track ran straight for a distance then curved to the left and crossed another old road and, without a signal, the runners collected in the middle of the intersection because they were now out of sight of the blown bridge and it was time to lick wounds.

Cass sat heavily in the middle of the two roads, comfortably so, because it was mostly sand and clay instead of hard asphalt, that material having dissolved in the snows and rains of the previous decades making the road fit only for foot and hoof and wooden wheel now. Not trucks. And she sighed contentedly and looked around at the rest of the running people, fewer of them than before. "Where's Junior?" she asked the nearby knots. "Where's Grampop?"

The people would not look at her but pressed lips and

bandaged cuts or wrapped sprains and took great gulps of water and ate the gaggy paper-wrapped bars under the bright, wonderful November day and it could have been a picnic but the air about them was somber. She stood, a bit unsteadily, and spun to look about the piles of people. She did not see Junior or Grampop. She did not see a lot of people, including Dad and panic rose in her heart until a figure stumbled out of the woods dragging a bag, followed by a couple of others and relief flooded through her because it was Dad and a member of Inez's gang and then Inez herself which gave Cass a start because hadn't she tried to kill them all a mere day ago? Frowning, she stepped to where Dad attended Price sitting on the ground and having a wound on his arm bandaged. "See this?" Price said, holding up the bloody arm to Dad. "Lawless himself did that with a sniper rifle."

"Doesn't seem to like you," Dad observed which drew a laugh from Price but a frown from Inez and Cass felt for her jodo sticks because what was she thinking– to betray them again?

"We should get going," Inez groused. "Won't take Lawless long to figure out another way across."

Price tacitly nodded, his manner cool, and Cass figured he didn't trust her, either. "Ten minutes," he said, "get people water and rations and medicine, then we go."

Dad turned at that moment and saw her and ran to her and hugged her like it was her birthday and Cass felt all warm and safe. For a moment. "Your Mom?" Dad said frantically. "Over there," Cass pointed and Dad moved that way but she grabbed at him. "Grampop? Junior?"

Dad shook his head. "They were at the bridge when it blew, but they scattered with the others and people are still making their way here. They'll catch up." But his words were hollow and furtive and she knew they were meant to comfort and something caught in her heart.

At that moment, Tat came up and took them to where Mom was dressing some cuts on Slickie's face and while Mom hugged Dad, Cass hugged her brother. "Thanks for having my back," she said.

He winced as Mom returned to dabbing his face with something. "You'd do the same for me."

"Dunno ..." and they were jostling and joking and even got a smile from Mom and then they were hoisting packs and belts and helping each other to their feet and Mom made her take two more of those pills – Tylenol, as it turned out, the cure for everything – and Cass had to admit she felt a little better, except the excitement was subsiding and the exhaustion was returning.

And there were fewer of them.

As they formed into a loose group, Slickie and Tat and she became the rearguard again and she kept looking back, not for the approaching demons, but for Junior and Grampop. Distant figures struggled through the woods to reach them, by their shape gang members of one kind or another, but no shape she recognized.

They turned north and they walked.

Late afternoon.

Clouds had formed and the breeze had turned colder and she shivered as they drew near the bridge over the James. More people along the way, not part of their group, farmers and their children, a couple of cadres fleeing at their approach and Price sent a few gang members at a time to break into the co-ops for supplies; they told the farmers what was happening and they silently gathered their children and wagons and set off in other directions. "Leaving a bunch of spies," Little John grumbled and Cass had to agree. The cadres, if not the farmers, would point out their direction of travel.

"They already know where we're going," Tat said, meaning the pursuing demons.

"Where are we going?" Cass asked because, heck, if the demons got to know, then so should she. Tat pointed and she looked and they were at the James. "Only place to cross," Tat explained.

"But, where are we *going*?" she changed the question with the emphasis. "Burnt Church?"

Tat looked at her and walked off, heading to the bridge.

It was one of the few bridges of the fabled golden age still standing across the James, but no one used it. The undersides were too crumbly and rusty for anyone to trust it, so a cadre had built a pontoon bridge next to it and, in the spirit of the New Man, was supposed to allow comrades to cross for free but, in the spirit of the Real Man, often charged something – food or a trinket or a favor, personal or sexual – for its use. Not today. F for Freddie had the cadre and his two sons on their knees, their hands interlaced behind their heads and Freddie's M16 moving threateningly from one to the other. That didn't shut up the old man. "You traitors! You scum!" he shouted over and over until Freddie butt-stroked him into unconsciousness. "Who's the traitor?" he snarled and raised the rifle to finish the man and his now quailing sons but Price called him off. Cass marveled. Freddie had a reputation for evenness.

This is what war does.

As she crossed the pontoon with groups of others, she looked at the adjacent bridge. Deceptive; looked solid and inviting but she and everyone for miles around knew not to trust it. The skills of bridge building and maintenance, of metals and load bearing and geometric structures, had died in the Event, as had most other skills. That puzzled her. Weren't there books all over the place and enough people from the golden age still alive to teach them, to show them? She'd once asked Dad about that.

"Takes thousands of years to build a civilization," he'd replied, "Just a night to lose it."

"Why, Daddy?"

He looked at her. "How many people do you know who can read?"

He'd meant her peers, the sons and daughters of the sons of daughters of the mythic age, who, unless they were gathered up and taken as a group to the education centers where they came back waving little red books and spouting slogans, or were "home schooled" as Mom called it, they didn't read. At all. They were like those two grousing, surly louts that Freddie held at gunpoint: mean, cruel, treacherous, ignorant.

Ignorant.

"When Rome fell," Dad had said and, thanks to her home schooling, she knew what Rome was, "the darkness came." And he'd looked across the ridge they were standing on at darkness covering the land. "For a thousand years."

And that's why the bridge was no longer useful.

Which was probably a good thing. Cass stood on the other side of the river and wondered if the Directorate, the Faceless, would be foolish enough to attempt its use. She had a satisfying vision of the entire demon army falling in concrete and metal into the river below, screaming. And it would be their only option because, as the last of the gangs crossed, Freddie made the sons unhook the pontoon and let it catch in the current and drift away, breaking up as it went, Freddie riding a couple of intact pontoon pieces on the water and disappearing around a corner but, don't worry, he'll catch up. And it occurred to her that the ones still on the other side of the river also trying to catch up, Junior and Grampop as two examples, would not catch up unless they found a convenient pontoon part or boat or ferry to get them across.

They would not catch up.

An unexplained lump formed in her throat as the two ignorant sons shook fists at them and shouted curses and she turned and joined the others marching through the normally busy river port town of Scottsville that was now strangely silent and empty, the bodies of two troopers in the middle of the street serving as warning. Cass barely glanced at them.

This is what war does.

North.

They marched dully, numbly, mostly on the small road but sometimes leaving it to follow a river bank then back to the road thereby throwing off their trail, avoiding the little settlements that showed signs of life but straight through the ghost ones, the taint of disease still hovering there and making normal people shy away so they were perfect cover and they swallowed their own fears and pressed on, ignoring the ghosts pointing at them from passing doorways. Night fell and still they moved, the clouds masking the stars and Cass stayed with the group mostly by feel and wondered how whoever was leading this gaggle knew where they were going.

Close to what she figured was midnight, they came to an even smaller road at another river (or the same one branching off, who knew?) and they dispersed to either side of it after crossing a small wooden bridge that they left standing because dropping it would mark their passing. Cass was prepared to sink gratefully into the spongy moss lining on her side of the river but Dad said for her to stand guard and she did, peering into the darkness across the cold, babbling water and wondering what she was supposed to look for because she could not see three feet in any direction. Someone came along after about three years and told her to go sleep and she moved under the rickety bridge barely six feet from her position and collapsed and was immediately asleep.

And immediately awake because something cold and sharp slapped her on the cheek and she was puzzled and frightened until the hiss of it in the water identified the interruption: sleet. She groaned. Possibly the worse type of weather because it covered everything in ice and wet and was no fun at all, not like snow, a conclusion everyone else came to and collectively decided there was no point lying around in the freezing mud being miserable: might as well walk and be miserable, so they did. Mom forced a Tylenol and a half a bar into her hand as they struggled up the ridge. "We're running out," she warned and Cass, disturbed, took and ate. They were running out of food. Of time. Of life.

Dawn came, dreary and wet and icy, and she watched the light change through bloodshot eyes set in her frozen, soaked body and saw refugees and vagrants and *les miserables* slowly materialize out of the dark and realized they were her family, her friends, her life, these scarecrows shivering and plodding along in a stupor. Exactly like she was.

Going up. They were climbing mountains now.

The small road went past abandoned houses and empty barns and these were the death lands that no one visited and the road died and they were across fields, the gathering ice and slope making the way harder and there was a consoling thought: if it was hard for them, it was hard for the demons and she blessed the clouds and ice that kept the dragons away and made the trucks useless and left the demons no choice but to slog along like Cass, cold and miserable and wanting to quit.

She hoped.

An hour, maybe two, as the light stayed dreary and they paralleled a creek and came to a big road, four lanes at one time in the past, part of the asphalt still intact, and they lost an hour there as Price sent people up and down to see if anyone was waiting but who, in their right mind, would be out in this weather? Oh, right, demons, and she shivered underneath a tarp that Mom had spread across a tree branch as they waited for the all clear and then they all scurried across with a haste belying their exhaustion and ran up the same small road on the other side until the forest covered them. Fear gives you wings.

Ever upward.

It got colder, the sleet sharper and she expected it to turn into snow at some point but no such luck. The road, by this time, had turned into clay and mud and she skittered off it for the more secure footing of the foliage alongside but she was still taking one step forward and two back, or at least that's what it felt like. She wasn't bothering to look behind her anymore because the demons could catch up and kill her right now and that would be fine. It gave her some satisfaction to see that Tat and Slickie weren't looking back anymore, either.

Sometime after noon, she guessed (because who could tell where the sun was) they came to some kind of building complex where several men, ten to twenty, came rushing out to see and this was it, they were dead. But they had the look of mountain men and Squint seemed to know them and there was a big group discussion right there in the middle of the road right at the complex's driveway.

"What's going on?" Cass asked Mom.

Mom frowned. "Whiskey makers," said disdainfully. Which meant outlaws, and no wonder Squint knew them. Cass was curious if these guys were the source of the popskull, which made Mom's disdain a bit hypocritical. Guess even criminals had their hierarchies.

While the discussion continued, she stepped over to Slickie. "Where did you go?"

He looked momentarily confused at her question and then understood. "All over."

"To do what?"

"Deliver messages."

"Were you successful?"

"Mostly."

And she nodded and stood back because the whiskey men's discussion had ended and several of the mountain men ran up their driveway and came back moments later with big field packs as Squint handed them weapons and ammunition belts and the mountain men took the front and headed off and they all caterpillared into a semblance of following them. Someone from the front shouted "Taylor's Gap!" Fine, as long as you know where we are.

An hour or so later and they were crouched at the side of a mountain, or what might as well be one, a tall berm several dozens of feet almost straight up and littered along the sides and tops with metal wreckage, piles of twisted cars and trucks, all rusty and overgrown and some of them precariously balanced over the edge, needing just a slight breeze to tumble them over. There were skeletons piled here and there, too, some of them macabrely stacked with skulls on top, apparently something that a local yokel, the whiskey men, for instance, thought a hilarious thing to do. Cass now knew where she was: Monsters' Highway.

Not its original name. It had a number once, back when it was pristine and beautiful and the golden age people used it to whisk themselves between sea and mountain but the Event and Breakout had turned it into a colossal traffic jam of desperate refugees and they had been found there, vulnerable and helpless, and this was the result. No one used the highway anymore, even though it was the straightest and smoothest way because it was nothing but death and Breakout monsters.

And they were going to cross it.

"You've got to be kidding me," Cass breathed.

Slickie looked at her, frowned, then shrugged and began scaling the berm. She looked at him as though he was crazy but Tat nudged her and she let out a '*tsk*' to let them know what she thought of this idea and followed.

It took about twenty minutes on the ice-coated scree to reach the top and she was downright exhausted and stopped there, as did everyone else, but they didn't do so because they were tired ... they did so because they were terrified. This was an evil road. Evil walked it, and one crossed it at their own peril. Even the whiskey men hesitated, crouched underneath the twisted bits of metal, combinations of railing and car, peering here and there, whispering among themselves. Cass felt a deeper chill. If the whiskey men, who lived next to the road, were fearful, then it was foolish to be here.

But what choice did fools have?

One of the whiskey men, the biggest and meanest-looking of them, nudged a younger and softer looking one (soft being a relative term among men so hardened) who looked at the older one like he was nuts, but then shrugged and struggled under a gap in the metal and disappeared onto the road. "Who are those guys?" she asked no one in particular, convinced the whole group of them was nuts.

"The old guy's name is Kaintuck," Tat answered. "That's his grandson, Larry, he sent on."

That wasn't exactly the question she asked, but it raised so many other interesting options that she turned to him. "Kaintuck?"

Tat shrugged, peering intently at the spot Larry

vacated. "Nickname. Because his whiskey is so good."

What the heck did that mean? But she opted for another question. "How do you know all this?"

Tat gave her a scornful glance and resumed his surveillance. Yes, it was a stupid question. Tat was everywhere throughout the year, so he knew everything.

She was deciding whether to demand that he share some of his all-encompassing knowledge when the kid – Larry – suddenly appeared above the berm, probably standing on something tall, and waved them up. She watched as Kaintuck pointed his whiskey men off to flanking positions and, as they scrambled over the berm's edge, looked at Price, who was crouched down next to the old man. He nodded and waved and the group began their ascent, staying in the lines they had formed while crawling up the berm. Cass followed Tat over the railing at the top …

… into nightmare.

The gray skies and cold wind and bursts of sleet set the stage, but this was hell. Pure hell. Piles of metal all twisted and tied together, the remnants of cars and trucks knotted all over the highway, some of them so entangled they made an effective barrier. But that wasn't the horror. It was the crosses, erected every ten feet or so and jammed into the wreckage, holding bodies that ranged from barely intact bones to much fresher ones, ripped and corrupted, the agony still clear on their rotting faces. Crosses as far as Cass could see, up and down both sides of the big highway until lost in sleety mist.

She stopped. She gasped. As did most of the others in her line, jamming up right here at the berm.

"Keep moving!" Tat whispered fiercely, frantically.

"Who did this?" she breathed, paralyzed. "Directorate?"

"No," Tat said grimly, pushing her roughly in the

back, "Something much worse."

"What—" she was about to ask what that could possibly be, when a shot rang out. Whirling along with everyone else in that direction, she saw Larry, still on top of the rusted cab of a truck, with his rifle up and smoke coming out the barrel. She followed its direction and saw … something. Blurred movement, foul and wrong, among the metal and crosses, flowing in their direction.

"Breakouts!" someone shouted and gunshots rang up and down as the far line of bent movement picked up speed and flowed through the wreckage and began howling. And she knew.

Monsters.

They weren't supposed to exist anymore. They were stories told to unruly children at night to make them behave because the Breakouts will getcha if you don't watch out! Sub-humans. Back on that day of horror when they crashed through the Zone walls and brought death on the wind, bearing before them their God, the corpse of their leader mounted like a banner on a cross at the head of their column, they brought death to an already dying world, spreading their murder and disease throughout the lands until what was left of them faded into the badlands, the deserted places, and into myth.

No more.

Cass watched transfixed as the stumbling, limping line of howling werewolves broke over metal and asphalt and came for her. To eat her. To rape her for days and then eat her, then put what was left of her on a cross and hoist her up, still alive, parts of her missing as a sacrifice to whatever Moloch these things still worshipped. Gunfire behind her and she turned to see half of her line now faced about, engaging a similar line of monsters converging on them from that direction. They were flanked. They were eaten.

"Shoot! Shoot!" Tat yelled at her and leveled his own rifle and let off a burst and Cass raised her MP5 into the face of a monster … if that's what you called a face, a gaping hole where an eye used to be, half of one lip gone to reveal filed-down teeth like fangs, patches of hair shaved ugly, and a leering, lustful light in the one good eye that was almost on her, claws for hands reaching for her and an inhuman holler rising from that open horror of a mouth and she pulled the trigger and the face misted into bone and blood and she brought the line of her fire into the mass of monsters coming for her. Coming for her.

In terms of a battle, it wasn't much of one. Cass reloaded twice and fired at the sub-humans until Tat screamed "Move!" and she bolted across the asphalt, weaving her way in and out of metal piles and monsters along with everyone else in her line, firing right and left as they tumbled down a berm and up the next one to another set of metal and monsters and asphalt and then past that and down the next berm, down and down, falling more than running but that was okay because it got her away from the howling mob faster and all of them piled up at the bottom and untangled themselves and ran onto a small road, maybe the same one they'd followed up to the first berm, on the other side of the Monsters' Highway and they were a mass of terrified humans frantically seeking safety in the woods.

Cass looked back once and saw the monsters lined up on top of the highway, yelling triumphantly and waving makeshift machetes and spears and slings at them and freshly cut heads aloft and they had a girl, someone Cass did not recognize, hoisted above them, already naked and screaming and Cass saw one of the sub-humans reach up with one of the crude machetes and slice her breast off and shove it into his mouth. That could have been me, she thought and paused and raised the barrel of her machine pistol to end the girl's torture but Tat slapped it down and bellowed, "Run!"

They ran for what seemed like a week. Up and west, through woods and creek and on the occasional road, on slippery dead weeds and grass, past dead neighborhoods and the occasional pond and creek and river, sometimes glimpses of the Monsters' Highway to their left from which Cass swore she could hear their howls and right on through the remains of a giant lumber yard where they turned sharply north for what seemed like another week over another highway and fear, fear because highways were monster lairs but not, apparently, this one and then sharply west across fields until they and the woods petered out and they were in a large clearing with concrete bases and rusted piles of electric towers marching off to the north and west and the dark clouds, getting darker, against the far mountains. Everyone stopped here, a natural stop because it was the only place open and wide enough to accommodate their number.

Which was a lot less than when they began the day.

"What was that?" she gasped, wheezing for air, the terror of the past few hours now giving way to exhaustion and she had to rest, had to.

Mom was there but said nothing, merely gave her a canteen that was almost empty and she greedily sucked its contents down before she realized this might be the last of it and she looked at Mom guiltily but all Mom did was nod and re-sling the canteen about her neck and look off, grieved and sorrowed and Cass knew better than to ask that question again.

But she did ask another. "Did we have to go that way?"

Mom did not respond and she looked about. Tat and Slickie were still with her and Dad was a little ways off and relief flowed through her, but she wondered if she would feel that way if she knew the name of the girl the sub-humans were now busily raping and eating over the next three or four days so she decided not to ask for the name but, instead, "Did we?"

No one answered. They all looked anywhere but at her, mostly off to the left at the base of the first tower where Price stood with Kaintuck and Squint, looking grim. "Ten minutes!" Price shouted holding up the requisite fingers, then turned and pointed up the line of tumbled towers. "Then we go!"

"What?" Cass was incredulous. Ten minutes? And go where? They needed to rest and reload and bind wounds and go back and kill the subhumans and put the girl out of her misery and exact a terrible vengeance.

A hand fell on her shoulder. Dad's. "We gotta keep going," he said softly.

"But, Dad—"

He made an impatient movement, shutting off her protest. "The Faceless know where we are now."

And she understood. The gunfire, as short as it was, had echoed and re-echoed and told the pursuing demons their prey was at the Monsters' Highway. All the demons had to do was brush aside the sub-humans, an easier task for them, note the pieces of the girl still left on the road, and follow the hasty tracks.

To them.

"Then why did we go this way?" she asked again, but no one answered. No one would.

Ten minutes later, in the increasing dark, they left.

Night, a black, dead one, and she was dead. She knew it. Her body didn't so it kept going. But it was a pointless waste of energy because she was dead. All of them were.

The clouds remained and the sleet came in waves and

it grew colder but she no longer felt it. The dead feel nothing. But the dead know everything. And she knew they were pursued. She didn't see the pursuit; no sudden flashes of light behind them, no sudden tracers, nothing like that ... didn't even hear anything, but knew it all the same. Even knew who it was: The demons.

The clouds to the east lightened a bit and she discovered that she was on top of a bluff, somewhat cleared, with remnants of buildings clumped on this edge. The bluff continued rising to the west, giving the impression of a sudden drop off at the peak. Not exactly a cliff, but steep enough. Woods in that direction, thick ones, tough. She hoped they weren't going that way, or any way, for that matter. Let's stop, just stop. Right here.

Price stood in front of the buildings she was heading toward, looking back the way they came, arms crossed, frowning. Cass was so exhausted she could barely see him. He didn't look like he was going to stop.

The dead know no rest.

She followed Slickie to one of the building walls and collapsed with him and several others on the leeward side, sheltering from some of the wind but not the occasional sleet burst. There were patches of mist here and there, making the place dreamlike and Cass was convinced this was a dream. Had to be. No human could feel like this while awake. "Anything to eat?" she asked no one in particular, and no one answered. She decided on a different tack. "Where are we?"

"Calf Mountain," one of Squint's guys, Kenny something, replied. He was laid full out in the middle of the flat space between two walls, taking the full brunt of the sleet and not caring one whit.

Cass shrugged. She didn't care one whit, either, and huddled against Slickie who was in a stupor and fell into one herself. For about two seconds, then there was a sharp whistle and someone clapping their hands in the most annoying manner and yelling, "Gather 'round!"

"No," Cass said but levered to her feet and shuffled with the rest of the group out of the walls and to the flat area on the other side where Price and Dad and Inez and the other so-called leaders stood and looked at them, grim. "This isn't going to be good," Slickie muttered.

It wasn't.

"We can't get away," Price said, flatly. "We have to fight." A pause. "Here."

There was very little reaction from the hundred or so of them deployed around the leaders, whether from exhaustion or resignation, didn't matter. They all looked dully at Price and waited to hear their death sentence.

"Here's what we're going to do," Price said, "We're going to split into three groups. The first one is going to bunker up in those buildings," a gesture at the ruins behind them, "and make a lot of noise. There's an old hiking trail behind the buildings," another gesture that Cass didn't bother to follow, "all overgrown but you can still see it. One group will go north on that trail about a hundred yards, the other, south, same distance, and wait. When the first group comes running that way with the Directorate following, you'll hit the enemy in the rear and flanks. Wait until our guys get past before you do that. Hit them hard, kill as many as you can, then run west. There's an old road there. Cross it and then it's a steep drop down to a valley with a town and a river. Get to the river and follow it north." A pause. "If you can."

No one spoke. No one complained. It was suicide, but as good a plan as any.

Tat and Little John were in the first group, Slickie in the second, Cass in the third. They muddled about setting weapons and ammunition pouches and Cass fell in with her group heading to the left and the old hiking trail,

Larry in charge. The sun had broken out of the clouds and the world was red and icy but the mist was clearing with patches of deep blue above them. "A good day to die!" Larry called out, somewhat cheerily, but there was a falseness to it. Cass looked at him. He was putting on a tough front, but she could read the worry in his eyes.

"I don't want to die today," whispered Sweet Pea marching behind Cass. She carried a rifle three times too big for her and looked as if she would fall over at any moment.

"None of us do," Cass whispered back. But there are certain inevitabilities, something she did not whisper. She decided, instead, to evoke the same false hope as Larry. "We've got a chance. Shoot as many as you can and then run for the town and the river."

"What's the name of the town?" Sweet Pea asked.

Larry, at the front of the column but close enough to hear, responded, "Dooms."

Fitting.

3.6

The Season of Battle

Cass could not see a thing, which was a bit odd because there was plenty of light now, morning light, plus the trees here had shed most of their leaves. But the light was only at the top of these surprisingly thick woods, which had so many wide-branched evergreens sewn through the pines and hardwoods that leaf loss didn't matter. All she could see were the spots along the surprisingly wide trail behind her through which sunlight had filtered. In front of her was a green wall, which wasn't good because the plan was for them to run to the clearing allegedly on the other side of the wall and catch Major Lawless in the flank. Cass doubted they'd get ten yards in before they were separated and tripping over roots and lost. Lawless would come in here at his leisure and pick them off.

A good day to die, all right.

Cass looked resentfully down the line at Larry, propped on a boulder bordering the woods and looking intently at the trees as though he could see something. Why was this guy in command? Cass was just as capable of leading a suicide charge blindly through unknown woods and into the arms of seasoned murderous assassins as he was. Probably because he *was* a guy.

Probably because he knew the area.

Cass had to grudgingly concede that point. Larry

knew this old trail, telling them that people used to walk all the way to Maine or Georgia on it, surprising Cass that he knew the names of two old states. Apparently, the whiskey kid could read. And he'd been smart enough to send a couple of guys out past the green wall to watch for the demons and come running back when it was time to attack. Cass hadn't thought of that. So maybe this wasn't a boy/girl thing; maybe the kid knew what he was doing.

Please let him know what he was doing.

"I'm cold," Sweet Pea, crouched next to Cass so close that she might as well be wearing Cass's clothes, whispered, then shivered to emphasize that. Welcome to the club, sister. Whatever warmth the rising sun offered was trapped in the upper branches. Could be 90 degrees up there, but it was sub-zero here on the ground. They would all be frozen solid to the trail, unable to rise, especially this little munchkin of a girl beside Cass carrying a rifle that had to outweigh her by about thirty pounds.

Cass nudged Sweet Pea's weapon. "What is that?"

"It's an M4A1, the fully automatic version, 5.56 with the 4-position stock and a C-More sight, rails, everything. I was going to put a 203 on it, but didn't have time."

Cass stared at her. Sweet Pea shrugged. "It's my job to know these things."

"I thought you were an accountant."

"What did you think I was accounting?"

Cass shook her head. "Stuff we were stealing. Stuff we earned from the popskull trade. Not weapons. I didn't even know we had them."

"No one did," Sweet Pea answered.

Okay. Cass resumed surveilling the front. Well-kept secrets. There'd always been rumors in the gang about hidden stashes, but most of that centered around Price's fabled gold reserve. That he'd parlayed it into an armory was never mentioned, never even hinted. Yet, here they were, all equipped with the latest in weapons technology … well, the latest as of the Event, which was the last time anything technical had been invented. Some of the old stuff was still obviously viable because the Faceless had helicopters, but old stuff like that was reserved exclusively for the State, not unwashed peasants or stringy-haired skinny girls whose only apparent expertise was starvation. She cast an admiring glance at Sweet Pea. Who'd ever think she was a master armorer? "What's your name?" Cass asked her.

The little girl looked puzzled. "Sweet Pea. You know that."

"I mean your real name."

"That is my real name." A pause. "It's all my mother ever called me." And she turned with a dismissive air toward the trees.

Cass figured there was a story in that somewhere, a hard one. She was tired of hard stories, though, and decided to drop it. Heck, she was overall tired. If Lawless didn't shoot her, she'd die of no sleep. Humans weren't designed to be this exhausted.

"*Hsst!*"

She was instantly awake, the blood pounding in her head as she looked down the line and saw Larry on the boulder with his hand raised in warning. Sweet Pea jumped a bit and looked as if she might die of fright right there, but then her lips compressed into a terrible resolve. Cass pressed into her own terrible resolve, swung her machine pistol to the front while checking if the magazine was still there and the remaining ones within reach.

Directly in front of their position they heard a swishing among the lower branches and Cass raised her barrel but Larry yelled, "Don't shoot!" and hers and several other barrels went back down. One of the scouts materialized suddenly between the trees, his hands and face torn and bloody and his eyes wild and he waved at them. "Come on!" he shouted and turned and plunged back through the trees.

They all looked at each other. "Come on!" Larry roared and they were up, stumbling and tumbling over the edge of the trail and the boulders and then running straight through the trees, in seconds their faces and hands as bloody as the scout's but they kept on, eyes on each other so they would not get lost, not lose each other, while pelting through the woods more or less in line, following the barely glimpsed scout as he angled them back toward the north.

A sound. A thrum, staccato and sharp, then blurred, and an underlying roar: men and women yelling. Angry yelling. Up ahead somewhere. Occasionally gunfire, very clear and very loud, came in odd waves but mostly sound was muted …

… until they reached the edge of the woods and poured onto the field bordering it. Where they all stopped. And looked.

Smoke and fire and people running and screaming, that was the overall picture. There were specific images within it. To the right at the edge of the bluff buildings, shattered even more than when they first found this spot, burned, figures here and there, some draped in odd ways over wreckage, with a knot of people in black uniforms, half of them with their faces covered, standing at the back surveying the field. In the middle of the knot stood a tall man, unmasked, but unmistakably Major Lawless. To the left, the border of the woods fronting the trail, gunfire and people running, the shabbily dressed ones who were Cass's gang and her family in front, turning and firing, the black uniformed ones in Directorate and Faceless garb behind them in hot pursuit firing back. And right in front of Cass …

The demons' flanks exposed; the demons unseeing and unaware that she stood there, and at her mercy.

A shout, louder than the general ones from the combatants to the front and Cass looked. Major Lawless was jumping up and down and gesticulating wildly. He had seen them emerge from the woods and was trying to warn the demons.

Too late.

Without a command, without thought, the entire line of them, about thirty, lowered thirty weapons and fired at almost the same time.

An invisible avalanche smacked into the side of the demons, rolled over them and knocked them down. Heavier rounds eviscerated and tore and ripped while the lighter ones cut through like stilettos, taking two to three of them in line at a time. The air misted with blood and bone and screams and the pursuit jammed up as the dead and the wounded fell into their comrades who turned to see this new threat.

Mistake.

Because, on the other side of the field, the second group, Slickie's group, emerged from their own wood line and opened up, right into the backs of the confused demons.

Simply. Murder.

That was the best description of it as Cass's machine pistol stopped firing and she looked and saw it was empty and she cleared the magazine and slapped in another and fired, just fired. It became quickly apparent that the objective was to fill the space between the two wood lines with as much indiscriminate, widespread, and rapid fire as possible. A hazardous tactic, of course, because the two groups were essentially shooting at each other across the field, but the Directorate bodies served as a backstop. Not all the time, and rounds slapped the trees and the ground around her and she wondered how stupid it would be to get killed by her own people, or to kill some of them herself, like Slickie. So keep the bullets low and into the Faceless, not your brother.

Someone was screaming, but not from fear, a battle cry, and Cass looked and it was Sweet Pea, cute little nothing Sweet Pea who was pure Valkyrie as her heavier weapon thrummed low and constant, the magazines changed in blinding speed and her monster bullets slamming the enemy to the ground in row after row. Cass's own Valkyrie scream rose to her throat as she reaped.

The line of gang members running for the trees suddenly wheeled about and brought up their own weapons and fired into the mass of roiling demons, while a group that had already been there emerged and stood beside them and the demons were in a box, a kill box, taking fire from three sides. They should all die.

They didn't.

Some of the demons in the middle grabbed the survivors and tossed them into semblances of lines as officers and sergeants emerged and shouted orders, the difference between professionals and amateurs, because now the kill box became a square and Cass faced a line of soldiers, real soldiers, bringing their weapons to bear on her.

The world exploded.

A flash and a giant hand slammed Cass straight into the ground like a fence post. If her feet had been wood, she'd be up to her neck, but she wasn't wood, she was flesh and bone and she collapsed, her head compressed and her breath gone and she figured she'd been shot. But no. As she toppled over on her back, she saw tree limbs and leaves and fire raining down and all she could figure was that the trees blew up. Puzzled, she looked over at Sweet Pea, who had sprouted about thirty wounds in her scalp. She was mouthing something at Cass. Mordor? Murder?

Mortar.

Cass raised her head and rubbed dirt out of her eyes and strained and yes, there, next to Major Lawless's little command group, two tubes rising out of the ground with some people attending them. As she watched, the one on the left belched smoke and Cass shrugged because that didn't seem so bad …

… until the tree line across from them erupted like a volcano.

"Slickie!" she screamed and wondered if he'd been hammered straight into the ground just as she had been. He was taller, so his head should be up in the blast area, pulverized. She tried to see but there was too much smoke over the battlefield now, and lines of fire were snaking out of the smoke and reaching for her. Oh right, the demons were now shooting into the woods from their little square. Hmm, if she'd been standing, she'd be shredded right now. Maybe the mortar had saved her life.

Kawhump … *BAM*! and the trees to her right evaporated in flame and splinters, many of which shrapneled past her, ripping the other trees apart. Wow. Might be a good idea to remain right here on the ground.

Boom! Followed by *BOOOOOM*!

What the heck?

Raising her head again, Cass was puzzled to see a long metal tube cartwheeling over the top of the building while Major Lawless and his friends scattered all over the place as more things exploded where the mortar had been. As she tried to figure out what had happened, the second mortar suddenly erupted in flame with a sharp crack! followed by the same *BOOOOM*! as its ammunition exploded and the tube followed its brother into the sky. Now what was causing this? Movement on the far side of the building across from the tree line, Cass focused on it and suddenly understood.

Junior. And Grampop. Both aiming rockets at the Directorate.

She wanted to jump up and cheer and call, "Yoo hoo!" to Junior but that would be inordinately stupid, so she lay there and cheered, or, at least, she thought she did. Her mouth was open and she felt columns of air rising through her lungs but she couldn't hear anything except a loud clanging and the sounds of explosions and guns and man, war was noisy. At least she was adding her two cents.

As she watched, smoke streaked from Junior's and Grampop's tubes across her line of sight and somewhere into the field where fire blew up like miniature atomic explosions, two of them, and she realized that they were attacking the square. Great! Bust them up and maybe Cass could get out of here alive …

… and Junior and Grampop dropped their bazookas and went running like crazy people for the wood line immediately to their left, as if the hounds of hell themselves were after them …

… Oh no, not the hounds. Demons.

Hundreds of them poured around the side of the building where Major Lawless knelt, screaming into a radio. Hundreds of them. Hundreds and hundreds.

My God, how many demons were there?

Let's not find out.

She looked at Sweet Pea, who stared, round eyed, at the influx of new demons. Cass nudged her. Sweet Pea looked over. "Run," Cass said.

They both rolled over on their shoulders simultaneously, scooping up weapons and packs and ran like the hounds of hell were on their heels because they were. The members of their group, whoever was left, had reached a simultaneous conclusion about leaving and they all streaked onto the trail, some of them heading for Maine, others to Georgia.

"No!" Larry yelled, "Follow me!" And he plunged into the woods on the other side of the trail. Didn't have to tell Cass twice and she and Sweet Pea and the others zipped right behind him, fear giving them wings and balance as they kept one eye on the blur of Larry and the other on the death behind them. Shadows back there dodged in and out of the trees, the ones not shooting at them obviously gang members, the ones shooting obviously the enemy. Ice still on the ground made the going hard, the way rough with boulders and holes and it was more of a controlled fall than a run but a blessing because it slowed the demons down as much as it did them and kept most of the demon's bullets from reaching them, They kept their feet, they stayed with it, they ran.

And were suddenly out of the woods and onto a road, asphalt broken here and there but still graded, a stone wall on the far side bordering it and overlooking a steep valley broken up by concrete tower bases and their fallen metal frames zigzagging down to a flat land interspersed with buildings where the newly risen sun winked on a far ribbon of water.

The river.

The gang piled up here, the three groups converging from out of the woods at the same time, mixing their ranks and roiling along as they tried to figure out what to do. "The river!" was shouted by dozens as gang members pointed fingers down the slope and some of them dropped over the side of the wall and slid down, intent on the distant water. Cass stood watching, then frantically looked around to locate her group. Ah, there, Larry, standing below the wall waving everyone on, Sweet Pea already well past him and all elbows-and-knees hustling for the bottom. Cass turned to the right and ran to the group falling out of the trees and clambering over the wall. "Mom! Dad!" she shrieked.

Someone grabbed her roughly by the shoulder and spun her around and her arms came up because it must be a demon but no. "Dad!" she shrieked as he seized her by both shoulders and put his face into hers.

"Run to the river! Go north. North! Stay on the left bank. Go to Burnt Church! Burnt Church!" and with that he pitched her over the wall.

She fell hard, landing on a pile of rocks and trees, skinning everything, cutting herself so deep on the arm that blood flowed freely. She tumbled in an effort to regain her feet and hurt herself some more and looked up and could see Dad and Little John standing on the road with a few others as more gang members cleared the wall, all of them dangerously close to falling on her and she whipped off the pile and stepped back and saw Daddy up there, faced around, a rifle held to his shoulder ...

... and watched as he was torn to pieces by about one million bullets.

"No!" she screamed. "No!" She screamed over and over as Little John, next to the shredding piece of meat that was once her Dad, brought his machine gun to bear and fired and fired at whatever he could see and his head was suddenly gone and there was a *brap*! *bang*! of a grenade and body parts flew over the wall and she screamed and screamed.

Someone had her. Slickie. And Mom.

They were a mass heading down the slope toward the far water, Cass hoisted between the two of them, looking back and screaming for Daddy but Mom and Slickie held her the tighter, carried her along as the terrain exploded around them with bullets and tracers. Cass caught glimpses of the Directorate troops that had reached the wall firing down on them and there was no way they would survive this, no way. In moments, they would be shredded. Like Daddy.

They dropped hard over a rise, all of the bullets flying well over their heads as they, along with dozens and dozens of other survivors, hit the rocky bottom. Mom pushed her hard against the wall. "Stay there!" she ordered and stepped back, looking up the wall at the top of the rise. Cass slid until she was seated on the ground, waves of shock pounding her into a stupor. Slickie squatted next to Cass, pulled her bloody arm to himself and examined it, then wrapped some cloth around her arm cut and knotted it tight, something that should have caused her to wince but she felt nothing. She looked at him dully. "Did you see what happened?"

"Yes," he said, grimly, and pointed at the bandage. "That should hold you for now." He also stood, staring up the wall.

The gangs were falling over the top and scrambling against the wall, pressing against her but she didn't care, simply brushed them aside so she could see. Some of the gang had joined Mom and Slickie, staring back up the slope, tense and braced, ready to do something; what, Cass didn't know. And didn't care. Daddy was dead. They were all dead.

She was cold and she shivered and didn't care. Sunlight burst suddenly over the rise, beaming from the top like a searchlight all the way down the slope and it was pretty but she didn't care. Sharp lines between shadow and sunlight now, a stark demarcation between the protection the rise provided and the exposure of the open ground before them. Cass watched as more and more gang members crushed into the protective shadows, a few of them joining the wall watchers, including Price, who strode into the middle of the watching line, his eyes fixed on the top of the wall. "Ready!" he yelled.

Cass blinked. Ready? For what?

Mom and Slickie and the twelve or thirteen people standing with them pulled grenades out of various pockets and belts, still looking up. Cass gasped. What are you doing?

An odd wavering and spiking ran along the sun line and Cass furrowed her brow. What was that? Shadows of some kind, long ones, thrown by the sunrise into the valley and the shadows were running and blending and clumping together until they suddenly resolved: people, lots of them carrying weapons and on the edge of the rise above her head.

"Now!" Price yelled and the grenades went flying, one set of about a dozen, followed immediately by another dozen up into the air and over the top of the rise. The shadows danced and gunfire erupted from the top, bullets flying wildly and not hitting anyone as a bunch of people up there began yelling and Cass suddenly understood about the same time as the first set of grenades went off: the Directorate had reached the drop off, and were about to get blown to kingdom come.

They got blown to kingdom come.

Not all at once. None of the grenades went off simultaneously. A few detonated within microseconds of each other but there was no single, loud explosion, just a quick and long series of *BRAP!BRAPCRACK!SLAP!* and an occasional *BOOM!* but the effect was the same: annihilation. Body parts and shrapnel and grass and rocks flew everywhere, mostly above her head but enough of the grenades exploded close enough to the edge that some of it rained down on the gangs and a couple of people were knocked over, blood spouting from their heads and shoulders. Didn't stop the launch of a third wave of grenades.

A wall of smoke and debris rising higher than the sunlight replaced the shadows. No more firing came from the top but there was a lot of screaming. Price stood for a moment watching, then swept his gaze along the pile of gang members. "Run!" he shouted, turned and was flying down the slope.

The gangs turned and collided, into and over each other, in a desperate effort to follow, Mom and Slickie swallowed up by them. The stronger ones pushed through and the more agile ducked and weaved and even the clumsiest got themselves sorted out and stepped off and were gone. Cass remained where she was. She didn't care.

Slickie materialized in front of her, grabbed her unbandaged arm and yanked her to her feet. "Let's go," he said and pulled her through the debris and pitched forward and they were heel-sliding and running down the slope, following the line of concrete bases and scrap metal. She didn't resist, didn't protest, even though she didn't care. She was actually somewhat pleased he'd remembered to get her.

The one advantage of heading downhill at such an angle was the lack of effort. Let gravity do the work. Keep your balance and pick yourself up quickly after the inevitable stumbles across such rough terrain. Heck, if she'd wanted to, she could have dropped down and rolled all the way down the hill. Of course, the rock outcroppings and rust iron would have torn her apart, but at least she'd make it. Most of her, that is.

Slickie made sure she made it, kept her upright and pulled her up from her falls. She returned the favor, helping when he fell headfirst several times but he really didn't need it because usually he shoulder-rolled and regained his feet. Pretty slick moves, Slickie. She gave him a boost up where she could, but mostly it was all him.

Those falling-down episodes gave her the chance to look back up the slope and see the pursuit. But, there wasn't any, not from what she could tell. Still a lot of smoke on the rise but the sunlight was strong and blinding and almost impossible to make out details. For all she could tell, an entire Division of Faceless could be pouring down the slope after them so maybe the best thing was to not worry about it until the chase became apparent ...

Which it did, right about the fourth concrete base, when the ground and air around her erupted in bullets.

Both she and Slickie did belly flops on the grass as the base wall right in front of her turned to concrete shrapnel and dust from millions of machine gun bullets blasted across its face. The grass was soft, still green and thick, all of the ice gone, but Cass managed to land on top of some tower residue and banged her chin pretty hard, to the point of seeing stars.

The machine guns raked the ground now and Slickie seized her by the shoulder and dragged her around the base where about thirty or forty others were sliding down the very steep berm that formed the downhill side of it. The valley fell at an almost impossible angle here for at least a mile to what looked like another ridge that fronted the farther buildings. The river twinkled enticingly beyond that. So, they were protected here; no bullets could reach them. Mortars could, though, and she looked up the base fearfully, expecting an explosion any second.

A line had formed at the bottom of the berm, about ten or twelve gang members, with their rifles up and pointing back up the base wall. Mom was one of them. Cass blinked at her. Daddy's gone, Mommy. I don't want you to go, too.

More gang members poured down the berm wall, clustering in the middle before flowing around the line of fighters covering their retreat. In fits, groups of them dropped down the slope in another pell-mell, barely-controlled fall to the buildings and the beckoning river. Cass wasn't the best reader of topography, but it looked to her that the fleeing gangsters were protected by various knolls and rock croppings all the way to the bottom and, once there, they were out of range of most rifles. If someone stopped the demons here, that is.

Cass looked at Mom again. No, Mommy, not you.

As if reading her thoughts, Mom pointed a ferocious finger at Slickie. "You have to go. Now. Take her to the river. Now." And she returned her intent, murderous gaze up the wall.

Slickie grabbed Cass's shoulder and pulled. "Let's go," he urged.

She shook out of his grasp. "No."

"We have to go, Cass."

"No. I'm not leaving Mom."

"She told us to go."

"No!" she shouted and slapped at Slickie. "You run and hide if you want to! I'm staying!" and she crossed her arms and huffed into a stubborn, unmovable crouch.

Slickie stood back, a helpless expression on his face and he made a helpless gesture at Mom who gave them both enraged glares but Cass did not care. She had already lost Dad and she was not going to run away while Mom stayed here to fight. She scrambled at her machine pistol and pockets and saw she had only one magazine left. So be it.

"You are no good to me here!" Mom screamed at her. "No good at all! You couldn't handle Dad getting killed so how are you going to handle this?" and she swept outraged arms at the fighting line, which was a suicide line; no one in it would survive the coming battle. Which should begin any minute now.

Shocked, Cass burst into frustrated tears and pawed

315

helplessly at the machine pistol to show Mom she sure could handle it but she had lost her grip. Someone materialized on her right side and she looked through her tear-blurred vision. It was Larry, leaning into her.

"Rise," he whispered, "Go to the river. And fight again." And he stood and held out a hand. She took it.

And they were past the suicide line, Slickie at their back and Cass glanced at Mom who did not waver, did not even look at them as they swept past and tumbled down a sharp ravine which, as Cass suspected, dropped them completely out of sight of the berm and its protectors. It was all she could do to keep upright, Larry grasping one arm and Slickie at her back as they slipped down the path and she had neither time nor chance to look back which would do no good because there was no way to see over the ridgeline and ask Mom with her eyes if she meant it. About halfway down, she realized Mom hadn't, that it was a strategy to get her moving and bitter tears sprang to her eyes but she kept going. To rise. To fight again.

Five minutes, five seconds, five years later, the shooting began.

Back up the hill and out of sight, but the sound carried well, intense and rapid and ferocious, and went on and on and she puzzled at that because the suicide line should have succumbed in about two seconds but no, the fight was still going another twenty minutes later and she was twenty minutes further down the slope where there was another drop off and they were over it and on a road, still mostly asphalt, and running for the buildings which were no longer far away.

It was getting dark.

Cass was surprised by that as they swept down the road to the buildings and the river because it hadn't seemed that long but yes, sunset was approaching and she could still hear battle back up the mountain. "Mom," she breathed, not in sadness, but admiration.

A barricade made up of old rusted cars and shorings of broken-up wagons and timber blocked a bridge in front of them. Armed men bristled all over it and she would have come to a screeching halt but Slickie urged her on and she saw more of them, more gang members, converging on the barricade. Price was there. So was Junior and Grampop and they had more tube weapons and were all of them bloodied and exhausted but they were clear-eyed and resolved in the quickly falling sunlight.

"Here," Price said and gave her a canteen and she didn't even question it but screwed off the top and drank deep and tasted something funny in it but who cares, who cares, and she took her fill and passed it to Larry. Price gave them a mirthless grin. "That'll hold you all night. You'll feel like crap around dawn, though." A bit startled by that, Cass thought it best not to query further.

Price pointed down at the bridge. "Get to the river bank. Go north. Travel only at night. Find Burnt Church. Find Collier Rashkil. Tell him you're with me." And he waved them on.

"How do we find the church?" Larry asked.

"I know where it is," Slickie answered and humped down the bridge. After a moment's hesitation, Larry picked up his pack and followed. Cass looked at Price, then at Junior and Grampop, intent on the mountainside and the sounds of battle still on going.

"Go," Price said softly. Then, after a moment, just as softly, "Daughter."

Cass let one tear fall, then turned and was gone.

3.7

Burnt Church

The hills were on fire.

Each flame originated from some building or another, usually a farmhouse and its barns but also warehouses erected here and there by cadres to centralize the theft of farm produce … in the name of the people, of course. Three or four complexes burned at a time, randomly distributed across the surrounding hillsides, acting like a ring of torches casting a lurid, hellish light on the thousands of people in the hollow below. Armed people.

An army.

Collier stood in the middle of them, arms crossed, unmoving. Silent. There was nothing for him to say: Eulen and Felicia and Darra handled the logistics, organizing the groups into units, directing them to supplies and weapons and commanders, taking census and intelligence reports, occasionally consulting with Collier who spoke one or two words to resolve the easy issues, Evelyn at his shoulder making notes of the harder ones that required more time and thought. Distracted, she looked off as new crowds approached, searching among them, sighing when she did not recognize anyone and giving her husband a puzzled, hard look but she did not ask anything. He would not have answered if she had.

"What do you think about shoring up the perimeter?" Darra.

Collier shook his head. "They won't attack us yet."

"You sure?" Darra's voice reflected doubt. Best time to break up a nascent rebellion was before it got itself properly organized.

"Yes. They would have to go through Winchester to get to us. By the time they figure out how to do that, we'll be gone."

"Where?"

"North," was all Collier would say. Not quite north, more east, he refused to say. Plans were best kept to oneself. That way, there was no chance of betrayal.

Betrayal.

Evelyn shifted next to him and he knew she wanted to ask her question: how will he find us if we move north? Collier would not answer that question. Not yet. But, soon, he would have to. And her heart would dissolve.

Lord, please do not let her ask the question. Ever.

Collier had done more praying these last two weeks than he'd done ever since his self-proclaimed pastorship. For the first time since he'd shouldered this burden, Someone actually listened, as if the obscure presence in Dad's Bible had made Himself apparent. Not expeditiously, certainly not with answers, but at least willing to lend an ear. And that was good enough. Lord knows Collier no longer had anyone else to talk to.

A group of about one hundred or so advanced up the road, the steep one that fronted the old burnt church that guarded this hollow. They were identical to every other group that had shown up here in the last few days: beaten, ragged, barely together. But defiant. The girl, Cassandra, the one who had brought Price's letter, was in the front ranks.

"You made it," Felicia said flatly as the group filed into the light.

Cass exchanged glances with a skinny kid next to her

about seventeen, blond with blue eyes shining even in this hell light. His resemblance to Cass marked him as the brother she'd mentioned ... what was his name? Slickie? Something weird like that?

Cass responded just as flatly, "Yes." A pause. "But not all of us." And the look between her and her brother was sorrowful. Collier knew that look. He'd exchanged it with hundreds of others over the years, with Davis and Jonesy and ... Rosa. Evelyn, soon enough, but hers would also be tinged with hate.

"Is Price with you?" Collier called across. Felicia looked back at him with surprise because she was doing the screening but saw the look on his face and stepped aside, waving Cass forward. Her brother stepped up with her. "No," the kid said, "but he'll catch up." Another glance of sorrow between brother and sister. So Price might not catch up. Ever.

Collier nodded and scrutinized them. My God, these kids have been through a sheer and recent hell. Their clothes were ribbons, their weapons mud-covered to the point the old sergeant in him went apoplectic but, look, the sorrow in their eyes. "You're Slickie, right?"

"Yes." The kid hesitated. "But my name is Homer," his eyes suddenly hooded and blank. "Please call me that from now on."

Cass suppressed a sob and Collier figured here was a tragic tale waiting to be told. It would have to get in line "Homer. All right. It's Homer from now on," Collier said softly. He paused and took in the gathering army. "You're the one who spread the word, and here we are." He turned back to the kid. "Thank you."

The hooded, blank eyes stirred a bit, but Homer said nothing.

"Did you ..." Collier hesitated, not sure how to ask the question within Evelyn's hearing. "... find everyone on the list?"

Homer shrugged. "Most."

Collier let that go without comment and looked over the boy's head at Cass's group waiting patiently behind. He pointed at an old man in the front. "Is that an RPG?"

"Yes," Homer said, "and we have more." He looked Collier full in the face. "And we know where to get artillery, too."

Collier smiled. "Of course. I'd expect no less from Price."

"It's not from Price," the boy responded with some ferocity. "It's from my Dad." A bit of a choke here. "And Mom." A definite choke.

Cass, round-eyed, grasped her brother by the sleeve and he turned to her and there, again, the look of sorrow, but now Collier knew its source. There's the tragic tale, right there, and off in some great distance, he heard Dad whisper his name. Collier needed to hear this tale, add it to his own. One day. When his own grief had subsided enough to take on someone else's.

"You are now a lieutenant, Homer," Collier said. "Your unit is now our First Recon Company and you are in charge. Colonel Cody!" Collier called out and Eulen snapped around. "General!" he called back.

Collier pointed at Homer. "These are the ones you've been waiting for. See to them."

"Yes, sir!" Cody barked and he waved at Homer. "Come with me, Lieutenant."

The boy hesitated and raised a querying eyebrow at his sister but Collier gestured him on and he nodded and stepped off and the group waiting with him shuffled into some kind of line to follow Eulen, who already had an arm around the kid, explaining what they intended. The kid's dropped jaw told its own story and Collier chuckled grimly. Just wait, kid, just wait.

Cass took a few steps with her brother but then turned and scrutinized Collier. "Are we the Ghosts now?" she asked.

In answer, Collier yanked his sleeve up and showed the tattoo, bloody and screaming in the bloody light.

"Ain't just him!" a voice called out from the middle of another group arriving and, startled, Collier whipped around because he knew that voice and the coal-black man – now sporting a head of magnificent gray curls – pushing his way to the front with his own sleeve pulled up and his own Ghost bellowing in the red light.

"Jonesy!"

And the person standing next to Jonesy. The short, fragile looking woman, deceptive, because her eyes were steel and fire and the blood of Aztec warriors raced in her veins, her own sleeve pulled up, her Ghost calling from across the years.

"Rosa," Collier whispered.

Characters in, More-or-Less, Order of Appearance

1. **Collier Rashkil**: see *Tu'an*.
2. **Philip Deavers**: born: Sep 23, 1980, Walpole MA. Son of Larry and Suzy Deavers, both of whom died in the Event.

History: from a blue collar family, joined the Army in 2000 because he had no other prospects, became a weapons instructor. His family's death by the al-Qaeda Flu left him bitter. Fought in Korea until evacuated, and ended up as a platoon leader in the Ghosts. Participated in Col Caldwell's betrayal of the Ghosts and ended up joining Col. Kant's embryonic intelligence organization now known as the Directorate. Involved in several assassinations of potential rivals to Col Kant and earned a somewhat undeserved reputation as a fixer.

Appearance: 5'10", thick curly hair with a face that comes to a point.

Weaknesses: concerned with his own well-being.

Strengths: Knows which way the wind blows, always gives himself an out.

3. **Rosa Vasquez de Alemeida Arce**: born NYC, Jan 8, 1976, daughter of Jesus Arce and Natividad Vasquez.

History: Upper middle-class family, numerous relatives. ROTC scholarship to City College, LT in Special Ops support when the Towers fell. At home when Flu hit, a Survivor. Fought her way out of NYC into New Jersey, holed up near Burlington. Lived almost the same existence as John Rashkil when Breakout occurred. Made contact with a reconstituted Regular unit, and quickly promoted because of her SpecOps successes against the Black Flags, which is what the pre-Red army was called. She and Collier became lovers after their third operation together. She was allowed to form her own group when the Reds attacked and personally asked for Collier to join. She was made S2 of the Battalion that eventually became the Ghosts.

Appearance: elfin, slight, 4'10", all tendon and sinew, medium brown color, large dark eyes. Extremely fast, Hapkido black belt.

Strengths: determined, competent, dedicated, a quiet storm. Feels ancient connections, sees the future, very strategic, fearless.

Weakness: tunnel vision, thinks everyone thinks like her, is constantly surprised by human evil.

4. **Colonel Harry Caldwell**, born: August 18, 1972, Sarasota, FL, son of Erskine and Lydia Caldwell.

History: Affluent family, attended Catholic schools and graduated 1994, from U of F. Joined Army, was in Kosovo. Fast promotion after Breakout and used his superior strategic and tactical sense to extricate the 1st Combined Arms Division from numerous difficult situations, earning them the nickname of the Ghosts. Became convinced of his infallibility and sold out the Ghosts thinking he could then take over the Reds. He was wrong.

Appearance: tall, thick. Short dark hair with suspicious eyes.

Weaknesses: not as smart as he thinks; more a useful idiot.

Strengths: complicated planner, knows people well.

5. **John Rashkil.** See *Partholon.*

6. **Randall L. Swift**, 2nd platoon, A Company, 1st Battalion, 1st Combined Arms Division: born Jan 3, 1990, Hastings, Nebraska, son of John and Teresa Swift.

History: Regular childhood, was about fifteen when the Event happened. Like everyone else, was outraged.

His mother died during Breakout and he joined the Army after that. Fought against the Red Army from the beginning. In Sergeant Jones's platoon but Collier always took him along on patrols.

Appearance: very tall and thin, pale hair and eyes, off-world stare.

Weaknesses: not very bright, cruel

Strengths: relentless in battle, extremely loyal to Collier.

7. **Cary and James Wilson**, known as #1 and #2: born Feb 4, 1985, and Feb 18, 1987, respectively, in Tumwater, Iowa, to a family of fifteen other brothers and sisters, parents Hank and Linda Wilson.

History: both draft-ganged and managed to stay together through the subsequent assignments. Took part in the southwest Army fight against the Mexican incursion before ending up in the Ghosts. Disappeared during the Pemberton fight.

8. **Sergeant Desmond Jones**, 2nd platoon, A Company, 1st Battalion, 1st CAD: born Feb 12, 1983, Dallas, TX. Son of Desmond and Willa Jones.

History: attending college in Dallas when the Event happened. Drafted during the first call-up and fought in the Saudi campaign. Assigned to Virginia when Texas was overrun by Mexico's composite Army and Phase 2. Became sick on return but recovered. Fought a lot of internal promotion moves and developed a cadre of trusted associates, including Collier.

Appearance: dark skinned black man with pop eyes and pencil-thin mustache. Tall and solidly built with quite an evil stare.

Weaknesses: still believes there is good in the people around him

Strengths: a bridger, knows how to get people to

work together, a warrior.

9. **Henry Price**, 3rd platoon, A Company, 2nd Battalion, 98th Truck, Army Transportation Command (ATC). Adopted son of Emmet and Wilhelmina Price, Farmville, VA.

History: Born Mar 22, 1987, son of Franklin Price and Teresa McDermott of Farmville. Both addicts, gave up their son to Franklin's paternal great-cousins. Emmet was a tobacco farmer and moonshiner, also ran some weed. Raised Henry in the business. Emmet was strict but fair and Wilhelmina was the perfect grandmotherly type. Henry was placed in the Provos when the war hit but, shortly before Breakout, was shanghaied into the regular Army. His entire family died from Phase 2 but he survived it because he was on special duty in the Midwest and holed up in a farmhouse. His special talents were recognized early and he was attached to Colonel Franklin Leideig's staff. Leideig was running contraband from the Zone out to the Midwest and resumed his activities when Phase 2 ended.

Appearance: fireplug, very tough, very strong, 5'6", 200 pounds, fat and muscle mix. Square, hairless face, reddish hair, thin, sharp features, extremely piercing blue eyes, very large, gives him a Big Eye painting look.

Weaknesses: self-centered with an urge to do right, which holds him in perpetual conflict. Loyal to a fault, usually attaches himself to the wrong person. Vindictive and hot tempered.

Strengths: relentless, long range planner and unusually adept at infiltration and sabotage.

10. **Cass Dinwiddie**: born Jan 1, 2015, in Lexington, daughter of Homer and Zoe Dinwiddie, part of Price's gang. Named Cassandra.

History: began working with the gang at age ten as a

runner and spy, showed a real knack for fighting with a club when taught by gang member Tatsuya Smith. At a very young age worked backup on ops and deliveries because she was so fierce and fast. She also has a natural affinity for engines. Repairs many of the simple water and steam driven engines the gang uses.

Appearance: She is thin and pale and blonde and blue-eyed.

Weaknesses: Needs to be supervised closely until the fight begins, then let her go. Impetuous, dangerously so, to the point she can jeopardize an op.

Strengths: Very strong, ferocious, loves to fight to the point of recklessness. Very fast reactions and judgment.

11. **Slickie Dinwiddie**: born Feb 2, 2013, in Buena Vista, son of Homer and Zoe Dinwiddie. Named after his father, but gets the nickname because he is a master thief, able to slip in and out without being seen.

Appearance: Looks like his sister but much taller and very thin.

Weaknesses: Unimaginative, so can't see implications.

Strengths: Very disciplined, stoic, deadly with a crossbow and a master of ropes.

12. **Homer Dinwiddie**, one of Price's LTs.: born Jan 1, 1985, in Lynchburg to Carl and Sylvia Dinwiddie, both of whom were classics professors at Liberty University. Named after the Greek poet.

History: He was sixteen when the Event happened. Both of his parents were arrested and executed by the third or fourth regime (Homer had lost track by then, as had most of the survivors) and he fled into the hills around Clifton Forge where he fell in with a gang of housebreakers. He took over the gang after a few years and they expanded their territory to include the area from White Sulphur Springs to Lexington. Because of their isolation, were spared most of the effects of Phase 2. His gang's specialty was raiding warehouses and buildings and they once emptied the armory at VMI, hiding the weapons (including artillery) in the mountains. Price came back to Farmville with the gold (see *Tu'an*), and Homer's gang tried to rob him but Price's gang defeated them. Price offered to make them part of his operation and Homer soon became indispensable.

Appearance: Blond and blue eyed with soft features. Average height, thin, keeps his hair very short because he doesn't want lice.

Weaknesses: his wife and kids, on whom he dotes. He is the reason Cass is ill-disciplined. Too easy-going with them and brooks no criticism of his family, becoming violent if someone does so.

Strengths: brilliant planner, who games housebreakings to the nth degree. Can write rudimentary Greek and Latin. Fiercely loyal to Price, regards him as more worthy of allegiance than the government or the country. Knows computers, at least the programs and codes available through 2001. Does not know mechanics but is a good theory guy. A natural chemist, also, with a knack for explosives and burnings.

13. **Rickard Lawless**: born Apr 4, 1975, Flint, MI, son of Rick Lawless and Emily Stotten. Father was a Ford factory worker who lived apart from Emily but occasionally showed up to take Rick out. He had a sporadic affection for the boy and loved to take him shooting, which was his main passion. Passed that on to his son.

History: Lawless's affinity for firearms led him to join the US Army in 1993, was sent to Bosnia where his tactical skills got him sent to US sniper school. Passed with flying colors and involved in many off-the-books operations. During the Event, was stationed in Korea and became part of the Peninsula war, one of the last evacuated. When the civil war broke out, quit the Blues in disgust because of the corruption and became part of the SW Army fighting the Blues in Texas. His behind-the-lines heroics came to the attention of Kant who personally recruited him to the elite counter-revolutionary unit of the First Directorate, nicknamed the Faceless. HQ'd with Kant in Fredericksburg, he is only sent out to trouble spots.

Appearance: very tall, thin, with intense green eyes and pepper hair. Very thin eyebrows, which gives him an intense stare.

Weakness: must be part of a larger organization and takes his orders without question, tactical thinker, not strategic. Can only think what his boss thinks.

Strengths: ruthless and thorough and one who considers every possibility, making it very difficult to surprise him.

14. **Colonel Franklin Leideig**, Staff Officer, ATC, Ft. Benjamin Harrison: born September 20, 1954, Champlain Illinois, 3rd son of Carl and Mabel Leideig.

History: attended Illinois State 1972, Business degree. Joined active military, assigned to various units as Logistics officer. Started black-marketing while on tour in Korea. Resigned after ten years and joined Illinois Guard where he kept up a pretty good trade in military equipment while running various shipping businesses in Illinois. Married twice, four children. Activated after 9/11, survived both Flu and Phase 2 with severe effects, left him weak and tubercular. Took over Central Army's logistics coordination which left him in a good position to start a lucrative black-market with the Zone and continue it after Breakout and his own recovery. Picked up Price, who turned out to be one of his most reliable couriers, after Breakout.

Appearance: tall, thin, eagle-like features, always

coughing from the Phase 2, moves slowly, gray-haired and stooped, betraying his 6'4" frame, 190 pounds, filmy pale eyes, very penetrating, though.

Weaknesses: greedy, self-serving, motivated only by gain.

Strengths: good judge of character and ability to pick people for his schemes, of which he has many going at the same time.

15. **General of the Army Frederick Santos Kant**, North American People's Army, Democratic Republic of North America, field headquarters: born Oct 31, 1970, Chicago, IL. Eldest son of Frederich Wilhelm Kant and Natalia da Silva Santos. Father possibly fought on Russian side during WW2.

History: Family very unusual, dedicated socialists who belonged to various Communist parties. Frederick is a genius, speaks German, Brazilian, English. Very rich family, went to prep schools, Princeton, Oxford. 1995, joined US Army as Infantry Officer. During the Event was a Captain in the Green Berets. Helped organize first Zone Guards. Got put on Staff, rapid promotion. When Reds destroyed the Blue Army, led a coup of selected officers against staff, slaughtered them all and turned over the remaining Army to Reds and, through ruthless maneuvering, to his present position as dictator. Ascetic, but once in a while enjoys a good bender, including rape of prisoners. Never married, no children.

Appearance: Looks a lot like General Grant, short, stubby beard, expressionless. Tending to fat, but extremely strong.

Weaknesses: arrogance and condescension make him blind to other's capabilities. Constantly underestimates his opponents.

Strengths: brilliant, a military genius of complete ruthlessness. No feelings, single obsession with the

Revolution.

16. **Washburn Reynolds**: born May 5, 1965, in Romney, WV. Son of Cole and Lizzie Reynolds, both farmers.

History: Washburn grew up hard and tough on a farm that barely made enough to feed him and his seven brothers. He became an expert tracker and hunter in response, supplementing family meals with his take. He never left the Romney area and dropped out of high school, turning himself into a much sought after hunting and fishing guide. As a result, he developed a greater prosperity than he ever thought possible, generously sharing his bounty with his parents and brothers and his church. Washburn's time in the forest turned him into a Christian mystic. He married a local girl and had five children. When the Event happened, he fled into the woods, urging his parents and brothers to follow, but they thought he was overreacting. He survived Breakout there, his parents and brothers not so lucky. His wife and children were all murdered by Breakout thugs and Washburn went on a rampage, killing everyone he came across, thug or Blue or Red. After years of this, he had a mystical experience on top of a mountain as he was drawing a bead on an unsuspecting Blue, and decided to stop hunting people. He heard about Collier's church and crossed the mountains to reach him.

Appearance: big, grizzly bear big. Looks like one with his full black beard and long hair.

Weakness: an almost fanatical belief that everything is the Lord's will, which can sometimes hamstring his actions and lead him to wrong conclusions.

Strengths: superior tracker and recon man with a view of God and Nature that makes him fearless. Straight talker, one that Collier can rely on.

17. **Ben Whittaker**: born Jun 6, 1985, in Winchester,

VA, son of Leslie and May Whittaker, who ran an insurance company in Kernstown.

History: Whittaker occasionally worked in his parent's office pre-Event, and then became a volunteer and gofer for the various military and civilian agencies that used Winchester as a staging area. Got to know everyone. Hid in the mountains after Breakout (which wiped out Winchester leaving it quarantined to this day and turning it into a storage and smuggling area for those willing to brave the place). Whittaker came back and ingratiated himself with the various Blue and Red forces that traded possession of the Valley during the war. Secretly a Blue, he provided intelligence until the Blues lost. Collier showed up five years after the war ended, and Whittaker latched on to him as the last of the Blues.

Appearance: affable, smiling, easy-going look and manner that makes everyone trust him. Black, light-skinned, tightly curled hair.

Weakness: is too confident. Thinks he's always one step ahead.

Strength: a loyal patriot dedicated to the restoration of the Constitution, willing to take any risk to move the country back along those lines.

18. **Eulen Cody**: born July 7, 1955, to Ewell and Loretta Cody, Down Holler, KY. Pig farmers, but good and upright people, who had ten sons, all of whom went on to wonderful careers in all levels of government and the military. Both parents died well before the Event, and Eulen's brothers all died as a result of it or the war.

History: Eulen joined the Marines when he graduated high school in 1973, spent ten years and then transferred to the CIA. Was a special ops guy over the next ten years, conducting operations mostly in Latin America before getting assigned to an analyst desk. Fled DC after his wife and daughters succumbed to the Event and got out of the area before the Quarantine was established, ending up in Hagerstown. Fled to Carlisle Barracks after Breakout and became an intel officer for various Blues units on the Ghosts' flanks. Briefly knew Rosa. After the Ghosts were destroyed, drifted back down the Valley and heard about Collier. Knew his name so joined the church.

Appearance: an old man, dyspeptic, gray haired and wrinkled and suffering from various old man ailments like arthritis.

Weakness: still applying old school principles to a world that no longer follows them. Still thinks there's a chance civilization will prevail.

Strength: extremely experienced and tough as nails.

19. **Felicia Delacourt**: born Aug 8, 1984, in Roanoke, VA, to James Delacourt and an unknown mother, maybe named Fae. She could never get the info out of her dad. Her dad owned an 18-wheeler. Felicia has numerous half-brothers and sisters, none of whom she could keep straight but with whom she forged a very successful guerrilla unit.

History: Felicia became an adept diesel mechanic well before she turned fifteen, primarily because her Dad was too cheap to pay one. She became his right-hand and his favorite, which was a testament to her because he was a chauvinist and a difficult man, but a hard worker and a genius with vehicles. Her father was gang-drafted and disappeared into the military, leaving Felicia to fend for herself, which she did successfully by her mechanical abilities. Breakout occurred and she and her surviving family members fought their way across the Appalachians until they reached Woodstock, which they took over. Formed a trade alliance with Collier then joined the church.

Appearance: Rather tall, smooth-faced black female with a prominent Afro.

Weakness: Does not trust anyone in authority. Tends to go her own way, forcing issues best left alone.

Strengths: very organized and action oriented.

20. **Darra Barar**: born Sep 9, 1980, Vancouver, BC. Son of Noor Singh Barar and Taj Barar, both engineers.

History: attending McGill University in Montreal studying civil engineering when the Event happened. Canada and the US came to blows along the border in several places and Darra was drafted before completing his studies. The border incursions subsided into an uneasy truce until the Mexican War started and the Canadians came in as US allies. Darra was sent to the Arizona front and was caught by Breakout. Surviving Phase 2 and the war, he drifted north and east trying to make his way back home but got caught up in the civil war and hid in the Upper Valley, steadily drifting north in an attempt to reach Montreal. Eventually reached Kernstown and ran into Collier who recruited him to improve infrastructure. Still intends to go north.

Appearance: tall and owlish with thick black frame glasses.

Weakness: heart not in it. Wants to go home, even though he knows home doesn't exist anymore.

Strengths: analytical, especially regarding physical structures like fortifications and approaches. Explosives expert.

21. **Evelyn Rashkill**: nee: Walker. Born Oct 10, 1987, in Waynesboro, VA, daughter of Michael and Eleanor Walker, who were teachers at Waynesboro High School. Michael was an assistant football coach there and knew Collier from games held at the field.

History: fourteen when the Event happened and witnessed much of the conflict around Waynesboro as Draft Gangs continually assaulted the town over the next four years trying to gather recruits. Her dad taught her to shoot and, on a few occasions, they joined forces with the Fishburne cadets, where she first saw Collier. Breakout happened and Evelyn fled with her mother and her two sisters and parents into the woods near Swift Run Gap but was ambushed by Breakout thugs. Evelyn hid in the rocks and watched as her family was raped and butchered. She avoided the same fate but caught Phase 2 and wandered delirious through the mountains until she ended up at Elkton, where she spent the war living alone in the ghost town. She hunted and traded meat with passing Blues and sniped Reds, turning into quite a stalker. She ended up drifting back to Waynesboro at some point and ran into Collier as he was searching Fishburne and securing the weapons he found there.

Appearance: elfish and wan with big hazel eyes. Soft spoken, the tragic about her.

Weakness: broken by her time in the mountains, rather hide than confront.

Strengths: regards Collier as her savior but knows his heart is elsewhere. That's fine, that is the wound these days. Willing to kill and die for him.

22. **Zoe Dinwiddie:**, born Feb 2 1984 in Washington, DC to Julian and Leslie Marcs, both mid-level administrators for the Department of Transportation. Not really a member of Price's gang but helps out.

History: She and her parents were in a Zone Camp after the Flu and caught up in Breakout, her parents massacred in front of her. May have seen John Rashkil's death. Zoe fled south and, after enduring rape and abuse, escaped from a slave camp that Homer's gang had attacked. She refused to leave him after that and they married.

Appearance: As dark as her husband is light, making everyone wonder where her kids came from. Helter-skelter eyes, and ferocious.

Weakness: terrified of strangers, which is why she does not help out much. Afraid for her kids.

Strengths: insanely protective of her family and the gang. Will die before giving up any information.

23. **John Rashkil II**, nicknamed **Second**: born Nov 11, 2015, in Kernstown to Collier and Evelyn Rashkil. Father works as a composter for the local cadre, and is secretly the pastor of a hidden church. Evelyn is a homemaker who works in a nearby weaving mill during cadre work surges.

History: Chafing under the strictures of his father's discipline, he has turned into a self-taught outdoorsman because of the many times he skips work to roam the woods. In typical teenage rebellion, he favors the Republic, primarily because his father does not.

Appearance: inherited his grandfather's size and deeply sunken eyes. Has blondish hair and a golden skin tone.

Weaknesses: irascible attitude and stubborn well past a fault.

Strengths: Strong and combative and questions everything.

24. **Art and Bart Rashkil**: twin boys, born Dec 12, 2017, to Collier and Evelyn Rashkil. Named after Collier's Uncle Art and his favorite cartoon character, Bart Simpson. The two reflect their namesakes. Art is a moody rebel who's only happy when he is building things. Bart is a prankster.

25. **Tatsuya Smith**: born Mar 3, 1980, in Washington, DC. Son of Michael and Keiko Smith, both Japanese interpreters working in DC. Father was a kendoist, taught son everything.

History: Living at VCU when the Event killed his parents. Tat was draft-ganged into a unit that turned Red after the battle of Richmond. Deserting, Tat fled to the mountains where he lived as a survivalist warrior monk. Ran into Homer near Lexington and agreed to join the band. Does most of the fight training.

Appearance: 5'8", thin but very muscular, tightly slanted eyes and Japanese cast. Looks full blooded, even though he's only half-Japanese.

Weaknesses: very stubborn, hard to move him off an opinion to the point he can be a detriment. Is particularly protective of Zoe.

Strengths: ferocious fighter with a great tactical mind.

26. **Little John Bawdry**: born Jan 13, 1988, to Carrie Bawdry, father unknown, in Lexington, VA. Mother was a waitress and worked at the Dollar Store but was a good and tough mother.

History: Bawdry was a big kid with good natural strength but had a righteous soul, as implanted by his mother, and used his strength to stop bullies. A middle school coach convinced him to play football and he developed into a very strong and fast young man until the Event ended most formal schooling, although Little John loved reading and continued to educate himself. He became a one-man police force in Lexington, attracting a couple of others who helped him keep order until the War broke out and then he joined the Blues. Fighting in Virginia and Delaware, John went home after the Ghosts collapsed and resumed his police work in Lexington. Fought Homer's gang on numerous occasions until the Reds took over the town and then he deserted to Homer. Part of the gang that Price trapped and so impressed by Price's organization that he stayed on.

Appearance: very tall, very big, muscular with a shaggy head and beard. Exudes strength.

Weakness; still believes in law and order.

Strength: very effective tactician and fighter.

27. **F for Freddie. Freddie Sizemore**: born Feb 14,

1984, to Roger and Helen Sizemore of Farmville, both of whom owned and ran a local grocery store.

History: He grew up with Price in the Farmville area and occasionally assisted Price and Pap in their businesses. A very bright student and interested in medicine, he stayed in school after the Event until the wars started and Draft Gangs came looking for him. His parents hid him in the woods near Sandy River Reservoir and successfully deflected the gangs until both were gunned down by one particularly nasty group. F stayed in the area and avoided the war, forming alliances with other runaways until he had an excellent sneak thief group that raided Army warehouses. Almost a Robin Hood character. He heard about Price when returned and made contact.

Appearance; Kind of goofy with buck teeth and a shock of hair that falls forward like the prow of a ship.

Weakness: too deliberate, and prefers to be off by himself.

Strengths: insightful and logical, able to draw conclusions from evidence.

28. Sally June Winthrop: born Mar 15, 1986, in Farmville to Henry and June Winthrop, who were farm machine dealers in the area. Both died of Phase 2.

History: Sally June was a sometime girlfriend of Price's while growing up but became more attached to Beau Armee and ended up spending a lot of time with both of them as Beau's girlfriend. Draft Gangs killed her father when the Event happened and confiscated his business. Her mother fled with her and Beau's family to the woods around Raines Tavern, and driven to Brier's Creek when Breakout occurred. They joined forces with the Squint gang to the west and became the nucleus of Price's gang. Sally was the first to recognize Price when he came back and was instrumental in getting the others to ally with him. Runs her own section, but has three kids with Beau: Junior, Sarah, and Faith.

Appearance: big girl, blonde, boney and strong with blue eyes and too much hair.

Weakness: still has a soft spot for Price.

Strengths: tough as nails and downright cruel against her enemies.

29. **Beau Armee**: born Apr 16, 1985, to Julian and Geri Armee of Farmville, a water manager and his artist wife.

History: a goody two shoes who excelled in all areas of academics and sports and was strangely drawn to Price, the two of them becoming best friends in school. Ended up with Sally as his girlfriend. Escaped with Sally's family to Raines Tavern when the Draft Gangs killed her father. Beau's father and mother went with them. Beau's Dad was 101st Airborne post-Vietnam and taught a lot of tradecraft to the group. Mom died of Phase 2 and the father still lives quietly near Brier Creek. Beau has three children with Sally. Sally brought the newly arrived Price to the gang and they immediately accepted his proposal of forming a smuggling ring united with other friends of Price's.

Appearance: dark and smiling with a fresh face that's almost Howdy Doody.

Weakness: still naïve.

Strengths: well versed in many subjects, including chemistry, and is an excellent infiltrator.

30. **"Squint" – real name Taylor – Raeburn**: born May 17 1980, son of Hiram and Ellie Raeburn, logger and moonshiner and cousins of Pap's. Both killed by Draft Gangs.

History: Squint got the name from a permanent disability that causes one eye to almost close. He is related to Pap and was heavily involved in the smuggling business until the Draft Gang killed his family and seized him. He was in the Richmond battle and, after losing that, decided to go home. He ended up in the Cumberland State Forest area where he could hide out from both Blues and Reds. He heard about Sally and Beau and made contact and they formed a loose confederation. When Sally told him Price was back, he immediately brought his gang of hunters and woodsmen into his employ. Expanded the gang's reach as far as Luisa.

Appearance: tall and tanned with a bald head

Weakness: not very bright.

Strengths: superior guerilla fighter.

31. **Inez Williams**: born June 18, 1982, in Lynchburg to Julio and Maria Williams who ran a thrift store and antique shop. Both died from Phase 2.

History: Inez worked most summers with her parents, learning the value of things and the importance of smuggling the more expensive – and usually stolen – items to exclusive customers., Formed a syndicate when the Event happened that broke into the exclusive customers' houses and raided their valuables for sale to customers in enclaves outside of the quarantined areas. Most of her gang was wiped out in Phase 2 and she hid in various places until she formed enough of a strike force to attack the Breakout thugs. Regained control of Lynchburg and ran it as her little fiefdom until Price showed up. Interested in getting Price's gold, she pretended to be an ally until it became apparent that she would never obtain the treasure, so she decided to become a more reliable partner, although she tends to go her own way.

Appearance: short-haired Latino, lined eyes and tending to fat.

Weakness: more self-centered than makes for a good partner.

Strengths: very independent and can take her own actions that support the group.

32. **Rodger Dodger**: born July 19, 1983, in New Market to Sam and Edna Angel, a car mechanic and his seamstress wife. Both died in Phase 2.

History: Rodger got the nickname for his thievery, something that got him into constant trouble and resulting stints in juvenile hall. He specialized in shoplifting and smash-and-grabs. The Blues set up near his home after Breakout and he became a shakedown artist of the soldiers and a burglar of their compounds. Ran into Inez and formed an alliance where he would steal back items she had sold to the Blues. Price had a couple of run-ins with him while working for Leideig. When the Blues lost the war, Dodger specialized in stealing their equipment and selling information to the Reds. Regarded by the Directorate as an informant.

Appearance: affable and smiling and everybody's friend.

Weakness: everything. The guy is a toad.

Strengths: survival instincts and can spot the double cross

33. **Corporal Terrel Quince**: born Sep 21, 2012, in Richmond, VA, son of Uvalde and Winona Quince, who ran a salvage business along the James River.

History: Born in Red occupied territory, he learned scavenging from his parents, who were assigned metal reclamation projects by the Red Army command. As the Red Army became the State, his parents grew in status because of their efficiency and Terrel was allowed to attend Red schooling, especially the few machinist courses available. Came to Directorate attention because of his knack with basic steam powered engines and picked up by Major Deavers, who also taught him trade craft.

Appearance; mixed Latino and black, keeps his hair cropped short. Very smooth skin. Looks like a kid.

Weakness: arrogant to the point he dismisses others.

Strength: good mechanic.

34. **Private Ulster Reynolds**: born Oct 22, 2010, to Mary Reynolds and an unknown Red soldier in Petersburg, VA.

History: Abandoned by his mother at birth, Ulster was raised by a couple of meth heads who sold him on occasion to soldiers and others for gold or trade goods they used to get chemicals to make meth. Both killed in a lab explosion when Ulster was ten and he became an accomplished knife man for various gangs wishing to kill off the opposition. Caught by cadres during an attempt on a commissar's life, he was picked up by the Directorate for his skills, especially his trade craft. Became Deavers's personal bodyguard and trusted valet.

Appearance: dark hair, wide, thousand-yard eyes, very pale.

Weakness: easily swayed by someone in authority

Strengths: sociopath.

35. **Colonel Victor Sams**: born Nov 23, 1990, Toronto, CA. Son of Victor and Maria Sams, bus driver and wife, both died of Phase 2.

History: Was part of the Canadian forces that closed the border with the US after the civil war between the Blues and the Reds broke out. Intrigued by the Red's philosophy (his father was a trade unionist) he deserted the Canadians and joined a Red unit attacking Ft. Drum. Rose through the ranks as an effective Directorate officer, part of their uniformed branch. Commander of Directorate troops in the Lower Valley.

Appearance: French, small features, although overweight, has pig eyes.

Weakness: women and liquor. A dissipate. If he wasn't so effective, Kant would have him shot.

Strengths; ruthless and cruel and loyal to Kant.

36. **Wooster Tutwiler**, Private, Directorate, house mouse to Colonel Sams: born Dec 24, 2011, in Fredericksburg, VA to Alicia Tutwiler, an accountant, and an unknown rapist.

History: Raised by his mother in the somewhat intact town of Fredericksburg, she became a maid and paramour to various Red commanders when the town was established as the Red capital of the US (DC is still too dangerous, filled with mutated variants of Phase 2 and Breakout monsters). His mother taught him how to read and write and do accounting books. He had a knack for office work so, at the urging of his mother, he was picked up by the Directorate. Abused by the many Red lovers his mother brought into the house, he developed a hatred for the Reds and their philosophy.

Appearance: meek and mild and owlish with glasses he picked up in the ruins somewhere that do not fit him and are not quite his prescription.

Weakness: fearful

Strengths: vengeful.

37. **Lieutenant Ben Cadgers**: born Jan 25, 2006, to Marcus and Yolanda Cadgers in Spotsylvania County. Both died in Breakout.

History: Passed around from distant relatives to complete strangers throughout his childhood, his last "family" enrolled him in a Directorate education camp when he was ten years old. Spent his entire life moving from one camp to another and eventually ended up a Lieutenant in the Directorate Logistics Corp. Still a Lieutenant because he's in a support role, even though he is very good at it. Takes a lot of abuse from superiors.

Appearance; Mixed race. His mother was Dominican and he speaks some Spanish. Tall and lanky with wavy black hair and an unfortunate complexion. Not handsome but exotic.

Weaknesses: Very afraid of authority.

Strengths: Questions authority, especially Marxist doctrine and has a strong core of defiance.

38. **Samuel Underbridge**, Trooper: born Jan 25, 1983, in Wythe, VA, to Samuel and Melissa Underbridge, handyman and wife. Both died of Phase 2.

History: Underbridge was raised as an assistant to his father but hated him and shirked his work as much as possible. Thrown out of the house at seventeen, he was snatched up by the Army and made a member of a Draft Gang because of his cruelty. Joined the Reds after the battles around Richmond but was court-martialed for theft and insubordination and drifted into the Troopers.

Appearance: Skinny and mean-faced.

Weakness: cowardly and a shirker.

Strengths: viciously cruel

39. **Hank Cadwaller**: born Mar 1, 1990, in Strasburg, VA, son of Henry and Helen Cadwaller who ran a gas station on Route 11 and are currently retired, living in a still-intact part of the collapsing gas station, making them two of the oldest people in the Shenandoah Valley, as well as a rare pre-Event married couple with a living son also born pre-Event.

Appearance: Looks overweight, but it's actually muscle, balding and smooth faced with a constant look of worry.

History: like typical civilians of the time, Hank fell into his parents' line of work after all other options were eliminated by the Event and the wars. That he had his parents available to teach him merchandising was an advantage, and he quickly became an important cadre. Somehow, he managed to avoid military service of any kind, another rarity of the times, and was assigned to the upper valley area after organizing Red distribution centers in Strasburg.

Weakness: craven.

Strengths: willing to go the extra mile to prove his worth.

40. **Junior Armee**: born Feb 26, 2015, in Raines Tavern, son of Beau Armee and Sally Winthrop.

Appearance: Short but strongly built, a mop of wild black hair falling into his face and merry blue eyes. Sunny disposition, like his Dad.

History: grew up absorbing the tradecraft of his grandfather, so has a special knack with ambushes and wood lore. Trusted by his father to run part of the gang in counter ambush operations. Well-read and has great forgery skills.

Weakness: Too sunny

Strengths: relentless.

41. **Sweet Pea**: Born August 20, 2010, in Richmond, the daughter of a woman named Olive and an unknown Red soldier who raped her. Olive escaped the sex-worker camp and made her way to Farmville where she hid out until she died from tuberculosis when Sweet Pea was ten. Never called her daughter anything else but Sweet Pea.

History: scrabbled around Farmville stealing and selling herself to whoever would give her a meal until Price ran across her and took her in. Mom had taught her how to read and do math so Price gave her a job inventorying his stashes. Knew she would be loyal to him, no matter what.

Appearance: malnourished and frightened, washed out stringy hair and dark, tearful eyes. Very thin, looks weak.

Weakness: terrified of everyone.

Strength: fiercely loyal to Price.

42. **Julian "Grampop" Armee**: born Mar 27, 1958, Asheboro, NC, son of Wade and Linda Armee, civil engineer and his stay-at-home wife. Both died in a car accident when Julian was eighteen years old.

History: Julian had just graduated high school when his parents died in the car accident in 1976, and, a week later, he joined the Army and stayed for ten years as an Airborne Ranger sergeant, a heavy weapons specialist. He met Geri Lind of Farmville while accompanying a friend from Ft. Bragg to a Radford U party and married her a year later. After Beau was born, he resigned from the Army and attended UVA to finish his civil engineering degree and was hired by the county as a water manager. Escaped with his family and the remnants of the Winthrops to Raines Tavern after Farmville was ravaged by Draft Gangs. After Breakout killed his wife, he ended up contacting Blues forces around Richmond and fought with them as a behind-the-lines patrol leader while maintaining his presence in Raines Tavern. He went back to Raines Tavern when the Blues were defeated and provided material support and training to his son's gang while establishing a private sanctuary on Brier's Creek. When Price came back, at the recommendation of his daughter-in-law he took charge of the weapons and the gold and became their guardian.

Appearance: tall and lean and grandfatherly "old soldier" looks, very bushy white eyebrows, receding hairline.

Weakness: Thinks it's still the 90s.

Strengths: innovative soldier and strategist.

43. **Carter Gough**: born June 30, 2005, in Farmville, VA to Lydia Gough and an unknown Zone Guard. Lydia was living on one of the Zone Camps at the time and, after she became pregnant, made her way out and to Farmville where she met the Armee's and escaped with them to Raines Tavern.

History: Raised by the Winthrops after his mother died of Phase 2, Carter became an accomplished second-story man, raiding Blue and Red compounds. Price recruited him directly when he returned and he serves as a courier between the two families.

Appearance: a little short of six feet, wiry, with reddish hair and freckles.

Weakness: not the brightest bulb in the pack.

Strengths: knows he's not the brightest bulb in the pack.

44. **Kaintuck Bup**: born April 28, 1954, in Charlottesville, VA, to Roger and Delilah Bup of Scioto, NY. Roger was a WW2 veteran who perfected the art of distillation in France and brought the skill with him back to the US. Owned a truck company and taught distilling as an illegal hobby. Died during Breakout.

History: Kaintuck graduated from UVA with a Business degree and, after spending a couple of years in the Army, took over his Dad's trucking business. Too old for the Draft Gangs, he fled into the mountains south of Charlottesville when Breakout occurred, hiding out to avoid the Breakout monsters. During the civil war, he became a guerilla leader, striking at the Reds around the Charlottesville area and carving out enough territory that he was left alone. He took over the Whiskey Works and used what his Dad taught him to revive them, creating a lucrative underground business.

Appearance: rail thin and leathery with a mean cast to his face that reflects a hard heart.

Weakness: sometimes too hard.

Strengths: ruthless with an almost photographic memory of the surrounding countryside. Hates the Reds.

45. **Larry Bup**: born May 29, 2010, in the Whiskey Works to Roger the Second and Ellen May, a local girl. Larry is Kaintuck's grandson.

History: Raised in the Whiskey Works hard and cruel by both his hard and cruel parents, Larry managed to hang on to a bit of humanity and curiosity, something his hard grandfather recognized and taught him to read and understand science, hoping to pass on the Whiskey Works to him. Larry, though, does not have the degree of hardness Kaintuck thinks he needs so he is constantly riding him in an effort to develop that. Roger Second assists.

Appearance: crew cut and built tough, there is a softness to his eyes.

Weakness: too willing to hear the other person's side of things.

Strengths: sees the possibility of civilization, restoring life to its pre-war glory. Willing to fight for that.

46. **Kenny Haskil**: born July 1, 2000, Spotsylvania County, VA to Ken and Loretta Haskil who both worked for the county road crew. Both died in the Event and Kenny was raised by various relatives until Breakout left him on his own at seven years old.

History: Haskil fell in with another group of orphans eking out a hand-to-mouth existence in the woods south of Fredericksburg until Squint found him and recruited him and others to run gang activity around Luisa. Competent and effective smuggler.

Appearance: dark like a gypsy, has a full head of hair but his handsomeness is marred by several facial scars caused by knife fights.

Weakness: linear thinker.

Strengths: good fighter and loyal to Squint.

ABOUT THE AUTHOR

D. Krauss resides in the Shenandoah Valley. He's been a cotton picker, a sodbuster, a librarian, a surgical orderly, the guy who paints the little white line down the middle of the road, a weatherman, a door-kickin' shove-gun-in-face lawman, an intel analyst, a school-bus driver, and a layabout. He has been married over 45 years to the same woman, and has a wildman bass guitarist for a son.

Website:
http://www.dustyskull.com

Goodreads:
https://bit.ly/3bkPDCm

YouTube: Old Guy Reviews Books
https://bit.ly/3y3KHLY

MeWe: dkrauss

OTHER BOOKS BY D. KRAUSS

The Frank Vaughn Trilogy
Frank Vaughn, Killed by His Mom
Southern Gothic
Looking for Don

The Partholon Trilogy
Partholon
Tu'An
Col'm
The Ship Trilogy The Ship to Look for God
The Ship Looking for God
The Ship Finding God

Story Collections
The Moonlight in Genevieve's Eyes
and other Strange Stories
The Last Man in the World Explains All
and other strange tales